The Paladins of Naretia

Book one in the Naretia series.

www.tpkeane.com

Massachusetts, USA

First Edition

Printed in the United States of America

Cover Design by www.ebooklaunch.com

Library of Congress Cataloguing-in-Publication Data Available

Library of Congress Control Number: 2016900714

ISBN: 978-0-9971793-0-9

10-ISBN: 0-9971793-0-9

To my wonderful husband, Peter, who stood by my ambitions, and selflessly gave up A LOT of his time to be my sounding board.

To Mark and Ryan, the bringers of joy, inspiration, cups of tea, and cuddles

Chapter 1

A stiff, snow-laden wind pushed against Olórin as he walked out into the night. It was bitter and persuaded him to wrap his heavy, brown cloak around him more tightly. The tidy mountain village of Valeskeep hunkered down against the icy winter squall; its hunched, thatched backs oblivious to the journey he must take. *'Just three ingredients,'* he thought. *'Three treasures hidden for eons in the ancientness of Naretia. Two I can find easy enough, but pry less easily from the hands that covet them.'*

Olórin shivered, his eyes followed the path the gusts took up the steep mountains. Somewhere within the jagged claws that scored the thick clouds above, lay the first ingredient. To obtain it he must meet his beloved Goddess, Edwina. He must face her, and his weaknesses. She will judge him, know him, and Olórin so desperately wanted to be seen as worthy.

He cast his blue eyes back to the window, through which the warming glow of a fire fought against the darkness outside. A few tankards of courage staved off the ice from his innards, but the feeling was fading fast. He burned the memory of the jovial tavern into his mind, for fear he would never see it again, before digging his walking stick into the drifting snow ahead of him.

If there had been a road, it was lost now to the knee-high white powder crunching beneath his feet. The only guide he had to find it was the rows of sloping cottages, which stuck out of the whiteness like enormous frozen mushrooms. Shutters latched and all noise of life muted by the gale, the homes of Valeskeep appeared abandoned. But, of course, Olórin knew they weren't.

A biting wind whipped at his long beard and stung his wrinkled cheeks until they became numb. The orange glow of the street lamps was dulled in the smothering blizzard. He pulled himself along the narrow streets, breathing harder with every step, one hand keeping a firm grip on his battered hat. Where the brim used to be wide and stiff, it dangled now, drooping over his face like a soggy biscuit. The proud point which had once stood to attention on the top of his head was deflated, battered and hung behind him like a cape. As decrepit as his hat was, he would not part with it for all the gold in Naretia. It had been with him since his days of apprenticeship and contained all of his supplies. It was also the only thing keeping his bald head warm.

The giant straw mushrooms, shut tight against the storm, billowed sideways smoke from their chimneys, belying their desolate exterior with the signs of life and warmth from within. In the brief moments when the wind died down, he could make out the aroma of burnt wood and hearty evening meals wafting down from the stacks. '*How nice it must be to live a life of obliviousness,'* he thought.

The truth was that he was bitterly jealous of the happy ignorance he saw with each passing town. It seemed to him that, for the past six years, his life had consisted of nothing more than passing by all the things that made it worth living: Huddling around a warm fire with loved ones, drinking a robust wine with good friends, and the ordinary comforts he only dipped his toe into now and again, so he didn't forget. These were the sacrifices he had no choice but to make.

It wasn't long before the rows of thatched cottages melted away behind Olórin. Beyond the outskirts of the town, deep in a lonely mountain pass, he heard a familiar sound which drew his eyes toward the sky. As the winter winds began to howl, the sound of the rhythmic beating of enormous wings defied its doggedness and came closer.

Olórin stopped and waited. From within the snow-heavy clouds above, he saw the silhouette of man with black wings descend toward him. Snow swished and swirled in every direction until his black leather boots landed with a muffled crunch. Olórin could only make out the creature's two slatted, amber eyes as they came toward him. It was a sight that normally filled the hearts of men with fear, but Olórin did not fear this man.

"Good evening, Aramus," he said, the frosty winds almost taking away his words.

"Olórin Talfan, have you had your fill of pleasantries for today?" a cool and deep voice said, having no trouble with the thiefly gale.

"I could do with a damn sight more," he answered, heaving a heavy-booted foot from the snow and restarting his laborious march up the mountain.

The winged man clasped his uncovered hands behind his back, as though it might have been a summer's day. Although Olórin worked hard to keep his thin frame upright against the winds, Aramus seemed none-too-bothered about the turbulent weather: His powerful strides were even and sure.

While Olórin struggled to find his grip on a path that seemed to want to reach the clouds in a terrible hurry, Aramus's shoulder-length, black hair tussled in the gusts. It was the only part of him which relented to the storm. A slightly hooked nose accentuated his hawkish features, but his broad jaw eased this appearance somewhat. He had the look of his father about him, the dark God Dantet, and this was what many had come to fear. *'So they rightly should.'*

"Why not take more time?" Aramus asked. "We can scale the mountains tomorrow. The weather might be more favourable then, and I'm worried a journey like this would be too much for you, old man."

Olórin stopped and faced Aramus, only a little annoyed at his condescension. Although, he thought of him as a man, he knew this boy to be only seventeen-years-old, a baby really compared to his nearly two hundred and ninety-eight years of existence. His youthfulness, however, was evident in his ability to be patronising without realising.

A thin, brown satchel nestled along his spine between his wings and was tied firmly with a leather strap across his broad chest. In all the time that Olórin had known Aramus he had never once seen it leave his person, not even for a moment. But having survived the life Aramus had, Olórin wasn't surprised about the young man's possessiveness over his only property.

A memory of Aramus as an eleven-year-old boy came flooding back to Olórin then; one of how he had been surrounded by twelve fully grown men who had given in to superstition. Their only intention was to kill the cursed child they knew nothing about. It was the first time Olórin and he had met, and it was not a pretty scene to happen upon. Three of the young man's assailants lay gutted on the ground, and if Olórin hadn't interjected, he was sure the others would have soon followed.

In the six years he had known the young man, his emotions and features remained stoic. He never outwardly showed that his terrible life, the acts he had committed, weighed on his mind for one minute. It never rested well with Olórin, or the prophecy infused in his mind, that the young man appeared incapable of feeling anything. But now Aramus seemed to show compassion for Olórin's need for companionship, and homely comfort. It gave him hope that Aramus wasn't so much like his dark father. More importantly, it gave him hope that the small shred of humanity he had inherited from his mother was proof the prophecy could be avoided. If not, then every living creature in Naretia would surely perish.

He studied the young man's features for a moment longer, searching for any hint that his concern was genuine. But as always, despite his words, Aramus's expression was indifferent.

"We are in troubled times, Aramus," Olórin began. "Dantet is raising his dark army, and now his soldiers hide in the shadows of Naretia. Only the mountains of the east and the elven woods to the west have been untouched by it." Olórin continued walking, his expression darkening with every step. "Even the capital, Lothangard, has had its veins muddied by his blood, and the infection is spreading death throughout the land. I fear that it won't be long until these vile forces reveal themselves. When that happens, the last refuges of mortals will be plunged into the midst of a war they knew nothing about. We have no time to dwell in places meant for families and old friends. Our path takes us far away from such pleasantries."

"And what path would that be, old man?"

Olórin was quiet for a time. He had never told Aramus the particulars of the vision he had had over two hundred years ago, long before the young man was born. He had never wanted to tell him that he was destined to be the catalyst that would see Dantet rise again, and the end to all life in Naretia. It was a burden Olórin did not wish Aramus to carry. It was enough that he was feared and hated by anyone who clapped eyes on his large black wings and amber eyes, the same physical traits his father bore.

Olórin had only ever told Aramus that his father had cursed him when he was born, causing him to not feel the way a mortal should. What he didn't tell Aramus was this gave the young man the ability to become as remorseless and as cruel as Dantet himself. Not only that, but it would also imbue him with powers no mortal should ever have. He had hinted that this curse might be an unfavourable trait for a happy life, but had never told him of the scarred landscape and the burnt corpses he saw when his eyes grew heavy at night.

"We go east, deep into the Saraethian Mountains, wherein we will search for the meeting place of the Gods."

"Why would the Gods need a meeting place on mortal soil?" Aramus asked.

"Because sometimes mortals behave like petulant children and need to be sat down and talked to directly."

Aramus laughed. His voice echoed loudly in the mountain pass and the sound of it was strange to Olórin's ears, as it so very rarely happened. Much of the young man's emotions were hidden, but Olórin was convinced that they *were* there, somewhere. They had to be because he was half-human, after all.

The road had long since disintegrated into a snow shoot lined on either side with sheer faces of grey stone. Acid winds raced down the trail, whistling the lonely song of a blizzard. Olórin's foot slipped and if it weren't for Aramus's steady hand catching him by the arm, he was positive that he would have slid all the way back to Valeskeep.

"Come on, you old goat," Aramus said, shifting the strap of

his satchel across his chest and stepping behind Olórin. "If we stay walking you'll be three hundred before we get to our destination."

Before Olórin had a chance to object, he found himself soaring through the frigid air, like a mouse caught in a hawk's claws. Such was the power and the speed Aramus took off with, that his hat blew right off his bald head. He only barely managed to grab onto it with his free hand before the bitterness of the night struck him.

As Olórin looked down at the disappearing glow of Valeskeep, he felt the overwhelming need to vomit. The rapid take-off turned into a graceful glide at dizzying heights, and Olórin could breathe more easily again.

"Aramus," he shouted, trying not to look down, "how many times do I have to tell you? You can't just pick up someone and fly off with them. It's considered rude, you know?"

Aramus didn't say anything, and Olórin hit him with his twisted walking stick, giving a snort of indignation. Olórin's discomfort wasn't just because he dislike flying. He was all too aware that he was getting old, and he didn't like to be reminded of it. Especially not by the likes of a strong, young man such as Aramus.

"Old man," Aramus said calmly from above him, "hit me again and I'll drop you."

Olórin was the one not to reply this time. '*Indeed and you would,*' he thought. It was for that very reason that Olórin had sacrificed so much of his life. He had no choice, because under the rule of the Goddess Edwina, wizards weren't permitted to murder. Olórin had to find another way to save them all. But there were others who didn't want him to succeed. He could feel the ever-nearing reach of a young girl, who was not under the same constraint as the wizards. And Olórin feared her resolve to remove their heads would soon see her victorious.

Chapter 2

The palace throne room was cloaked in a thick silence. The only sound came from the gentle lapping of flames of golden trays of fire oil, dangling from the marble rafters. There were no banners of green and gold hung from the walls, as there had been in years gone by. There was no audience creating a gentle hum, nor did the armour of the King's Guard clatter to kill the silence in the shadowy hall. It was void of all furniture and grandeur, save a small hill of marble steps that led up to a tall, golden throne adorned with green fabric over its seat.

A girl, with a waterfall of red, curly hair spilling over her shoulders, sat in the large chair. Two intensely blue eyes peered out from under the curtain of red, and burned into the wooden doors at the far end of the room. Her slim frame, too slight to fill the throne, was clad from her neck down in close-fitting red, metal armour. A long golden sword rested by her right leg, glinting in the poor light like a statue that might suddenly come to life and slay all who dared look at it.

She waited, gripping onto the golden scrolls at the end of her armrests more tightly with every passing second. Though the oil lamps burned, they could not completely light the dark hall, and that was the way she preferred it. The shadows clinging to the corners of the empty room appreciated it too and waited for their chance to creep forward. In her mind, she saw them tentatively extend a murky hand out when the light flickered dimly, only to retract it again as the oil fires refused to give up on their quest.

Two years she had watched those shadows try to reach her, to no avail. The memories of the past horrors that befell within the walls stayed hidden inside their murky world. She had once been afraid to re-enter the throne room, but with each passing season her patience grew thinner, and she became more ruthless. The shadows, while they still whispered echoes of her heartache, no longer frightened her. It was the brightness that she feared the most. Seeing, in full light, the place where her nightmares had been born, was too much even for her. But she was the queen, and a queen needed a throne.

In the beginning of her rule, she was perpetually flanked with advisors and guards. But she needed no guards now, nor did she need the passive advice of old men wanting peace. The time for peace had long since passed, and her abhorrence for her subject's distaste for blood grew with time.

A loud clunk, followed by a deep wooden groan, came from the far end of the room. A sliver of unwelcomed light intruded into the darkness, stretching its niveous spear along the centre aisle. It was followed by the small, round figure of some creature edging its way past the door.

She waited.

The creature sniffed and snuffled around the air as it fumbled its way inside. Two wide, shovel-like hands, toyed with each other, making their long talons click like an old woman's knitting needles. This was harmonised terribly with the patter-clink of the creature's broad feet, which ended in eight long claws that matched its hands perfectly. The tapping and patter-clinking made its way slightly left of the centre aisle, bumping its bulbous, furry frame into marble pillars as it went.

Her visitor was slow, too slow for her liking. She curled her fingers under the scroll of her armrest and the cool metal dug into her palms. The creature neared the throne and as its face emerged into the brighter light, its black beady eyes rested on the occupier. It hesitated, its angst making it emanate noxious gasses from its rear end in small spurts, as was common with its species. A bushel of black whiskers undulated in a deranged manner as its long nose tentatively snuffled the air in front of it.

"Q-Queen Aria?" it asked in a squeaky high voice.

Two large yellow teeth protruded from its upper lip as it spoke, making it impossible to tell if the creature was open mouthed on purpose or not.

"What news?" she replied in a flat tone.

The creature stumbled backward when she spoke.

"My, my apologies, Your Majesty. I'm afraid with my poor eyesight I did not see you there," he said, bowing so low that his snout almost touched the floor. More gasses escaped his rear end with the effort.

"I care not for your excuses, moleman. What news? And you had better not make me ask you again." Aria's tone seethed with unspoken deadliness.

The mole man jumped up to attention and a loud rasping noise echoed against the marble walls. Aria wrinkled her nose at the smell that was becoming more pungent. *'Stink ridden, flea infested, windbags,'* she thought. *'What useless creatures.'*

"Y-Your Majesty," the moleman began. "My people have scoured the city of Lothangard, they've eavesdropped on every wizard, and alerted all the trolls, ogres, harpies, and worgen in Naretia to your request."

"What about the dwarf mines?" Aria asked, narrowing her blue eyes.

"Ah," he replied, twitching his snout. "Ah, you see, well, that one I'm afraid is a bit, em, complicated."

The moleman shut his beady eyes and cowered in front of her.

Aria said nothing. She didn't move. She waited.

"Y-You see, em, it seems that, well, I don't know quite how to put this," he continued. "But, it seems that the dwarfs have put protection around their lands to keeps us, and every non-dwarf, out. I guess, well, you know, that being the only other creature which burrows beneath the ground, they thought we might steal their treasures from them. It's not true of course. Well, maybe just a little, but it's mostly lies and the dwarfs have always been a little paranoid if you ask me."

"I *didn't* ask you," Aria said coldly. "Enough of your stories, you little pest, have you heard anything about the wizard or the winged man?"

"Eh, well… n-no, I'm afraid not."

The moleman curled into a ball at the foot of the marble

stairs and quivered violently. It seemed that fear had also clammed shut his rear end in that moment. All that could be heard was whimpering and the gentle lapping of the flames from the oil fires.

"What do you mean, no?" Aria hissed, leaning forward in her throne. "Have you not been scouring Naretia for five straight months now? How can you not have heard anything? What about the lands to the north?"

The moleman unfurled, but only just enough to let his face come out.

"The ice plains of the north are like rock, we cannot burrow through them, Your Greatness," he replied.

"How many of your people are carrying out my orders?"

"All the men and the available women have left their homes to follow your most benevolent lead, Your Highness. But the winged man and the wizard have the advantage of the sky, a place we cannot go."

"Even if they are sky-bound, they have to land at some point," she shouted. "What of your children, do they search as well?"

The creature unfurled and looked at Aria with an astonished expression.

"N-no, Your Majesty, because they are children."

Aria swooped down from her throne with her golden sword in hand. Quicker than a lightning strike, she pointed it at the furry neck of the moleman. A small blob of his green blood oozed from the tip of the sword and trickled down his fat torso.

"My army is positioned and waiting," she said. "Send the children too, *all* of them. And I don't care if the imaginary dragons that people say live in the ice plains, pick you off one by one. Send your people to the north. They *must* be found. Do I make myself clear?"

The moleman froze like a statue.

"Do you hear?" Aria shouted.

"Y-yes, of course, Your Majesty. Right away, Your Majesty."

Aria was contemplating whipping off one of the moleman's fingers as a reminder of his duties, when a small tittering noise emanated from behind her throne. She knew who it was and instantly withdrew her sword.

"Begone, moleman, and do not return until you have some good news for me."

"Y-yes, Your Majesty, as you wish, Your Majesty," he said, scrambling to his feet.

The moleman dashed out of the throne room faster than his little round body had probably ever gone before. He bumped his way against the marble pillars, and just as he closed the large wooden door behind him, he let out a gaseous rumble that would have rivalled an ogre's.

Again the small tittering noise came from behind the golden throne.

"Do you think that's funny?" Aria asked, sheathing her sword into the black scabbard on her hip. The snigger grew louder and louder, until the full volume of a child's laughter rang out in the empty hall.

"Why don't you come out?" she asked, taking two steps at a time back to her throne.

There was no answer.

"Oh, I see," she said. "You want me to come find you?"

A small shuffle was the only reply.

"All right, but you know what I'll do to you when I find you, don't you?"

Silence again.

"I'll take my sword and run you through," she said, jumping behind the throne.

There was no one there. Aria circled the golden chair until the room around her spun, but to no avail. She couldn't find the owner of the voice anywhere.

"Come out, come out, wherever you are," she sang.

A shrill scream made her look upward. Perched precariously on the very top of the throne, that was at least three heads taller than Aria, was a young boy. A crazed smirk crossed his face as he lunged his whole body at the queen, soaring through the air like a pouncing cat.

"Aaagh, die you wicked queen, die," he roared, landing squarely on her torso.

His weight sent her tumbling backward onto the ground with a loud clatter of metal armour. Tiny fists flew in Aria's direction, but she fended them off easily. Grasping the young boy under his arms, she picked him up and flung him to the side before flipping over and righting herself. The young boy landed on his feet and, within a second, was running at her again. A mop of curly red hair jostled violently as he ran.

"Oh, no, whatever shall I do?" she said, running away from the young assailant.

With a maniacal laugh, he pursued Aria around the throne, time and time again, until he finally caught up with her. Producing a small wooden sword from his belt, the young boy swung it wildly. She dodged his attacks in swift movements left and right.

"Death to the Blood Queen," he roared.

Aria stopped in her tracks and faced the young boy. She caught his wooden blade in her hand as he thrust it toward her abdomen, stopping it dead.

"What did you call me?" she asked, furrowing her eyebrows.

"The Blood Queen," the young boy replied, relinquishing his sword and his fierceness immediately.

"Where did you hear that name, Pearan?"

"I, I, I don't want to get anyone in trouble," Pearan replied, looking at Aria under his red eyebrows and sticking out his lower lip, like he was about to cry.

"You won't get anyone into trouble," she said, kneeling in front of the young boy and cupping his face in her hand. "Tell me, who said this name?"

"A lot of people; the servants, the tutors," he replied, fixing one of her curls that had fallen in front of her eyes with his small hand. "I think everyone calls you that name. Is it bad?"

"It's not a nice name, and if you weren't my brother I would send you to the gallows for it."

Pearan's jaw dropped and his eyes began to water.

"Really? But I'm only seven. You wouldn't really send me to the gallows, would you?"

Aria thought about it for a minute.

"No, of course not." She wasn't sure that that was the truth. "But if you hear anyone saying that name again, you tell them that I'm going to come and have a talk with them if they repeat it, okay?"

"Okay," Pearan replied earnestly. "Aria?"

"Yes."

"What does it mean?"

Aria let her hand drop from his face and looked into the wide brown eyes of her brother. She wondered if she should tell him the truth. Tell him that it was a name given to her by her people because of all the blood she had shed across Naretia. His face was so innocent in that moment. A cute button nose, the same as her own, was dotted with freckles, and his long fluttering eyelashes would make any lady jealous. It would have made Aria jealous too, only she had the very same features. The only difference between them was that her brother had her father's eyes, while she had her mother's.

"It doesn't mean anything," she answered finally. "It's because I dress in red. But I don't like it, that's all."

"Oh, okay then," he replied, plopping himself onto her throne.

Aria gave him a curious look. The kingdom had come to fear her reign. Great warriors trembled at her power, and dark creatures bowed to her will. Yet, here was a small boy, unafraid and oblivious to what his sister truly was; a monster, according to her people. And that's the way she wanted to keep it.

"You know, you've gotten very good at hiding. If I didn't know any better, I'd swear you were more like a rogue than a prince."

"That's what Daddy was, wasn't he?" Pearan asked beaming proudly at his sister. "He was a rogue before he married Mommy?"

"He was," Aria replied, ruffling his hair. "And you are just like him."

Pearan's smile faded and he fixed his eyes on his black, leather boots.

"I miss them," he said quietly. "Do you think they can

really see us from the afterlife?"

Aria felt the sting of tears at the back of her eyes. She missed them too. But she secretly hoped that there was no afterlife, so they wouldn't see the terrible steps she had taken against her treasonous subjects. They had been kind and wise leaders of Naretia, before they were murdered, and they wouldn't have liked the kind of ruler she had become.

"I'm sure they can," she replied in a whisper.

Pearan smiled broadly then.

"Good, cos I have something to tell Mommy." He stood on the seat of the throne, stretched his neck as long as he could, and took a deep breath in. "I didn't eat my carrots today Mommy!" he roared at the top of his lungs before sticking his tongue out and rasping loudly.

This sent Aria into fits of laughter. It had always been a tiring battle for her mother to get Pearan to eat carrots, and it had become something of a joke between the two of them, even after her death. Pearan had always despised his red hair and thought that eating carrots would only make it worse.

"Go on you little scamp," Aria said, lifting him off her throne. "Go back to Governess Margaret. It's time for your lessons, and *I* have some more training to do."

"Awe," Pearan sulked as he walked toward the door, "I hate lessons."

"So do I," Aria said.

The palace halls were as devoid of decoration and people as the throne room. Long corridors of limestone blocks, mourned a time when they were more frequently used. The narrow windows looked sorrowfully into the overgrown gardens that once housed fabulous parties. Aria remembered them well. She remembered running around the feet of visiting dignitaries in fine robes, pulling on the long beards of old wizards, and horrifying the elegant elves by waving cured sausages around their heads, knowing perfectly well that they did not eat anything that had once lived. Even as a young child, she was known to the palace as a handful. But no one could have suspected the kind of handful she would eventually become, not even the all-seeing wizards.

Aria walked purposefully through the empty corridors, passing the equally empty state rooms with dusty furniture and drawn blinds. She ignored the ancient suits of armour that had been left to rust. It was the purple smoke that rose from the wizard's tower which drew her attention and irked her the most. Even though she was the queen, she couldn't rid her palace of the infestation of treasonous magic-men, their power was too great. Despite their close proximity, however, she hadn't seen a wizard in many months. They were wise enough to keep to themselves and stay out of the reach of her sword.

Aria hurried toward the central courtyard that had once been the fighting arena. It was still winter, and without the summer birds jovial song the arena was oddly silent. Her metal armour clinked noisily in the doldrummy courtyard. In years gone by, it would have been filled with the boisterous army of the King's Guard. Manly roars would resonate between the limestone walls, and clashing swords would have rung until darkness came. But now it was silent and empty. Her guards had abandoned her on the orders of the wizards.

The only living creatures left in this once mighty fighting arena now, was Aria and Edwel – although Edwel wasn't living, strictly speaking. He was a golem, created by the wizards nearly ten thousand years ago to protect the ruler of Naretia, and all future rulers thereafter. He was also unlike most golems. Aria suspected that either the wizards, or the thousands of years he had lived, had changed him somewhat. He talked, pondered questions, and constantly spouted theories of how to be nauseatingly happy. So odd was he, that she wouldn't have been surprised to, one day, find him frolicking in a field of wild flowers, singing some repellently happy tune. But he was also her fighting instructor, and her only remaining companion: The only one capable of disagreeing with her and living to tell the tale – if it could be called living.

"Good morning Aria. Isn't it a wonderful day? The sun is out, the frost has made the world shine, and my mould is slowly dying away," he said, turning toward her.

Aria scowled at him. Edwel clasped his grey stone hands in front of him. His enormous body crunched, grinded, and his powerful stone muscles bulged as his arms came together. A ground-trembling clunk shattered the silence as he took a step toward her, grinding his square toes into the cobbled floor. Edwel was an impressive sight. Half a size bigger than any man, his grey stature would have been intimidating, if it wasn't for the stupid grin across his square head. His stone lips crackled and broke with the effort of smiling, his expression looking a little ridiculous to Aria.

"How are you this fine morning Aria?"

"Tired of your optimism," she said, striding toward the table of weapons behind Edwel. "Why can't you just be like normal golems, Edwel? All this cheeriness and incessant talking is irritating."

"Are you not in a good mood today, Your Highness?" he questioned, fashioning his face into a frown as much as he could.

"What exactly is there to be in a good mood about? My father is dead, my mother too, the kingdom despises me, and the three castes have refused to help me. The world waits and holds its breath until I turn eighteen, in ten months' time, when I will be forced to marry some dim-witted nobleman's son. And then they will look to *him* for leadership instead of me. I am quickly running out of time to do what needs to be done. The only help I can enlist is from the Dark Ones, but they are all but useless and undisciplined. So, what exactly, I ask you, could be *good* about this morning?"

Edwel pondered the question deeply, as he did every question that was posed to him, and scratched a stone finger against his stone chin.

"You are correct," he began, stomping noisily around the courtyard. "The three castes have disapproved of your quest; the wizards, the elves, and even the feisty dwarfs. But at the risk of sounding unoriginal, the night is always darkest before the dawn, My Queen. I am still confident that you shall succeed, and when you look back on this time, you will be proud of the unyielding determination that you showed in the face of great danger.

"However, it is my duty, nay, it is my pleasure to remind

you that regardless of your struggles, this day is still a good one. The sun still shines, ignorant of your labours, the birds will return to sing someday, and my mould still falls away from my back. If you reach the end of your journey without noticing the fleeting beauty along the way, well then, it would be easy to lose yourself to bitterness. And what kind of ruler, what kind of girl, would come out at the other end of your battles?"

Edwel grinned stupidly and froze in his place, waiting for Aria's reply. In that moment he truly looked like a statue to her, not breathing and so very, very silent. She had half a mind not to reply and leave him standing there, looking like an idiot. Edwel only ever came to life when the ruler of Naretia was near, or was in mortal danger.

As much as he irked her, Aria knew he was right. But unlike the overly appreciative golem, who would admire every blade of grass if he could, Aria didn't have to look quite as hard for her joy. Despite the darkness that surrounded her, there was *some* light left in her life. Just one, Pearan. He was the only one left who could make her laugh now, make her forget the brutal things she had done, make her feel as though she was still loved in this harsh world.

But now was not the time to think of fond things.

"Shut up you great big boulder and let's get on with the lesson," she snapped.

"As you wish Aria," he replied, giving a stone-grinding bow. "You have mastered the sword, the bow, and even your fists to a near expert level. But now we must work on your mind." Edwel took a defensive stance in front of Aria. "Battle rarely plays itself out as an equal number of parries and lunges. Fighting dirty is not a nobleman's desire, but it is a warrior's upper hand."

Without warning, Edwel jumped higher than Aria had ever seen him jump before. He landed behind her and the ground shuddered under his weight, making her legs wobble. He kicked her in the back with a swiftness that belied his size, and Aria was sent careening into the table of weapons. The swords, axes, and shields went scattering onto the stone floor with ear splitting crash. Aria swung around quickly to face Edwel, her sword raised, but he was nowhere to be seen. Grimacing from the pain in her back, Aria could feel the rage of frustration building inside of her already.

"Hiding maybe for cowards," his voice echoed from some indiscernible location in the courtyard, "but it also allows you to fight another day, *and* gives the advantage of surprise."

Suddenly Aria felt herself being picked up from behind by her metal chest plate. The wind whistled by her ears as she soared through the air until she hit the far wall with a painful thud. Stars danced around the edges of her eyes and her head spun mercilessly as she tried to catch her breath.

A wild rage boiled inside of her as she gasped for air. It was the same rage that saw her decapitate her enemies on a regular basis. But before she could get her bearings to exact revenge on Edwel, his stone hand reached out to help her up. Aria took it and struggled to her feet again.

"A friendly gesture in a time of need maybe nothing more than a poisoned offering," he said, thrusting his other hand out and slamming it hard into her chest.

Aria cried out in agony and stumbled back a few paces. Her metal chest plate was dented inward, digging painfully into the ribs she suspected Edwel had just bruised. Tearing at the leather straps under her shoulder armour, she screamed in rage and ripped her chest plate off before raising her sword again. Anger didn't boil inside of her anymore, it erupted into a volcano of vengeance.

Aria swung her sword at the golem's head with as much strength as she could muster. It clanged impotently against his hardened skin, and bounced off. But that didn't deter Aria. She swung again and again, lunging, thrusting, and flailing the sword in whichever way seemed the most likely to do some damage, any damage. But it didn't. Her sword bounced and ricocheted off every time, and all the while, Edwel remained frustratingly stoic. She screamed in anger again before slicing the weapons table in two.

"Aria," he said with a look of disappointment in his stone eyes. "Your anger gets the better of you every time. I don't know how many times I have told you that if you lose your temper, you lose the fight."

"I don't care," she screamed at Edwel, hitting the table again. "I don't care how many times you've told me that. You'll just have to keep telling me it because my anger will not leave me. Not until *he* is dead. Not until I have returned the favour he bestowed upon my parents, with my blade. I won't rest, Edwel, I will never rest until his head is driven into one of the spires of the castle towers."

Edwel's stony gaze rested on Aria for a long time.

"Do you hear me golem?" she roared breathlessly.

"I do," he replied.

Chapter 3

"Honestly, Olórin, do I really have to go?" Aramus asked.

"Yes," Olórin replied, his enthusiasm lifting his legs higher than they would normally go.

"You could just go yourself, you know. I don't mind finding my own food and staying around the outskirts of the town, like I normally do."

"What would be the fun in that? Come on, Aramus. Some of the most wonderful things in life happen with a pint of ale in your hand."

"Need I remind you, old man, that ale has no effect on me?"

"Bah!" Olórin replied, batting his hand in Aramus's direction. "You just haven't drunk enough, that's all. Come. Let us try an experiment and see if we can't get you drunk tonight. Eh?"

"And the wings?" Aramus said, gesturing toward his back.

"Ah, I nearly forgot," Olórin replied, slapping his hand on his forehead. "Here."

He took off his droopy hat and pulled out a black cloak, which shouldn't have fitted, from inside. Aramus took the cloak and looked questioningly at Olórin's hat. Up until recently, Olórin had been content to live with the young man in a small hut many miles from Lothangard, and out of the way of prying eyes. They had only ever ventured into the public as needed. With all his comforts so close at hand, he had never had any need to use his hat in Aramus's presence before this. But Aramus was nearing the time when a prophecy would come to pass. With little or no change in his demeanour, Olórin couldn't leave anything to chance. It had become apparent that they *must* embark on the perilous journey he had tried so hard to avoid. It also meant that Olórin must remove the veil of normalcy he had tried to give Aramus.

"What?" Olórin said, shrugging his shoulders. "There has to be some perks to being a wizard, right? I shouldn't tell you this, but I also have a cauldron, some books, potions, spare clothes, and, amongst other things, a chicken in there."

"A chicken?"

"Why not?"

Aramus rolled his eyes and threw the cloak carefully over his wings. He covered his head with the moth eaten hood, and Olórin nodded in satisfaction.

"Just keep the hood down low and no one will see your eyes," he said to Aramus.

"I hate wearing this thing," Aramus huffed.

Olórin knew only too well and waited for Aramus's shoulders to slump under the memories that should have haunted him. '*Be strong, my young friend,*' Olórin thought. '*It will all be worth it in the end.*' But Aramus's shoulders remained as square as ever.

They strolled down the narrow, hilly streets of the small mountain village of Tasadia. The townsfolk were mostly Mountainmen now. It seemed to Olórin that the higher they climbed into the mountain communities, the more Mountainmen they saw. The tall, wide people, all with fair hair, green eyes, and adorned in thick fur coats, gave them peculiar looks as they passed by. Olórin suspected that the sight of an old man and a hunch back, who coward away from bright streetlights, might have seemed quite an odd couple to them.

"Evening," Olórin said, dipping his brim toward a pair of ogling ladies.

Mountainmen were commonly twice as tall as a regular man, and the origin of their size had been lost through time. It was believed that they were either the bastard children of man and fabled giants, or demi-gods gifted their size by some old world deity. Either way, a love of alcohol was also a well-known trait of the Mountainmen. If it weren't for their love of ale, which saw them become jovial and melodic, Olórin was sure they could have easily conquered the kingdom of Naretia. Thankfully for the kingdom, they had never shown any interest in defeating anything but a tankard.

The village sparkled with the frosty jacket it wore and Olórin was relieved that the wind had finally died down. His thick cloak and fur boots were sodden, and the cold mountain air had crept into them, trying to remove his toes. Frost bite would have been a certainty if the squall hadn't weakened. Olórin stared longingly into the warm glowing living rooms of the oversized cottages that lined the hilly streets.

"Tell me again, old man, why have you never found yourself a woman and settled down?" Armaus asked.

"Psht, too busy, far too grumpy and finicky for the delicate creatures that are women. I mean, could you imagine some poor lady having to deal with the likes of me?"

Olórin hocked noisily and spat half way across the street to emphasise his point. Seeing a glint of disbelief in Aramus's eyes, he proceeded to scratch his rear end and complain about the parasites that might be living there.

"Hmm," Aramus replied, sounding unconvinced.

"Anyway, I'm too old now to consider such things. But *you* on the other hand, you're at the right age to find a young lady friend," Olórin said, jabbing Aramus in the ribs. "How about we try and find you someone tonight, eh? In a mountaintop village like this, there is bound to be a surplus of girls needing husbands."

"Old man, don't you dare," Aramus said. "You know as well as I do that no woman would have me. I'm a freak, a bad omen, as evident by the cloak I have to wear just to walk amongst them. Better we just keep our heads down, get some food, and then be on our way."

Olórin was disappointed. If there was anything that could make his quest easier, it was if Aramus could find true love. Such a thing had a powerful magic all of its own and it was always good. Olórin had witnessed its lure turn a village lout into a hero, and Aramus so desperately needed to change, even if he didn't realise it. He sighed with deep-seated resignation because the young man was right, of course. Most women would have opted for an old wizard, rather than a strange creature like Aramus. It was unfair, but it was the truth.

"Very well," said Olórin.

The two walked in silence and soon the streets opened up into the large town square. Brightly decorated carts filled with food, clothes, wine, toys, weapons, and a multitude of strange items Olórin recognised from his youth, crammed every square inch of the quadrangle. The air was heavy with the smell of pan fried nuts, freshly brewed ale, and smoked curiosities. More than the smells, voices boomed, one louder than the other, with the names of the different products for sale.

"Oh look," Olórin squeaked with delight, quite by accident. "It's Winter Fest, the Mountainmen's celebration of the end of winter's end. I hadn't realised so many months had passed. Come, Aramus, come and see the delights of such a wondrous event."

"Olórin, I can't. It's too bright, there are too many people."

Olórin ignored Aramus and trotted toward the coloured stands, instantly lost in the red, gold, and orange silks that floated in the gentle wind. He gazed over the mottled stalls, and sniffed in deeply the scents that he remembered only too well. The smell of caramelised nuts conjured recollections of his days as an apprentice wizard. Dried fish on a stick brought back the memories of he and his friends quelling the potent maladies of ale by eating a variety of food on a stick. Olórin laughed as he remembered accepting the challenge of eating a fried rabbit gonads on a stick once.

"Do you know… "

Olórin was about to tell Aramus about the surprisingly sumptuous taste of fried "Ruts", as he had so donned them, when he realised that Aramus was no longer behind him. Craning his neck over the tall Mountainmen, Olórin spotted Aramus hiding in the shadows beyond the reach of the bright street lights. If he hadn't have known to look for him, the young man would have been invisible.

"Aramus, coo-wee, over here. Yes that's right over here. Come, don't hide in the shadows, my friend, not when there is so many wondrous things to see."

The crowd between Olórin and Aramus took bewildered glances at the two. The young man put his head in his hands and shook it. *'Oh, perhaps not quite so loud next time,'* thought Olórin. Regardless of the embarrassment, or perhaps to save himself some more, Aramus reluctantly joined Olórin in the busy market.

"Look at these," Olórin said, pointing at the menagerie of products lining the streets. "Why, it's been more than a hundred and sixty years since I've hand the pleasure of tasting pickled snails. And look, stuffed barbequed apples, how wonderful."

"Dare I ask what they're stuffed with?" Aramus asked sulkily.

"Pig snout of course!"

"Of course, why wouldn't they be?"

Olórin noted the tone of distaste in Aramus's voice and scoffed at his limited palate.

"Two dozen snails and a stuffed apple please," he said to the jolly looking Mountainman behind the stalls. "Oh, and if you have any beetle candy I'll have a packet of those too. You know, Aramus, I've always wondered how they get the snout into the apple. There never appears to be any damage to the skin of the fruit and yet, they have assured me, every time I asked, that it's not done through magic."

Aramus didn't respond.

"Five shekels for de lot," the rosy-cheeked Mountainman said, leaning close to Olórin with an unsteady gait, a fatuous grin, and an overpowering whiff of ale coming from his breath.

Olórin tossed the oversized man five silver coins and collected his brown paper bag with a satisfied sigh. He stuck his nose into the produce and inhaled as though the smell alone could sustain him.

"Ah, now that brings back memories," he said, handing Aramus a stuffed apple.

Aramus refused, all the while glancing nervously at the pressing crowd. A few green eyes returned Aramus's wary look. He was careful to keep his hood lowered and his back away from prying hands.

"Come," said Olórin gently. "If I remember correctly there is a little tavern near here called, The Monkey's Nuts. Fantastic food and even better ale, quite too and out of the way. What say we have a drink or three there, you know, to the warm the old bones?"

"I'd say that sounds like a good idea," Aramus replied with a hint of relief in his voice.

The two companions left the bustling market and made their way down narrow winding streets, lined with more oversized cottages. The smell of smoke wafting from the chimney stacks, mixed with the crisp mountain air, brought a smile to Olórin's lips and a warm feeling in his heart. *'How long has it been since I celebrated Winter's Fest?'*

Olórin had always loved the Mountainmen's winter festival. In his youth he used to travel here every season with his Mountainman wizard friend, Gustoff. Whilst the rest of the kingdom wallowed in the cold and damp, locking themselves away in a hibernation, Olórin found warmth in the high mountain settlements. There was never a door shut in his face, nor was his tankard ever left empty. Perfect strangers would hug him and invite him back for a hearty meal. For to know the Mountainmen was to truly know family. It was for that very reason that not many Mountainmen took up the call of wizardry when it came. They preferred the simple life instead, unlike the human or dwarf wizards, of which there were many.

But that was over two centuries ago now, and Gustoff had not lived the long life Olórin had. He had been one of only a few wizards to answer the Mountainmen's call for help in the genocide that was perpetrated by the ogres some one hundred and fifty years ago. With the aid of a wizard, turned by the alluring powers of Dantet, the ogre's had emerged from the world below.

But living in this world was not a natural thing for ogres. Without the heavy hand of Dantet culling their population, their numbers grew too large to hide in the darkened city streets. The mountain offered them a new home where they could flourish. But they were ferocious neighbours, and the fever of bloodthirst infected a large portion of them.

Hunting in packs, they came upon the Mountainmen settlements and sent word back to their leaders about a new abundance of food. Although the mighty Mountainmen had put an end to the war, their population had been cut in half by the end of it. Since then, they had become more cautious about inviting strangers into their homes, especially if they were wizards. Now, instead of open doors and warm smiles, the only movement from the houses was the twitch of an off-white curtain as the two strangers walked by. The war happened a long time ago and the reasons for their stiltedness had been lost through the ages by most, but not by everyone. Wizards were not welcomed anymore, not since they decapitated the dark wizard responsible for their losses.

Olórin didn't expect anything less. There wasn't a day that went by when he didn't feel the weight of guilt for pursuing his quest instead of aiding his friend. But obsession had blinded him, and most of the wizard caste, to anything other than the prophecy. It was that regret which made his steps feel heavy in a place he used to call his second home.

They rounded a sharp corner and Olórin stopped short.

"Ah, good, it's still here," he said. "The Monkey's Nuts."

The two story thatched building looked as though it had been through a few fires in its time. The straw roof was tattered and bare in spots, while the once white walls were caked in soot. Red shutters dangled precariously from their hinges, missing slats, and in desperate need of a new coat of paint. Olórin didn't remember it looking quite so shabby, but then again, it *had* been a long time.

"You sure this is a tavern?" said Aramus.

"Never judge a dwarf by his height, Aramus. Some things might just surprise you."

Aramus gave a snort and wrinkled his hooked nose at the building. Olórin had to admit that he probably would have had the same reaction if he was introduced to the pub in its current condition. Regardless of the taverns appearance, however, Olórin heard the cheerful sounds of men singing and tankards colliding from inside, and that was enough for him.

He pushed the timeworn, wooden door open and smiled.

Inside, the tavern hadn't changed a bit. Sawdust still covered the grey slate floors, large tables with even larger benches lined the yellow walls, and a great fire burned inside an enormous hearth against the far wall. Tall Mountainmen lined the circular bar in the centre of the room, their heads nearly reaching the wooden rafters. They paid no heed as the two strange men entered, too busy besting each other in arm wrestling matches or drinking games.

The tavern was busy, but Olórin saw his usual table set off to the back and made a beeline for it. Just like he remembered, *this* table was the only one made specifically for the smaller derrieres of non-Mountainmen folk and, as such, was all but useless to the usual clientele.

"Sit," he ordered Aramus, who dutifully followed his directions.

Aramus kept his back to the wall and his hooded eyes to the crowd. He shifted nervously in his stool and pulled the hood down further. Olórin felt a pang of pity for his young companion. *'To always have to be so guarded.'*

"Vot vill it be?" a female voice interrupted his thoughts.

A large woman with thick, blonde hair tied up in a two haphazard buns on the sides of her head, tapped her large foot as she waited. She was young and pretty, maybe a little older than Aramus, but at least a half size taller than him. She wore the traditional Mountainwoman brown skirt and white shirt with intricate embroidery throughout. She threw side-ways glances in Aramus's direction, more out of interest than caution.

"Two pints of ale for me and my deformed friend here," Olórin said loudly enough for everyone to hear.

A sudden pain shot through Olórin's leg.

"Stop drawing attention to it, will you?" Aramus hissed under his breath.

The young Mountainwoman paid no heed to their dispute and disappeared through the crowds of large men toward the bar. Olórin rubbed his leg before resting his hat and his staff on a chair beside him.

"Aramus, if other people's curiosity makes you

uncomfortable, then the best way to end that curiosity is to point out the answer. People lose interest once the mystery is no longer a mystery."

Aramus huffed and pulled his cloak around him further. Olórin ignored his friends discomfort and turned his attention to the young waitress instead. She returned with two enormous tankards of ale and banged them down on their table unceremoniously, before taking another quick look at Aramus and leaving. Although the cups would have fitted nicely into the large hands of any Mountainman, Olórin and Aramus both had to use two hands to lift the brews.

Fuelled by three large ales, copious amounts of beetle candy, and the homely feel of the tavern, it wasn't long before Olórin found himself waving his half empty tankard in the air and jovially singing along to one of the Mountainmen's songs, occasionally throwing some stuffed apple into his hat to feed the chicken.

"Oh, on de tide of scarrabee,
De God, Krut, came from de sea,
He loved de Mountainmen young and old,
And gave them gifts dat were not gold.

"Take my strength, and my might,
Take my two green eyes for your sight,
Dese were de words he had spoke,
To de mighty Mountainmen folk,"

"Come, Aramus, sing with me," he said, elbowing Aramus in the ribs.

Despite having had four tankards of ale, Aramus remained unperturbed. Neither the ale, nor the bonhomie of the tavern, seemed to move him. Olórin sighed and turned to his young companion.

"Couldn't you at least *try* to have some fun?"

"I cannot be anything other than what I am, Olórin," he said flatly.

Olórin was caught by his words. He felt a lump in his throat and a sinking feeling in the pit of his stomach. *'But you must, my friend, the future of Naretia may depend on it.'* The sinking feeling deepened and Olórin felt a coldness edge in around him. His head swayed and his vision blurred. It was not dread or ale that was making him feel so ill.

"Oh, no," he whispered. "Not now."

Olórin felt himself slump forward onto the table and, as the world disappeared around him, he heard the distinct noise of his tankard crashing to the floor.

"Old man, snap out of it. Not here. They'll realise you're a wizard and who knows what they'll do to you," he heard Aramus whisper in his ear. "Oh for the love of the Goddess Edwina, at least close your eyes, they've turned all white again."

Olórin felt a hand slide over his eyes, and then he was surrounded by darkness. But in that darkness he could still see a silvery outline of the place he had just left. He watched as he floated above his body, which Aramus had propped up against a nearby pillar, and above the heads of the unsuspecting patrons of the Tavern.

"Is your friend okay?" the Mountainwoman asked as she came to collect the fallen tankard.

"Yes, yes, he's fine," Aramus lied. "Just too much ale, that's all."

"Hmm," the young woman said looking at the pair. "I suppose Mountainman ale is a bit strong for you little folk. But *you* seem to be okay. You must have de strong stomach."

"I guess so," Aramus said, looking at his empty cup.

"I like a man vith de strong stomach," said the waitress, leaning over suggestively and picking up Aramus's tankard. "How about I get you anoder vun?"

Olórin's vision from above their table, drifted off with the sound of Aramus stuttering nervously. The tavern disappeared in a mist of swirling silver lines, and Olórin found himself outside the front door again. The frost glistened in his vision under the moonlight, like a painting made entirely out of diamonds. He felt no coldness anymore.

Hollowed out silvery Mountainmen walked by, and even through him, unaware that he was there. The street lamps shone a dazzling light on carts as they ambled past, and the sounds of hooves clopping seemed distant.

Without warning, Olórin fell beneath the earth. Although he was surrounded on all sides by the dark soil, he could still see beyond it. His vision painted a silvery outline of something small burrowing its way underground, like some artist had drawn a moving picture on a black canvas. The creature came closer and closer. It wasn't long before Olórin knew what it was, and the sight made his heart pound fiercely in his chest.

"So, ver are you two from?" the waitress's voice cooed.

"Look, you seem like a nice girl, but really, I'm not right for you," Aramus said uneasily.

Olórin was only half aware that he was back in his body. Coupled with the copious amounts of ale he had drunk, he found it hard to snap back into reality. His limbs were heavy and his head, too dizzy to allow him to speak.

"I tink dat I should be de judge of dat," she said.

Olórin opened his eyes to the sight of the young waitress sitting at the table beside Aramus. She leaned over, and gently pulled his hood down behind him.

"No, wait…" Aramus said, raising a hand, but not stopping her.

Aramus closed his eyes and clenched his jaw. '*Don't be repulsed, don't be repulsed,*' Olórin thought over and over hopefully. The young woman took Aramus's chin in her hand and raised his head up to look at her. He opened his eyes, and for a moment, Olórin saw the hope he had so longed to see there.

And then it happened.

"Dantet!" she whispered at first, her eyes and mouth opened wide.

She snatched back her hand like Aramus's face had burned her and got up from her seat, backing fearfully into the crowd.

"DANTET!" she roared to the patrons of the tavern. "HE HAS DANTET'S EYES."

Aramus remained stoic. His shoulders didn't slump, his eyebrows didn't furrow. In fact, he remained more emotionless then Olórin had ever seen him before, and Olórin knew that that wasn't a good sign.

The patrons turned to look at the person the waitress had screamed about, and each of them mimicked her fearful expression. Some of them backed away, other's put down their ales and reached for their swords. The remaining few just stared open-mouthed at the young stranger with slatted amber eyes. It was only then that Olórin's groggy mind reminded him of the vision he had just had.

"We must leave," Olórin croaked.

"Whatever gave you that impression?" Aramus said, throwing his cloak off and flexing his large black wings to a startled crowd. He reached out a hand to Olórin and helped him onto unsteady feet. "Yes, that's right take a good long look," Aramus spat at the crowd. "Why don't you all run home and grab your pitchforks and torches? That's what you want to do, isn't it? Well, go on then."

"Aramus, we must leave, *now*," Olórin said more forcefully.

"They're not going to do anything, old man, too worried about the wrath of Dantet, aren't you? I pity all of you, you know, letting superstition dictate your thoughts and actions. Pathetic!"

"ARAMUS!" Olórin boomed, silencing the whispers that were flittering around the tavern. He grabbed hold of Aramus's black leather tunic and pulled him closer. "We have to go *now*. One of the queen's molemen is making their way here as we speak."

"You saw it in your vision?"

"Yes. Forget the Mountainmen. Pick me up and fly away from here as fast as your young wings can carry us. Do you hear, Aramus?" he said, grabbing for his staff and hat.

Without needing another word, Aramus scooped Olórin into his arms and burst out of the Tavern in a torrent of flapping wings. Olórin knew that if he asked Aramus to take to the air with him, the gravity of the situation would be clear.

Turning his head back toward the tavern as it disappeared out of sight, Olórin spied a mound of soil erupt from under the cobble stone in front of the door. A small, furry ball emerged from the mud. But before it could get a good look at which direction they were headed in, Olórin pointed his staff toward the ground.

"IGNEOUS!" he shouted.

A sliver light snaked from his hand, down the twisted wooden knolls of his staff, until it gathered at the burl like streaks of lightning chasing each other. The deadly sphere pulsated and shot toward the mound, its sound tearing through the air as if it were fabric. Olórin wasn't sure if he hit the moleman with enough force to stun him. Regardless of its capacity to remain upright, he was sure it wouldn't be able to follow them at the very least.

Chapter 4

The quiet, narrow streets of Tasadia rang out with the perfectly timed cadence of armoured boots on frozen cobbled roads. The ominous sound was only interrupted by the heavy, mistimed steps of Edwel the golem.

From beyond the closed shutters of the large cottages, Aria heard the whispers of, "The Blood Queen is here," as she passed by. As much as she wanted to slice out their slanderous tongues, she didn't. She was preoccupied instead with finding this tavern in which her enemy had last been spotted. The moleman, whose fur had been singed almost clean off, ran on all fours to stay ahead of the queen's determined pace. He looked more like a small pig than a moleman, and the snorting and grunting of his heavy breathing made him sound like one too.

Behind her, an army of ogres, dressed in black armour, marched in rows of four. Their bulbous, green heads, adorned with two small horns and tiny black eyes, bounced in time with the march. Long, sharp teeth jutted from their mouths in such a deranged manner, that it gave the impression of a being whose creator had modelled them in the dark. They weren't as tall as the Mountainmen, but their mere presence seemed to strike terror into the hearts of every man, woman, and child they came across in Tasadia.

These monsters didn't know fear, too stupid to think of it, and that is exactly why Aria found them to be her perfect army. Like the body of a dark snake with a head of red, glinting armour, they wound through the streets until they stopped outside a rundown tavern on the outskirts of the town. The moleman skidded to a halt.

"H-here, Your Majesty. This is where I saw them," he stuttered in a squeaky voice.

"And you're sure it was them?" she asked, unsheathing her sword.

"I, I, saw two people flying into the night, and one of them was a wizard. He, he did *this* to me," the moleman replied, gesturing to his naked body.

"How can you be certain of what you saw? From what I am told your people are almost blind," she demanded, leaning forward and pointing her sword to his throat.

"A girl," he replied quickly, stumbling backward with desperate fear in his black, beady eyes. "A girl inside saw him. I heard them talking about it afterwards."

"Did she now?" Aria said, feeling the excited pull of discovery draw her toward the tavern.

Inside, the patrons sang around a circular bar. Sawdust covered grey slated floors, and a fire roared in a large hearth at the far wall. The singing and crashing of tankards quieted when she entered, and a grave silence took the place of the merriment. Aria strode in, followed by four heavily armed ogres, and Edwel.

"I am looking for an old wizard and a hunchback," Aria began. "I've been told that he was spotted here some two days ago. Is this true?"

No one answered. The patrons stared at Aria with a collective hardness that couldn't have been missed; their green eyes shooting deadly glances between her and her army.

"I-it was that one," the moleman said, slipping between the ogres thick legs and pointing to a young Mountainwoman at the back of the bar.

Aria approached the young girl, who was at least a half size taller than her and twice as broad. She studied her brown skirt, white shirt, and two blonde buns on the side of her head for a moment, and then smiled pleasantly at her.

"Did you see them?" Aria asked sweetly.

"How dare you," a man's voice came from behind the bar.

Aria followed the sound of the voice, unable to hide her sneer, to see an older Mountainman gripping onto a dirty dish cloth so tightly that his knuckles had turned as white as his long plaited hair.

"I'm sure you're not referring to *me* in that manner," Aria replied with a small laugh.

"How *dare* you," he repeated more firmly.

The patrons collectively put down their tankards and stood soberly in their place, like they had never touched a drop of ale in their lives.

"I am your queen," Aria said with a deadly tone, "and I shall dare what I please. Which includes doing what is necessary to protect Naretia."

"Dese filty ogres murdered our people, slaughtered dem in an unprovoked attack. And now you bring dem here, into our land, our homes, and treaten us vith anoder battle dat saw entire clans viped from existence? No quveen of mine vould insult deir people like dat."

"Your people were betrayed by the wizard caste, as I recall," Aria said, stepping toward the Mountainman behind the bar. "It was one of them who unleashed the ogres to begin with. And if that wasn't bad enough, they abandoned you to your fate. The Mountainmen were forsaken by the only ones with enough power to stop the ogres.

"From your own history, you should know not to trust the wizard caste. The wizard I seek was one of those who ignored your call for help. He is also harbouring a murderer, one that I am trying to bring to justice. Why should you show him any loyalty?"

"Because he is de lesser of de two evils," the man replied, pursing his lips into a thin line. "Better to be ignored, den to be slaughtered at de vim of a little girl who bathes de land vit blood, and shames de good name of her family."

Aria felt the anger boil inside of her. She clenched her hand around her sword, and her heart pushed hot blood around her body until she was near bursting point. Edwel's resounding stone footsteps sounded muffled in her head as he approached.

"Your Majesty," he began in a sunny voice. "Please remember that these are good, hardworking people. They only misunderstand you."

Aria ignored the golem and nodded at one of the ogres.

The ogre swiftly raised his bow and shot an arrow through

the Mountainman's neck. His eyes widened and blood spilled quickly down the front of his shirt. The silver haired goliath choked and spluttered for air he could no longer take, before collapsing onto the floor. A few Mountainmen ran to his side but emerged a moment later shaking their heads and clenching their fists. Aria heard the whispers of her hated moniker bubble from the gathering. The young woman she had come to question, screamed a bitter, heart-broken cry.

"Oh, Aria," she heard the golem sigh.

Ignoring him, Aria took swift steps back toward the Mountainwoman, raised her sword, and pointed it at her chest.

"Did you see them here?" she demanded.

The Mountainwoman stared between Aria and the dead Mountainman. Her eyes were wide and tears glistened at the edges. Aria pressed the point of her sword more firmly into the woman's chest and curled her lip into a sneer.

"Dat was my fader," the young woman whispered.

Aria was only a little bit surprised to find that she didn't care who the old man was, despite the fact that she had lost her own parents in similar circumstances. All she cared about was getting the information she came for.

"Answer me," she demanded.

"Dere vere no such people here," the Mountainwoman said with more defiance than Aria was expecting. She glanced questioningly back at the moleman who held his hands up defensively.

"You lie," she seethed.

"Do I?" the Mountainwoman said rebelliously. "Krunk, did you see anyvone here?"

Another old man, with short, white hair, stepped forward with a determined look.

"Only Mountainmen have passed tru dese doors, until today," he said.

"Dere, see? I told you. Dere vas no vizard, or vinged man here."

Aria smiled wickedly.

"I never said anything about a winged man," she said with a quiet deadliness.

Without warning, Aria pushed her blade deep into the chest of the young woman. The woman grabbed the blade and gasped. Her watery green eyes watched her blood spill over the gold blade, and followed its line until they met with Aria's gauntlet. The only noise which broke the silence in the tavern, was the sound of her wet, gurgling lungs as they fought against the inevitable. With a steely look, she used her last breath to spit blood in Aria's face before collapsing onto her knees, and falling to the floor, dead.

Edwel let out another sigh of disappointment.

"No!" shouted a few patrons.

All of a sudden, the room was filled with Mountainmen scrambling for whatever kind of weapons they could lay their hands on; wooden stools, old knives, anything. A spear shot through the air directly at Aria's head, but before she had time to react Edwel's stone body appeared in front of her and it bounced off his chest.

Aria wiped her face tersely and nodded toward the ogres at the door. With a deafening roar they leaped forward, swinging their mighty cleavers through the sea of defiant Mountainmen. They cut them down, one by one, and the Mountainmen fell like corn stalks in harvest. But the ogres didn't just stop with an honourable kill. Now infused with a bloodlust, they dug their razor teeth into the necks of the fallen Mountainmen, and savagely began to devour them.

Aria strode across the tavern and pushed open the door, leaving the ogres to their job. Sheathing her sword back into the scabbard on her belt, she turned and faced the remaining soldiers. They stood, gazing at the carnage that was visible through the open tavern door, and desire was written all over their hideous faces.

"Aria, was it really necessary to…" Edwel began only to be stopped by Aria's raised hand.

"If you should undermine my authority like that again, Edwel, I shall be forced to leave you at the bottom of an ocean for all of eternity. Do you understand me?"

Edwel nodded, contorting his stone face into a frown.

"I am here only to serve the rightful heir of Naretia."

“We move on,” Aria shouted at the ogres, clutching a small golden amulet that dangled from a gold chain around her neck. “The wizard and the winged man passed here not two days ago, so they cannot be too far ahead.”

Like they were under some hypnotic spell, the ogre army marched in perfect unison at her command. She led them through the winding narrow streets, heading in the direction the moleman had last seen them fly. Behind her the war cries of the four ogres, still mauling bodies in the tavern, echoed in the distance, and she left them to their fate.

Lost to the bloodlust that often takes over the ogre’s feeble minds, making them the most feared creatures in the kingdom, she knew it wouldn’t be long before the remaining Mountainmen in the town, found their weapons and ended their lives. Four ogres in a deep frenzy they could handle, but any more than that would have made it a futile battle. If she remained in Tasadia much longer, the rest of her militia would succumb to the bloodlust and devour the entire town, like they had done over a hundred and fifty years ago. She had to lead them away. After all, it was the least that she could do for her subjects… even if they didn’t appreciate it.

Chapter 5

Fresh powdered snow fell from the burdened branches of countless fir trees as Aramus landed between them. The forest was thick, and the tree branches bounced gratefully upon their release. The silence of the uninhabited mountaintop was only broken by the sound of Aramus breathing heavily, and Olórin groaning as he made to stand from the young man's arms. Having been nearly exclusively carried across the many peaks of the eastern Saraethian Mountains, Olórin had all but forgotten how old his bones truly felt. The sensation of being warm was also a distant memory.

"Do you… want to tell me exactly… what we are looking for," Aramus panted.

Although Aramus was a strong man, Olórin could see that the weak mountain atmosphere was taking a toll upon him. There was only so high his powerful wings could fly without losing their purpose to the lack of air, and it seemed that Aramus had reached his limit.

"You know why we are here, Aramus."

"Yes… I know you think you can cure me with some stupid potion of yours, but what *exactly* are we looking for?" he asked, resting his hands on his knees.

"You will know it when you see it," Olórin replied, making to climb further upwards.

Aramus grabbed hold of Olórin's arm and spun him around to look into his eyes.

"For the Goddess's sake, old man, why must you be so cryptic? We have been travelling these accursed mountains for two straight days now… without so much as a decent night's sleep. Do you even know… where you're going?" he demanded.

Aramus appeared to be unable to regain his strength in the high altitude, his normally tanned face was blanched with the cold. Olórin found it somewhat disconcerting that *he* now appeared to be the stronger of the two, and had finally found a weakness in the young man. *'Perhaps the closer to the heavens we soar, the further away he gets from his father and the weaker he becomes?'* But Olórin also knew that it didn't do to dwell on such matters. He could never use this information to harm Aramus in any event.

"We are heading to the highest peak of Naretia, to the point where the heavens meet mortal soil. In case you haven't noticed, it's not an easy place to find, and not many have travelled there. So, while I do not exactly have a map to follow, I *do* know that it lies within these mountains... somewhere."

Aramus released Olórin's arm and squinted his eyes upward, trying to see the end of their journey through the hazy air. It was the first time in this young man's life that Olórin had seen a hint of worry in his expression.

"We'll soon be above the highest clouds at this rate, but the peak is still a days' climb. I am guessing that we will only be met with the same barren rocks as we saw on the other mountaintops behind us. What makes you think that this place even exists?" he asked.

"I've heard of it from many legends," Olórin replied, digging his staff into the deep snow again and following it with determined steps. Aramus was silent for a long time.

"Are you mad?" he finally shouted. "Only a fool believes the made up tales of drunkards and cowards that try to cover up their failures with elaborate tales." Aramus paused to catch his breath again. "You have dragged us to near the point of oblivion on the well-researched and trustworthy words of a *legend?* Old man... I knew you were eccentric, but I had no idea you were senile too."

Olórin didn't bother to look at Aramus. He didn't have to. He knew that the young man's face would hold an expression of shock and anger, or at least it should have.

"The minds of mortals are limited to what we can see and hear," he said, trudging onwards. "It is true that we are great story tellers. But in the field of originality, I'm sorry to admit, we are somewhat lacking. Most stories are often retells of other, older stories, twisted and turned to hide its true origins. But when a legend appears that is entirely different, so fantastical that it could *not* have been dreamt up by some dreamer in a dingy scroll-laden cell, I have always come to suspect that there might be some truth to them."

"You suspect?" Aramus replied, catching up to the old man. "By your own reasoning, the more unlikely a story is to be true, the more you believe that it is? And so, you have dragged me all the way up here… on a suspicion?"

"Yes! But won't it be a wonderful adventure regardless."

Aramus snorted and Olórin smiled, but together they continued up the mountain. It was a disconcerting change, for Olórin, to see Aramus as the one to struggle. His breathing, still laboured from the thin air, made his footsteps clumsy. On occasion he stumbled over a snow-buried tree root, and Olórin would have to catch him before he fell. '*Now you know what it is like to be a weak human,*' he thought. '*But you shall overcome your weakness in time, and my only hope is you remember it.*'

The two companions climbed higher and higher, until they emerged above the clouds. Far in the distance, the sun's energy had all but been extinguished; its bright yellow colour had turned amber, burning the landscape with its hue. The savage, jagged teeth of the tall mountain ridges made to swallow the ochre ball, as it dipped below the horizon. After a time, it was completely consumed, allowing the darkness to throw its cloak over the world.

As if to spite the full moon lighting their path, the harsh winds tried to turn their tears into rime and blind them. Each slippery step was taken more carefully, and more slowly. The coldness turned into a bitter monster that tried to attack them, viciously slicing at their skin with its frosty claws. Aramus, unable to withstand its onslaught, stumbled on the sheer mountain ridges more than Olórin cared to think was safe. But still they climbed, until the face of the crag became precariously sheer.

The crag itself, it seemed, wasn't best pleased to see them. Like it had a mind of its own, it threw a boulder in their direction and tried to knock them off. But the tumbling rock was met with Olórin's glowing staff, shattering it into a thousand tiny pieces. From somewhere high above them, the companions heard a primordial howl, followed closely by an echo of five or six distinctly different howls.

"What was that?" Aramus asked, craning his neck to see beyond the sheer ridges above them.

Olórin slammed the point of his staff into his young companion's back and pushed him hard into the cliff, just as another boulder tumbled within inches of Aramus's head.

"It is not the mountain that tries to knock us off the ridge. Worgen are the guilty party here," Olórin replied, hugging the icy rock in turn.

"No, it can't be. Worgen don't come this far up from the forest. It's why we flew over it."

"It seems that the queen's proficiency in convincing creatures of the underworld to do her bidding, is more accomplished then I had anticipated. I suspect that the breeze is carrying our scent toward them and they know exactly where we are, even if they can't see us."

Olórin glanced at Aramus, but he didn't see the fear written across his young face, as he would have expected from anyone else. There was no worry, no anger, no anxiety at all at the revelation that they were being pursued by half-men, half-wolf creatures, whose only talent was for disembowelling their prey in the most painful manner. The only discomfort shown was in the paleness of his face, the blue tinge around his lips, and the shiver in his fingers as he pressed his chest against the icy mountain.

"What kind of creature does not fear his own death?" Olórin thought sadly. *"Even those that dwell in darkness and feed on destruction, fear the end."* But Olórin was only too aware of the kind of creature Aramus was and why death had no meaning for him. This boy, this man, that he had known

since the age of eleven, might never know *that* kind of fear no matter how much he tried to teach him. Not, at least, until their quest was completed.

A large boulder sped past Olórin's ear, jolting him from his thoughts. Three more followed, but those were each met with a silvery bolt from Olórin's staff. The explosions sounded out with the sharp, crackle of lightning. Rock fragments and dust covered the two companions as they clung to the cliff edge. The onslaught was unrelenting as more and more boulders flew past their heads at ever increasing quantities.

"They are gathering," Olórin shouted above the sound of the explosions. "They're trying to pin us down until the whole pack is present. They won't attack until then, and we must hide before that time."

"And where exactly do you expect us to hide up here?" Aramus asked sarcastically.

Olórin shot him an unappreciative glance before scouring the jagged ridges above them. "Up there," he said, pointing to a cliff edge. "We shall make camp in that cave up there. It's downwind from where I believe they are waiting for us. The ice is technically water, so if I seal off the mouth of the cave the worgen should lose our scent. But we have to move quickly, before they see us, and can aim better."

"*Should* lose our scent?"

"Do you have a better idea?"

"We could just kill them." Armaus's eyes narrowed and a hint of something deadly glinted in the amber that was illuminated by the full moon. "Between the two of us we could handle them."

"No, Aramus," Olórin said firmly. "I will not kill just because I can. And besides, you are in no fit state to battle a dandelion, never mind a ferocious pack of worgen. You must trust me that right now is *not* the time to fight, but to hide."

Aramus nodded reluctantly and, with fumbling hands along the cliff wall, he carefully followed Olórin along the narrow path. The trail fell sharply away on one side, to whatever fate lay beneath the clouds. Olórin fought hard to stay on the path whilst blasting the boulders at the same time. At one point

Aramus lost his footing and slid onto his stomach, his legs dangling off the edge. His fingers dug into the frozen path to gain some kind of grip. But despite his efforts, he slowly slid toward the edge.

Olórin felt his heart jump into his mouth as he grabbed hold of Aramus's leather jacket and hauled him back onto the path. The two companions huffed with the effort and relief, before a falling boulder reminded them of their urgency.

Clambering inside the cave, Olórin pointed his staff toward the mouth and a silvery light burst from the burl. Within a matter of minutes, a thick, blue wall of ice grew across exit and crackled against the cold breeze outside. Muffled howls made their way through the thick wall. Eventually, much to Olórin's relief, they began to sound further and further away.

Even though it was not as warm as a tavern, Aramus and Olórin were both thankful to be out of the bitter breeze that had betrayed them. With numb, fumbling fingers, Olórin took off his hat and rummaged inside of it. Aramus collapsed against one of the icy walls, and wrapped his dark wings around his shivering body tightly. *'I remember seeing you once like that before,'* Olórin thought. *'It was the last time I ever saw you so vulnerable too, until now. But you were only eleven then, and a much more vicious creature.'*

A sharp nip at Olórin's finger brought him out of his thinking. Apparently the chicken living in his hat didn't appreciate the disturbance of his hand.

"Ouch, accursed fowl," he said through chattering teeth. "Now, where is that fire? No, that's a broom, and that's my collection of *The Thirteen Tombs of Wizard's Decrees*. Some spare underpants. Wait, here it is. No, sorry, that's not it either… you don't want to know what that is. There's some parchment, a chamber pot, OUCH, the accursed chicken again, a tankard, the vegetable patch, and… ah, yes, finally, here it is."

Olórin tipped his hat upwards and pulled his arm out. Hovering just above his outstretched palm was a fully built, and lit, camp fire. He let it hover for a moment, enjoying the heat that radiated from it. Plopping his hat back on his bald head, he picked up his staff and banged it once on the ground. The ice and snow under it, curled away in the pattern of a small circle to reveal the long forgotten grey mountain stone underneath. Taking care not to singe his beard, Olórin placed the lit fire down onto the stone.

Almost immediately, Aramus crawled toward the heat. With his wings outstretched and his hands precariously close to the flames, he let out a long, shivery sigh.

"Better?" Olórin asked.

"How long have we been cold, old man, and you had that fire in your hat all this time?" he asked, now mostly recovered from his breathlessness, and giving Olórin a pointed look.

"The magic in my hat only preserves the items I put in there as they are. As soon as I take them out I cannot stop the fire from burning, my young friend. Nor can I whip up another one at will; magic cannot produce something from nothing. Had I taken out the fire earlier, then we wouldn't have it now when we needed it most," he replied, rummaging in his hat again.

"Have you got anything else warm in there?" Aramus asked hopefully.

"Alas, if you recall, you left my cloak in The Monkey's Nuts. But I do have some eggs from the chicken, some bread, and a jug of elven firewater to warm the blood," Olórin replied, pulling out a large metal pan from his hat and plopping it over the fire. It landed with a resounding *hiss* as the cold metal met the warm flames. With little care he threw the eggs, shell and all, into the pan.

"Warm the blood?" Aramus said incredulously. "I think you mean set it on fire."

"Ah, yes, pure firewater is indeed too much for our kind. But *this* particular brew was made by my dear friend Tallain, the alchemist. He assures me that, while it will still singe the tough hairs off a dwarf's beard, it is perfectly safe for us to drink."

Olórin pulled out a small, brown bottle. It had a large red X haphazardly drawn on its syrupy green label, like it had been marked in haste. Aramus eyed the potion suspiciously.

"Is this friend of yours an elf?" he asked.

"No, no, of course not. I think we both know that elves don't compromise on much, so altering their beloved firewater is out of the question: Too high and mighty with their purity and unadulterated ways of living, and all that. No, Tallian is a fellow human living in the queen's keep, in Lothangard."

Olórin unscrewed the top of the bottle. A small hissing sound rang out against the icy walls of the cave, followed by a small green cloud which escaped the bottle top.

"You mean he's the queen's prisoner?"

"Yes, yes, I suppose he is. But he's also a fine alchemist, and a damn good man to know. Not at all the treacherous poisoner *she* made him out to be."

"Poisoner?"

"Well, even the best of us have a bad day every now and then. I suppose he didn't mean to poison her head advisor on purpose."

"You suppose?"

"In truth, the two of them never really got on, something about one of them stealing the others wife, so one can never be truly certain. Drink?" he said, offering the small bottle to Aramus, who scrunched up his nose and shook his head.

Without so much as the smallest hesitation, Olórin drank from the brown bottle. Almost immediately, his face burned, and he did a little hop before sitting down next to the fire. A pleasant hot tingle coursed through his veins and, as he jabbed the sizzling eggs with a wooden spoon, he was sure that the ice would melt under his bottom from the heat. Aramus watched Olórin warily, like he was waiting for him to die, and huddled closer to the fire.

"You really ought to learn to trust people more, Aramus," Olórin said, holding out the firewater to him again. "I would never lead you astray."

"It's not you I'm worried about," he replied, eyeing the bottle. "It's your friend Tallian, and the true reason the queen has him locked up, that I don't trust."

"I am alive, am I not?"

"I suppose," Aramus replied, taking the bottle and sipping

it at first.

Within a matter of seconds Aramus had polished off the contents of the bottle. His face shone with a healthy warm glow, and his posture relaxed. His two large wings folded neatly behind his back again and he even almost managed a smile. But it wasn't long before his smile faded.

"Olórin, why do they hate me so much?" he asked quietly. "The queen *really* hates me, doesn't she? But she's not the only one. Why do they all want me dead?"

"I won't lie to you," Olórin said with a deep sigh, still poking the eggs on the pan. "I am afraid that you are simply a victim of your heritage. Although, the queen does seem to have taken a rather severe dislike to you that I cannot explain. But in large, people react to you with the most irrational of feelings, fear."

"You mean because of who my father is?" Aramus asked, breaking a chunk of bread off and scooping up one of the eggs with it. "But I am *not* my father. I've never even met him. So, why would they think I am in anyway like him?"

"Because you look like him, Aramus. And because you suffer the same affliction that saw him become the lord of the underworld, ruler of the most feared and hated creatures in existence."

"Is this the same affliction that you're trying to cure me of with your potion? Why won't you tell me about it? I have a right to know."

Olórin bit into the fresh eggy bread, peppered with egg shells, and mulled the contents of his mouth sluggishly. He was waiting for Aramus to get impatient, or to get angry with him for not answering. But as he had expected, Aramus was silent, and waited patiently for his answer.

The truth was that Olórin had thought long and hard about telling the young man about his father, about the reasons why they lived as outcasts since he was a young boy, about why his mother abandoned him, and why every creature on the surface of Naretia ran in fear at the very sight of him. But long ago, many decades before he had met Aramus, he had decided that Aramus's change must happen naturally. It couldn't be forced or influenced by the knowledge of what was expected of him. It is easy to pretend to be something you're not when your life may depend on it. But true change only happens when one is not coerced by outside factors.

Now, however, it seemed that the pinnacle time of the prophecy was drawing near, and without any evidence of change regardless of Olórin's precautions. *'Perhaps I have been wrong not to tell him,'* Olórin thought. *'Perhaps the knowledge will offer him motivation?'*

"Do you remember when I got you that pet Razorbeast?" Olórin asked.

"I do," Aramus replied, tearing a chunk of eggy bread off with his teeth. "It was purple, with more than a dozen sharp razors all over its back and head."

"Do you remember what happened to it?"

"I killed it for biting me. What has that got to do with anything?"

"*That*, I'm afraid Aramus, has everything to do with it." Olórin dropped his bread in the pan, his appetite lost at Aramus's indifference toward life. "You see, I got that pet for you to teach you how to connect with another living creature. I knew the Razorbeast would eventually bite you, they're nasty little blighters at the best of times. But I wanted you to come to love it enough that you would forgive it, regardless of how many times it bit you."

"What in Goddess Edwina's name would make you want to do that?"

"I did it *in* the name of our Goddess Edwina."

Aramus was silent for a moment. His slatted amber eyes studied Olórin in the dim light of the camp fire, and his jet black eyebrows furrowed. What Olórin had to say next prevented him from looking at Armaus directly, so instead, he watched the fire create shadows in between the powerful muscles of his chest. His black shirt was open just wide enough for Olórin to know that this boy, even though he was only seventeen years old, was more physically a man then most peers his age. Given the life he lived, he had to be.

"What exactly do you mean by that?" Aramus eventually

said.

"Let me tell you a story," Olórin replied with a long sigh.

"I'm too old for stories, just answer me."

"This story *is* your answer."

With a suspicious look toward him, Aramus nodded.

"Long before creatures dwelled on the surface of Naretia, there were two gods that hung in the sky. One was Edwina, the creator and the nurturer, the other was Dantet, the passionate lover and the destructor. Together they lived in harmony, and their love filled the skies with a light so bright that it would burn the eyes of a mortal man. The two celestial bodies saw perpetual day come to pass on this world, and the soil was nothing more than dust.

"But Edwina, whose love was abundant, wasn't satisfied to live in an existence with only one other being. So she bore Dantet's children, twins, whom she named Vesta, meaning devotion, and Amor, meaning love. The two stars were born and shone more brilliantly in the sky than any other star that could be seen, and Edwina revelled in their love.

"Dantet, however, was not pleased. He grew jealous of the love Edwina showered on her children. This jealousy painted dark pictures in his mind, which bent and twisted his sense of reason until he couldn't take it anymore. One night, as his lover Edwina slept, Dantet murdered his two children in the hopes that Edwina's love would now be focused entirely upon him, and him alone.

"When the Goddess woke to find her two babies slaughtered, the skies wept for a century. She cast Dantet into a dark underworld where he would never see her light again. She took his powers from him, his fire, his ability to feel, to love, so he could never hurt her again. She took his memories, his heart, and his soul too, until there was next to nothing left of him. It is said that the hollow moon is all that remains of Dantet's physical form, only ever casting a reflection of the light it once had."

"That's a very nice story Olórin, but what has it got to do with me?"

"Don't interrupt! Where was I? Oh, yes. Edwina, wasn't

content to let her heart fester in grief. But without Dantet's seed she could no longer become pregnant herself. So, instead, she created corporeal life on the world where her tears had moistened the once dusty ground. She named her new children's playground Naretia, and watched over us. She also gave some of us unmatchable gifts, so that we may protect ourselves better than her own two children had been able to.

"To the dwarfs she gave bravery, strength, and loyalty. These three traits have proven to be indispensable in resisting the call of Dantet and his dark creatures. It ensures that they can work beneath the ground, close to his dark world, without succumbing to his influence. We, the wizards, were given magic in the most general and powerful sense. We dabble in everything from runes to the good old fashioned abracadabra stuff. We are not born into it, however, rather the ability grows within those chosen by the hand of Edwina herself. But with such abilities comes the inevitable hunger of greed, and the desire to rule all others, grow.

"So as not to abuse our position as the protectors of this world, like Dantet had abused his, we wizards are forbidden to murder. We cannot be complicit in the murder of another either. If we do, then our powers, and the lives of the entire wizard caste, are forfeit. In the midst of battle, however, the Goddess sees reason and does not hold us responsible for the actions of heated minds, only our own.

"Additionally, the elves were given power over nature, with the stipulation that they must remain as pure as nature itself. That is the reason they do not eat meat, nor do they partake in drinking ale, smoking pipes, or any activity which could be seen as unnatural or impure. They are the balancers and, unlike wizards, can kill. But they only do so to maintain the balance of this world. They too are cursed, and should they break their creed, they are instantly turned into Dark Ones, orcs to be exact. That is how the three castes of Naretia were formed, and we have protected its people since the dawn of our time."

"I still don't…"

"I said not to interrupt. I am old, Aramus, and follow a

certain train of thought. Yes, I know I ramble, but I am getting to the point, I promise. Now, where was I again? Oh yes. More than two hundred years ago, just after my apprenticeship finished, and I was enjoying the fruits of wizardom, I had a vision. It was the most powerful vision anyone had ever had and it lasted for days. The wizarding community was awash with stories of my eyes and the ancient words that escaped my lips. People even came from near and far to see me as I lay in a trance.

"The Goddess Edwina spoke to me directly during that vision. She told me of a child that would be born in the future, a child with the blood of Dantet. You see, up until then, Dantet had been content to dwell in his underworld. Without his heart he no longer had the passion he once had and could no longer desire for anything more than the darkness. Nor could he remember why he had been so obsessed with Edwina. But the guilt of murdering his two children was a more powerful magic than even the Goddess Edwina had first thought. It festered within him and created a want, a need, which he could not understand without his soul.

"In the reflection of the moon, Dantet saw the life Edwina had created on Naretia, and something stirred inside of him. He too wanted to create life, to regain something he had once lost, but could no longer remember. He tried to create it using the flesh from his corrupt body, and so the Dark One's were born. But he was not satisfied.

"One night, as Edwina had predicted, Dantet set forth a loyal minion from his darkened world and had him bring back a human woman. Without her permission, he planted his seed in her and returned her to live amongst Edwina's children. Before long she gave birth to a baby boy, a boy she instantly feared. This young boy was different to any other creature in the kingdom of Naretia, and the Goddess was fearful of the chaos she had predicted in his future. She saw that, like his father, this young boy would ensure her own children would all be slaughtered because of him.

"Regardless of her fears, however, Edwina refused to kill Dantet's child, like he had killed Vesta and Amor. That is why she chose me, a wizard forbidden to murder, to stop this prophecy. She didn't not tell me when, or where, this baby would be born, so I wouldn't be tempted to prevent his birth, thus killing him by not allowing him to exist in the first place. So, for over two hundred years I have foregone the pleasantries of a normal life while I searched for this baby, following the path my Goddess has laid out for me."

"And *I* am the baby you speak of?" Aramus asked quietly. "I am the curse of Naretia? You found me that night when I was forced to kill those men who surrounded me. The prophecy you saw was about *me*, wasn't it?"

Olórin nodded and laid a gentle hand on Aramus's shoulder, but he pulled away.

"That's why people fear me isn't it? They think I'm going to slaughter them all."

"Not everyone is aware of the prophecy," Olórin replied. "It was because of fear that I kept it secret from all but the wizards. I couldn't risk anyone taking matters into their own hands."

Aramus shot the old man an impatient look and stood up, pacing the small cave.

"But they can *see* what I am, can't they? They think because I don't get angry that I am incapable of feeling, like my father. They think that because I am apathetic that there's something sinister about me. And you think it too, Olórin, don't you?" he demanded from the old wizard, pursing his lips together.

Olórin said nothing, he would never lie to Aramus.

"But I am human too. Maybe I appear to be indifferent because that is the way the world has taught me to be? Maybe I don't get angry because my anger has led me to do terrible things in the past, things that I regret. Maybe, I hold no faith in this world because it holds no faith in me. My mother killed herself at the sight of me, and my remaining family beat me daily to rid me of my *demons*. These are the memories that I keep locked inside, the reasons why I am the way I am, and not because of who my father is."

Aramus ran his hands through his thick hair and took a few

deep breaths.

"If Edwina has seen me do terrible things… maybe the world *would* be better off without me," he whispered.

Olórin watched, almost dumbly, as the young man pulled out a small dagger from his black leather boot and placed it into his wrinkled hand. Aramus knelt down in front of him and wrapped his hand over both the dagger and Olórin's unwilling grip, pointing the knife to his throat.

"Go ahead," he said. "Kill me. Naretia would be better off, and you will be freed of your burden."

The dagger pricked Aramus's neck and a small drop of black blood ran down its blade. Olórin watched the young man's Adams apple bob up and down as he waited for his death. His eyes scrunched closed and a single tear rolled from the corner, trickling down his cheek. Olórin had never realised that Aramus was so bothered by the reasons behind people's hatred toward him. But in that moment, something in the trembling of Aramus's fingers gave Olórin hope that the prophecy could indeed be prevented.

"Are you scared to die?" Olórin asked in a whisper.

"Of course I am. What man wouldn't be?" he said, closing his eyes and waiting.

Chapter 6

"Get a move on, you pathetic shower of miscreants," Aria shouted.

The ogres marched nosily in rows of four and kept time with her pace up the mountain. Their perfectly timed footfalls rang out amongst the thick trees and scattered whatever was nesting inside the forest. A handful of dead ogres dotted the path behind them, dead from exhaustion. Still they marched through the woodland, driven by an unnatural desire to obey Aria.

"Your Highness," Edwel whispered as he trudged along beside her. "This is not an ogre's preferred environment. They cannot keep up with this pace. The cold is too much for them and they need to rest, *you* need to rest."

"I will not rest until I reach him and one of us is dead," Aria spat at the golem. "They are only ogres, Edwel. Honestly, do you care so much for all living things that you're actually bothered by what happens to these filthy beasts?"

Edwel pondered the question leisurely. He tapped his finger against his stone jaw and turned the opening of his mouth downward, as much as was possible. Aria didn't wait for his reply. The desperate desire to catch her prey filled her heart and wouldn't allow her to find a reason to delay. She could feel how close she was to the winged man now, and was determined that nothing was going to stop her relentless pursuit. Not even the welfare of the army which unwittingly followed her.

"I suppose I *do* care that they are being mistreated, but not for the reasons you might think," Edwel finally answered. "While I am aware of the ground we have gained over your nemesis, I fear that when you finally reach him your army will be too exhausted to be of any use. Not only that, but when you are done with these ogres, do you expect that they will just forget what you have done to them?"

Aria stopped and stared at the golem, her army came to an abrupt halt behind her too. If she could only keep marching, keep trudging through the bitter cold nights and eat only when weakness tugged at her muscles, then she was sure to catch up to the monster who had killed her parents. But even with the fire of her defiance fuelling her body, her chest grew tired of breathing so heavily for so long. She wondered if Edwel was right, would she would be able to fight Dantet's son in such a weakened state?

"I don't intend to let the ogres live once they have gone beyond their usefulness," she seethed. "But we can rest, if you think prolonging the inevitable is kinder." Aria turned to her army. "We stop and make camp here," she ordered.

With a collective sigh the ogres broke rank, some of them even collapsed to their knees, but Aria wouldn't let them rest for long. She clutched the golden pendent around her neck and ordered them to collect firewood and food. The night was slowly losing its battle with the sun and Aria knew that she wouldn't sleep once it did. *'A few moments of rest,'* she thought, *'just a few.'* Sitting down next to a large, fallen tree, Aria leaned against it and closed her eyes, allowing herself to be overcome by the darkness that lay behind them.

It was an ungodly chorus of snarls and howls which wrestled her from the darkness. Daylight burst through her eyelids as they opened, forcing her to shield her eyes. *'How long did I sleep?'* Aria didn't have time to think on it much before the sight of her ogre army in utter chaos, snapped her back to reality.

Deep amongst the army of large, green bodies, were the even larger, hairy forms of worgen. A natural adversary of the ogres, the worgen stood tall on their hind quarters whilst powerful, clawed hands sliced and jabbed into the mass of monsters surrounding them. Long, hairy muzzles curled around deadly white teeth as they flashed in the morning sunshine. Like a meadow of poppies amongst the weeds, a sea of ferocious red eyes faced off against the deadly swarm of green and black. They wore no armour, they didn't appear to need it as wave after wave of stupid ogres fell at the point of their talons.

Aria watched, stunned for a moment, as the worgen made easy work of her army; sending them catapulting into the air with one or two missing a leg, or a hand, as a result. Odder still was the sight of Edwel standing between the two warring parties, frantically waving his arms and occasionally catching a vaulted ogre. He was trying to keep the peace and separate them all, but was failing miserably at his task.

Aria snapped out of her daze. Getting to her feet, she strode amongst the savage ogres (who on occasion would mistake her for an enemy and lose their life at the point of her golden sword for their error). Making her way toward Edwel, Aria gripped onto her necklace and roared, with deadly fierceness, "ENOUGH!"

The forest became quiet again and all of the creatures looked to her. Edwel, although he didn't breathe, panted like he had exhausted himself; pandering to the illusion that he so desperately desired – to be alive. Aria ignored him and turned her attention instead to the largest of the worgen in the pack. His black fur was peppered with grey, and now splattered with green ogre blood too. His mighty chest heaved with the exertion of killing her army. He trailed his wild red eyes on her as she approached.

"What is the meaning of this?" Aria demanded of him.

"Your Highness," he growled without bowing. "My name is Luscious, and I come here upon your request."

"I think you are mistaken, Luscious, I didn't request the aid of the worgen."

"Not directly you didn't, no," he replied, taking a step toward her. Edwel made to put himself between them, but Aria raised her hand to stay him. "You see, Queen Aria, we have had word from the molemen that you are seeking an old wizard, and a winged man."

Aria, in turn, cautiously took a step toward Luscious.

"I am, what of it?"

"I may have some information that would be of benefit to

your search."

Aria felt a small twinge of impatience mixed with excitement, brew in her chest.

"Tell me," she urged.

"I will, gladly, but there is something I would like from you in return."

Luscious curled his hairy lips into a smirk, like he believed he had the upper hand with this nugget of information. He straightened his back and stood at full height next to Aria, not deigning to use the proper etiquette of lowering himself when addressing a queen. The excitement inside of her turned sour, and was instead replaced with ire.

"So, you think that you can negotiate with the queen of Naretia, do you? Standing behind me is an army of ogres who blindly follow me. I have cut clan chiefs from their invented thrones, and each one of them bargained for their lives, to no avail. But *you* think that you can do better? Tell me, Luscious, what makes you believe that I won't kill you where you stand, like all the others I have slaughtered?"

"Because I have something that they do not. I *know* the whereabouts of your winged man, and I won't tell it to you until you agree to my demand," he said with a low growl.

Aria tightened her fists into a ball and her teeth clenched together. She wanted nothing more than to plunge her blade into this insubordinate child of Dantet, but she knew she couldn't. From what little she had learned of the worgen, Aria knew that she was undoubtedly talking to the alpha, the pack leader. If she killed him, not only would she never get her answer, but the rest of the pack would be on her in a second. No, killing Luscious was not the answer *this* time.

The worgen were renowned for their untrustworthiness, and often liked to play games with their prey before devouring them. Dangling her greatest desire before her was just a means to blind her and make her step over the edge of a cliff she had not seen yet. She was determined to not fall for their trickery, and instead extract the information on her own terms using the one thing that would ensure their obedience. If games were what these worgen liked to play, then she would play a game not to their liking.

Quite incongruously Aria laughed out loud, like she had heard something hilarious whispered into her ear which no one else had heard. Luscious took a step backwards, confused by her reaction.

"Aria, please, be merciful," Edwel said quietly, knowing full well what her laughter meant.

Aria quickly silenced him with a dark look. Gripping onto her golden necklace, she turned her gaze on the alpha.

"You fool," she scoffed. "Kneel!"

As if someone had pulled invisible puppet strings attached to his limbs, Luscious knelt before Aria. His subservience was met with the alarmed and bewildered looks of not only his pack, but of himself too.

"You two, step forward," Aria commanded the two nearest worgen, and they obeyed diligently. "I asked you nicely to tell me what you know, Luscious, but you just had to be greedy, didn't you? I will not be parting with treasures or favours today, or any other day, do you hear me? I try so hard to be a kind and benevolent leader, but you, *all* of you, take advantage of me. Do you think the tales of my atrocities across Nareita were only stories, perhaps exaggerated? Well they aren't. If anything, they do not tell the true gruesomeness of my wrath."

"Aria, I beg you," Edwel protested again.

"Be still," Aria commanded.

Instantly the golem became as motionless as the mountains that surrounded them. Aria knew he wouldn't move again until she called for him, or until her life was in immediate danger.

"Isn't it the alpha who gives the commands in your pack?" she asked, turning her attention back to Luscious.

"They will only ever obey *my* word," he replied defiantly.

"Is that so?" she said with a wicked grin. Pushing some of her red curls from her eyes, she stared at the two worgen she had called forward. "Disembowel the worgen standing beside you," she commanded of one of them. "And *you,* stand where you are and allow him to do it."

"No! Wait! What are you doing Lobok?"

Although Aria couldn't tell male from female, as all

worgen looked alike to her, it was obvious from the more high-pitched voice that this worgen was a female. The worgen struggled, her clawed hands pulling at her legs, but they were as rooted to the ground as an ancient tree.

"I can't stop it, Tarra. Please, Luscious, do something."

Tarra's screams filled the silent forest as Lobok drove his talons into her stomach.

"Enough! Stop this and I'll tell you," Luscious roared.

"Making more demands I see," Aria seethed.

As the screams continued, Aria had to look away from the two, but she didn't stop them. She fixed her eyes on Luscious instead, who continued to beg and plead with her desperately. Aria blocked both his pleading and the screaming from her mind.

Finally, silence followed the last screams as they disappeared beyond the mountains, and Aria heard Tarra's body fall to the floor with a sickening thump.

"*Now,* you will tell me what you know, won't you?"

Still kneeling, Luscious's eyes were transfixed on the scene beside him, and his mouth opened in disbelief. The sound of Lobok's gentle weeping resonated inside of Aria, but she shut it out with the reasoning that the blame lay squarely on Luscious for not answering her.

"They were mates," Luscious said in a whisper, "and worgen mate for life."

"Why would that matter to me?" she replied flatly.

A moment later, Aria heard a second sickening thump. When she glanced over, she saw the dead body of Lobok draped over Tarra's. He had sliced his own neck and taken his life with the very talons that had ended his mate's. Aria's stomach churned at the sight, and a muddlement of confusing and conflicting feelings crashed, like waves, against the walls she had erected.

"You, petulant, child," Luscious spat. "Do you not know that there are consequences to your actions? Now their young will grow up without parents to guide them. And I can assure you that they will most certainly be fixated on your death, just the way you are with this winged man." The alpha wolf tore his red eyes away from the horrific scene and fixed them on Aria. "Tell me, oh benevolent queen, how does it feel to have become the monster that you hate so much?"

Aria clenched her hand around her sword so hard that the hilt dug into her palm. *'How dare this creature of Dantet accuse me so wrongly? He doesn't know what he's talking about. He's wrong, he's wrong.'* The churning in her stomach became a whirlpool, defying her resolve.

"I am *not* like him," Aria seethed. "He is a monster who cut off the heads of your king and queen. He sliced out their eyes as a keepsake, and walked away to freedom. The wizards refuse to bring him to justice, and the kingdom has allowed him to walk amongst them, unchallenged. It is all of *you* who have betrayed me, my parents, and the rule of Naretia. I am only seeking to right a wrong. I am *nothing* like that monster."

"And now we are all to suffer for your justice, are we?" he asked solemnly. "How does that make you any better than the monster you pursue?"

Aria raised her sword and slammed the hilt into the side of Luscious's wolf-like face. Red blood spilled from his lip as she hit him again and again. Unable to defend himself after being commanded to kneel, Luscious returned each blow with a deadly stare instead. Her attack on him felt hollow. Still weak from exhaustion, Aria stopped her onslaught and breathed heavily as Luscious continued to stare. Reaching under her breastplate, She dangled her amulet where Luscious could plainly see it, before slowly wrapping her fingers around it. It was obvious from his wide eyes that he knew the power it contained.

"Tell me. What do you know of their whereabouts?" she panted, wiping a spot of his blood from her chin with the back of her hand.

"They have sealed themselves in a cave, high above in the mountain ridges," he replied reluctantly, spitting blood from his mouth. "They think we don't know where they are because of the ice, but we do."

"How far away are they?"

"My pack can reach them in two hours, but your obedient

ogres are too clumsy for the narrow mountain pass. It would take them nearly a day to reach it."

Aria looked back at her army. They were as motionless as Edwel as they waited for her next command. While the ogres, with their simple minds, were easier to control then the worgen, she knew that they would indeed be too slow. Edwel would also find the narrow track difficult; his wide stone feet wouldn't be able to grip the icy path. She had to leave them behind, she had to get to the wizard and the winged man, now, and trust that she would be able to control the worgen long enough to complete her task.

Chapter 7

It always amazed Olórin how well Aramus could sleep, his nights unbroken by nightmares of the terrible life he had lived. Even now as Olórin watched over the young man curled up by the dying fire, his powerful chest rose and dipped evenly. His large black wings fell gently behind him as he slept, and his handsome face was a picture of serenity. *'How handsome he truly is,'* Olórin thought fondly. *'It's such a shame that no woman will ever see what I see.'*

But Olórin was no fool. There was a reason Aramus slept so well, and he had to admit that it worried him. Inflicted with his father's curse of a heartless existence, he could easily have slaughtered men, women, and children at a whim, and without a single sentiment of remorse too. Should he reach the age of maturity without learning the value of life, or love, then Naretia would surely be doomed.

To have killed Aramus as he held the dagger to his throat would have been easy. It might have even saved the world from the prophecy that followed this young man like a shadow. However, killing him would have not only ended Olórin's life, but also the lives of the wizarding caste. Such was the Goddess Edwina's unyielding belief in the sanctity of life.

But a flame of hope lit itself inside Olórin's chest for the first time since he had embarked on his quest over two hundred years ago. Last night, Aramus had shown a side to him that Olórin had not seen before. He had shown remorse, anger, frustration, and even fear of death. All the things that he had been trying to coax out of him for the past six years. It was Aramus's human side and, although it had only shown itself briefly, it gave Olórin great faith just to know that it *was* there.

The only thing potentially powerful enough to bring Aramus's human side closer to the surface, was the tug of true love. But even if, by some unfathomable reason, he *did* find true love, it was no guarantee that his dark side would be permanently squashed. Regardless of how it might have helped, Olórin knew it was unlikely to ever happen. Women, it seemed, were more terrified of him than men or children – presumably as a result of the violent stories of how Aramus's mother had conceived him. This only served to reassure Olórin that his potion was the *only* resort left to take. But his faith that they would find all the obscure ingredients needed for it in time, was beginning to wane.

"Aramus," Olórin said, gently shaking the young man's shoulder. "Aramus, the sun has risen and now we must too."

As though he were never sleeping, Aramus opened his slatted, amber eyes and blinked only once at the bright light that shone through the ice of the cave entrance. Without so much as a yawn or a stretch, he got to his feet and righted the backpack between his shoulder blades. He held out a hand to help Olórin up and Olórin accepted it gratefully. His old bones and the cold were long enemies of each other, and today the cold had gained the upper hand.

Taking off his wizard hat, Olórin threw the frying pan and the remnants of the uneaten bread into it. He plopped it back on his head, like it weighed nothing at all, leaving behind only the charred remains of their fire. Pointing his staff toward the icy impasse, a thin, silvery line snaked out from it and melted the ice at its touch. Within a matter of seconds they were free to walk back out onto the precarious, frozen ridges of the crag.

"Where to?" Aramus asked.

"Up, we go up," Olórin replied.

*

Aria was beginning to miss having Edwel about and that confused her more than anything. His incessant cheeriness and talking would often drive her to distraction, not to mention his constant advice on how to be a benevolent leader, which often made her want to throw up. But now that she was alone, surrounded by creatures who would love nothing better than to slice open her neck, she missed the security of the great big, stone oaf.

"You will need to pick up your pace if you wish to reach them on time. I cannot guarantee they will still be in the same place as we left them otherwise. Daylight has a strange way of motivating you humans. It is something I will never understand. When you're on the run, why travel in daylight when it is easier to be spotted?" Luscious asked rhetorically from behind Aria.

The mountain ridges got steeper and steeper as Aria navigated the treacherously narrow path. A long line of worgen snaked behind her, each one on all fours, and each one eyeing her with vengeance clearly written in their red eyes. *'All I have to do is control the alpha and the others will follow his lead,'* she thought, not truly believing that she could. *'Just until we get as far as this winged man and then, once I have killed him, I will order Luscious to kill his pack himself, before making him plummet to his death from the mountain top.'*

"How much farther?" she asked.

"At *your* pace, another three hours."

Aria stopped and turned to look at Luscious.

"Well, you will just have to carry me then," she said matter-of-factly.

Luscious laughed hard, as did the rest of his pack behind him.

"I am not a horse, and even if I was willing to carry someone on my back, I would not foul my coat with *your* filth."

"Shut your mouth," Aria shouted, grabbing the amulet around her neck tightly. Almost instantly Luscious's lips closed and, as much as she could see him try, they wouldn't open again. "Now, bend down and carry me on your back, dog."

A whisper of low growls came from behind Luscious, but

none of the other worgen dared move. The alpha's muscles strained under the invisible force that was pressing down on his shoulders and hips, making him crouch low to the ground. His large claws dug into the ice and snow under the pressure, almost dislodging a large chunk of it off in the process. With his head satisfactorily lowered, Aria threw a leg over the mighty beast and gripped tightly onto his coarse, black mane.

"Now run," she whispered in his ear.

*

Olórin had not looked up to see where he was going for some time. The path had all but disappeared, and now they were left to pick out stable footing amongst the sharp juts of ice and rock. On more than one occasion, Olórin had placed his fur boot on what he thought was a flat bit of solid ice, only to have it fall away from under him.

Aramus too was having a difficult time climbing the mountain. Although he seemed to have regained the use of his lungs, he was visibly weaker and often needed to steady himself against large boulders of ice as they climbed. It was only when Aramus disappeared from Olórin's periphery with a grunt, did the old man stop his assent.

"Aramus," Olórin shouted, rushing to look over the large chunk of ice the young man had disappeared behind.

Clinging onto the edge of the cliff, Aramus feet were scrambling to find a foot hold while his wings flapped impotently in the thin air. Olórin extended his arm out over the edge and grabbed hold of the young man's jacket. With one mighty heave, he helped him back onto the ridge for the second time.

Aramus lay on his back for a few moments, breathing heavily.

"Thank you," he said. "It seems that the weaker I get, the stronger you become, old man."

"Indeed, but I suspect that it is only because we are getting closer to the Goddess Edwina," he replied, getting to his feet without so much as a creak from his old bones now. "It's a strange feeling really. It's like I have regained a couple of hundred years of my life. Maybe I should take this opportunity to show you a jig that I was famous for as a teenager."

"I'd rather you didn't," Aramus said, gesturing with his hand for the wizard to stop his sudden floundering of knobby knees and flat-footed tapping on the perilous ice.

"Aramus, you've hurt yourself," Olórin said, immediately grabbing hold of the young man's extended hand, and examining a small wound that oozed black blood.

"It's only a scratch. I think I'll live," he said, taking back his hand.

Olórin huffed audibly and turned his nose toward the sky in the indignation of not being allowed to mollycoddle the young man as he had done when he was a boy. It was only then that he saw what lay beyond the last ridge, and it made his eyes widen and his heart beat fiercely.

"Darzithal!" Olórin said in a whisper.

"Dar-what?"

"Look, up there on that plateau above us. Can you not see it? *That*, is Darzithal, the meeting place of the Gods and the mortals."

High above them on the very top of the mountain, the peak became oddly flat as though someone had cut the top off with a sharp sword. Perched on the plateau, an opaque and shimmering dome twinkled in the morning sunshine. It looked to be solid, like ice, not moving in its shape. But the surface swirled in small pearlescent eddies, as though it were made of turbulent water.

"Do you see?" Olórin asked, still staring open mouthed at the glorious sight.

"I do," Aramus replied impassively.

Olórin shot Aramus a pointed look.

"You do realise that Darzithal is an ephemeral place, only appearing at the decree of the Gods, don't you? The fact that it is here is a great thing, Aramus."

"If you say so," Aramus said, shrugging his shoulders.

"Goddess Edwina, give me strength." Olórin sighed in exasperation. "Come on then, I'm sure the Goddess is busy and can't wait around for us forever."

The two companions scaled the last of the precarious

ridges until they stood on the more stable ground of the plateau. The light shining from the shimmering dome was almost too much for Olórin, who had to shield his eyes for a moment. Aramus also squinted against the bright light, but took a few steps closer to the dome. He reached out his hand to touch it.

Without warning, a bright and powerful spark of lightning shot out from the swirling wall and struck Aramus's outreached hand. He pulled it away and grimaced in pain, holding his hand close to his chest.

"It's broken. Either that, or no one is home and they don't want us poking around while their gone," Aramus said through gritted teeth.

Olórin looked between the dome and Aramus's injured hand. It was the same hand he had cut after nearly plummeting to his death earlier. Small rivers of dried blood still ran down his fingers. He couldn't believe after coming all this way, the Goddess would refuse them entry. After a moment, Olórin stepped toward the dome and pressed his hand on the shimmering wall. It was cool, soothing, and gave way at his touch.

"It is not broken," Olórin said sadly. "It is averse to having the blood of Dantet pass through it."

"Wonderful," Aramus grumbled. "So, what then, I wait outside like a dog while you have your little powwow with the royal highness of sulkiness?"

Olórin was on him instantly. He grabbed a handful of the black linen shirt Aramus wore under his jacket, and pulled him closer.

"You mind your tongue when you speak of the Goddess Edwina," he hissed. "She is the creator of life, the giver of love, and bears the sadness's of this world with the enduring strength of a mother. She has known the ultimate sadness of death, brought on by the jealous, wallowing actions of an egotistical God. Do not judge her for her preferences without having first felt her pain. Am I clear?"

"Perfectly," Aramus replied quietly.

"Now," he said, letting go of the young man and digging

out a small glass bottle from the point of his hat. "I will be as quick as I can, but know that in there, time does not operate in the same manner as it does out here. So I do not know how long I will actually be."

Aramus nodded, having the look of a scolded child, and Olórin took a deep breath before he stepped through the shimmering wall.

*

Luscious stopped abruptly, nearly sending Aria toppling head first over him. Ignoring her fumbling arms and legs as she tried to right herself, he sniffed tentatively at the ground and then turned his red eyes on her.

"What is it?" she asked, before remembering that she had forbidden him to open his mouth. Grabbing her amulet, she said, "Speak."

"Blood," Luscious said, stretching his jaw muscles. "Black blood."

"He's hurt?"

"Not really, it's only a small bit. But now that I have his blood scent, I can track him anywhere."

"Good," Aria said, feeling a smile tug at the corners of her mouth. "What are you waiting for then? Find that monster and I shall release you from your duties."

Taking large bounds over the juts of ice, his sharp talons provided a powerful grip on the slick surface. Luscious followed a path that led toward the peak of the mountain. Aria's fingers grew numb with the cold air and she found it hard to hold on. *'How am I going to fight him like this?'* she thought. *'My muscles ache from tiredness, and my fingers are too numb to hold my sword. What am I going to do if I* do *find him?'*

"You never asked me what my demands were," Luscious said.

"Why would I be interested in your demands?" she asked coldly.

"Believe it or not, Your Highness, we actually want the same thing," he answered, taking a few more bounds over ice boulders. "It is true that we worgen are the creatures of Dantet, and as one of his subordinates we hear his every command. But some of us do not blindly follow him. We have our own minds and desires - unlike the brainless ogres that you have commandeered as an army. Granted, there is nothing I would rather see then a little more chaos and destruction in this world, but the plans our master has told us about are not in *our* best interests."

"What plans?"

Luscious laughed, taking a sudden spurt of speed up a steep incline.

"I am not so stupid as to tell you that much and suffer his wrath. But what I will say is that his plans pivot on a prophecy told about his son, Aramus, the winged man you seek." Aria had not heard of any prophecy and wondered if the all-knowing wizards were also aware of it. "If that prophecy should come to fruition, then I do not believe any creature on the surface of Naretia would survive it. I have come to like living on the surface, as have the rest of my pack, and the only way to stop the prophecy is to kill Aramus.

"So, you see, we have the same goals, you and I, we both want him dead. But he cannot be killed by my hand as it belongs to Dantet. If the Dark God heard of how we conspire against him, we would suffer greatly for our treason. We are taking a great risk helping you, and so my demand was only to make sure, without a shadow of a doubt, that you *do* kill him and leave no ogre behind to report back to our master."

"Oh, I didn't know," Aria said quietly.

Edwel had always told her that she was too impetuous, and remorse for her overreaction at the camp began to creep around the certainty of her actions. Tarra and Lobok need not have died, and now, more than ever, she knew that killing them had been wrong. Aria bit her bottom lip, forcing the heavy feeling of guilt to be replaced with pain.

"No, you didn't know, and that should be something you learn from. You need not rule your kingdom with suspicion in everyone, Your Highness. Some will have purity in their hearts, others treachery, but for the most part people will come to you as a means to an end. All you have to determine is if that end is beneficial to you too. But you will never find that out if you dominate them without dialogue, and murder them before they have said their piece."

Although it was basically the same thing Edwel had been trying to teach her for two years now, somehow it sounded different coming from an enemy. It sounded more truthful, real, and sage. After all, what did Edwel know about real life? He was nothing but a stone man, created by self-righteous wizards, who only pretending to be alive. But Aria didn't have time to think on it long, because as Luscious bounded further upwards she saw something she had been waiting to see since *that* day.

The silhouette of a young man, against a large shimmering dome on the highest plateau of the mountain, became clear. Wrapped around him like a cloak were his two enormous black wings. Her heart leapt into her mouth at the sight of him. So close now, she could almost taste his black blood, and it was pre-emptively satisfying.

Chapter 8

It was neither cold, nor was it warm inside the dome. There was no breeze, but yet, Olórin felt a distinctive prickle of his beard as though gravity itself had lost its grip on it. His old joints moved fluidly as he stepped into a world where pain had been expunged. A blanket of calmness wrapped around his shoulders, and it felt like home. Streaming in from the walls themselves, an opaque light bathed the air in a niveous haze. There was no snow underfoot anymore, no trees or rocks in sight, just an endless landscape of white that Olórin both walked and floated on at the same time.

Somewhat disorientated, Olórin took a few tentative steps deeper into the dome. It struck him as odd that his footfalls made no noise, nor did his clothes rustle as he moved. He tried to speak, but heard only silence. Tucking the glass bottle under his arm, Olórin clapped his hands together as hard as he could, but still there was no sound.

He didn't know how long he had stood there before something moved in the light and a figure slowly emerged. Olórin didn't hear himself suck in his breath, but he knew he had. A tall, slender woman glided through the brightness with the same ease that a cloud would soar through the sky. The lady's long straight hair glimmered silver and mirrored the same silver that shone brightly in her pupil-less eyes. Her porcelain skin was unmarked by imperfections and shone the same irradiances as the haze around her. Her features were delicate; a small pointed chin, thin silver eyebrows, and lips of an intense azure blue.

She did not wear clothes, as such, rather she wore the blinding whiteness as a misty gown. But still, the silhouette of her naked body could be seen. '*An alluring vision for most men,*' Olórin thought. '*How could Dantet* not *have fallen in love with her?'*

Quickly realising that he had been staring, open mouthed, at the Goddess for longer than was polite, Olórin bent down on one knee and bowed his head as low as it would go. He wasn't expecting to meet the Goddess Edwina herself, but instead find a small stream or spring from which he could gather the waters of life. Although the very idea of meeting his Goddess had riddled him with nervousness in the past, having finally met her, his heart thumped patiently and his mind became oddly clear and calm.

"My beloved Olórin," a strange voice said.

It was certainly female, but instead of sounding in his ears it whispered all around him. Her voice was powerful, but quiet, like the ominous rustling of leaves before a raging tempest.

"Stand," she said.

Olórin rose to his feet and stood before his Goddess. In the minutes that passed while they stared at each other, he wondered why he felt so at peace and began to think that perhaps he might have died. The thought of it, and the warm feeling he got as he stood next to Edwina, lifted a weight from his shoulders and eased a heaviness in his chest. His worries about the world outside the dome, about Aramus, who was waiting in the cold, melted into a serene feeling of bliss. He could have stayed that way forever.

"You have come for the waters of life, my child."

She tilted her head gently, but her blue lips never moved. Her voice emanated from everywhere around him and inside of him, and it filled him with joy to hear it. He tried to speak, but again, no sound came from his mouth.

"Your voice cannot be heard inside these walls," she said, taking slow, graceful steps deeper into the dome, Olórin followed. "It is not time for you to speak, but rather to see and listen."

She glanced at Olórin with a knowing look in her silver eyes, as if she could feel the wave of questions that was trying to burst from him.

"I have watched you carefully and have seen the sacrifices you have made. Some of them were selfless, while others were only a convenient excuse to not be truthful," she said, continuing to walk. "Love is love, Olórin, and I do not frown upon any of it. But I do not come here to talk about love. I have come here to help you see, and to strengthen your resolve as I fear that you will need it in the end."

The Goddess waved her hand in a long, slow movement over the expanse of white in front of her, and suddenly an image of Aramus appeared. His large, black wings, extended to full width, and his amber eyes glowed with a deadly fire that burned from within. A powerful wickedness exuded from him, and Olórin did not recognise the young man he had come to know in the vision standing before him.

"Dantet's child is nearing the age of maturity," she began. "With that, he will inherit some of his father's abilities. While I have rid Dantet of his own powers, I fear that they shall rise again within Aramus. Mortals, however, were never meant to have such Godly powers. And so, if his son is allowed to live he will be wild and out of control."

Without warning Aramus's apparition burst into flames. Orange and yellow tongues wrapped themselves around his hands, his feet, and set his wings alight without burning them. Olórin took a step back and stared, wide eyed, at the image. Aramus smiled a poisonous grin, and raised his fiery hands high above him, threatening to engulf both Olórin and the Goddess in the raging fireball he conjured.

"This power, the destructive element, can lure the most noble of men into losing themselves within it. It is hungry, all-consuming, and unprejudiced in choosing its victims. If you fail in your quest, then Aramus's human side will be lost to this enchantment. Dantet will use him as a conduit to seek revenge on me, and he intends to burn everything that I love to the ground."

Taking his cue from her words, Olórin watched as Aramus's fireball exploded and spread through the air until the dome around them was a raging inferno. Behind the young man, an image of the kingdom of Naretia burned, consumed in a greedy blaze. Screams and cries of pain came from the flames under his feet, as burning hands reached up to beg

Aramus for mercy. But he ignored them all with a cold look that Olórin had seen only once before. It was the day they had first met, when he came upon him in a quiet suburb of Lothangard, dripping in the blood of several dead men who lay scattered around him.

"If that should happen, then my sadness will surely break me *and* the hold I have over Dantet. He will have his freedom to step foot on mortal soil, and I will be powerless to stop him."

A deep sadness filled the dome and the image of Aramus, and his fire, died like they had been washed away with enormous tears. Olórin felt the weighted sorrow, like an anchor in his chest. It was the first time he felt something other than peacefulness since entering the dome, and it pulled him down until he couldn't breathe. Tears, that were not his, ran down his old cheeks and he crumpled to his knees.

It wasn't until the hand of Edwina lifted his chin that he saw the very same tears as his own, roll down her porcelain cheeks – only hers shone like crystals. Olórin couldn't help but watch them trickle slowly toward her chin, mesmerised by their beauty and brightness. *'How can something so sad be so beautiful?'* he thought.

"The waters of life," she said, gesturing to the glass bottle Olórin held in his hand.

Quickly realising what the Goddess was saying, Olórin uncorked his empty bottle and held it under her chin, ready to catch the tears as they fell. *'The waters of life are the Goddess's tears,'* he thought, as three luminescent tears turned solid and dropped into the jar soundlessly. *'She must have cried for a long time after her children's deaths to have created so many creatures in Naretia.'*

When the forth tear fell from her chin and tumbled into the bottle, the Goddess stood up and walked away from Olórin. The sadness that had weighed him down and crushed his chest, went with her too. Before she disappeared into the white mist altogether, Olórin quickly corked the bottle again and placed it gently into the point of his hat. Getting to his feet, he followed her.

"There will come a time, Olórin, that you will have to make a choice," she said gliding through the mist. "You must choose carefully and know that there is more at stake here than *his* life and the lives of the wizard caste. Be sure to weigh all of your options, even the unthinkable ones. And while there is one decision I cannot condone, you may have to take it regardless. If you do, know that I am at peace with it."

Olórin opened his mouth to ask her "what decision might that be?" But frustratingly nothing came out. He tried to shout louder, feeling a desperate desire to not disappoint his beloved Goddess fill his heart. While in her presence, the urge to blindly follow her directions was more powerful than anything he had ever felt before. But she hadn't given him any directions. There were things he desperately wanted to ask her, things he needed to know and not all of them were about Aramus.

"My child, Olórin, I thank you for the sacrifices that you have made and are going to make," she said not hiding the sadness in her voice. "And if we should not see each other again, either as you live or after you die, know that I love you more deeply than you can imagine."

Those were the last words the Goddess said before gently kissing Olórin on the forehead. He closed his eyes and through the rosy, blood tinted hue of his eyelids, Olórin saw the light around him fail. The warm feeling of her lips on his forehead drifted away, like the tumbling sands off a dune in a stiff breeze. The bitter air and the weakness in his old bones, blasted him back onto the mountaintop. But still, he didn't want to open his eyes again, he didn't want to see reality. So peaceful it had been inside that dome, like returning to a childhood home that held only warm, happy memories. He wanted to live in the Goddess's eternal bliss forever. But the ugly sound of swords clashing, and cries of pain, forced his eyes to open again.

Chapter 9

"Surround him," Aria roared as she and her unwilling band of worgen approached the winged man. "Do not let him escape or your lives will be forfeit."

Like the black furry pincer of a giant monster grabbing an object, the worgen circled their prey. Aria jumped from the back of Luscious and, in a flash of gold, her sword found its way firmly into her hand. The man she had been searching for, that had been living in her nightmares since the day he had killed her parents, was only a few feet from her now. Her heart beat fiercely, and adrenaline pushed the coldness from her body until she burned from head to toe with a fire born of vengeance.

The worgen growled at him, their hackles raised and their teeth bared. But the demonic creature that stood at the edge of a shimmering dome, was ready for them. Where his wings had been wrapped around his body to stave off the cold, they suddenly opened to full width, revealing a silver sword that gleamed in the bright light behind him. Aria would have thought he looked like a celestial being if she hadn't seen his acts of brutality for herself. *'How deceiving looks can be,'* she thought.

With one mighty leap, Aria bounded over the last boulder of ice and landed squarely in front of her quarry.

"I hope you and your wicked father are on good terms, winged man, because you are about to meet him face to face," she hissed.

Without waiting for an answer, she swung her sword wildly, forgetting everything that Edwel had ever taught her. All she could see, all she could focus on, was the vision of his black blood spilling, unreservedly, over the pure white snow beneath him.

"My name is Aramus, and I do not know my father," he replied, blocking the riotous swings, some of which came precariously close to his head. "But I do know you, Queen Aria."

The thought of this murderer affiliating any part of her to him was enough to make Aria's stomach churn. She knew, being outnumbered as he was, that he was trying to manipulate her, searching for the smallest window of escape by distracting her with talk. But he would find no such opportunity from her, of that she was determined.

Aria thrust her sword toward his stomach and chest, but each time his sword would block her attacks and a resounding *twang* would sound out her failure. The more she heard it, the more it angered her and the wilder her swings became. Soon the mountaintop rang out with the sounds of metal on metal, like the isolated bell of a chapel in the wilderness.

"I remember you," Aramus said.

Aria could see him breathing heavier with the effort of fending off her attacks. Small beads of sweat clung to his forehead, and his slatted amber eyes followed her sword closely, not straying to watch where he was going.

"I remember you from a time when I was lost and afraid."

Aramus's foot caught a lump of ice and he fell backward. Aria seized it as an opportunity to strike and, more quickly than lightning, she swung her blade downwards. Aramus rolled onto his side and her sword met with solid ice. She made to decapitate him as he stood, but he was too quick. He ducked and before she had a chance to bring her sword around again, he pushed her roughly away from him.

Aria stumbled sideways, but she didn't fall. Now back on his feet again, Aramus was in clear distress. His breathing wasn't just heavy, it was laboured, and Aria smiled. For years she had been preparing to battle the "Winged Man", whose legend had struck fear into the hearts of children and men alike. But now, as she saw his strength wain from the attacks of a seventeen-year-old girl, she was somewhat disappointed that killing him was going to be so easy.

Aria thrust her sword toward his chest again. This time he

didn't have the strength to react quickly enough. Instead of using his sword, he turned sideways and her blade missed its fatal mark. But she did manage to slice some of his black leather tunic from his shoulder instead and cut into his flesh.

Aramus cried out in pain, knocking her blade away with his before grabbing his shoulder. To her delight, Aria saw trickles of black blood ooze between his fingers and drip onto the snow as he stumbled backward. Standing at the edge of the sheer mountain cliff, and looking weaker than ever, he tried to fly away. But his wings flapped futilely in the thin mountaintop air.

"It seems that where birds cannot fly, neither can the mighty Aramus," she laughed.

"I am sorry," he said in a whisper that oozed regret.

His words caught Aria off-guard.

"What do you mean, you're sorry?" she demanded of him.

Aramus, still clinging to his injured shoulder, dropped his sword to the ground in surrender and fell to his knees. His powerful chest rose and fell with more than just exhaustion. If Aria didn't know any better she could have sworn he was about to be overcome with emotion.

"I know the pain and hurt that I have caused you, that I have caused the kingdom," he began. "At the time, I believed that there was no hope for me, that everyone wanted to see me dead for no reason. I had been hunted and vilified all of my life, but that's no excuse. But when your parents, the king and queen, freed me from the prison they put me in, I seized the opportunity to escape at the cost of their lives. My life up until then, made me feel as though I couldn't trust them. I convinced myself that I had no choice but to do what I did. And for that, I am truly sorry."

"You LIE!" Aria shouted, holding the point of her sword under his chin so he had lift his head and look at her. "Do *not* besmirch my parent's name. They did not hold you captive. I was there, behind a tapestry in the throne room. I heard what they said to you. They wanted to help you, and you repaid their kindness by decapitating them."

"Enough talk," Luscious growled.

"Your parents *had* captured me and held me captive for more than six months before they decided to be benevolent," Aramus said, ignoring Luscious and wincing as Aria's sword pricked his skin. "Do you know how the guards treat prisoners in the king's keep? Well, now imagine what they did to the son of an evil God. I was alone." Aramus's voice became quite. "Because of my own childish petulance, and some ridiculous argument, I was separated from the only person in this world who *didn't* want to kill me.

"When I was brought before your parents, I didn't truly believe that they wanted to help me. I feared for my life, and my desperation took over my senses making me commit that terrible crime. And for that, I apologise without reserve, or any expectation of forgiveness."

"You stole their eyes," Aria seethed, taking a step closer to Aramus, running her blade along his neck until he gasped with pain. "What kind of monster takes someone's eyes?"

Aria studied her enemies face carefully. His black eyebrows furrowed together and his mouth opened slightly. A look of utter confusion crossed his face.

"I… I never took their eyes," he said, shaking his head slightly. "What use would it be to take their eyes?"

"Liar!" Aria shouted. "The guards told me what they had discovered after I ran to alert them. They told me that their eyes were missing. You were the only one in the throne room when I left, and now I am going to slay you with the very same sword that you used to kill my parents, my father's sword."

"But you weren't there. You ran off before you saw who took them, am I right?"

"How could I stay after seeing their heads' fall to the floor?" Aria said, her voice more uneven then she had intended.

It was something that Aria had regretted all of her life. The horror of what she saw, only haunted her slightly less than her cowardliness at running away when her parents needed her the most. It was a quality she vowed would never surface again.

"I am guilty of a lot of things and I admit to them with remorse, just as I admit to killing your parents. But if I would confess to murder, why would I deny a lesser part of my crime? I have been accused of a lot of ridiculous things; hiding the sun, creating plagues, turning sheep black. I will gladly atone for my crimes, but only the ones I am guilty of," Aramus said defiantly.

He dropped the hand that was holding his wounded shoulder and held both his arms out wide. Aria could see a shake in his fingers as he knelt on the hard ice, waiting for her to kill him.

"Maybe the world is right," he said, his voice barely louder than a whisper. "Maybe you would all be better off without me. If that's the case, then maybe it's only fair that my life should be taken by the hand of one of my victims… and I forgive you for it."

'Forgive me! Forgive me? What does he mean forgive me?' Aria thought angrily. *'I'm the one who should be forgiving him, not the other way around. How dare he!'* Aria clenched her teeth together and raised her sword above her head with two hands. Aramus closed his eyes and, for a moment, Aria was struck by the fact that he looked almost normal. Were it not for the two large wings protruding from his back, he could have been any other citizen in Naretia.

Aria hesitated. *'Why would he forgive me?'* she thought, feeling the anger inside of her begin to subside. *'Do I need forgiveness? Was Luscious right? Are the atrocities that I committed, worse than what this man has done?'*

"What are you waiting for?" Luscious roared from the line of worgen. "Kill him!"

Before Aria had the chance to act, Luscious broke ranks and bounded forward. With a savage snarl he dug his sharp teeth firmly into Aramus's injured shoulder, and shook him viciously. Aramus cried out in pain, but he didn't fight back. He didn't punch, kick, or try to run away from Luscious at all.

"STOP!" Aria cried out, kicking the worgen squarely in his muzzle.

Luscious howled and released his grip on Aramus, who crumpled to the ground. The worgen turned to snarl at Aria and she noticed one of his large canine teeth was missing; still stuck in Aramus's shoulder, no doubt.

"*I* am the queen of Naretia, worgen. It is *my* responsibility to see to it that this man dies, not yours," she shouted. Luscious reluctantly bowed, melting back into the line of worgen, and Aria turned to face Aramus again. "I will not allow a murderer to walk free in my land, regardless of his repentance. Judgment day will come to each of us, Aramus, and I can only pray that when mine comes, it will be as quick as yours."

It felt wrong to say his name aloud, like it was the most vile curse word known to man. Aramus staggered to his feet again and ignored the black blood spilling from his shoulder. Further weakened by Luscious's vicious attack, his unsteadiness made him waver from side to side. Eventually, though, he became stable enough to look Aria in the eye.

"I understand," he said, holding out his arms again.

Taking a step toward him she placed the tip of her sword in the centre of his powerful chest and steadied both of her hands on the end of the hilt, ready to drive it in. Aramus closed his eyes and swallowed deeply.

"Nooo!"

The voice of an old man echoed in the mountain air. Aria had only enough time to turn and see that the shimmering dome was no more, before the old wizard standing on the plateau raised his staff and brought it down hard on the ground. A shockwave of rock, ice, and frigid air, came rushing toward them. Aria, and her platoon of worgen, were sent flying backward. The force of it, tumbling them over large boulders of ice. Her scrambling hands barely found a large shard of ice to cling to as her legs dangled over the edge of a sheer drop. At the same moment, she watched Aramus being blown off the mountain side; his limp body plummeting toward his rocky doom.

*

Olórin watched in horror as Aramus was blown backward by the blast from his staff. Without thinking, he ran down to where the young man had fallen, and dove, head first, after him. Soaring through the air, fearfully anticipating that he would soon meet with one of the jagged cliff edges that whizzed past his head, Olórin caught up with Aramus's limp body. He grabbed hold of the young man around the waist, and pointed his staff in the direction of the serrated rocks that were quickly approaching.

"ONIS," he boomed.

Almost instantly a plume of dirty, grey clouds gathered under them. The vortex spun violently, engulfing the two in a matter of seconds. A powerful blast of icy air slowed their fall. Like an autumn leaf caught in an updraft, Olórin and Aramus fell downwards until they landed at the foot of the mountain with a small drop, whereupon the swirling vortex melted from existence like it had never truly been there.

From high above Olórin, the sound of the queen's furious cries rang out in the still air. The fall had given them some time to escape her, but not much.

"Aramus," Olórin said, laying the young man down gently in the snow. "Aramus, speak to me."

Olórin waited for what seemed like an age. His heart thumped widely in his chest as he pressed down on Aramus's injured shoulder to stop the bleeding. Regardless of how hard he pressed, however, blood still spilled between his fingers, and soon it began to feel cold and sticky.

"Old man," Aramus groaned half-coherently. "You do realise that *I* am the only one who can fly?"

"Yes," Olórin replied with a small laugh of relief. "Although, my magic has taught me to fall gracefully, has it not?"

With his eyes still closed, Aramus turned the corner of his mouth into a crooked grin.

"We must leave this place at once," Olórin said looking around him. "It appears that the queen's reach has already come as far as the mountains and it's no longer safe to journey in the open."

"I… I'm not sure that I can walk," Aramus said, grimacing.

"No, of course you can't. But with a little help from our friend over here, we will move more quickly." Olórin raised his hand toward a long-haired mountain goat with its muzzle buried deep in the snow, trying to find some grass to graze on.

"A goat?" Aramus laughed weakly. "You expect that a goat will be able to carry me? I think the fall has loosened the last ounces of reason secured in your brain, old man."

"Aramus," the old wizard sighed. "Although your proclamations about my senility had always been said in jest before, I never knew that you truly believed them."

Closing his eyes, Olórin began to repeat a low rumbling chant which echoed inside the nearby rocks. The mountain goat raised its head from its work and looked at the two men. It stomped its hoofs irritably, like it had an itch that it just couldn't reach, and slowly it began to grow. First its two curled horns grew until the weight of them made its head bow. Next its legs widened and stretched, followed closely by its torso and head. Soon the hardy animal had grown to twice the size of any horse. When it was all done, Olórin lowered his hands and breathed heavily.

"Okay, I take it back, old man," Aramus said, before passing out.

Chapter 10

Aria stumbled down the last of the jagged mountain alone. Her worgen companions released on her command, she frowned until the muscles in her brow began to ache. Not sure it was such a good idea to allow the worgen to go free, a fierce argument between her reasoning and her gut instinct, raged inside her mind. Something had changed during her encounter with the worgen which saw her reasoning win out over her instincts.

She had always known that her actions would have consequences, but seeing them up close when Lobok had taken his own life, made them tangible and real. Luscious could have easily commanded his pack to tear her to pieces as she descended. But the air carried no sound of four legged beasts pursuing her, only the lonely songs of hardy winter birds.

Luscious had promised, under the amulets influence, to use his formidable tracking ability to find Aramus and the wizard. Aria expected that he might not return to her at all, and take it upon himself to kill the winged man by some other means instead. But as he had mentioned before, there was a reason people came to the queen to seek help.

Luscious wanted Aramus dead almost as much as Aria, but he couldn't kill him by his own hand. He had to trust that Aria would be true to her word and she had to trust him in return. But something about Luscious's behaviour on the mountain didn't strike her as true.

She had had her sword at hand and Aramus was surrendering, but yet, Luscious wasn't satisfied to allow her to kill him on her own terms. It was almost as if he *wanted* to bite the winged man for no apparent reason at all. If he had intended to kill Dantet's son himself, why not strike a fatal blow by tearing his throat out instead of biting his shoulder?

Aramus was unarmed, and unable to protect himself. *'Surely Dantet's hold on his followers could not be so fragile as to allow one of his minions to defy him, could it?'* she thought.

Now more than ever, Aria wished she hadn't frozen Edwel in the ogre camp below. He had always been her compass, and was infuriatingly always right in his judgment of others. He had tried to stop her cruelty toward Tarra, but Aria hadn't listened. Now, because of her rash actions, a new enemy of hers walked Naretia, biding their time until her usefulness had come to an end.

Aria strode into the ogre camp, her shoulders slumped and her eyes fixed to the methodical movement of her feet. She was so distracted by the day's events it took her a moment to remember why her army was so quite. Like a gathering of hideous statues, the ogre's stood where she had left them a few hours before, as did Edwel. She wandered in front of her army and examined the golden amulet around her neck for a moment.

A treasure found in the vaults of Lothangard's castle, which had allowed her to break free from the overbearing reigns of the wizard caste. For so long they had controlled everything, including the King's Guard; the whispers of their seers overruling her authority. The all-knowing, all-powerful wizard's regime was absolute, and all those who questioned it were excommunicated from society. Not even *she* had been immune to their iron fist when she demanded Aramus be found and executed. Her defiance saw her stripped of an army, and her influence.

"Why should I allow it to continue?" Aria whispered allowed, still examining her amulet. "I am the ruler of Naretia, not them. I am the one who people should look to for protection and guidance. But the wizards took that away from me. Why allow Aramus exemptions that the rest of us are not privy to?"

The golden amulet glinted in the morning sunshine. The head of a horned monster with amber eyes glared back at her from the triangular base, an image of Dantet himself. In the palm of her hand the metal felt hot, as it always did, like someone had put it into a bowl of boiling water. The weight of it was disproportionate to its size, making Aria wonder if it was the magic inside that made it so heavy.

It was a dark-haired junior wizard named, Mullrode, that had led her to discover the amulet. He was a self-important wizard, whose sharp nose seemed to favour the highest point it could stretch. Strangely, she had never seen Mullrode in the palace before, or ever again after the discovery. But there were more wizards' than regular people in the city of Lothangard, and one unremarkable wizard could have easily been overlooked.

'Why would he have shown me how to find it if wizards are forbidden to murder?' she thought, wrapping her hand around the pendant tightly. She had been too impatient and headstrong to think of it before. But the convenience of finding such a weapon in her own palace, just as she needed it, now bolstered the embers of mistrust. *'It is my duty as the ruler of Naretia to find out the truth, and I will.'*

"Awaken," she commanded.

Without warning, the ogres collapsed onto the ground, exhausted from having stood up for so long. Aria hadn't meant to freeze the ogres too, but, as stupid as they were, they thought that she was speaking to them when she commanded Edwel to be still. Edwel's stone body turned toward Aria with the sound grinding breaking the silence. His mouth turned into a grin when he saw his queen.

"Have you succeeded in your task?" he asked in a sunny voice, not one bit perturbed by the fact that she had ignored his advice and frozen him to the spot.

"Not today," she replied. "But soon."

*

Olórin was tiring, and holding the spell over the mountain goat was taking every last ounce of his energy. The task took considerable concentration, and the sight of Aramus slumped over the grey, hairy back of the goat was not helping matters. A long line of black blood matted the wiry fur, and Aramus's wings jostled limply every time the goat leaped over a fallen tree or a small stream.

"We must make camp somewhere so I can tend to your wounds," Olórin said.

They had left the mountain some two days ago, and travelled southward toward the dwarf mines. It was at least another three days trek, and Olórin feared that Aramus would not make it. He had haphazardly bound the young man's shoulder with some rags as they made their escape, but the bleeding had never stopped. Aramus had grown weaker and weaker as time passed, and Olórin suspected that a fang of a worgen was the reason why – the venom of which could cause unstoppable bleeding.

He knew he had to stop and pull it from his shoulder if Aramus was to live. But the queen would not let up in her hunt for them, and if the worgen were aiding her, they wouldn't be far behind. From the amount of blood Aramus had lost, it was apparent that it wouldn't be an easy extraction. He would need time to recover; time they did not have.

Ahead, a green wave of tightly packed trees, shrouded in fog, loamed ever closer. Olórin recognised it as The Shrouded Forest, and a sinking feeling made itself known in his stomach. Despite the lack of time on their side, Olórin knew stopping inside of the forest would be out of the question. If only they could ride through it quickly and reach the safety of the underground dwarven city of Balbuldor. There, they would at least have *some* protection from the queen's army of darkness. If the dwarfs despised anything more than thieves, it was the monarchy who taxed their wealth. They even went so far as to ignore their demands, and had crowned their *own* king, much to the queen's annoyance.

"Three days is too long," Olórin said to himself.

Directing the mammoth goat toward a large, hollowed tree at the edge of The Shrouded Forest, Olórin leaned closely to its ear and whispered. Almost immediately the goat stopped in its tracks and, as gently as it could, it lowered its body to the ground. Olórin used the tough goat hair to climb down to the ground, resulting in an indignant snort from the beast, and carefully slid Aramus off its back shortly after. No sooner had he rested the young man's limp body inside the hollow of the tree, then the goat retuned to its normal size.

"I thank you, my hardy little friend, you may go now," Olórin said, waving off the goat. The goat was startled to find itself far from where it normally grazed and, with wide eyes, suddenly bolted away from the two men at a great rate. Olórin hoped its blood-stained coat would draw the worgen away from them, and give Aramus the time he needed to heal. But worgen weren't stupid, and he couldn't rely on chance.

Olórin scanned the forest and smiled. If there was one place in Naretia that could provide everything he needed to heal Aramus, it was a forest. He knew this vast one very well too. Lost here during one of his wizard training sessions, he had come to make this forest his home for some three months before the Elders eventually found him. But he was also very aware of the sinister creatures that lay within the haze, and knew it was better to stay at the edges. Aramus was ashen and pale, and wouldn't be able to move anytime soon.

Leaning on his twisted staff to support his weary bones, Olórin got up and began to search the forest grounds for ingredients. After only a short amount of time he returned to Aramus with a handful of herbs, berries, and fruits. Tossing them onto the mossy ground, Olórin took off his wizard hat and rummaged through it, only occasionally cursing the chicken. Producing a small mortar and pestle, he got to work crushing the ingredients.

"What are you doing?" Aramus whispered faintly.

"Ah, you're awake. It would be better if you were still sleeping," he replied, concentrating on his work. "I have to take the worgen fang out from your shoulder, otherwise you'll keep bleeding, my friend. This pulp is to help with the pain when I do, and the infection after."

"If it's anything like ale, then I'm not sure it will work on me."

"I know," Olórin replied quietly. "But there's no harm in trying."

Setting down his tools, Olórin broke off a chunk of wood from inside the tree. He quickly removed as much bark and splinters as he could before presenting it to Aramus.

“Bite down on this,” he said. “It’s not going to be pleasant.”

“Wait,” Aramus said, turning his head away from the stick. “I want to keep the tooth.”

“What? Why?”

“It’s the first time I’ve ever really been injured. Think of it as a souvenir, so that I don’t forget what it was like because I don’t intend to get injured again.”

‘A small taste of human suffering,’ Olórin thought. He nodded and, satisfied with his promise, Aramus bit down on the lump of wood. Olórin could see a small amount of fear building in the young man in the way his chest rose and fell tersely. His fingers dug into the moss below him, revealing the soggy soil beneath the green blanket. Olórin knew the poultice he had made probably wouldn’t have the same effect on Aramus as it would with any other mortal being, but he had to try. If the tooth hadn’t dislodged on its own with the uneven clomping of the goat’s gait, then it was most likely lodged into the bone, and would cause an immense amount of pain while extracting.

Olórin took off the makeshift bandages and ripped Aramus’s shirt to reveal the wounds in his shoulder; eight punctures (four on the front and four on the back of his shoulder) and a long straight laceration from a sword that reached from one end of his collar bone to the other. The laceration looked superficial enough, but the puncture wounds resembled the mouth of some dark cave. It was clear which wound had the offending tooth lodged in it, because there was only one of those caves still oozing black blood. Surprisingly, the rest of his injuries had already started to close of their own accord. Olórin suspected Aramus’s ability to heal may have more to do with his heritage than anything else.

“Okay?” Olórin asked, scooping a glob of green pulp in his fingers.

Aramus took a deep breath and nodded. Olórin smeared the paste over all of wounds and heard the young man grunt in pain. He’d had this pulp on an injury before and knew that it stung terribly. But it was nothing compared to what Aramus was about to feel. Taking one hand and placing it firmly on the centre of Aramus's chest, to hold him steady, Olórin raised his other hand over the young man's shoulder.

Fingers spread wide, Olórin began to chant. His words whispered around the forest, like the rustle of autumn leaves as they were disturbed by some small creature passing through them. Over and over again he chanted until all his words muddled into one long stream of vowels and constants. Olórin could feel Aramus's powerful chest muscles tense under his hand and his breathing quicken. He could feel a heat rise up inside the young man as the pain grew worse.

Olórin visualised the tooth and willed it to come out, to follow the same path that it had entered, and to do it quickly. But the tooth was stuck, and would require more force. Olórin's chanting became louder and Aramus groaned against the pain. He writhed beneath the old man's touch, and his face contorted into an expression of pure agony. Aramus's feet pushed against the forest floor the louder Olórin became, and he struggled to keep him still. He arched his back and his wings flailed, surrounding them both in a tornado of fallen leaves and dirt.

Finally, Olórin began to shout his commands to the object inside of Aramus's shoulder and it began to move. Bit by bit, the tooth wiggled inside Aramus's bone. He let out a scream of pain just as it burst out of him and into Olórin's outstretched hand. Then it was over and Aramus collapsed unconscious against the tree. All around them The Shrouded Forest had become eerily silent as its startled inhabitants had run from Aramus's screams, no longer content to just watch them cautiously.

Olórin crumpled into the hollowed tree next to Aramus, and examined the bloody tooth in his hand. It was as long as his fingers and incredibly sharp too, like the blade of a knife. After a time Olórin slipped it into Aramus's pocket, fulfilling his request to keep the gruesome trophy, but something more peculiar caught his eye as he did.

Lying on the ground beside him was the stick Aramus had bitten down on. Olórin picked it up and scrutinised it carefully, his brow furrowing and his mouth pursing into a thin line. Indented into the wood was the outline of Aramus's teeth. But the impression wasn't made by sheer pressure alone, like he was expecting. Instead it appeared to have been scorched as if Aramus's teeth had turned to fire and burnt it.

The vision Goddess Edwina had shown him came flooding back to Olórin. He recalled the image of Aramus wielding a terrible fire, and the thousands of hands burning beneath him, begging him for mercy. Olórin felt sick, like a stone had landed squarely in his stomach. He knew that the son of Dantet was rising from within the handsome façade of this young man, and feared it would soon take him over.

Olórin stared at Aramus for a long time and considered his options. *'How easy it would be to kill you now,'* he thought.

chapter 11

It was almost half a day before Aramus was strong enough to walk on his own. By that time the sun was on its final few steps toward the horizon, and the forest creatures had begun to settle into the safety of their dirt and twiggy homes. Of course, Olórin knew the *real* reason they hid, and it was not because they were diurnal. It was because the nights in The Shrouded Forest were anything but peaceful. It would have been a wiser decision to seek refuge in a wild bear's den than to continue walking through the forest at night. But Olórin and Aramus were left with little choice. They could either stay put and be discovered by the queen's minions, or take their chances through fabled *Crying Mists.*

"Aramus," Olórin said, using his staff to pick out even ground amongst the tree roots in the dying light. "When the darkness comes you must promise to trust me, no matter what you see or hear. Things are not always what they seem in this place, and the mist has led many men to their doom."

"I would trust you with my life, old man," Aramus replied, cocking his head to the side and giving Olórin a crooked grin. "But I am not afraid of the dark, and whatever lies between these trees will not change once the sun sets. A tree is just a tree, what more could the forest hide?"

"Ah, so young," Olórin said, casting a cautious eye toward the inky sky. "Do you know that the elves believe everything from the grass blades to the trees themselves, has a soul? But in their belief, all souls are not equal either. Those born with a heartbeat are closest to the Goddess Edwina, and their heart symbolises her love. Those born without a heart are either free of sin or closest to the God Dantet, and are not under her protection. This is the reason they do not eat anything which once had a heartbeat, and dedicate their lives to killing Dark Ones.

"In the same way that the elves believe the trees around

them, the grass, and the grain, all have souls or a thriving for life, they also believe that the ground beneath contains memories of times gone by; memories that far outlive the oldest creatures of Naretia. These memories date back to the time of creation, and contain secrets that our feeble minds, and written records, do not hold.

"In a way, I believe the elves are correct. Something powerful truly exists beyond that which we can see and hear. Not only do I believe the ground has memories, but I believe the world also has its own magic. The mist that lives between these trees is the forest's magic, and it isn't always kind, Aramus. The deep scars across its face, which man created with their axes to build homes, has not been forgotten, and the mist is laced with the desire to retaliate.

"But when the darkness comes, so too do dark creatures who are able to bend the mist's magic to their will, and create all manner of chaos. They twist the moons light to make you see untruths, they fill your ears to make you hear lies, and strangle your lungs so that you cannot scream. But most important to remember is that their only goal is to ensnare your senses and to end your life, Aramus."

"I see, a friendly lot then," Aramus replied. "But that also makes me wonder what the elves would make of me. Where would I lie on their spectrum of souls? I have a heart that beats and part of me is human, but I am clearly the son of Dantet, and therefore their enemy. I wonder, would they dedicate their lives to killing me?"

Olórin didn't answer straight away. The truth was that he didn't know what the elves would make of Aramus. The young man would be a paradox to their entire belief system, and one they might not welcome to quickly. No, it was definitely safer to bring Aramus to the dwarfs first. Perhaps with an encouraging nod from two castes, the elves would be less inclined to shoot an arrow through Aramus's skull upon first sight of him.

"Dantet does not have a heart, Aramus, but yours beats strongly in your chest," Olórin eventually said. "It may take some convincing on their part, but I believe that will come to see what I see. They maybe puritans, but they are also fair."

"So, just win them over with my charming smile and my wit then?"

"Indeed."

The two walked on in quiet contemplation for what seemed like an age. The sun reached its final destination and the mist thickened in the moonlight. The silvery moisture, which hung in the air like a ghost, became so dense that Olórin could almost make out the individual water globules swishing and swirling in front of him. It clung to his skin leaving him feeling cold and damp, and invaded his lungs against his will.

It was getting difficult to see any more than a few feet in front them, and the silence soon became eerie. Nevertheless, Olórin wouldn't risk lighting their path with his staff and alerting the creatures around them to their presence. Keeping a constant ear out for any unusual noise, Olórin was thankful that the only sound he heard was their own footsteps in the stillness.

To his right he could still make out Aramus's figure. It seemed that the further away he travelled from Darzithal, the stronger he became. He took confident strides through the blinding mist, his wings lifted proudly on his back. His shoulder had all but healed, no longer needing a fresh bandage every few minutes. Aramus's chest didn't heave with the same effort of breathing through the smog, like Olórin's did. His amber eyes searched the greyness, focusing on objects that Olórin just couldn't see. Soon, he was being led once again by Aramus's deftness. His old bones creaked and complained in the dampness, and Olórin felt every bit his age.

"Did you hear that?" Aramus said, stopping dead in his tracks.

Olórin listened carefully, turning his head this way and that, but only the muteness of the mist reached his ears.

"I hear nothing," he replied.

"It's gone now," Aramas said after a few moments, cautiously taking a few steps forward again and stretching out his injured shoulder. "I thought I heard someone crying, but I guess I was wrong."

Olórin felt a lump grow in his chest. He knew what was lurking in the mist, waiting to find them, and hoped they would reach the edge of the forest before it did. The legendary crying of the mist was a sound that he had never been privy to hear, and the only reason he had survived so long in The Shrouded Forest during his apprenticeship.

"Let us move more quickly, Aramus," he said, his voice more uneven then he had intended. "Pay no heed to the sounds around you. Quickly now!"

Aramus nodded and picked up his pace. Olórin struggled to keep up with him. The moon hid behind the canopy of leaves above them, and it wasn't long before Aramus was a few meters ahead; far enough away that Olórin could only just make out his form.

"Aramus, we must stick…"

"There it is again," Aramus interrupted.

Olórin heard the young man's footsteps quicken.

"Aramus, wait!"

"It's a woman," he shouted back, now completely out of eyesight. "She's crying, like she's in pain. Come on, we have to help her."

"ARAMUS!"

But it was too late. Olórin heard the young man break into a run to follow a sound that *he* could not hear. His heart pounding in his chest, Olórin ran after Aramus, blinded by the fog and the dense trees.

The forest broke into a clearing, the bright moonlight having burned away the choking mists. In the centre of the clearing Aramus stood gazing up at a creature Olórin hoped they would not meet. Hovering above him was a woman whose skin had all but been stripped off her body, revealing the hideous muscle underneath. Two bat-like wings, ending in sharp claws Olórin knew to be poisonous, flapped in slow rhythmic movements. She wore armour constructed from the bones of her previous kills, humanoid and animal alike. Strung like fine beads around her neck were the shrivelled hearts of the many men she had lured to their death.

The creature's hideous mouth gawped open, singing her

honey-sweet song to entice Aramus. It was a silent song that held no power over Olórin as he could never be enticed by a female. Her large, clawed hands reached out to Aramus, and he was not repulsed.

"ARAMUS!" Olórin cried out, raising his staff in the air.

The creature shot a deadly look at the wizard. From her sharp toothed mouth, an ear splitting shriek resounded through the still air. To Olórin's astonishment, a dozen more creatures suddenly appeared between himself and Aramus. Without warning, they grabbed both of Olórin's arms and splayed them wide. One of them knocked his staff from his hand, while another wrapped her claws around his mouth.

"She's beautiful," Aramus said, just barely louder than a whisper. "She says she's lost and needs my help, Olórin. She doesn't fear me. She… she likes me."

Olórin watched the creature edge closer to Aramus. The young man smiled at the beast. He made to reach out and stroke her face. Olórin thrashed against the claws to free himself and soon the hand around his mouth lost its grip.

"Relinquam!"

As if he had suddenly been turned into searing metal, the creatures around him shrieked and pulled away. They writhed and hissed with vengeful fury, circling around Olórin and barricading his way to Aramus.

"Aramus, do not let her kiss you or she will end your life," he shouted over the screeches. "She's a harpy. All of this is an illusion. Aramus, do you hear me? Aramus!"

Between the skeletal arms and thick black wings of the circling harpies, Olórin saw Aramus step closer to the creature. He wore a smile that Olórin had wished to see on his face since he had first known him. But now it sent a wave of panic through the old man's chest. Aramus believed this creature loved him, as did all the men who had crossed her path.

"So beautiful," he said longingly. "She doesn't want to hurt me, she's just lost and alone. Why won't you let me help her?"

"She is here for only one thing, Aramus, and that is to end your life."

Fuelled with a large surge of panic, Olórin searched the

ground for his staff, to no avail. He watched helplessly as the creature ran her long talons through Aramus's shoulder length hair, down his neck, and finally resting on his chest.

"She says that you're jealous, that you don't want happiness for me because you have never found true love. Why is that, Olórin? And why would you do that to me? All I've ever wanted was to be accepted… loved. And now that I have found someone, you want to take it away from me?"

Olórin saw Aramus's brows furrow and his fists clench. *'This harpy's magic is more powerful than any I have seen before,'* he thought. *'She must be a queen.'* That realisation alarmed the wizard more than anything, because queens normally don't rise above the world of Dantet; not unless it was by his orders. Her considerable powers of persuasion would undoubtedly raise whatever human yearning Aramus had, and accentuated it until he was terminally under her spell.

"Aramus, I want nothing more than for you to find true love, but this is not it. Think about it. You have met this creature for less than a moment, and yet, you are already in love with her? Some other dark power is at work here, Aramus. Please, I beg of you, despite what you see and hear, you must trust me."

Olórin watched as his words were drowned in the chorus of ever swelling octaves from the circling harpies. The shredded lips of the queen edged closer to Aramus's, and no matter how he roared, Olórin's voice was lost in the terrible music of her minions. Like a snake emerging from a cave, Olórin watched helplessly as a pink, vaporous tendril emerged from the queen's open mouth, and entered Aramus's.

A terrifying electricity rose up in his old chest. Try as he might to focus his energy on the queen, without the boost of his staff, his efforts were easily blocked by her self-sacrificing cronies. Olórin reached a hand through the tornado of sharp talons and black wings. He had to get to Aramus. All would be lost if he allowed this creature to take him. With a deafening screech, one of the harpies dove toward Olórin and struck him across his face. He felt the searing pain of three long claws scratch him across his cheek, but he had no time to dwell on it.

"Aramus," he shouted. "Do *not* kiss her."

Through the tornado of monsters, Aramus eyes locked on Olórin's and he saw them flinch. Olórin wasn't sure if it was his words or the sight of the wounds the harpy had caused him which snapped Aramus from the depths of his trance. Whichever it was, Aramus drew his sword and, without hesitation, plunged its blade deep into the chest of the harpy queen. *She* seemed as surprised by Aramus's actions as Olórin. Immediately the other harpies took to the air, screeching like they had all been set on fire. Each one of them clutched their chests and turned their dead, horrified faces toward their queen.

Her black eyes slowly lowered and followed Aramus's blade, up the muscles of his arm that were now straining under her weight, until they rested on his cold, slatted amber eyes. The pink tendril receded from Aramus's mouth and instead, whipped violently in the air. She let out a final shrill shriek before falling to the ground, dead. Moments after, her followers dropped from the sky and they littered the hazy forest floor with their limp, hideous bodies.

The silence returned to the forest and the mist swallowed up the echoes of the harpies' last cries. Aramus doubled over panting and clutching his injured shoulder, before standing to survey the scene around him. For someone who had just skewered the woman he thought he loved, Aramus seemed remarkably unperturbed by it all. Then again, Olórin knew how he rarely showed emotion. But with something like this he was expecting, well, more.

"Olórin, are you okay?" Aramus said.

"Yes, yes, I'm fine. Just a scratch, that's all," Olórin replied, fingering the wounds on his cheek. "More importantly, how are you?"

Olórin gestured for his staff that he now realised had only been a few feet away from him.

"Fine," he said flatly, handing Olórin the staff.

"Are you sure? The pull of a queen harpy can have lasting effects on a man's heart."

"I said I'm fine. Just leave it."

Aramus's curt response was a small relief to Olórin.

"As you wish," he said with a sympathetic tone. "Come, the dwarfs are at least another two days walk, and I'm sure it won't be long before one of the queen's subordinates discover what has happened here. We must move quickly now. We still have to breech the dwarven barrier outside of Balbuldor, and that in itself is going to be difficult."

Without needing another word, the young man turned and began to make his way through the clearing, leaving Olórin to pick his way over the dead bodies strewn around him. Aramus took a last furtive glance at the harpy queen before he left. Olórin could have sworn that he saw him wipe a small tear from the corner of his eye. But his hand had moved too quickly to be sure.

Chapter 12

The trail left behind after the wizard and the winged man, was clumsy and made it easy to follow them. Even without the mammoth goat hoof-prints, black blood still showed her the path they had taken. Aria should be overjoyed that it was so easy, but she wasn't.

"Is there something troubling you, Aria," Edwel asked, the concern in his voice belying his sunny expression.

"I am the queen of a belligerent people, Edwel, of course there are things that trouble me," she replied.

Behind her, the army of ogres marched dutifully, but the sound of their footsteps irked her. It was only by the power of the amulet that they stayed in such perfect formation – an unnatural thing for ogres to do. Like her rule over her kingdom, their obedience was a ruse. She had begun to doubt the righteousness of her quest, even her methods, and it seemed that Edwel had picked up on her uncertainty.

"You have been the queen for two years now Aria, and yet, I have never seen you bite your bottom lip with such ferociousness. Are you sure that there isn't something else bothering you?"

Aria let out a weighty sigh. There was no hiding it from the golem.

"As a matter of fact there is," she whispered. Edwel leaned closer to her as they marched, seemingly understanding that she didn't want the ogres to hear. "I fear that there are other forces at work here, Edwel. Something else is guiding either my hand, or the hand of the wizard."

"Whatever do you mean?" he replied in what he thought was a whisper, but really was louder than his normal voice.

"Quiet you big boulder," she hissed. "I mean, that I don't believe I was handed this amulet by accident. Why would

Dantet allow the creation of an artefact that could take his power away from him? And if he didn't create it, how *did* it come into being? And why would the wizards give it to me? Aren't the wizards forbidden to murder, or help someone to be murdered? Surely they would be signing their own death warrants by giving me the power to kill Aramus."

Edwel straightened himself again and pondered the question. He did not answer for the longest time. He trudged through the open fields, unaware of how his heavy frame bent and broke large stalks of corn. He waded through slow moving rivers, still tapping his stone jaw as he submerged under the water, and broke countless branches of thick trees as they made their way through The Shrouded Forest, before finally arriving at a conclusion.

"Although the amulet originates from dark magic, of that there is no denying, perhaps it was not Dantet who created it. There have been many stories of wizards who have delved into the darkness in order to gain power. I have lived for thousands of years and have seen such wizards. But with this dark power comes a price. It twists their senses until their humanity dies in the gloom, the ogre rising over one hundred and fifty years ago was a direct result of this condition. Perhaps that is what is happening here, and Dantet has had no hand in it?"

"Then how do you explain *this*?" Aria said, pointing to a clearing that opened up in the midst of the forest.

Strewn on the floor amongst the moss and the protruding tree roots, were the bodies of thirteen harpies: Each one holding an expression of anguish across their flayed faces, and each one clutching at their chests too. But as far as Aria could make out there was only one that had an actual wound.

"These, like the worgen, are the children of Dantet," she said, stepping carefully between the corpses. "Surely you don't believe that he has lost control over them too?"

Even the ogres wore expressions of disbelief at the sight of the massacre. Stupid as they were, they were not so brainless as to think nothing of the sight. Edwel followed Aria, picking his way carefully between the rotten arms and legs. His stone mouth turned downwards and his square head shook gently from side to side. If he had had any eyebrows Aria was convinced they would be knitted together with worry.

"I cannot explain it Aria," he said. "See here, this one with the gaping hole in its chest, this is a queen harpy. It's most unusual to see one above ground and usually only under the orders of Dantet himself. Killing a queen would end the lives of its entire hive, and that would be a major blow to him. Harpies are one of his most loyal creatures, often becoming his bedfellow. So if this was by his order, then I'm truly afraid of what it means?"

Aria clenched her fists until she felt her nails digging into the palms of her hand. *'Aramus must die for what he has done,'* she thought. *'But what if I am just a pawn in someone else's plan?'* Anger surged inside her chest. *'I will not be manipulated, but I will not be cheated of my justice either.'*

With clenched teeth Aria drew her sword and, releasing a ferocious scream, she decapitated the nearest dead harpy. The harpy's mottled skull did a very unsatisfactory bob before lolling gently to one side, now free of its body.

"You will return to Lothangard, Edwel, as fast as your stone legs will carry you," she said between her clenched teeth. "You will fetch me the wizard named Mullrode, the one who revealed the existence of the amulet to me. I have some questions for him, and he will answer me or lose his life."

"As you wish, My Queen."

Edwel turned and stomped through the forest in a westerly direction, chasing the dying sun. Aria knew that he would not need to stop and rest. His stone muscles would not exhaust themselves, and he would probably return with his quarry before the end of the next day. Until then, she and her army would follow the path the old wizard and Aramus had forgotten to cover up.

*

"Why can't we just fly over it?" Aramus asked.

Olórin stood on a sandy road on the outskirts of a small village called Bartertown, with Aramus hiding in the nearby bushes. Even from their distance, the old wizard could see the unmistakably stout silhouettes of a few dwarfs mixed in with the regular sized humans. The village itself was only three streets long, with little more than a tavern, a trading house, and a blacksmith to supply its commerce.

"You have not yet recovered your full strength, and I don't fancy plummeting to my doom. Not only that, but if we fly, how are the dwarfs to know that we are coming?" he said, pointing his staff in the direction of the village. "This is the nearest outpost to Balbuldor, and it is frequented by trading dwarfs. They are somewhat paranoid at the best of times, my young friend, and if they should see you flying above them in the air, they will undoubtedly take it as a hostile invasion."

Olórin reached into the bushes and grabbed hold of Aramus's arm, pulling him out onto the road for all to see. Aramus checked the road up and down to make sure that it was clear. Even though it was, he still tried to flatten his wings against his back as much as possible.

"Dwarfs have gotten a bad name really," Olórin said, ignoring Aramus's unease. "But they truly are a most hospitable people; so long as you have no intention of stealing their gold, diamonds, or fabled unbreakable dwarven iron from them. However, they do not trust easily, and surprising them is their least favoured way of making new friends. By walking through the village it won't be long before a dwarf, or two, reports us back to their city. That is how they will know that we mean them no harm. Oh Aramus, for the Goddess's sake, would you come out of those bushes."

"That's easy for you to say, old man," Aramus said, reluctantly stepping back out onto the path. "People don't scream at the sight of you, do they? They don't want to pierce your heart with a blade, or hang you by your neck either, I'm guessing. If I show myself in broad daylight like this, things could get very dangerous, very quickly."

"You have lived your entire life in the outskirts of Lothangard, have you not?" Aramus nodded his head whilst still nervously looking about him. "The city, though it has its own charms and attractions, is a very culturally bland place to live. You can undoubtedly find anything you need there, from elven potions to dwarven swords, but you will very rarely see an elf or a dwarf within the city walls. There is no need, you see. Not with trading posts such as this.

"Therefore, the people of Lothangard are not accustomed to seeing a variety of creatures walking their streets. So, you can understand why they would be utterly terrified by *your* appearance. But in a village like Bartertown, variety is a commonplace and I will wager that you will only get a few curious stares."

Olórin glanced at his young companion and, by the knitting of his eyebrows and his dark expression, he could tell that Aramus was unconvinced. Olórin didn't blame him, he wasn't sure he believed himself either. While he knew that distant trading posts are more accepting of the unusual, Aramus's unique appearance might be too much, even for them. But the young man stayed on the path regardless of his concerns, and followed Olórin into the village.

The sandy road gave way to cobble stone thoroughfares, scared deeply with two parallel lines from the wheels of many heavy carts. A distinctive aroma of horse droppings and smoke, appearing to predominantly come from the blacksmiths furnace, hung in the air. Olórin knew it was the type of stink that would linger on his clothes long after he had left. The tall five story buildings, either side of the streets, were wooden and all slightly off-kilter. Long lines of freshly washed clothes hung high between the buildings, dancing like celebratory flags in the fetid breeze. With the amount of laundry visible, Olórin dreaded to think how many families lived on each floor.

For a small village, the noise of metal slamming on metal, carts rattling, and trading partners arguing amongst themselves, was almost deafening. Olórin began to wonder if they would be noticed at all as they strode through the streets. But sure enough, the further they travelled into the village, the quieter it became.

People stared with open mouths as they walked by, some sheltering their children's eyes from the sight of Aramus, and Olórin could feel the tension build inside his young companion. From the corner of his eye, he saw his fists ball so tightly that they shook, and his jaw clench repeatedly.

“Smile, Aramus, you look like you’re about to murder everyone,” Olórin whispered under his breath.

Olórin smiled broadly, feeling a small sting in his wounded cheek, and tipped his hat to two ladies in fine dresses. The splendid ladies stood motionless in the streets, with their hands over their reddened lips and their heavily-painted eyes wide enough that they threatened to pop out altogether. Affluence was worn outwardly in Bartertown.

Aramus, in turn, attempted to smile at the ladies.

“Good Goddess, Aramus,” Olórin said after the two ladies ran into the nearest building. “You looked like a devilish cat waiting to pounce on its prey. How about you leave the smiling up to me instead, eh? All you have to do is stand next to me and try not to look so threatening, or stiff.”

“That’s easy for you to say,” Aramus replied. “And I don’t look like a devilish cat. I’m just not used to smiling at people, that’s all. So forcing it is somewhat, unnatural to me. I can’t help it if *that’s* what comes across.”

“Indeed,” Olórin said.

With a street full of curious eyes watching them, Olórin and Aramus took refuge in a large store in the centre of the village. The walls were lined with dusty boxes of curiosities, grubby glass bottles of fermented produce, and colourful rolls of fabric. Dusty floorboards creaked under their feet as Olórin and Armamus walked in. Three large wooden counters, with glass fronts displaying the more expensive items, lined the walls. Behind them were three older gentlemen. Each one had a magnificent white moustache that curled up to a point on either side, fine red britches, matching jackets, and a black gentleman’s hat atop their three heads of bushy, white hair.

“Good evening,” all three said in unison. “How may we help you?”

Not only did they look identical in every way, even down to their twinkly grey eyes and pointed noses, but they all appeared to know what the other was doing without the need to look. The man on the left, having just made a sale to a stout woman, tossed her produce toward the man in the centre. He in turn caught the object, without looking, and took payment for it. Once the woman had paid, he lobbed it to the man on the right, who packaged it neatly without a single glance.

"Good evening to you, fine gentlemen," Olórin said, taking a step toward the man on the left.

The stout lady, having only just seen the new customers as she was leaving, let out a squeak of surprise and bustled out of the trading house in a hurry. The only customer left was a burly, blonde-haired dwarf, who remained open mouthed and firmly stuck to his spot as he ogled Aramus.

"Oh dear, it seems we have startled one of your customers. I do apologise."

"No matter," said the first man.

"No matter," chorused the other two.

"How can we help you this fine day?" all three said together.

"Are they normally like this?" Aramus asked under his breath.

"Ah, you'll have to forgive my young friend here," Olórin said with an apologetic laugh. "He's never met a Trithonian before."

"No matter," they said in unison.

"What's a Trithonian?" Aramus asked quietly.

"*We* are a Trithonian," they replied in unison. "Psychically linked, physically in tune, and spiritually the same."

"I am he, and he is I," the first pointed to the last.

"They are me, and I am them," said the second.

"We are all, and all are one," said the last.

Aramus threw a confused look at Olórin.

"Think of one mind sharing three bodies," Olórin explained.

"A good analogy," said the first.

"Now, if we can be so bold, may we ask, what are you?" all three asked, pointing to Aramus.

Aramus opened his mouth to reply, but nothing came out. Olórin suspected it was because he didn't quite know how to explain what he was. Here was this unusual creature standing before him, separate but one, able to explain what it was and with a solid understanding of where it came from. But yet,

Aramus was lost with that question.

"I don't know," he answered quietly.

Olórin felt a pang of sympathy for his young friend.

"But we *do* know where we are headed," Olórin interrupted. "We seek an audience with the dwarven king of Balbuldor, and we would like to bring him a gift."

All three men laughed like they were one, and the dwarf customer snorted as he absently perused a nearby trinket.

"You know the king?" the Trithonain asked.

"No, we haven't met, persay. But I'm hoping that he has heard of me, and will grant me an audience regardless."

"And who are you?" they asked.

"My name is Olórin Talfan."

The tree men looked at each other, their mouths opened to exactly the same amount as the others. A heavy footed shuffle let Olórin know that the dwarf had suddenly left the shop in a hurry. With precise steps, the Trithonian huddled together at the back of the shop, whispering in hushed tones and taking the odd glance back at Olórin.

"If I didn't know any better, I'd swear they looked scared of you," Aramus whispered.

"Perhaps they are," Olórin replied with a knowing smile.

Before Aramus had a chance to ask another question, the Trithonian bustled forward with a large bottle in their hands.

"Here, for you," they said meekly. "Please take it, free of charge. This is the finest bottle of whisky for miles around, and the king is an avid lover of the drink. Please, we want no trouble, nor do we cause any trouble. Take it, with our compliments."

"Why, what a lovely gesture," Olórin said taking the bottle and sliding it into his hat. "I thank you my kind friends. It is lovely to see how your people have come to be so generous. And might I add, I am pleased to see your moustaches have grown back so nicely too."

Each of the men touched their well-groomed lip hair protectively and tittered with a nervous glance at one another. Olórin nodded to them and left the trading post, followed by Aramus, who looked more confused than ever.

"Are you going to tell me what *that* was all about?" he asked.

"The Trithonian didn't used to be just three," Olórin said, keeping his eyes fixed on the road ahead as they left the village. "It once occupied hundreds of physical forms and was called the Centhonian. So many crimes it got away with, so many alibies to choose from. Its numbers had to be reduced, you understand?"

"You killed the others?" Aramus asked with surprise. "I thought wizards couldn't kill."

"Killed? No, indeed not. Think more along the lines of squashing lots of grapes into one bottle, and you will understand what I did."

"Oh," Aramus nodded. "If someone had done that to me I think I would have remembered them. But the Trithonian didn't know you until you said your name."

"Ah, yes. It was many years ago, back when I first became a full wizard. I'm afraid a lot has changed since then, and most of it has been on my face," he said, gesturing to his wrinkled appearance. "Anyway, let us not dwell in the past because it only serves to rouse ghosts, and what use are they? They will neither feed us nor comfort us. We must make our way to the badlands now, because *that's* where we will find the entrance to Balbuldor."

*

They had marched for many hours without a break, and dehydration had murdered more ogres. But they were so close to him that Aria couldn't stop her pursuit for something as mundane as water. There was no Edwel to persuade her otherwise either. The footsteps in the sandy road ahead of them were deep and unmoved by the gentle winds. One pair of shoes walked the path boldly, while the other criss-crossed between the bushes. Further down the road, it seemed that the second had lost its shyness, and now the two pairs of prints walked together.

Aria had been so intent on tracking Aramus and the wizard, that she was almost inside the village before she realised there was one there. It was only when the tracks disappeared and gave way to cobbled stone, did she look up. Everywhere around her, people bustled, carts rumbled, and loud clangs emanated from the sole blacksmith in town. Fused with the smell of horse dung and smoke, the acrid air made Aria wrinkle her nose in disgust.

"Spread out," she said. "Look for any clue that they have been here and report back to me."

With a collective grunt the ogre army fanned out through the town, roughly tossing large baskets aside, and barging their way into people's homes. Shouts of objections and a few screams of terror, rang out from the small village as Aria made her way toward the centre.

"Your Majesty, Your Majesty," came the voice of three men speaking as one. "How lovely it is to see you here. To what do we owe the pleasure?"

"I am looking for a hunchback and a wizard," she said, curiously eying the identical men in red suits.

She had a particular distaste for men who spent too long grooming their facial hair. In her opinion, men who fastidiously drew attention to such an outwardly feature did it to draw the eye away from something else. These three men had the most immaculately groomed moustaches she had ever seen, which made her mistrust them immediately.

"Have you seen them?"

"Oh, we were hoping you would ask that," they chortled in apparent delight. "There is no need to keep searching, we will tell you everything. A hunchback has not passed through here, but a wizard and a winged man have. Are they the ones you seek?"

Aria felt her heart leap into her mouth.

"How long ago did they pass?" she asked, taking a step closer to the three strange men.

"Not less than two hours ago," one of them replied. "They are heading toward the badlands."

"And they are seeking an audience with the king of Balbuldor," the two others said.

"King?" Aria snorted in disgust. "There is no king beneath the ground. *I* am the only monarch of Naretia."

"Our apologies, Your Highness, we meant no offence," they replied with a bow.

Aria ignored the reverence of the three oddly dressed men and focused on the more imperative question at hand.

"Did they tell you why they are looking for him?"

"No, they did not," the three said. "But you should be aware that *this* wizard is no ordinary wizard."

"What do you mean?" Aria narrowed her eyes.

"*This* wizard is none other than Olórin Talfan," the three whispered.

Aria took a step back from the men again. She eyed each one of them, carefully scrutinising their features for any tell-tale sign that they were lying. There was no twitching of the eye, no glancing to the side, no fiddling of fingers, nothing that would indicate a falsehood. It was then that Aria felt her heart sink and her resolve falter.

She had known that Aramus travelled with an Elder wizard, as was denoted by his brown cloak. But never having had a good look at the wizard, she was entirely unaware that the Supreme himself had decided to travel with this murderer. In the hierarchy of the wizard caste, the Supreme Wizard was as powerful as they get, as close to a God as any mortal can achieve, and most probably the only one who could stop her from avenging her parent's deaths.

Aria absently clutched at the amulet around her neck, silently called for her army of ogres to cease their searching and advance to her location. They diligently obeyed, and soon an orderly line of ogres stood behind her. But even with the surge of power she always felt when she used the amulet, Aria couldn't help but feel impotent.

"You are worried, Our Queen?" the three said.

"You think he is unbeatable?" said the first.

"We know that he is not," the three said together.

"I am tired of being fed riddles," Aria hissed at the three men, before roughly pulling the middle one up by his neatly pressed shirt collar, choking him. "Tell me what you know or I will see to it that the Trithonian becomes only one. Yes, that's right, I know what you are." The three men held their hands over their necks, gasping, like all of them were being strangled at once.

"Gladly, gladly," they whimpered. "We do not wish to seem mistrustful, only we are ancient and speak with the words of different ages. We promise to be more forthright, Your Majesty."

"Tell me then, how do I defeat Olórin? How do I slay the Supreme Wizard of Naretia?"

Even as she said it, the words seemed wrong somehow, like having to put ones hand through flames to reach a prized jewel. A small voice warned her that she would get burned if she tried to take on the Supreme Wizard, but she so desperately wanted that jewel.

"His biggest weakness lies in his heart," they said through gasps. "He will do anything to save that young man. He will lay down his staff and willingly give himself to the mercy of your sword, all for the sake of love."

"Love? How does that help me?" she said hotly, dropping the middle man with a frustrated shove. The three men stumbled backwards and collectively sighed with relief.

"When you hunt deer, where the arrow lands will be the difference between failure and success," said the first.

"If you hit it in the leg it may stop running for a time, but it still can kick and hurt you," said the second.

"If you hit it in the shoulder it may carry on running and escape you," said the third.

"But if you hit it in the heart, it will stop dead," they said together. "Ignore the wizard as you battle, and focus your attention on the young man. Holding his life to ransom is the key to defeating the Supreme Wizard."

Aria contemplated what the three men had said, but in the heat of battle she wasn't too sure how much use their advice would be. Her ultimate goal was to kill Aramus, but in order to do that she would have to go through Olórin. To get past Olórin they say she would have to hold Aramus to ransom, although, she wasn't convinced that they knew exactly how deadly Aramus was. It was a no win scenario. Aria ran her hand through her curly, red hair in frustration before fixing her blue eyes on the three men again.

"Why do you want to help me? I thought the *wizards* were the rulers of this land, not me. Why risk defying them?" she asked.

"More than two centuries ago," the first said with a scowl. "Olórin Talfan wronged us more deeply than you can imagine."

"Now, we are trapped within these three," they said in unison. "Our voices are many and the walls of these bodies echo our sounds loudly. A being, such as ours, is not meant to be confined like caged animals. It is a torture that is unrelenting, and all for the sake of a little bit of thievery. But with his death, his spell shall be broken and we shall, once again, be free."

Aria wasn't sure she liked the sound of that, but before she had a chance to think on it, a series of heavy stone footsteps racing down the cobbled roads of the village caught her attention.

Edwel's large stone body appeared in the distance. On his face he wore a stupidly sunny grin, and over his shoulder were the blue robes of a dark-haired junior wizard. Mullrode kicked and hit the golem furiously, shouting obscenities at the stone man for "interrupting his work and kidnapping him". Edwel was non-to-bothered by the insults or the thumping. Choosing to ignore it, he waved at Aria and, with a cheery call yelled, "Coo-wee".

"Do you know him?" the Trithonain asked with a snigger.

"I do," she replied flatly, "And if you are not gone from here by the time I take my next breath, I will ask him to sit on all three of your heads until they pop like rotten eggs."

Aria took a beat and when she glanced behind her, the only remaining sign of the three strange men was the trading house door swinging closed behind them. Overly groomed facial hair or not, the Trithonian couldn't be trusted with the information that she might have to force out of the struggling wizard.

Chapter 13

"Aria." Edwel skidded to a halt in front of her, sending shards of broken cobble skittling across the road. "Wonderful news, I have returned with the wizard called Mullrode, as you requested. *And* he most graciously offered to craft a new head for me. I'm thinking, perhaps one with a nose, and not quite so square."

Aria pinched the bridge of her nose and shook her head. Edwel, so pleasant and optimistic, was not accustomed to sarcasm and took everything literally, including threats to his physical being. It was a characteristic that had annoyed Aria a great deal. But now, seeing his stupid grin whilst simultaneously manhandling a struggling junior wizard, it brought up a feeling of pity instead.

"I don't think that's quite what he meant, Edwel," she said with a gentle sigh.

"Oh, right then," Edwel said. His stone mouth turned downwards as he dumped the wizard unceremoniously onto the ground in front of Aria. It was the first time in her life that Aria had heard true disappointment in his voice.

"Q-Queen Aria," Mullrode spluttered, his voice high and nasal. "I-I had no idea that the golem was sent by you. My apologies, Your Highness, if I had known I would have come with him willingly."

Aria looked the man up and down. He appeared to be in his early forties, young to have passed his apprenticeship, with jet-black hair that reached only as far as his shoulders. His short, black beard was parted into three plaits and finished off with red beads that clinked annoyingly together as he spoke. He had the look of a man who spent most of his time indoors, away from the sun and any form of exercise.

"Who else do you know that commands a golem?" Aria

asked accusingly.

Mullrode spluttered and raised his hands in a limp gesture of "I don't know". His severely arched eyebrows followed his hands movements. Aria noted a nasty bruise under one of his grey eyes – presumably a result of his struggles with Edwel.

"I did tell him, Aria," Edwel said defensively. "He told me that he didn't give two…"

"Ahhh, it doesn't really matter what I said," Mullrode interrupted with a nervous laugh. "What matters is that I'm here now. So, how may I be of service, Your Majesty?"

"You can start by telling me how you came by this amulet?" she asked, gesturing toward her neck. "In all the years, and in all the wars that raged between us and the Dark Ones, I have never heard tales of it before. Yet now, as the son of Dantet makes himself known, it conveniently does the same. And just before my eighteenth birthday too, after which I would no longer be the sole ruler of Naretia."

"I don't know what you mean, Your Majesty," Mullrode scoffed. "The amulet has always been in the castle vaults. Why, I have seen it there for many years. Perhaps it is because the amulet lay in an obscure part of the vault, in an area that hadn't been touched for some thousands of years? I only discovered it when Olórin himself asked me to catalogue the unending contents of the palace bowls."

"Why would Olórin ask you to do that?" Aria asked, taking a step closer to Mullrode, who still sat on the ground. "Something about what you're telling me does not make sense, wizard. Any apprentice, or servant, could have done that job. So, why would the Supreme, all-knowing leader of the wizard caste ask a junior wizard to perform such a remedial task instead?"

"I don't know, but Olórin has never liked me much. In the time that I studied under him, he seemed to delight in belittling me," Mullrode answered, squirming a little.

Aria narrowed her eyes and drew her sword.

"Tell me how you truly came to know about this amulet," she said slowly. "Answer me now, or I will slit your throat."

"I came to know of it from cataloguing the vaults, Your

Majesty, I swear," he said, his voice getting slightly higher with each word, and his hands beginning to tremble as he held them up defensively.

"Fine! If you won't answer to me, then perhaps you will answer to a Dark One," Aria seethed, gripping her amulet. "Perhaps being undone by the very thing that you allowed me to control might loosen your tongue."

"Aria, please," Edwel said. "He says he doesn't know."

"I don't believe him," she spat, before turning to the nearest ogre. "You there, walk forward and remove this wizard's tongue. He apparently has no use for it at the moment."

Dutifully, one of her ogres walked forward with large resounding steps and a gleam of want in his eye. His black armour clinked loudly in the now silent town. Traveling on the gentle breeze Aria could hear whispers of the name she had come to loath and know so well – The Blood Queen. She could feel the angry eyes of the residents staring at her from behind their dirty window panes.

"No please, don't, I beg of you," Mullrode whimpered, scrambling away from the approaching ogre. "I swear to you, I know nothing more of the amulet other than its existence. I wasn't even sure that it worked. Please, My Queen, Please!"

Aria ignored the wizard. She didn't want to have to resort to torture, but she also knew that fear was a powerful way to loosen a man's tongue, and nothing about his story seemed honest right now.

Without warning, the wizard fell onto his back and pulled up his sleeve. He held up his arm and revealed a bizarre symbol etched in black ink on his forearm. Within an upside-down triangle two lines were drawn, each one curving away from the other at the top, like the horns of a goat. The wizard closed his eyes tightly and waited. When the ogre saw the marking, he stopped in his tracks and blinked stupidly at the wizard.

"What are you waiting for?" Aria shouted at the ogre. "I said to remove his tongue."

The ogre took another step forward and then hesitated

again. He glanced between Aria and the wizard in an intense moment of sheer confusion. Brandishing his cleaver, he took another step forward and scratched his forehead before thumping it a few times with the heel of its hand. The ogre moaned and groaned like his brain was about to explode. Mullrode remained calm and still, his branded arm held up toward the ogre. Quiet unexpectedly, the ogre ended the baffling standoff by swiftly driving his cleaver deep between his own two eyes. His green body swayed for a moment and a smile of relief crossed its toothy, blood-stained face. He collapsed, dead, in a heap in front of Aria.

Edwel stood between his queen and the wizard to protect her from whatever magic Mullrode had cast, but Aria walked around him and stared at the fallen ogre in disbelief.

"What did you do?" she screamed at the wizard. "I thought only the amulet could control Dark Ones. How is this possible? Answer me!"

"My apologies, Your Highness, but I didn't much feel like dying today," the wizard replied, standing to his feet and dusting himself off. "This is a protection mark against all creatures of Dantet. It is called a Custos, and should a Dark One try to harm any person bearing this mark, they will instantly feel an overpowering urge to commit suicide. It is a brutish spell, and one of my own invention, but in these uncertain times it is a necessary one. Most wizards who fight against the rise of Dantet will bear this mark. Tell me, do you know if Olórin Talfan has one? I have studied under that self-important blowhard for many years and I can unequivocally tell you that I have never seen one."

Mullrode's tone changed at the mention of the Supreme Wizard's name, like it had made the taste in his mouth turn sour just by saying it.

"That has to make you think, does it not, My Queen?" Mullrode said more coolly. He strode away from Aria and Edwel to examine the line of growling ogres. He smiled at them, holding his long, pointed nose firmly in the air in the same manner as Aria had remembered from the first time they met.

"Olórin *is* the one who sent me into the vault to discover that amulet. He is also the one who protects the son of Dantet and, as the leader of the wizard caste, he is the one who prevents you from achieving justice for your parents. It has become obvious to me, and to many more within the wizard caste, that something otherworldly has persuaded him to save that monster.

"We believe that Olórin has fallen prey to the seductive whispers of the Dark God. His actions belie the integrity he spouts. I know that if *I* was the Supreme Wizard, I would have taken the death of Naretia's king and queen more seriously."

"And what, pray tell, would you have done differently, Mullrode?" Aria said, keeping her eyes mistrustfully fixed on the wizard as he meandered casually back toward her. "All wizards are forbidden to murder, are they not?"

"You are correct, My Queen. Such wisdom in one so young," Mullrode said, facing Aria. Knowing that humouring him was more fortuitous in extracting information, Aria had to try very hard not to snarl at his condescending words. "As it happens the wizards of today follow the stringent law of the Goddess Edwina, but they don't have to. Magic cannot be created from nothing, but Edwina is not the only source of power in this kingdom. There is a new faction emerging from within the wizard caste called, The Order of Everto. And, like all new ways of thinking which threaten the sentiment and tradition of old men, it has been falsely associated with Dantet."

Edwel looked meaningfully at Aria, or as meaningfully as his rigid stone face would allow. She remembered his warning about some wizards who, in their thirst for power, favoured the law of Dantet.

"Let me reassure you, Your Majesty, that the order does not, nor will it ever worship that foul beast Dantet," he said as though he could read her thoughts. A few grumbles of disapproval rippled through the stoic line of ogres at the insult, but Mullrode ignored them. "By denouncing Edwina's rule we are no longer governed by any God, but rather by the magic we syphon from Naretia itself, and there is much of it here. So it is in our best interests to ensure the safety of our world and, by extension, the ruler of it.

"But regardless of how Olórin may *try* to prevent it, a new reign is coming to the wizard caste, and, as old men often are, the Elders are frightened of what that will mean for them. They grow desperate to keep their long-winded traditions and power over the common folk, which have afforded them such an unquestioning rule. That is why they have created these lies about the order, vilifying us without any evidence at all. I also suspect that it is those very same wizards whom Dantet has turned.

"However, I am just a humble servant to the true ruler of Naretia, and Olórin's motivation is not for me to decide. *You* are the rightful heir, and only *you* can decide which of us truly works in your favour and in the favour of Naretia. I only ask that you carefully consider the evidence so far."

Aria wondered if Mullrode *was* telling the truth and, just like the worgen, dissention was also creeping into the unwavering rule of the wizards. Aria was only too aware how young blood often sites change in a society of traditions, as she had done within her own palace. She also wondered if the unseen hand, which had created the fateful eddies in her path, hadn't also steered Aramus's actions too. It would mean that, as a pawn, he was innocent of premeditating the terrible crimes he had committed. But he had still committed them and, as such, should be punished.

'Why have I only learned of this dissention now?' Aria though. *'You may have the same goal as I, wizard, but I fail to see how helping me would benefit you.'*

"Had *I* been the Supreme Wizard," Mullrode continued, "the winged man would not have been allowed to go free. I would have imprisoned this criminal for life, at the very least. There are also many spells that could have been cast, which would have left him writhing in pain for an eternity as punishment. When the new order comes to power, as it inevitably will do, if you make *me* the Supreme Wizard, I can swear our eternal allegiance to you and you alone."

And there it was.

"Tell me, Mullrode, should I decide to make someone else the Supreme Wizard, would you still swear your allegiance to me?" she asked.

"Of course," he answered with a bow that almost lowered his nose to normal level, but not quite. "As long as you reign, you are, and always will be, my Queen."

"Is that a threat, wizard?" Edwel said, taking a step closer to Mullrode.

Aria didn't stop Edwel approaching him this time. She also got the distinct impression that he was hiding something more sinister within his words.

"No, no, of course not," Mullrode replied, taking a reluctant step away from the stone golem. "I only mean that we, as wizards, will outlive the ruler of Naretia. But no matter who is in power our loyalties will always lie with the crown."

"Then you won't mind me testing your loyalties, would you?" Aria asked.

"I welcome it."

"Tell me how to defeat Olórin in battle."

Mullrode paused for a moment, flitting his sickly grey eyes between the golem and Aria.

"You hesitate," she said, narrowing her eyes.

"I do," he replied. "But only because to know how to disarm Olórin is to also know how to disarm any wizard, and it would leave us all vulnerable."

"Tell me, and you will be free to return to Lothangard."

The junior wizard pursed his lips into a thin line and shifted uneasily on his feet.

"Very well," he replied, sliding a pale hand into the pocket of his blue robes. "In the beginning, when Edwina entrapped Dantet, she created a magical barrier between the two worlds. A shield called the Valefire, through which Dantet, or followers, could not cross. In the soil next to this barrier lay small pockets of a metal ore. Over eons this ore absorbed some of the barriers qualities, making it as impervious to all kinds of magic as the barrier itself. When the dwarfs discovered this ore they smelted it down, and so Etherium was created.

"This scarce metal was only ever known to have been

made into two sets of armour, one for the dwarven king and one for his champion. But by good fortune, and a sympathetic patron, the Order of Everto came upon one of these suits of armour, and it was fashioned into weapons for us. This is just one of the Etherium arrows," he said, withdrawing a silver metal shaft from his pocket. "As with all the other arrows, it has been enchanted with the Valefire shard to make it a formidable weapon against any mortal creature in existence."

The thin rod shone brilliantly in the sun, and sung with the hint of a creature that was living. It was tinted blue and, although he called it an arrow, it had no fletchings that Aria could see, nor did it have a sharpened head either. For all intents and purpose, it looked like a simple rod, and Aria wondered if Mullrode was trying to fob her off with some junk he had picked up along the way. But she remembered hearing of a powerful gem called the Valefire, known only to the leaders of the castes and her father. It was a broken fragment of the Valefire shield itself, that protected Naretia from the dark creatures of Dantet's world. If Mullrode knew of it too, then he must be telling the truth.

"The arrow will pierce any armour, magical shield, or hide, and is impervious to misdirection," he continued. "Thrown toward your target, it will strike it true every time. For most creatures one blow from the arrow will end their life, but for a wizard of Olórin's formidable power, I suspect that it will only weaken him for a time."

"How do I know that you tell the truth?" Aria asked. "And how is it that you conveniently come to carry it right at the point where I would need it?"

Mullrode smiled and turned his back to Aria's army of ogres.

Without warning, he threw the arrow away from him, and it soared through the air with a long, high-pitched zing. Aria watched as the slender metal rod turned course of its own accord and took aim at the nearest ogre. The ogre too noticed that it was coming straight for him at an ever-increasing speed and tried to hide behind the soldier next to him. The arrow skirted around the soldier and passed through the head of its target without slowing down. Without slowing, it returned to the outreached hand of Mullrode in one seamless movement.

The town grew silent as the ogre stumbled backward, green blood oozing from either side of his temple, and he fell to the ground, dead. The rest of the ogres bellowed, and made to advance on Mullrode before Aria stopped them with a raised hand. Edwel stepped closer to his queen in a vain attempt to protect her. Even though Aria knew the weapon would most probably find her regardless of his stone body, she was still grateful for the presence. Never in her life had she seen a wizard kill, and the sight disturbed her.

"You see, Your Majesty, the arrow will never miss." Mullrode smirked. "It is something that every member of the Order of Everto carries because we are a constant target of ill-wishers. It is not convenience that sees this weapon on me, but rather necessity. I would not part with it easily, but for you, My Queen, it is yours," he said, handing the arrow to Aria.

Aria took the metal rod and examined it closely. It was heavy, cold, and etched along the shaft were a multitude of unfamiliar, swirling markings that seemed to embrace the blue metal, like the many arms of an octopus clinging to some treasure. It was indeed a formidable weapon and would be of a lot more use then the Trithonians advice.

"I must warn you, though," Mullrode continued, "that I do not believe the arrow will survive its encounter with Olórin; his power is too great. And so, it is imperative that you only strike at the most opportune moment. Otherwise, I fear your efforts to thwart him will be in vain."

"Tell me, Mullrode," Aria said, eying both the strange weapon and the wizard suspiciously. "What good fortune led this metal into the hands of the order? I am familiar enough with dwarfs to know that such a find would only leave their hands if they were cold and dead. Who is this patron that has given you such a prize?"

"Why it was their king, Your Majesty," Mullrode answered flatly.

Chapter 14

The dusty roads, parched from lack of rain, soon gave way to a dark landscape devoid of trees, grass or any indication of life whatsoever. The intense sunshine of southern Naretia was swallowed greedily by vast fields of blackness, which refused to let any light reflect off its glassy surface. Dark waves, frozen in place by some magical spell, stretched out as far as the eye could see, and looked as though it could have consumed every vector of life instantly.

Though they had not yet stepped onto the ominous terrain, the intense heat radiating off the surface blew suffocating air in Olórin's direction. Dwarven legends tell of how they used the blood of the fiercest demon, the heart fires from the hottest volcano, and the strongest diamonds from their mines, to create this impenetrable obsidian landscape. There were many legends too about men spending weeks, and all of their resources, trying to break though the surface so that they might lay hands on the dwarf's riches. But all perished in the end.

"What is that?" Aramus asked, squinting against the bright sunlight.

"*That,* is the city of Balbuldor," Olórin answered, pausing to riffle through his hat.

The heat had forced Olórin to relinquish his thick cloak and fur boots into his hat, in favour of lighter clothes. Aramus, however, seemed unperturbed by the heat, despite his black leather jacket (which now had a sizable hole in the shoulder) and heavy boots. Olórin felt faint just by looking at him, and wondered if his tolerance for the climate wasn't another trait passed down to him by his father.

"I see no city, old man."

"No, of course you don't," Olórin replied, fishing out a small bundle of pink wool with a sigh of relief. "It wouldn't be protected very well if it were just lying around in the open, now would it? The city lies beneath the ground."

"How do we get there?"

Olórin plopped his hat back on his bald head and proceeded to detangle the lumps of pink wool until four knitted tea cozies emerged.

"With these," he said handing two of them to an astonished looking Aramus. "Don't look at me like that. I'm not crazy. The dwarfs have enchanted this obsidian with an Infernos curse. Should any living, or non-living thing rest upon its surface, it will superheat it until the object melts or bursts into flames. So, I would suggest that you put those on your feet before you walk any further."

Aramus shot Olórin a sceptical look. Throwing his eyes to the heavens Olórin sighed and shoved his staff into his hat. He slipped on his own tea cozies and walked, unharmed, onto the obsidian. Reaching into the pockets of his robes, he pulled out a small item, and tossed it toward Aramus.

A round, yellow pebble skidded to a halt no more than a foot away from the young man. Slowly the black rock beneath the pebble began to change. It turned a bright crimson colour and an intense heat began to emanate from it. Olórin watched as Aramus shielded himself from the rising heat with his arm. Within seconds the pebble shattered into a thousand pieces from the heat.

"You must take care not to accidently drop anything onto the surface," he continued. "Don't sit down, or lean on anything, because it is only these pink shoe coverings that prevent us both from being burned alive. You can thank my good friend, Zerran, for these."

"Was Zerran a wizard too?"

"Heavens no. Zerran is a somewhat dim-witted farmer that lives in the middle of Lothangard, where he has no fields to plough. But what he lacks in common sense, he makes up for with his gift in creating heat-absorbing tea cozies. Although, I think it may have more to do with his one and only livestock, Bella the sheep, who lives in his kitchen. According to Zerran's neighbours, Bella was involved in some kind of horrendous incident involving the raspberry bush and an overprotective wizard. Since then, she's lost her taste for raspberries, and given Zerran nothing but magically imbued pink wool that protects from all things hot. Fascinating really. Of course, being the dim-witted soul that he is, he lacks the imagination to fashion anything but tea cozies from it."

Aramus paused and opened his mouth like he was going to say something. After a moment longer he closed it again, straightened the strap of his backpack across his chest, and put the pink woollen covers over his black boots.

"All right, old man, where to next?" he said with a defeated sigh.

"Next, we must get lost. That is the only way to find the entrance to Balbuldor."

Aramus rolled his eyes before cautiously stepping onto the black obsidian. With little more than a sigh of relief at not bursting into flames, he followed Olórin into the featureless landscape.

They had only walked for a little over twenty minutes before they became aware of the sound of ogres screaming in the distance. The two companions spun around in unison, and standing at the outer reaches of the obsidian border was the queen of Naretia. Her red armour glinted brightly against the dark landscape, and a long line of cleaver wielding ogres paced excitedly behind her.

Olórin watched as she pointed to another ogre and gestured him forward. He diligently marched onto the obsidian without fear, but within seconds was consumed in a blaze. His arms and legs hit out wildly, and his bloodcurdling roars of pain reverberated over the glassy landscape. Olórin couldn't look, so instead turned his gaze toward Aramus, who appeared unruffled by the torture that was happening.

"We must quicken our pace to get ourselves lost," Olórin said, taking Aramus by the elbow and turning him in the opposite direction. "I'd wager that she doesn't know my friend Zerran, but she is also resolute to reach us. I don't doubt that if she could create a path of dead ogre bodies to reach us, she would."

*

Aria screamed in frustration. She had everything she needed to defeat Olórin and capture Aramus, but now they were too far away. She fingered the Etherium arrow and wondered if it might be able to reach the wizard and weaken him from this distance. But even if it could, she was too far away to be able to take advantage of it, and to have come so far only to be stopped by something as innate as rocks, infuriated her.

"You there," she shouted at the nearest ogre, "find a way to them."

The ogre grinned a stupid, toothy grin and saluted the young queen, like he had been the first to be asked. Raising his cleaver above his head, and letting out a brutish roar, he ran across the dark rocks as fast as he could. Within seconds the black surface under him turned a bright crimson colour and the ogres cries of war soon turned into screams of anguish. Aria clenched her jaw so tightly that she thought it would never open again.

"My Queen," Edwel began in an aggravatingly calm voice. "This is enchanted obsidian, there is no way for us to cross it."

"There has to be," she shouted at the golem. "If *they* can cross it, so can we."

"They may have knowledge of magic that we do not," he replied. "But never fear, we can just wait for them to emerge again. They cannot spend an eternity beneath the ground."

"Wait? Wait?" she said, picking up some nearby pebbles and throwing them at the obsidian. The pebbles exploded one by one as the black rock beneath them reacted to even the smallest one, confirming that she couldn't use Edwel to cross it either. "And where exactly should we wait? The badlands are vast. Should we circle around and wait to the east or the west of them? Or perhaps we should just wait here, because they are *bound* to emerge in the exact same spot as they left, right? I have no idea where they will be headed once their business with the dwarfs is finished, do you?"

Edwel clasped his hands in front of him, like a scolded child, and solemnly shook his stone head.

"Two years I have been waiting to gain the upper hand over that murderer Aramus. Two years! But it seems that I am to be blocked at every pass by whatever forces protect him. Why?" she screamed at the skies. "What would you have me do? Should I ignore his crimes and content myself to sit on a golden throne, pretending to be ignorant? Is that the kind of ruler you would have me be? Answer me, Edwina!"

Aria's last words rang out across the barren landscape, but there was no reply. She was resigned, the goddess Edwina had forsaken her mission too.

Her chest heaved with the effort of breathing in the heat. Sweat rolled down her neck and disappeared under her armour. Despite Edwel's multiple requests, she had refused to remove it; choosing to be battle ready at all times instead. She was beginning to regret her decision now as her mind, made mad from the heat, conjured the sound of hundreds of hooves galloping closer and closer. She knew that it couldn't be, because animals needed grass to graze and water to drink, but there was nothing in the arid southern region of Naretia except sand and black obsidian.

Aria watched Olórin and her enemy disappear beyond the blackness. She hung her head in defeat and fell to her knees, a small tear escaping the corner of her eye. A queen shouldn't cry, especially not in front of her army, but the girl inside her wouldn't allow her the dignity of stoniness and she hated that.

The sound of galloping grew louder as the heat reached its choking hands around Aria's face. She ignored it.

"Aria!" Edwel whispered, pointing his stone finger toward something in the distance.

The sound of four legged creatures racing toward them grew louder still, as did the grumbling from the line of ogres. Aria stood up and squinted in the direction Edwel pointed. A small flutter of something made itself known in her stomach, she wasn't quite sure if it was fear or delight. Kicking up a cloud of dust from the path behind them, was an army of worgen. And leading the charge, was Luscious.

"Be still," she ordered her army.

Their voices hushed and their weapons lowered instantly.

Within minutes, Luscious and his pack, of at least thirty worgen, skidded to a halt in front of her.

"Queen Aria," Luscious growled, the corner of his lip curling to reveal the missing canine tooth. "I see the wizard and Aramus have escaped you."

"Do you come here to gloat, Luscious? Because if you have, I have better things I could command you to do with your time," Aria warned.

"There is no need for the amulet, Your Majesty. I have no intention of harming you or your pride. In fact, I come bearing wonderful news."

"Is that so? Please, do go on," she said, eyeing the large number of worgen with a small amount of trepidation churning the contents of her stomach.

"We know where they will travel after the dwarfs," he said, absently scratching his pointed ear with his hind leg. "But I fear they may gain the support of the half-men and, should that happen, you will need more than a subservient army of mindless beasts to defeat them. Small as they might be, the dwarfs are nothing short of powerhouses built to level mountains. Although they are not warriors by trade, if you should put a sword in their hands instead of a pickaxe… well, you can imagine the damage that they could do."

"Nothing short," Edwel sniggered at the unintentional pun.

Aria shot him a pointed look which stopped his scoffing instantly.

"Where do they travel to next? And how did you come across this information when I have scoured every inch of Naretia and heard nothing?" she asked.

"Like the worgen, not all of the dwarfs follow their god blindly," Luscious said, turning toward the setting sun, "I find that sugar has always been more appealing to flies then a swot. However, the real truth only comes to light when the flies are made aware that the swot is still nearby. Gold is a very persuasive incentive for the dwarf's."

Luscious, followed by his army of worgen, skirted around the grumbling ogres.

"Aren't you coming?" he asked Aria.

"Where to?"

"There are a number of underground passages from Balbuldor which lead outside the reach of the obsidian. They are well guarded and commonly used by the dwarfs. But there is only one passage that leads to the west, toward Elwood. If we beat them to it, I am sure we can ambush them."

"They go to the elves? Are they mad?" Aria said, waving on both Edwel and her army. "Of all the creatures in this kingdom, the elves are most likely to strike Aramus down where he stands."

"It is true that the elves are puritans and may not allow the son of Dantet to take a single breath of their air, but they may also take the word of the Supreme Wizard over their own instincts. Either way, it is imperative that we make sure he dies. We cannot afford another mistake like the one on the mountain. If we can get to him before the elves do, to ensure the job is done properly, all the better."

"But he will die by *my* hand, Luscious, remember that," Aria sneered.

"I would not have it any other way, Your Majesty."

*

The heat was unbearable and the shimmering mirages in his periphery only served to make Olórin more unsteady. How he longed to be able to take out his staff and lean against the stubborn burls. But he knew he couldn't. The only thing that could touch the enchanted obsidian were the two pink tea cozies covering his feet. Even the ends of his brown robes had been singed off where they had accidently trailed along the ground. While Olórin struggled to stay upright, Aramus appeared to be immune to the heat. Despite the fact that Olórin was sure it was only getting hotter the more they walked, his young companion did not break even the smallest sweat. And that troubled him.

"How long have we been walking now, about a day?" Olórin asked, wiping his brow with his sleeve.

"Two hours," Aramus replied.

"What? Are you sure? I was positive that it was longer than that."

"I'm sure," he replied. "The sun has hardly moved in the sky."

"Yes, you're right. It's just hanging there like a maddening itch you cannot scratch."

If Olórin had had the energy he would have balled his fist at the sun and cursed it for existing in the first place. But as luck would have it for the sun, Olórin couldn't manage to do anything more than plop one pink foot in front of the other, and breathe.

"Let me carry you, old man," Aramus said, stepping toward Olórin.

"What? Wait! Don't be daft, get your hands off me. I don't need carrying. I said no, Aramus. Goddess be, why won't you listen to me? Aramus, put me down this instant."

Despite his objections Aramus did not listen to him and, in some small way, Olórin was glad. He didn't know how much longer his old body could have sustained the heat without collapsing to the ground and erupting into a ball of flames.

"Fine!" Olórin relented. "But if you're going to carry me you must promise not to fly."

"Why don't you like flying?" Aramus asked.

Olórin's fear of heights stemmed from being hung upside down off the wizard's tower in his youth, but he had never told Aramus about it. He had never told him why he was so disliked as an apprentice, and he didn't think now was the time either.

"Because flying isn't natural," he answered, keeping a firm hold of his hat. "If humans were meant to fly we would have been born with… oh."

It was the sight of Aramus's jaw clenching repeatedly that alerted Olórin to his mistake. He could tell that the young man was trying to hold in some persistent emotion, which wanted to burst from his chest, and it flooded Olórin with guilt.

"I'm sorry," Olórin said quietly. "I didn't think…"

"Don't," he spat. "Don't backtrack now for the sake of my feelings. It's true, isn't it? Humans aren't meant to have wings, are they? That's why people are scared of me. Well, one of the reasons anyhow. That's also why my childhood was spent scavenging for food instead of in the warm embrace of a loving mother and father. That's why I slept under bridges and behind barns every night, while other children were tucked up in their beds, isn't it?"

"The prejudices of man are cruel," Olórin said, his voice more quiet then he had intended. "You didn't deserve to be treated like that, Aramus. No one does."

Aramus was quiet for a time. In his eyes, Olórin could almost visualise his memories of being a small child, shivering and huddled alone under a bridge in the depths of winter. If Aramus's heart couldn't break, so Olórin's did for him.

"None of that matters now. You're going to cure me with this potion of yours, aren't you?" Aramus said, giving Olórin a crooked grin. "And then I'll be just like everyone else, won't I?"

Olórin hesitated, his mouth ajar and his stomach suddenly clenching.

"I will, won't I, Olórin?" Aramus asked again, turning his slatted amber eyes squarely on Olórin and knitting his dark eyebrows together. "I mean, that's the whole reason we're travelling to these God-forsaken lands, isn't it?"

"It *is* the reason we travel, Aramus, yes. But if I am to be completely honest, I do not know how the potion will affect you physically." Olórin could feel the tension build in Aramus's arm muscles. He heard the young man's breathing becoming terser with every step and knew that it wasn't from the effort of carrying him.

"What do you mean?" he asked quietly. "What would be the point of all of this if people are still going to fear me?"

"As the son of Dantet, you are plagued with his curse of soullessness. As such, you cannot appreciate love, happiness, and all the mortal pleasures of life. More importantly, should you die before you take the potion, then your being would undoubtedly be returned to Dantet, where you would suffer an eternity of his cruelness. But with it, the Goddess Edwina would surely see her light within you and embrace you as one of her own children."

"So," Aramus said slowly. "You would give me a potion

that would allow me to feel how much I am hated, to truly know my aloneness, until the day that I die in the hopes that I would be redeemed in the afterlife? How long will I live, old man? I am the mongrel son of a mortal and a God. Which side do you think my longevity will take after? What if I can't die? What if I am immortal, like my father?"

"I, I do not know," was all Olórin could mutter.

He had hoped that Aramus might long for a chance, any chance, to connect with humanity, but never once stopped to think that he could be condemning him to a life of loneliness – an eternity of isolation and rejection.

Olórin pondered on this for the longest time. The Goddess had told him that he must not stray from the path he was on or it would spell the end for mortal life. But he was beginning to think that perhaps Aramus would be the collateral damage in her bid to save them all. *'Would the Goddess truly care so little for a living creature, even if he* was *the son of Dantet?'* he thought.

Although he had always known his Goddess to be loving and kind, he was beginning to suspect that *that* was the true reason he was not permitted to speak when they had met. Perhaps the answer to his questions wouldn't have been to his liking, and knowing them would have condemned her children to their deaths. *'Would a loving parent really sacrifice someone else's child for their own?'* Having never had his own children it was a question he knew he couldn't answer.

"I would rather have you live an eternity with the smallest chance that you might find happiness, then condemn you to one with no hope of it at all," he finally answered.

It was the truth, and Olórin clung to it desperately. Aramus, however, didn't appear to share in his optimism. Olórin didn't blame him. Had he been faced with the same bleak outlook, he might not have been so calm. In fact, Olórin was positive that *he* would have thrown the greatest hissy fit known to man.

The two walked in silence for what seemed like hours, or rather Aramus walked whilst carrying Olórin. The heat from both the sun and the enchanted obsidian, made it almost impossible to breathe. Olórin was beginning to empathise with the lobsters he had seen thrown into pots of boiling water in the queen's palace.

"It will soon be night, where is this entrance?" Aramus asked.

Olórin couldn't be sure, but he thought that there was still a hint of irritation in Aramus's voice.

"Do you know that feeling you get when you think all is lost, and a knot ties itself in your stomach?" Olórin asked. Aramus shrugged indifferently. "Well, the entrance will only make itself known at that point. While the dwarfs do not encourage visitors to their kingdom, they are not without their sympathy for those who manage to cross their land."

"And what if one of us cannot feel that desperation?"

"Ah, well, I actually hadn't thought about that. I'm not too sure if both of us need to feel hopeless. Em, well, that is a bit of a conundrum, but we have come too far to turn back now. My old body wouldn't be able to tolerate another day of this heat. Oh Goddess, perhaps we *should* turn back and look for another way in. But we've come so far I… wait, I see it, over there Aramus."

Olórin gestured to a small grey stone which had suddenly appeared amidst the endless obsidian, and breathed a sigh of relief. He hadn't banked on it being *him* that would panic, but was relieved nonetheless, to see it. That is, of course, if *it* was the opening to the underground city.

If the truth were to be known, Olórin had never been to Balbuldor. His only knowledge of its whereabouts had come from drunken conversations with far travelling dwarfs. He was only too aware that *those* dwarfs had more heed to exaggerated tales and win an extra tankard of ale from listening patrons. But regardless of how he came to know about it, the sight of the round grey stone was like a much needed rain shower on a stifling summers day.

Aramus carried Olórin toward the stone and looked questioningly at the palm-sized rock, before carefully standing him up again.

"If that's supposed to be a door, I don't think I'm going to fit through," Aramus said.

"No, no, of course it's not a door, that's just the knocker," Olórin replied, fishing through his hat again and producing his wooded staff.

Taking careful aim at the small stone, Olórin raised his staff high above his head and, after only a moment's hesitation, brought it down hard onto the rock three times. With each strike, a resounding boom echoed across the obsidian landscape, like a mallet striking a gong. Olórin could feel the vibrations reverberate through his chest.

"What now?" Aramus asked after a while.

"Now we wait," Olórin replied.

"What are we waiting for?"

"Aramus," Olórin said, giving him a weary look, "These mines run deep and the dwarf's legs are short. It's going to take them some time to answer the door."

Aramus rolled his eyes again, and Olórin was beginning to wonder if the young man really *did* think that most of what came out of his mouth was nothing short of fantastical poppycock. Olórin, highly offended at the idea, thrust his staff into his hat again and crossed his arms tersely across his chest. He turned his back on the young man and huffed loudly. That is the way they remained until a sudden shift in the obsidian, and a deep rumbling, unsteadied Olórin. If it hadn't been for Aramus's quick reflexes, he would have landed his bottom squarely on the obsidian surface, to a rather uncomfortable rump-roasting end.

Below their feet the black stone slowly shifted and changed. It swirled and shunted alarmingly until a set of narrow steps began to burrow their way down into the ground in a spiral. The two companions took a step back, so as not to be accidently swallowed by the invisible, ravenous worm they imagined was chewing up the obsidian in front of them. Slowly, the din of stones shattering and grinding, came to a halt. The silence was only broken by the shuffle-clank sound of heavy iron-clad footsteps from below. Whomever was approaching was taking his time and huffing loudly along the way.

After a time, Olórin could see the dim glow of a lantern on

a stick begin to emerge from the dark staircase, and following closely behind it was the stout figure of a fiery-haired dwarf. The mass of red hair rocked from side to side as a short legged, half-man struggled up the last few steps. His beard almost seemed to walk before him in a bushel of wiry, red whiskers, peppered with his last meal.

From within the hairy hedgerow, two beady blue eyes and a bulbous, red nose poked out. The hirsute dwarf huffed and puffed as he reached the last step. He leaned a solid, broad hand against the centre pillar of the stairs whilst he regained his breath. Clad, from his neck down in dwarven armour, Olórin had no doubt that the effort of ascending to the surface in such attire would have exhausted even the strongest of ogres. He waited patiently for the short man regained his composure.

After some lung-squeezing huffs, the dwarf finally cleared his throat.

"Whot do ye want?" he demanded.

"We seek an audience with your king, kind dwarf," Olórin said humbly.

"Och, aye, and I want a twelve foot keg of ale every night tae sooth me, like a wee babies bo'le, but I'm no' gonnae get that either," he replied gruffly. "The king has heard of yer coming and will no' be bothered wih' yer business. Be off wih' ye now. We have no use for peddlers and, and, whatever *you* are," he said, gesturing toward Aramus.

Olórin gripped Aramus's wrist to stay the offensive retort he could see was ready to leap from the young man's mouth. Dwarfs were not the kind to take insults lightly, however much they might dole them out. They would usually settled their differences in battle; something Olórin and Aramus could ill-afford in the heat of the obsidian landscape.

"Good sir," Olórin said kindly. "I would normally never bother such an important man as your king, nor indeed yourself, but we are here on the gravest of matters. I am no ordinary peddler, although I have been known to sell the odd potion of fortune or two. I am Olórin Talfan, the Supreme Wizard of Lothangard, and this is my friend Aramus. It is imperative that we speak with your king on a matter which will not only affect those above ground, but also the dwarven city below it. Believe me, your king will thank you for allowing us in and exercising your wise judgment in this matter."

The dwarf scratched his beard, dislodging a crust as he pondered the problem. Olórin knew that, in general, appealing to dwarfs' vanity and greed would have more sway with the half-men then his grand title. But the age old paranoia of their people was no guarantee that his tactics would work.

"Potions of fortune, ye say," he said, eyeing Olórin suspiciously, ignoring the more imperative subject at hand. "And whot is it, exactly, that is so fortuitous about these potions?"

"Multiplicity," Olórin replied simply. "It multiplies whatever good fortunes the drinker has already."

"Right!" he said, straightening his armour and taking a step toward Olórin whilst holding out his hand. "I'll be having one of those, and then ye can come in tae see the king."

"Olórin, is it really necessary to…"

Olórin waved off Aramus's objections about bribing a dwarf, and the dwarf, in turn, shot Aramus a poisonous look. Taking a moment to riffle through his hat, Olórin produced a small phial containing a glistening golden liquid.

"I must warn you first," he said, handing over the phial, "to only take a small drop at a time. Too much fortune, even if it is the good kind, can be bad for a man."

"Aye, aye, I heard ya," he said, shoving the phial into the entanglement of his beard.

Although he could have been carrying a pouch around his neck, Olórin knew it was more likely the phial was, instead, caught up in the bristle, along with his last meal.

"Well, ye had best follow me then. Come on, down the stairs, you first strange fella. That's right, come off the nasty surface before ye burn yer britches, and in the name of the wee man, would ye ever take off those pink slippers. Ye'll be laughed outta the place, ye big Jessies."

Aramus grumbled profanities under his breath at the dwarf's insult, but followed his instructions and whipped off the pink tea cozies. Olórin, on the other hand, was quite fond of his new foot coverings and was slower to comply. They were a damn sight more cheerful looking then his brown wizard shoes, which curled up into a point. He could never understand why women were the only ones that this particular colour was suited to. *'Be it black, pink, turquoise or puce, a colour is a colour,'* he thought. *'Why one has to be denoted for a gender is nothing short of sexism.'*

Knowing that he wouldn't solve the discriminations of custom at that moment, or in the present company, he took Aramus's pink cozies and thrust them into his hat along with his own.

"Thas way," the dwarf said.

The dwarf pushed past them both and led the way down the spiralling stairs. It was made out of the same obsidian stone as the surface above them, only without the Infernos curse for which Olórin was very thankful. Although the blackness of the walls and ground was engulfing, the roof above them was a smoky grey. Olórin could see the setting of the sun through the transparent ceiling. He could see for miles around them and marvelled at how the emerging stars resembled diamonds lodged into the stone.

Aramus followed after the half-man and Olórin took up the rear of the small party. The dwarf huffed and puffed, his heavy metal armour clanked nosily as he waddled down the narrow flight of steps, which seemed to go on forever. His lantern swayed from side to side and made Olórin quite seasick.

"My apologies, kind sir," Olórin said, his voice echoing for a long time down the darkened passage ahead of them. "I'm afraid that I did not catch your name."

"Bernard Barrelbasher," he replied between puffs. Olórin could hear Aramus stifle a snigger and hoped that the dwarf's hair-stuffed ears didn't pick up on it too. Seemingly oblivious to Aramus's amusement of his name, Bernard continued to amble clumsily down the stairs. "I'm second in command of the Stair Guards of Balbuldor."

"My, that sounds like a very important position to have."

"Aye, aye, it is. Mind you, I could easily get tae first in

command if I wanted, but I dinnae want tae do that. Once yer at the top of the Stair Guards ye cannae switch yer duties. And everyone, who's anyone, knows that it's the King's Guard who get the best pay. Bunch o' uppity, namby-pamby, girly-boys if ye ask me. All they do is stand around looking like a shower of polished doorknobs and pretend they're better than us hard-working folk."

"Hmm, I see," Olórin said, now feeling quite nauseous with no end in sight to their gyratory descent.

"But you wouldn't mind joining them?" Aramus tone was laced with the acknowledgement of Bernard's hypocrisy.

"Whot do you think? I have five wee ones, a wife that would near eat me outta house and home these days, and an extended family of fifty-two that try to peddle their accursed cured sausages tae me every day. I lost me taste for those blasted things as a wee lad because of me Da's inability tae say "no" tae them. But still they come, every bleedin' day, and not only that, they actually want *me* tae take over the family sausage business. Can ye believe that?"

"How dreadful," Olórin answered, wanting the talk about sausages to end quickly. "How much farther, Bernard?"

"We'll be there in two sakes of a lamb's tail," he answered.

More than ten minutes later, the three finally arrived at level ground. Olórin was so relieved to not have to walk in a clockwise direction anymore that he could have kissed the slick black obsidian beneath his feet, but he didn't. Instead he cast his eyes to the ceiling where the starry night still twinkled above them.

"Are you all right, old man?" Aramus asked. "You've gone a sickly colour of green."

"Ugh, don't say the word sickly, it doesn't help."

"Och, here. Dinnae go cowking over me nice clean stairs or I'll be making ye clean it up wih' yer tongue. Ya hear me?"

"Unfortunately," Olórin replied, holding his hand to his mouth.

"Right, thas way," Bernard said, waving them onwards.

Aramus caught hold of Olórin's elbow and helped him forward. Olórin smiled and glanced at the young man appreciatively. He noted that Aramus seemed taller in the dark mines, or perhaps his own stoop had gotten worse, he couldn't quite tell. But one thing was for certain, Aramus had a glow about him, like he had taken a potion of fortitude. His shoulders seemed broader, his muscles seemed stronger, and even his slatted amber eyes glowed more ominously than ever. It brought a flashback of the vision he had had of Aramus whilst in the presence of the Goddess Edwina. Olórin said nothing, but inside his innards ran cold, and this time it wasn't because of the nausea.

Bernard led them out of the stairwell and into a wide corridor, dumping his lantern along the way. Its black walls stretched up to an impossibly tall translucent roof, which was at least a hundred times Olórin's height, if not more. A network of pipes ran along the dark walls, supplying a multitude of gas lanterns that burned with an incessant hiss.

Olórin couldn't help but marvel at the dwarf's ingenious engineering. He was amazed at the resources they found beneath the ground, and wondered if these gas lights couldn't be used to replace the oil lamps and candles above ground. In the orange glow, large divots and hollows along the wall stretched shadows across them. For all intents and purpose it looked as though the tunnel had been chewed instead of mined, leaving the walls uneven and serrated.

"Why do such short people need such big corridors?" Aramus asked, dropping Olórin's elbow once he had stopped listing to the right.

"There are things far larger then Bernard down here," Olórin answered.

"What kind of things?"

"Beasties!" Bernard replied. "Beasties as big as thas tunnel whose jaws can easily crush stone. So I wouldnae be getting any ideas about thieving from us or ye might end up as their supper."

The three walked in silence after that. Although Olórin couldn't help but visualise being shredded by whatever kind of monster Bernard had mentioned, he noted that Aramus seemed as calm as if they were walking through a meadow of wildflowers. The corner of his mouth turned up into a handsome smirk, and his glowing amber eyes perused his surroundings lazily. That same chilling warning he had felt before, ran up and down Olórin's spine now, like a trickle of frigid water.

After a lengthy walk, the three emerged into an enormous cavern of black obsidian. Several irregular stairwells clung to the sheer wall, like ivy, and led to a large city resting on a plateau below. As large as the city was, it was crammed with rows upon rows of tightly packed stone homes. They lined winding streets, making the city look like an oversized thumbprint. Smoke billowed from the chimneys and rose high into the air. It culminated into a dense cloud which bubbled on the caverns roof, hiding the stars from view. The cloud fought to escape the city of Balbudor through small holes high in the wall, but despite the effort, the air still tasted of soot.

Snaking around the homes, from which the voices of many animated dwarfs could be heard, was a thick stream of lava that encircled the city. The hot haze tried to suffocate Olórin, and he couldn't fathom how any living creature could survive in such a place.

"There she be," Bernard said, pointing to the centre of the underground city. "The king's palace."

Nestled in the middle of the expanse of ordinary homes, was a tall building. Its gold walls shone brilliantly in the light the lava cast upon it, and three enormous golden spires pierced the smoggy clouds above. Even its narrow windows sparkled to such a degree that Olórin was convinced they must have been made out of diamonds. In all his years he had never seen such a spectacle of wealth.

"Ye'll be wanting tae follow the stairs down there and make yer way to the palace," Bernard said. "I can bring ye no farther cos I have tae be off tae me duties again. *Heaven forbid* should the stairs need another sweepin'."

"Thank you, Bernard," Olórin said.

The plump dwarf made his way back toward the stairs, mumbling disgruntled utterances as he went. Olórin looked toward Aramus.

"Well, I guess there's nothing left to do but find the king."

Chapter 15

Olórin was hoping that the dwarfs wouldn't pay much attention to Aramus as they walked through their underground city. But how could a community of half-men *not* notice two tall strangers wandering their streets? Especially as one of them had large black wings and eyes that glowed like the lava. He was at least grateful that they didn't point and stare, or run screaming in absolute terror at the mere sight of him. But there was the odd shuffle of small children, with bristly moustaches, being herded back indoors by their equally hairy parents as they approached; not to mention the distinctive clatter of silver as it was shoved into various hiding places. Aramus returned the befuddled stares at the whiskery children. He nearly followed them into their houses to get a better look too, and Olórin worked hard not to laugh.

"Are *all* the children like that?" Aramus asked.

It was only dwarfs crossed with other species, such as a humans, which seemed to be immune to the tufty look that usually accompanied their kind. But none of those children lived underground with the rest of the hardened dwarfs; the particulars of their heritage also seeing them need sunshine on more than one occasion in the year. These would be the dwarfs that most above ground dwellers would be accustomed to. And so, Aramus's marvel at the strange little creatures around him was to be expected.

"You should know better than to stare at the unusual," Olórin scolded.

Aramus let the grip of his probing eyes go immediately and stared at the ground instead.

"You're right," he replied quietly. "Out of all the people in existence, I know what it is like to be stared at like that. But it's so hard to look away. I couldn't help it, and now some small child might think that I believe him to be a monster. What kind of person does that make me?"

"Don't feel too guilty," Olórin replied sympathetically. "I think you'll find that they were staring at you too. The inhabitants of Naretia are all curious creatures and it should bring you some comfort to know that you are no different."

Aramus smiled weakly as they made their way through the streets of houses fighting for space. But as his guilt trained his eyes to the obsidian rock beneath his feet, Olórin couldn't help but notice that there was something very odd about Aramus at that moment. He couldn't quite put a finger on it, but something about the way he was carrying himself, the glow from his amber eyes, the lack of any sweat on his perfectly tanned skin, all cried a warning in his old head. But Olórin couldn't hear the words no matter how hard he tried.

"State yer business!" an authoritative voice boomed over the hustle and bustle of Balbuldor.

Olórin nearly jumped out of his skin. He had been too busy listening to the foggy voices in his head to notice the looming palace only three feet in front of him. Standing beneath an ornately carved, golden arch was a soldier. His dwarven armour was considerably shinier, and better fitted, than that of Bernard's. His physique was leaner too, and his straight, black beard was neatly plaited into long ropes, tied off at the end with bobbles of the same shiny metal as his armour. His large broad axe glinted in the dim light of the dark streets.

It was only after a moment of clearing his throat that Olórin realised there were, in fact, two of them standing by the heavy gold door. Each one gleamed in their armours brilliant lustre, and each one eyed him suspiciously with beady brown eyes that turned down at the edges.

"We have come to see your king," Olórin replied.

"King Thrais willnae see peddlers and…"

Both of the guard's small eyes widened at the sight of Aramus. Their tanned skin paled, and their mouths dropped open as they struggled to form whatever words they had meant to come out.

"Dantet!" the first guard finally hissed, pointing his axe

toward Aramus.

The second guard followed suit and thrust his spear toward Aramus's throat. Aramus stood still with his hands held in the air.

"Leave, now," the first soldier said. "No creature of Dantet will pass through these gates, nor any companion of his either. Whot fool let you in?"

"Please," Olórin said calmly. "We come on a very important matter. It was your wise Stair Guard, Bernard Barrelbasher, who gave us passage. He understood the urgency of our quest, and I assure you that your king will too."

"That dobber? Och, Angus's no' gonnea be happy wih' that," said the first guard.

"No, I reckon Bernard'll be cleaning jobbies outa the lavs till the end of his days fer that one," said the second.

"Who's Angus?" Aramus asked.

"Shut it, you," said the first guard. "Angus is the king's right arm, head of the King's Guard, and brother of Bernard. If it weren't for Angus, Bernard would still be stuck in the lower mines along wih' all the other oafs that havenea got the smarts to do anything better."

"We had no idea and meant no offence," Olórin interjected before Aramus could say anything else. "Please, tell your king that we are here. I am sure that he will reward you greatly for it."

The two guards looked at one another in silent contemplation. Olórin could see them considering if the *reward* might be worth taking the risk. True to their nature, the lure of possible remuneration was too much for the half-men.

"Right," the first guard said. "Ye two stay here and I'll go speak tae Angus."

The first guard dropped his axe and turned toward the gold door behind him. It was embossed with the image of a proud dwarf wearing a tall spikey crown. Using the knocker, which was the oversized crotch of the embossed king, he gave one mighty pull and the door swung open with a creaky protest. The second guard pressed the point of his spear into Aramus's throat to make sure that he didn't take advantage of the open door. Aramus grimaced as a small trickle of black blood ran down his neck. The sight of Aramus's dark blood was enough for the second guard to gulp and relinquish the pressure immediately. Aramus wiped his neck and locked eyes with the guard. The two stared at one another for an age, unable to look away, one because of anger the other because of fear.

After what seemed like forever, the faint sound of armoured footsteps grew louder from the palace ingress. Soon the first guard reappeared with another more powerful looking dwarf. His armour glinted with a blue hue, something Olórin had never seen, and his fiery, red beard was neatly plaited in the same way as palace guards. A large broad sword, the length of the dwarf himself, was strapped to his back along with a more proportioned shield. Olórin was sure that if ever there was a dwarf who was capable of ripping a man's heart from his chest, that *this* would be him.

"Olórin Talfan?" the more powerful dwarf asked, throwing a cautious eye at Aramus.

Olórin nodded.

"My name is Angus. The king has been expecting you."

Angus gestured for them to follow him into the palace. Olórin breathed a sigh of relief. He had given his last potion of fortune to Bernard and was thusly out of any more bribing material that a dwarf would be interested in. The second guard lowered his spear, but still kept it cautiously trailed on Aramus as they walked beneath the golden arch.

Olórin heard Aramus take a small breath in as they entered the brightly lit halls of the palace, and he could see why. Every wall was made of solid gold. Chandeliers of diamonds, rubies, and emeralds dotted the tall ceilings at three foot intervals. Larger than life portraits of past rulers, fighting for room on the walls, were trapped in heavy gold frames; each one wearing the same spikey crown as the other. The long since dead leaders also wore a stare, which, with dusty suspicious eyes, followed the two strangers as they encroached into their inner sanctum.

"Ye'll walk no' farther than I tell ye, and ye'll no' speak until spoken to, understand?"

Angus didn't wait for an answer, nor did he glance behind him at the two tall men who followed. He made his way to a pair of heavy looking golden doors at the end of the great hall and, with one powerful shove, pushed them open.

Inside, a large circular room opened up. Six enormous pillars moulded in the likeness of three dwarfs, foot on shoulders, strained to hold up the solid gold roof above. The heavy feet of the bottom dwarf rested on solid golden floors. They looked too heavy to be supported and Olórin wondered if the floor might eventually give way. Ten narrow windows, clearly made out of large diamonds interlocked with a thin mesh of silver metal, gleamed in the light of fifteen hissing gas lamps which dotted the walls.

From the corner of his eye, Olórin saw Aramus straightened his black, leather tunic and try to not look self-conscious in the opulent surroundings. Olórin too felt like the peddler the other dwarfs had called him, and attempted to right his floppy, brown hat, but to no avail. Wishing now that he had taken the time to replace his worn clothes, Olórin followed Angus into the room.

A sea of tufty dwarfs in shining metal armour, and bearded court maidens in fine silks, parted way as the two strangers approached the throne. Whispers of the name Dantet circulated the large room, and soon it was all that could be heard. Angus stopped three feet before a rotund dwarf who had perched himself on a collection of golden boulders, haphazardly melted together to form a high-backed throne. Dotted between the melted boulders were enormous precious stones, which glinted in the bright lights of the room.

The king himself appeared to be an old man: His beard was grey, the hair on his large dome was visibly thinning, and it all contrasted brightly against his dark skin. Perched on top of his balding head was the same spikey crown Olórin had seen in the portraits. It was a diadem whose construction was solely meant to boast of the wearer's wealth. To the less observant it might have looked as though a solid gold porcupine had taken roost upon the king's head.

"Whot does me right arm bring before me here?" the king's

voice boomed.

Clad in robes of red and gold, the king's lack of any physical prowess was overshadowed by the authority in his voice, and the menacing stare he gave Aramus.

"Your right arm brings you Olórin Talfan, the wizard, and his companion," Angus replied bending on one knee.

Although they hadn't been told that they must genuflect before the king, Olórin thought it a good idea. He gave Aramus a poke in the ribs and, together, they kneeled.

"His friend, you say?" the king said, rising from his throne. "Do ye mean to tell me that the Supreme Wizard of Lothangard has befriended the son of Dantet? I think my right arm has wronged me by bringing this demon into my palace. Perhaps I should cut it off?"

It became obvious to Olórin that the king never had any intention of seeing them, and it was only by the good fortunes of a greedy stair guard, and Angus overriding his orders, that they now knelt before him. Olórin was sure Angus would pay for his insubordination later. But something else the king had said made Olórin's eyebrows knit together. He hadn't told anyone in Bartertown the particulars of their quest. Although it was obvious that Aramus had physical traits of the Dark God, he had never mentioned that he was, in fact, the *son* of Dantet. Most people wrongly assumed that he was a reincarnation of the Dark God himself, or a minion. Unlike the startled courtiers, the sight of Aramus in Balbuldor didn't seem to surprise Angus, or the king.

"Och, that's right, wizard, there's no need tae look so surprised. When ya live so close to the lair of the Dark God, ye hear a thing or two. I know who he is and why you are here, and I want nothing to do wih' it. If yer looking for help, then ye've come tae the wrong place."

"Then you have heard about the prophecy, King Thrais?" Olórin asked.

"Aye, and I'll be asking me right arm to pick up me sword in a moment, and slay the winged man. There'll be no prophecy if there's no son tae carry it out."

Aramus glanced wide-eyed at Olórin, before quickly

standing and backing away from Angus. The king's right arm, however, was motionless, seemingly unconvinced that the king had actually given any order yet.

"You know that I cannot allow that, Your Majesty," Olórin said, standing between Aramus and the formidable dwarf. "Even if he should die, I am not convinced that his death would mean the end of the prophecy. The vision wasn't very clear, and it was had over two hundred years ago. I cannot say, with absolute certainty, that Aramus's death is not the *key* to Dantet's plan. In fact, I have come to believe that it *is* the Dark God's desire, because his children have not tried to aid his son, but rather have relentlessly tried to kill him."

"But that dinnae make no sense," the king said incredulously. "From whot I've heard, he'd surely want his son on mortal soil tae carry out his plans. That's whot I've heard. Why would he want him dead? I ask me right arm, whot do you make of thas?"

Angus stood and glanced back at the two strangers for a moment. His blue eyes lazily shifting between Olórin and Armaus before turning back toward his king.

"As we are so close tae the lair of the Dark God, I dinnae think it wise tae dance so close tae the edge of the cliff," he replied.

"Och, fer the love of the wee man, would ye speak proper," the king demanded.

"If Dantet should rise," Angus said slowly. "Where do you think his army will come from?"

"From under mortal soil," the king replied with a grave expression.

"And whot people will feel the first blows of his mighty fists?"

The king slowly glanced around at the worried looking courtiers, all grandeur and pride gone from his expression. "We, the dwarfs," he said in a quiet voice.

"Your right arm thinks that helping these two strangers will ensure the survival of our people," Angus continued. "But *I* am only an arm, and my king must use his head tae decide."

The king sat back down in his chair with a heavy plop, like

the weight of the world had suddenly landed on him. Olórin suspected that it had, and didn't envy his position.

"Whot would ye be asking of me?" Thrais asked Olórin.

"I would ask for the Valefire," Olórin replied flatly.

The king scoffed, laughed, and then almost choked himself with the array of noises of disbelief that bubbled out of him. His face went pure scarlet and his crown nearly toppled from his head.

"What's the Valefire?" Aramus asked quietly from behind Olórin.

"The Valefire, strange fella," the king replied, still occasionally letting out a choked noise of disbelief, "is said tae be the mighty shield of the Goddess Edwina, and is all that protects us from Dantet. Many thousands of years ago, the mines of Balbuldor ran too deep, and we reached the precipice between the mortal world and his dark world. Shielding that divide, was a wall of solid stone that shone like the moon in the night sky. My ancestors, not knowing anything of it, sought the advice of a wizard. That dark wizard persuaded them that such a stone was a gift from the Goddess, and *must* be taken with gratitude. They spent decades trying tae break the stone. They succeeded, and that is how some of Dantet's children came tae first roam mortal soil.

"We sealed the divide, of course. But even wih' the metal of the Gods, Etherium, it was no match for Dantet's determination. Tae thas day, dark things still rise, and only by regularly reinforcing the Etherium using a Valefire shard, and a spell given tae us by a dwarf wizard, can we hope tae keep his armies at bay. But wih'out it, I fear that his armies would find a weakness in the seal. And so, you can see what it is Olórin is asking of me, winged man. If the Valefire becomes lost tae us, then Dantet's army will be freed, and we will be overwhelmed."

The king took off his crown and scratched his balding dark dome with a frustrated sigh, before plopping it back on his head again. What he had failed to mention about the Valefire was that it was also a highly coveted talisman. Created by the Goddess herself, many a wizard had died trying to reach the underground city of Balbuldor to steal it, or persuade it from the king's vaults. Olórin was not immune to this desire, and he feared that his faithfulness to the quest might falter if he should handle something so hallowed. But the Goddess herself had told him to stay the path he was on, and he trusted her foresight.

"I cannae be quick wih' thas decision, wizard," he said, eyeing the tall visitors. "It's gonnae take some time. So, until then you two are tae be my guests. Angus, here, will be yer guide and tonight, we shall feast together as new friends ought to."

If there was one thing the dwarfs were known for, more than their paranoia, it was their feasts. Olórin's heart gave a small jump of excitement, and he couldn't help but beam broadly. It had been a long journey and he could do with some hearty dwarven ale.

"It would be our honour, and to thank you for your hospitality I bring a humble gift," Olórin replied, whipping off his hat and producing the bottle of whiskey he obtained from the Trithonian, much to the kings delight.

"Thas will no' sway my decision, you understand?" the king replied, eagerly gesturing for one of his guards to pass him the bottle.

"Of course," Olórin said with a bow. "Such a wise leader as yourself could never be swayed with a bribe."

Chapter 16

The night was spent feasting on spit-roasted boars and chuncks of heavy dwarven bread, all washed down with many tankards of heavily spiced ale. Olórin had delighted in seeing Aramus forced to dance by the undaunted dwarven children. Of course, he had convinced Aramus that he simply *must* dance, telling him that the dwarfs would be insulted if he didn't. But that wasn't even nearly true. The dwarven children, having too much fun to notice Aramus hiding in the corner, would never have asked him to dance if it weren't for Olórin suggesting that they do. But to see the formidable son of Dantet dancing the chicken dance with the children, his arms flapping wildly and carrying a permanent scowl across his face, was worth whatever recrimination might follow.

The old wizard laughed heartily as the children climbed onto Aramus's back and ordered him to fly around the room. One by one, Aramus delighted the children as he swooped around the tall palace feasting room, over the long tables of merry dwarfs, beneath the glistening chandeliers, and around the large fire pit in the centre; beside which the king drank deeply from the bottle of whiskey. At one point Olórin was positive that he saw Aramus smile at the children's delighted shrieks, and it did his heart good to see the young man having fun, probably for the first time in his life.

It wasn't until late at night, when the children were all shooed off to bed by their bearded mothers, that Aramus found his seat beside Olórin again. But instead of trying to melt into the shadows, he sat with an air of confidence now.

"Enjoyed that, did we?" Olórin asked, teetering slightly in his chair.

"It was the most humiliating torment I've ever endured," Aramus replied, giving Olórin a crooked smile.

"Good. I daresay that the children will not forget this night in a hurry either."

Aramus gave a small laugh and looked on, with an uncharacteristic broad smile, as the dwarfs continued to dance, clank tankards, fall over, and indulge in all manners of culinary debauchery. But Aramus's smile didn't last. His expression became more melancholic as he absorbed the sights around him greedily.

"Is this what it's like to be normal?" he asked Olórin. "To not have people run in fear of you, to be… liked?"

"It is," Olórin replied, his heart aching for the young man.

"Then I like it," Aramus said, taking in a deep, satisfied breath.

Without warning, Aramus was grabbed by his arm and whisked back onto the dancefloor by an elderly bearded lady. Even from so far away, Olórin could hear her "insist" on teaching Aramus how to dance properly. According to his kidnapper, he simply couldn't dance the chicken dance with a reputable lady. Olórin laughed, and Aramus reluctantly learned to dance, only occasionally stepping on woman's rather large feet.

The merriment soon melded into a fitful slumber. How Olórin had come to find a bed was beyond him, but when he woke he was met by the steely blue eyes of Angus, and a pounding headache.

"Time tae be up now," Angus said slightly louder than Olórin would have liked. "After thinking about it fer the night, King Thrais has agreed tae give ye the Valefire."

Olórin jumped up from the small wooden bed, rather more quickly than his head would have liked. It wasn't a difficult task because his legs, too long for the dwarven furniture, had already spent the night on the cold floor. The golden room spun around him in two different directions. For a moment, he was sure that his eyes must have followed his bifurcated brain, independently of each other.

"Here, drink thas," Angus said, handing Olórin a tankard of green liquid.

Olórin didn't argue, his head wouldn't have tolerated the

noise or provided him the coherency to, even if he tried. He took a large swig of whatever was in the cup and instantly his throat was set alight. It burned through to his stomach, and snapped his brain back together in a moment of sheer terror and pain.

"What in the name… hooo… of the good Goddess… heeeee… was that?"

"The cure," Angus replied flatly. "Dinnae worry, the burning will stop soon enough."

True to his word the intense heat that scorched Olórin's throat soon eased, helped along by three more tankards of water. In no time at all he felt as though he had not touched a drop of ale all night. It was disappointing really. Olórin quite enjoyed having the excuse to lounge around in bed for the day, because it so very rarely happened. But today was not the day for lounging. Angus had announced that the king had agreed to give them the Valefire, and Olórin was surprised that it hadn't taken longer. He wondered if Angus hadn't been whispering in the king's ear all night, or if the bottle of whiskey was indeed the ideal bribe needed. If that was the case, then he would have to return to the Trithonian and thank them.

"Come, yer friend Aramus is already up," Angus said, handing Olórin his hat. "I dinnae understand how he go' off so lightly after drinking nearly twice as much as you did last night."

"Ah, well, you see…" Olórin began before being waved off by the dwarf.

"Och, I dinnae wana know. Is no' my business. I'm just here tae see ye tae the vault."

"Right," Olórin said, finding his feet and following the dwarf out of the small golden room, having to duck his head under the door frame as they went.

Aramus was waiting outside the door, wearing a contented smile. It was the happiest Olórin had ever seen the young man, and reaffirmed in his heart that the path they were taking was, indeed, the right one.

The two companions followed Angus down a grand golden staircase, one that Olórin had no memory of climbing, and out of the palace grounds. Once outside, the oppressive heat returned to wrap its sticky hands over Olórin's face. After the bright lights of the king's palace, he had to lay a hand on Aramus's shoulder to guide himself whilst his eyes readjusted to the dark obsidian vista.

Angus didn't wait for them. He made his way past the two saluting guards who had refused them entry the day before, and took a path that appeared to lead deep into the noisy city. Olórin and Aramus hurried to keep up with him, Olórin waving pleasantly at the grumbling guards as he passed. But by the looks of their thunderous expressions, he expected that the two guards did *not* receive a reward for letting them in, and would love nothing better than to return his greeting with a rude gesture of their own. But they daren't with Angus nearby.

"Why does King Thrais call you his right arm?" Aramus asked Angus as they caught up with him.

"Because it is his right arm that wields his sword, his right arm that stays the unrest of his people," Angus replied. "I am his most loyal servant, an extension of himself, and therefore, the only one he can trust wih'out question."

"A most noble position to hold," Olórin said, feeling the weight of the heavy air as he struggled to keep up with the two young men. "One of great responsibility."

"Aye," Angus replied, giving Aramus a warning look, "and one that I dinnae take lightly."

Soon the three travellers came to a large stone building in the centre of the city. Its walls were constructed out of perfectly smooth obsidian bricks. There were no windows. Only a tall, black funnel on top of the roof marred the perfectly square building. Miners, dressed in dusty overalls and dinged metal hats with candles on the front, went two by two through the walls as though it were made of air. More miners came out the other side and, although they didn't appear to be spectres, Olórin couldn't fathom how else they could walk through something so solid.

"Come on, the king's waiting," Angus said, waving them on and walking through the wall himself.

With a quick glance at one another, Olórin and Aramus

followed. They were both equally surprised to find that the wall was not solid at all, it was only enchanted to appear so. It was a guise to fool outsiders into thinking there was no way down into the dwarven mines. Passing through it felt like walking through a waterfall of tepid water that neither relived the heat nor wet them.

Inside the room there was a large, metal box attached to a multitude of pullies and ropes. It dangled from the tall funnel Olórin had seen outside, and looked about as secure as a vine dangling from a rotten tree branch. The dwarfs ahead of them entered the box, slamming shut the metal gate behind them. A great rumbling sound signified their descent. Simultaneously, another metal box appeared from beneath the ground, and the tired looking passengers disembarked on the other side of the room.

"What magic is this?" Olórin said open mouthed.

"There's no magic here, wizard," Angus replied with a small laugh. "Just engineering. We call them lifters, and ye had better get in the next one before another round of miners take it. Where we go, they cannae follow."

Olórin and Aramus dutifully followed Angus into one of the lifters. Several miners tried to join them, but they were quickly stopped by Angus's raised hand. Sliding closed the flimsy mesh doors, the dwarf pressed the only red button on a side panel, and the box jerked. Olórin took in a deep breath and steadied himself on the nearby railings as they descended underground. The metal box passed levels where Olórin could see hundreds of miners shoving metal carts on wheels.

The carts, which were as tall as the dwarfs themselves and twice as wide. They were filled with mounds of dirt and various coloured stones. Dumped onto enormous sifting trays, which could have carried twenty wizards, the rubble was sifted over and back by burly dwarfs who grunted with the rhythm of the large mesh tray as it swung. Each level exhaled hotter air then the last, and, like the bones of a giant beast, a scaffolding of obsidian held back the dirt and rocks within.

During their descent, which seemed far too long for Olórin's liking, Aramus suddenly grunted and clutched at his chest. He bent forward and rested his other hand against the metal wall of the lifter, and Olórin could see him grimace in pain.

"Aramus, are you all right?"

Aramus didn't answer. He breathed rapidly through his clenched teeth, and gripped so tightly onto his tunic that his knuckles turned white. His jaw muscles tensed and he turned a deathly shade of pale. With a sudden sharp gasp, Aramus fell to one knee.

In a blind moment of panic, Olórin let go of the railings, forgetting his fear, and bent down to the young man. He rested his hand between Aramus's large black wings and was surprised to notice an intense heat emanating from him. Despite the heat, however, and the obvious pain Aramus was in, the young man's brow still had not broken a sweat.

"Aramus, what is the matter?" Olórin begged.

The sound of metal sliding on metal alerted Olórin to the fact that Angus had drawn his sword.

"Is he all right?" Angus asked, keeping his sword at the ready. "Is he sick?"

"Put that away, there's no need," Olórin snapped. "Aramus, please answer me."

"I'm… I'm fine, old man," he replied between gasps of breath. "Probably just a bout of indigestion from all that… heavy dwarven bread last night."

Aramus, still gripping his chest, tried to stand, but collapsed back onto the grated floor of the lifter again. He stifled a cry of agony. The hand that had propped him up, slid from the wall and clutched at his stomach instead. Olórin's eyes widened. Left on the wall was a perfectly formed imprint of Aramus's hand that had melted into the metal.

Aramus's pain seemed to get worse the further underground they went, presumably the closer to Dantet's world that they came. Olórin had seen what was coming, what Aramus was capable of, and if he didn't do something about it now he feared that they would all be incinerated in an inferno. He had to cut Dantet's hold over the young man.

"Stop this blasted contraption," Olórin shouted at Angus.

"Bring us to the surface at once."

"I cannae," Angus said, raising his sword. "Whot's the matter wih' him?"

"It's the change," Olórin replied, kneeling in front of Aramus. "It's not supposed to happen yet, not until his eighteenth birthday. It's too soon. Aramus, Aramus, hear me."

Olórin placed his right hand on Aramus's burning temple, and all around them the noises faded away; the grinding of the colossal gears, evaporated, the shouts of Angus telling Olórin to stand away from him, gone, and Aramus's cries of pain, now silent. It all melted into a nothingness, like they had been submerged beneath a vast ocean and the water had filled their ears.

"Aramus, hear me," Olórin said, his voice, willowy and only audible in their two minds. "You must control this. If you do not, it will consume us all. Breathe. Find that inner quietness to calm the storm."

Aramus looked up at Olórin, his amber eyes were alight with the same fire that the Goddess Edwina had predicted. The young man gasped small, desperate breathes through his teeth, and his handsome face contorted with the pain. A heavy weight landed itself squarely in Olórin's stomach, and a cold sense of dread chilled his body in spite of the heat.

"I, can, not," Aramus answered, his voice laced with agony. "It hurts, too much."

"Yes, you can Aramus. Think of a time in your life, any time, where you felt protected, safe, loved. Surely there has to be at least one. Let that feeling wash over you, like a wave quelling the fire."

Aramus smothered another cry of pain and shut his eyes tightly. Olórin dropped his hand and the quiet that had surrounded them was murdered by the churning gears, rattling metal, and Angus shouting to whomever was below them to clear the area.

Olórin watched as Aramus fought the pain, his every muscle straining with the effort, and wondered if there was such a memory inside the young man. A weakness filled Olórin then, the likes of which he had never felt before.

Normally he could connect with another person's mind for long periods of time, but whatever was effecting Aramus seemed to have taken its toll on him too.

The lifter came to a sudden, jerky halt, and Angus flung open the doors. Taking Olórin under his arms, he dragged him out of the lifter. Olórin objected, wanting to stay next to Aramus, who was still doubled over in pain. Unable to stand under his own strength, Olórin watched in horror as the young man's leather clothes began to smoulder.

Angus stood between Olórin and Aramus, and ordered the surrounding dwarfs to hide, his broadsword at the ready. Cautiously, he edged his way behind the young man and rested the point of his blade between his two wings.

"What are you doing?" Olórin demanded. "Do *not* kill him. He has done nothing wrong."

"Yet," Angus replied, some of the fiery hair of his beard singeing with the heat that Aramus was giving off. "But I cannae sacrifice the lives of the dwarfs down here, or of the king, for *him*. If he cannae control himself, I will have no choice, wizard."

Olórin whipped off his hat and brandished the staff he kept in there. He took aim at Angus and, in a desperate bid to save Aramus, a long silvery streak of light shot out of the staff and hit the dwarf squarely in his chest. But Angus did not fly into the air as Olórin had expected, he didn't even flinch.

"Etherium," Angus said, gesturing to his blue tinted armour. "Yer magic is no good on me."

Aramus interrupted them with a long rasping gasp, arching his back and splaying his arms wide, before collapsing onto the floor of the lifter, unconscious. With what little energy he had regained, Olórin got to his feet and rushed over to his friend. Using his staff, he knocked Angus's sword away before flipping Aramus onto his back. After a moment or two of Olórin gently tapping his face, Aramus slowly opened his eyes. An eerie fire still burned within the amber colour, but other than that he seemed to have returned to his old self again; no longer radiating any heat at all.

"I'm not dead, old man, so stop looking so worried,"

Aramus said weakly.

Olórin felt the sting of tears at the back of his eyes, and breathed a weighted sigh of relief. With a broad smile, he grabbed the young man by his shoulder and helped him to sit up. Aramus grimaced in pain with the movement, but after a short time seemed to recover from his ordeal.

"What was that?" Aramus asked.

"I'm afraid it was another attribute of your father's," Olórin replied.

"Will it happen again?"

Olórin nodded solemnly, and Aramus knitted his brow.

"What was it that you remembered?" he asked.

"What do you mean?"

"The memory that helped you bring it under control."

Aramus smiled at Olórin.

"It was you! The day that we first met when you saved me from those men. Even though I had killed most of them, you defended me when all others would have killed me. I know that I wouldn't have walked away alive if it weren't for you."

Olórin felt his heart swell with pride and love. *'And I would do it again, my son.'*

It took some considerable amount of persuading to convince Angus that Aramus's "affliction" was now under control, and he posed no risk to the king, or his riches. Olórin wasn't sure that it was the truth, but the sooner they could reach the vaults and were done with the whole affair, the sooner they could return to the surface. Only above ground, could they put some distance between them and Dantet's influence, and Olórin didn't want to let Aramus out of his sight until then. Angus, however, was unconvinced and kept his sword drawn as he led them onwards.

Not far from the lifters, they passed a large creature attached to an enormous, stone drive-wheel. Its bulbous body was clad in a spikey, overlapping exoskeleton, and it towered over them at least three times Olórin's height. It had no eyes, nose, or lips to speak of. Its facial features consisted of nothing more than a jaw, permeated with of rows of sharp undulating teeth that disappeared down its crimson throat. Six tree-trunk sized legs pounded into the obsidian ground as it turned the drive-wheel around and around, sending the lifter back up to the surface.

A juvenile dwarf was the sole operator of the Beastie. He sat on its back, controlling it with heavy metal chains that had been driven into its thick jaw, like some kind of gruesome horse's bridle. Although Angus had told them that the creature was only a small female, Olórin couldn't have fathomed one larger than that.

Aramus walked with a powerful stride now, and his eyes still burned with the fire Olórin had hoped would disappear. His whole physique oozed an internal power, something Olórin was severely lacking at that moment. He had never felt so old and drained of energy in all of his life, and the hot air threatened to suffocate him at every step.

"What is that noise?" Aramus asked.

"What noise?" Olórin replied, straining to hear over the unrelenting echoes of mining from the levels above them.

Out of the corner of his eye, Olórin saw Angus's grip on his sword tighten.

"Never mind," Aramus said, after a short hesitation. "Must be the miners."

Occasionally throwing weary looks at the young man, Angus led them passed a series of armed guards and into a tunnel that ended in a gargantuan golden door. Resting resolutely across the circular hatchway, was a large dragon claw of the same metal. Its sharp talons dug into the surrounding obsidian rock, holding the door firmly closed. Ten guards in polished silver armour, stood to attention outside the vault. Each one of them carried a broadsword and a menacing expression.

"Halt, ye'll come no farther," one of the guards shouted.

"We are expected," Angus yelled back. "The king's right arm brings his guests', as ordered."

"The king has asked that his right arm hold his visitors here while he rummages."

"So shall it be then."

Angus gestured for Olórin and Aramus to wait, and then

sheathed his sword with some reluctance. Seeing his guests arrive at the point of a sword would undoubtedly raise concerns for the king. But Aramus paid no attention to the half-man's misgivings toward him. Instead, his fiery eyes stared down a darkened corridor to the left, like he was trying to see the shadows within the darkness.

The tunnel appeared, to Olórin, to be completely abandoned. There were no miners milling in and out of the corridor, like there had been in other ones along the way. There were no torches lighting its path, nor any signs of life whatsoever. The only thing Olórin could detect from the tunnel was a stiflingly hot breeze that could have easily been the source of *all* the heat in Balbuldor. But Olórin also knew that Aramus's eyes saw through the darkness, as though it were day; another trait of his father's.

"What do you see?" he asked Aramus.

Before Aramus could answer, the massive dragon claw began to rumble and drew Olórin's attention back. Its scaly gold digits arched upwards, dragging its talons along the obsidian rock, until they rested well within the circumference of the vault door. A deep, reverberating groan filled the mines as the vault swung slowly open. From inside, a light, so intense that it stung Olórin's eyes, burst into the dark tunnel.

Olórin only caught a glimpse of the ocean of riches in the golden chamber before the rotund figure of King Thrais, and his spikey crown, emerged. He carried with him a small, brown pouch weighed down by an even smaller round object inside. As soon as he cleared the doorway the dragon claw slammed the vault shut, at a speed which belied its size, sending a deafening echo through the mines. Its talons stretched out to find their resting place in the obsidian wall again, and dug its claws back into the rock, before becoming still once more.

The king, surrounded by his ten guards, walked purposefully toward their party.

"I hope you understand, wizard, that I cannae entrust such a precious and powerful gift tae ye wih'out some reassurances that it will be returned," he said. "Therefore, my right arm will carry my treasure until such time as you need it. Once ye have completed yer quest, my right arm will return it tae me."

Olórin sighed audibly and gave silent thanks to the Goddess for the king's wisdom. Even now, although it was secure within a pouch, he could feel a warm tingling in his chest and a voice in his head, which he did not recognise, telling him that Dantet wouldn't stand a chance against him with this talisman. Resistance and fortitude were a talent best left to the dwarfs'. Angus's mouth, however, opened and his bushy, red eyebrows furrowed with confusion.

"Wih' respect, Your Highness, *my* duty is tae my king," he said. "How can I protect you if I am no' here?"

"By ensuring that the son of Dantet does no' fulfil his prophecy, you *are* protecting me, Angus. You are protecting all of us," the king replied. It was the first time the king had referred to his right arm by name, and it seemed, by Angus's expression, to hold some gravity with him. "Besides, your Etherium armour will make you immune to mortal magic should the wizard try to betray me. And your skill wih' the sword will best anyone who tries tae take the Valefire. I have enough soldiers' tae protect me until yer return, but I only have one soldier that I trust as much as I do you."

The king held out the small pouch and, after a moment of vacillation, Angus accepted it. Using its long leather strings, he wore the pouch around his neck and tucked it firmly under his chest plate.

"You must also choose a second, as is customary wih' all missions of thas gravity," the king said. "So that he might complete yer task should you no' be able to. Whot warrior say you?"

"My brother, Bernard," Angus replied without hesitation.

"Bernard? Him? Are you sure?" Thrais asked, his eyes widening and his face reddening. "I have had more cause to exile that bumbling, opportunistic catastrophe than any other subject. Surely ye can choose a comrade more fitting?"

"Bernard maybe short-sighted and always in need, but he is my brother and I trust him above all others," Angus replied. "If he swears you his word, then he will be true to it until his dying day."

Olórin remembered the stout dwarf at the top of the stairs and, although they shared the same blue eyes and fiery hair, the two couldn't have been more opposite in nature and in build.

"Very well, I will trust me right arm's decision."

King Thrais gestured for one of his guards to go fetch Bernard, and as soon as he was out of sight he turned to Olórin.

"Tell me, whot help will the Valefire provide, exactly?"

"Just as it separates the mortal world from Dantet's, so will it separate Aramus's human side from his father's. I have, in my knowledge, the ingredients for a godly potion, one that was given to me by Edwina herself. The potion is capable of splitting a man's soul, and the Valefire will keep the dark side from the light. It is my belief, and the Goddess's too, that Dantet's affliction, and therefore his hold over the young man, will be broken. After which, only the light of Edwina will reside within him, even if it is only half of her light."

"Interesting, but speaking of splitting souls," the king said, looking behind Olórin. "Where, pray tell, has yer peculiar friend gotten to?"

Olórin spun around, only half as quickly as Angus, to find that Aramus was no longer standing behind him. He hadn't heard him wander away, and that same cold feeling of dread he had had in the lifter, now filled his entire body.

"Aramus?" Olórin yelled.

A distant and primordial cry of pain responded from down the forlorn tunnel Aramus had been examining earlier. Angus's eyes widened, and the king took in a sharp breath when they heard where the noise came from.

"In the name of the Goddess, I pray he has no' gone down *there*," the king said in alarm.

"Why, what is down there?" Olórin demanded.

"*That* is where the Etherium seal to Dantet's world lies. I'd wager all my riches that his father's will has, somehow, enticed him there. Even while no' on mortal soil, Dantet's reach is still far."

Before the king could finish his last word, Olórin had spun on his heels and bolted down the darkened tunnel. Behind him, he heard Angus's voice ordering the soldiers to bring the king to safety, before the clang, clang, clang, sound of his armoured boots followed. The tunnel was dark and Olórin couldn't find his way, but panic prevented him from thinking sensibly. It wasn't until he went careening into an obsidian wall, and falling rather painfully onto his rear end, that he thought of using his staff.

"Illuminous!"

A flood of silver light burned through the passageway. It revealed a labyrinth of other tunnels crisscrossing in front of him, each one as dark and as forsaken as the next.

"Aramus?" he roared again.

The tunnels were silent. Olórin was lost, and hopelessness began to set in. Angus came to a skidding halt behind him and lifted him to his feet again.

"If he's been drawn tae Dantet, then he'll be down thas one tae the right," Angus said, leading the way.

Olórin followed after the half-man, keeping his staff raised to light their path. The distant sound of many more iron-clad footfalls following them, told Olórin that the king had dismissed Angus's advice to be brought to safety.

The deeper into the labyrinth they went, the louder Olórin could hear Aramus's gasps of pain. Heat, which had been so suffocating before, scorched his face now. The obsidian rock around them had begun succumbed to it; its surfaces becoming fluid and slick. In a deft movement, that even Olórin was surprised he could do, he whipped off his hat, dug out the pink tea cozies, and slipped them onto his burning feet, all whilst running and holding his staff at the same time. It wasn't a graceful movement, but a necessary one to prevent the hot rock burning a hole through his wizard shoes. Unlike the iron-clad feet of the dwarfs, the soft leather wouldn't hold up to much.

After what seemed like an impossibly long time, the pair came upon an opening to a cavern twice the size of the city of Balbuldor. Dotted along its melting black walls were the many ancient carcasses of Beasties and dwarfs alike. They were frozen in action, some trying to shield themselves while others wielded ancient swords. But they were all cemented in individual tombs of obsidian, and it spoke of a terrible battle that had once happened.

A blue tinted metal disk took up nearly the entirety of the cavern floor. Etched on its surface were markings that Olórin was only too familiar with; runes which were used to fortify cells and entrap Dark Ones. To his horror, he saw Aramus in the centre of the disk, bent double with pain and on all fours. The flames, which he had witnessed in Darzithal, now flashed and sputtered beneath the young man's palms, like a candle trying to remain alight in a stiff breeze. Aramus's dark wings smoked with the threat of a sudden blaze, while his whole body smouldered. His black leather clothes had peeled away in places, yielding to the heat.

"Aramus!" Olórin cried, taking a step into the cavern.

He was stopped by Angus's powerful arm blocking his path.

"You cannae go in. It's too hot."

It was at this point that the king, and his polished guards, joined Olórin and Angus.

"Whot witchery is thas?" he demanded. "I wasnae told that the demon had powers. If I had known that, I wouldnae have brought him down here, nor would he have remained in the city. Have you been hiding thas from me wizard?"

"No, I swear it to you, Your Highness," Olórin lied, feeling an overwhelming panic electrify his innards. "I believe Dantet has felt the presence of his son and has lured him down here in order to melt the seal, or worse, kill him. We must concentrate now on getting him out of here, and quickly."

Aramus cried out in pain. He raised himself onto his knees and arched his back. The flame that had flickered around his hands now sparked a chain reaction around him and within seconds, his whole body was alight.

"Aramus!" Olórin yelled.

Chapter 17

The inferno that erupted around Aramus sent a heat wave so intense toward Olórin and the dwarfs, that Olórin had no choice but to raise his staff and conjure a shield around them. But even with that, some of the heat from the flames still made their way past and singed his long beard. Olórin truly felt his weakness at that moment, his stomach ached with a desire to wretch, and his muscles quivered wanting to collapse. But he refused to listen to either of them. He *couldn't* listen to them, for to do that would spell the end to life in Naretia and see Aramus die. No memory of happy times was strong enough to pull Aramus from his father's grip now, and Olórin felt the panic rise up in his chest.

"We have tae get him outta there," the king roared. "Before he melts the seal and sets loose the monsters beneath."

Without needing another word, Angus turned to Olórin.

"Keep that shield up and protect the king," he ordered. "Or believe you me, I'll end yer friend's life myself."

The intent look in Angus's eyes told Olórin that he meant every word.

Reaching behind him, Angus retrieved his shield and brought it in front of his face. It glowed with the same blue hue as his armour. With it firmly strapped around his forearm, the dwarf stepped beyond the safety that Olórin's magic provided, and into the cavern. Olórin was helpless and could only watch.

The sweat ran freely from the dwarf's brow and down his neck as, step by step, he edged closer to Aramus. Still on his knees, Aramus's fiery wings flapped wildly as he writhed with pain. He clenched his fists and, time after time, a searing ball of flame would shoot out from inside them. The projectiles slammed into the obsidian walls around him, shattering some of the entombed statues into pieces, and scattering their ancient bones across the cavern. On more than one occasion, Angus had to use his shield to redirect one of the fireballs away from him.

Olórin prayed to the Goddess, with every fibre of his being, that his quest would not end here. He prayed that Edwina would grant Angus whatever strength he would need to reach Aramus and save him. It was all he could do. If he had more strength, perhaps he could have conjured a small ocean to suddenly appear in the cavern, cooling it for long enough to retrieve his friend. But as it was, he was finding it difficult just to keep the shield up, and the irony was not lost on him.

'With all the power granted to the Supreme Wizard,' Olórin thought, *'the fate of Naretia now relies on a half-man, a mortal, with no discernible magical ability, or power, other than his bravery.'*

With his heart leaping in his chest, Olórin gasped as the dwarf fell to his knee just as he reached Aramus. '*Goddess, no! Do not falter now, not when you're so close.*' As though he heard the old wizard's thoughts, Angus reached out his armoured hand toward the young man, keeping his shield raised with the other. The metal of his gauntlet burned bright blue before turning crimson. His fingers wrapped around Aramus's flaming wrist and the dwarf let out a sudden cry of pain. A wisp of smoke danced on top of Angus's fiery red hair.

With gritted teeth, and one stubborn foothold in the Etherium disk, Angus stood up and started to back toward Olórin and the king. Aramus's flaming body fell limply to the ground and Angus had no choice but to drag him. They reached the edge of the disk, and the flames, which had engulfed Aramus, extinguished; along with most of the searing heat.

Olórin's shield dropped and he rushed to Aramus's side, helping Angus drag him the last few feet into the tunnel. His clothes had been all but burned off him, save for a few charred leather patches. Olórin examined him for injuries as he lay gasping and choking on the floor. However alarming his appearance might have been, there were no burns, no scars, blisters, or any evidence of the fire on the young man's body, save for the black soot that covered him from head to toe.

"Aramus, speak to me," Olórin whispered, brushing aside some hair that clung to his ashen face.

Aramus shivered like he was cold. His teeth chattered as though he had been plunged into icy water, despite the fact that his skin still burned at the touch. His blackened arms clenched next to his chest, and his jaw muscles firmly clamped his jaw shut. His only response, a distressed grunt.

Olórin rummaged through his hat, desperation making his fingers clumsy, and produced a flagon of water. He poured it over Aramus's face, chest, arms, and legs until the young man's convulsions subsided. He was only half aware of Angus's gauntlet falling to the floor, his hand blistered from the heat.

"Aramus, why did you go in there?" Olórin asked.

"I… don't… know," Aramus managed to reply. "A… dream."

Olórin was only too aware of how Dantet could call his other children. Years of examining Dark Ones, in the keep of Lothangard, had given Olórin this insight. For the most part, the Dark Ones would reply willingly to Dantet's command, and only hear his whispered orders in their heads. But for those defiant few, and there had only been a few that Olórin knew of, it was as if they were locked in a deep trance; unaware of what they were doing or where they were going until the deed was done. Such was the power Dantet held over anything which his blood had given life to.

So concerned with what this meant for Aramus, Olórin didn't hear the many sounds of metal sliding on metal, as the guards swords unsheathed at the king's silent command. It wasn't until the points of those swords made their way into Olórin's periphery that he knew the dwarven king had lost his sense of hospitality in the events he had just witnessed.

"Ye must leave," the king said with a deadly tone.

"Please, Your Majesty, he is hurt and needs help," Olórin begged. "He was not aware of his actions."

"We will clothe ye, and give ye some supplies, but ye must be gone wih'in the hour," the king replied, ignoring Olórin's requests. “I will no’ have thas creature in my kingdom no more. ‘Tas a bad omen, and we are too close tae the Dark God tae flirt with omens like thas. I had hoped that my right arm wouldnae have brought such a threat so close tae his king and his kind, wi’hout knowing more about it. But I see now that there are some things even my right arm is blind to.”

Olórin glanced with pleading eyes between Angus and King Thrais, but he was met with an expression of regret from one and an unrelenting hardness from the other. There was nothing else for it, they would have to push on whether Aramus was fit for travel or not. Olórin only hoped that his young friend would recover enough to be able to walk under his own steam, because between Angus’s burnt hand and his own weakened state he knew there was no way they could carry him. The wide eyed stares of the king’s guard, told Olórin that there wouldn’t be any volunteers to assist them either.

With some persuasion from Olórin, Aramus managed to stand. He was still weakened, but under the unwavering point of Angus’s sword, the young man had stumbled his way back through the tunnels. He leaned heavily on Olórin as they ascended up to the underground city. Olórin tried his best to support the young man, but he himself had not recovered as well as Aramus; his limbs still felt like a young sapling in a tornado, unable to do anything but wilt.

In one of the many small stone cottages, Aramus and Olórin were given the opportunity to wash, change clothes, and gather some supplies, much to the disgruntled looks of its owner. The stout woman, with a blond moustache, piercing green eyes, and more chest than torso, glared at them from the corner of her living room whilst she tended to Angus’s burnt hand. When her job was done, she tersely crossed her arms in front of her large bosom. She said nothing to the two strangers, content that Angus’s pointed sword was enough of a deterrent.

It was obvious, by the looks that followed them through the streets as they were led away, that the sight of the king’s right arm leading two tall strangers from the city would be the topic of conversation for many months to come. Whispers of tall tales, about how they had come to steel the king's riches, had begun to stir already and made their way to Olórin ears as they walked the obsidian streets. The further they travelled, the more elaborate the stories became. This was another talent the feisty half-men were known for. Olórin overheard one passing dwarf insist that he had personally seen them hold a knife to the king's throat.

"You! I have a bone tae pick wih' you."

Olórin heard Bernard's heavy footsteps before he saw him. His rotund figure waddled from side to side as his gait made way for his size and heavy armour. More alarmingly, his fiery red beard, which had now been tied into neat plaits leaving no sign of past meals, was less red then his face. Two steel eyes contrasted brightly against all the crimsonness, and they stared, with fury, in Olórin's direction.

"Whot manner of poison did ye pander tae me?" he asked, huffing and puffing as he reached the travellers, pointing a short stubby finger at the old man. "I drank that stupid potion, and fer me troubles I got promoted tae First Guard, me wife is pregnant *wih' twins,* and me stupid cousins transferred ownership of that blasted sausage business tae me, wih'out even asking. There was nothing *good* about that potion of fortune, and I demand a refund."

"Ah! Bernard, how lovely to see you again," Olórin replied calmly. "I would gladly give you a refund, my friend, but seeing as how your payment was our entry to Balbuldor, and we are currently leaving it under guard, I fear that your refund has already been paid, even without your knowledge. May I ask though, did you drink the entire potion in one go as I had told you not to?"

"I… well… maybe, but that dinnae matter. When thas is all over ye'll be righting the horrendous wrong yev hexed on me house, ya hear me?"

"Indeed," Olórin replied.

"Brother," Angus interrupted, extending his free arm to Bernard.

"Brother," he replied, embracing Angus with a rugged hug that would have taken the wind out of most humans. "It's been too long since we last met. That king has hoarded you like he has hoarded his gold, the same gold that our hands dug from the soil fer him."

"Do no' speak unkindly of King Thrais, brother. Wih'out him our lives would be a lot less fortunate."

Bernard spluttered and sounded like he was trying to hold in vomit.

"Dinnae speak tae me about fortune. I've had me fill."

"I see good fortune has finally tamed that beard of yours?" Angus laughed.

"Pomp and circumstance see me wih' such a travesty of facial hair as thas, no' good fortune," Bernard replied, then looking somewhat sheepish added, "and Ravina."

Angus laughed hard, and Bernard threw him a dark scowl.

"I hate to interrupt this reunion," Olórin said, eyeing the nervous villagers around them. "But shouldn't we get moving? The hour the king granted us has long since passed, and I would loath to test his patience any further."

"Aye," the two brothers said in unison, clapping each other roughly on the back.

With Bernard leading the way, and Angus and his sword taking up the rear, Aramus and Olórin were escorted through the city, over a precariously thin obsidian bridge that traversed the lava river, and into a nearby tunnel. It took some time before the obsidian gave way to stone and dirt, and Olórin knew that they had gone beyond the safety of the dwarven lair.

*

A dense morning mist rolled down the hilly terrain, unaware that it caressed an army of foul creatures nestled between the tall tufts of grass. They had been waiting there for the better part of the night, unnaturally resilient to sitting in the dampness that it brought, unlike Aria.

She had taken refuge in a hollowed out tree, whose life had long since been drowned by the abundance of water, and preserved in the natural workings of the peaty bog. Despite her makeshift shelter, however, the cold had still crept into her limbs, and as the hazy sun rose she had never felt more in need of a hot bath, both to warm her and to rid her of the sticky mud. As much as it was a paradox in itself, she was in awe at the cleanness of her surroundings. The boggy air smelled pure and untouched by the industrial toils of man, and the green landscape rolled and dipped, uninterrupted by his engineering. If ever there was a place that Aria could say had been unspoiled by living creatures, it was this place. But all that was about to change.

"Good morning, My Queen," Edwel said cheerfully. "Isn't it a fine morning?"

Aria was about to tell him where to shove his "good morning" when she caught sight of the stone golem. Having stood outside her shelter all night, without moving, his heavy body had sunken into the soggy earth. All that remained of the massive stone man was his stupidly grinning head. It poked up just above the tufts of grass and she couldn't help but laugh. The stone man's mouth turned down into a sulk.

"I fail to see the humour in my predicament, Aria," he grumbled.

"Really? Edwel the positive, the jovial, the pensive, and always enlightened, fails to see the humour?" she mocked playfully. "Oh, Edwel. Surely you can see that a being whose sole desire was to understand what it means to be alive, finding himself one day to be only a head, is a little amusing."

Edwel's stone face became rigid as he pondered the question. His two black eyes searching the sky for an answer. In the time he had come to open his mouth again, Aria had ordered twenty of her ogres to dig him out.

"I suppose you are right," he replied with a small chuckle. The golem stepped out of his boggy prison with a squelch and a plop, his grey limbs dripping with brown mud. "In fact, I suppose that it could be the material of the finest court jester."

"Or life's satirical way of amusing itself," she replied under her breath.

Aria turned her attention back to the rolling hills beneath her. The exit to the dwarf mines lay some two miles to the south-east of their position. Luscious suggested that they lie in wait for them far enough away that any dwarfs guarding the exit wouldn't hear the cries of battle.

Only one path led through the vast bogland toward the elves, and it was paved with so many sunken limestone boulders that, beneath it, was more stone than bog. It would be unwise for the wizard to cross the quagmire anywhere else because, as Aria had learned by losing a few ogres to it, the bog consisted of deep puddles of muddy water that were too thick to float in. It had been a precarious task to find good hiding places without losing too much of her army. As it was, she was down to twenty-five worgen, fifteen ogres, Edwel, herself, and the Etherium arrow.

Despite the dwindling numbers, however, Aria was convinced that the king of the dwarfs wouldn't send an army to accompany Olórin and Aramus, given his allegiance to the Order of Everto. With that in mind, she was also certain they would easily outnumber them.

"Queen Aria," Luscious called out as she found her hiding place amongst her army again. "My scout has returned and he says that the wizard and winged man have left the dwarven city."

Aria's suspicion of how Luscious came to know the wizard's plans raised itself again, and she wondered if the dwarven king knew there was a spy amongst them, or if the king himself was the spy.

"How many do they bring with them?" she demanded.

"Two," he replied. "An overweight one and, if I am correct, the king's right arm."

"His what?"

"His right arm," Luscious said, snorting indignantly at her. "His most formidable warrior, the only one he has granted the right to wear the armour of the Gods. Although I am surprised that he has sent him. This dwarf is as much a prised possession to the king as his crown, and never normally leaves his side."

Aria was quite surprised too. If the king had truly given the Order of Everto his own Etherium armour, she expected that he would want to keep the other one near-by. Not only that, but if he favours the new order so much, why then would he help the son of Dantet at all? There was only one reasonable explanation which sprung to her mind. The king was betting on both sides; hoping, at the end of it all, that he would still come out in favour of the victor.

"How long until they reach us?" she asked quietly.

"Any moment now."

*

The fine mist, which hung in the morning air, bathed Olórin's face mercifully. With the heat he endured in Balbuldor, he had almost forgotten what it was like to be cool. Breathing the peaty air in deeply, Olórin let out a long sigh of relief.

"Ye'll have tae come and meet yer nephews and nieces," Bernard shouted all of a sudden.

Olórin glanced at Aramus, who looked as confused as he. The young man's eyes still shone dimly with Dantet's fire and his face still held a hue more pale than normal. But his appearance seemed less foreboding in the brown leather attire that the dwarfs had given him. Olórin too had forgone the usual Supreme Wizard robes in favour of something more colourful. Yes, purple with bright gold designs was the order of the day, and Olórin couldn't help but admire his long flowing robes as they billowed in the morning air.

"I cannae," Angus replied. "You know that I am bound tae the king."

"Beasties butt-cakes," Bernard scoffed. "Surely he doesnae need you tae wipe his arse fer him too. Ravina thinks ye dinnae like her, and the kids have never met ye, brother. What kind of king would want that fer a family, I ask ye?"

"It's more complicated than that, Bernard," Angus replied quietly.

"I know. But one day, one day is all I ask," Bernard said.

Olórin, feeling the third wheel in the conversation, took off his hat and began sorting out the contents into neatly ordered segments, ensuring that the chicken remained at the very bottom. He took out his staff and used it to pick his way over the uneven boulders, humming lightly as he went. But it was impossible not to overhear the two vociferous men as they spoke. Even the few birds that were resting in the sparse trees, undoubtedly on their way to more lush forests, were startled by their conversation and took off into the sky.

"You know that no one cares about the past," Bernard continued. "You're the king's right arm now. Yev earned the respect of yer peers and of the old folk. They dinnae care no more about the other kinda stuff."

"Be quiet, Bernard," Angus snapped. "I dinnae want tae talk about it."

"But brother, I swear, no one cares that you dinnea like girls and…"

"Shut it," Angus roared.

Olórin knew only too well how Bernard's ramblings would be a sensitive subject for Angus, and changed the topic of conversation before he could say another word.

"How are you feeling now, Aramus?" he asked.

"Like a Beasties butt-cake," he replied with a weak smile.

"Hush," Angus hissed.

"Sorry, I just thought I'd lighten the humour a little."

Angus raised his hand and the expression of concern he carried on his face silenced any further conversation. The half-man drew his sword and tilted his head from side to side, like he was trying to hear something very small. Bernard too reached for the broad-axe on his back, and stood at the ready. Olórin was surprised that their hair filled ears could hear something that he could not. Regardless of his deafness, a prickling sensation made its way down Olórin's neck, warning him that they were not alone.

The fierce cries of combatant creatures suddenly erupted from the quagmire around them, followed by the sight of an army of ogres and worgen emerging from the brush. As they charged toward the four travellers, Olórin spied the ominous glint of red, metal armour from atop the hill.

Chapter 18

Aria took in a deep breath, held the pendent around her neck tightly, and roared to signify the beginning of battle. The ogres were the first to respond, and two rows of ugly green creatures descended the small hill toward her enemy. The worgen lagged behind the ogres, choosing to encircle the party of four instead of running into the midst of them. Aria watched with salivating glee as her trap sprung. Only Edwel remained by her side, moving his feet occasionally, so they wouldn't get sucked into the waterlogged soil again.

The ogres closed in around her enemies and their mighty cleavers were met with the meagre defence of a broad-axe, two swords, and the silvery projectiles from the old wizard's staff. The peaceful mire rang with the sound of war cries, clashing metal, and the peculiar sound of Edwel squelching in the mud. No longer able to contain her fervour, Aria moved to take long strides toward the battle, only to be stopped by Edwel's stone hand.

"You cannot command your soldiers if you are in the midst of the brawl," he said.

Aria batted his hand away with a growl, but stayed in her spot. She knew that he was right, but she couldn't help wanting to be closer. She wanted to see the whites of Aramus's terrified eyes, to smell the blood as it trickled from his body, and hear his last pathetic cries for his vile father as he whimpered into death's arms.

But she was to be disappointed.

The two dwarfs battled with mighty swings, which saw the arms of her obedient ogres vault into the air, their bellies splayed open, and cleavers cut from their hands. Aramus too seemed to have the upper hand against the stupid beasts, although he again appeared to be weak, stumbling occasionally onto the floor.

Frustration saw Aria grip her sword more tightly, but something else caught her attention as she watched the winged man. From within the torrent of his flapping wings, and his powerful twists and turns with a sword, something flashed momentarily, and Aria could have sworn it looked a lot like fire.

*

"There's too many," Bernard shouted over the din of the snarling ogres.

"Keep yer hand tae yer weapon, brother, and yer eyes to the monsters," Angus ordered. "Even if there are too many, the only options we have is tae fight, or die."

Olórin could feel his heart pound in his chest as though it had turned into the hoofs of a terrified horse. Swinging his staff behind him he caught two ogres squarely in the chest with a silvery blast. The ogres stumbled backward, only temporarily stunned by his magic, and came for him again. *'A weakened wizard isn't much use in a battle meant for killing,'* he thought, breathing hard.

Aramus jumped in front of Olórin and, with a wide sweep of his sword, he took the ogre's heads clean off their bodies. No sooner had their open-mouthed craniums thudded sickeningly to the ground, than another ogre advanced. Despite his rescue, Olórin knew that the battle was hopeless. They were outnumbered, and it was only a matter of time before the queen's army would see victory.

Still weakened from his ordeal in Balbuldor, Olórin was left with little choice but to expel the last of his energy with magic. He grasped his staff with two hands, raised it high into the air, and then brought it down hard with a ground-shaking rumble. A silvery dome exploded from the burl and expanded rapidly around them, sending a cascade of surprised ogres stumbling backward.

At the queen's command the ogres got to their feet and pushed their shoulders against the shield. One by one, they slowly made their way through, as though they were only shifting an invisible boulder that blocked their path. Olórin knew he was not yet strong enough to stop them all, but slowing them down might give the dwarfs a fighting chance to do what they do best.

From half way up the hill, Olórin heard the Blood Queen scream in frustration and order her worgen to join the attack. Olórin strained against the added pressure as they too pushed against his shield. But the effort was draining him fast. He felt as though some malevolent machine had found the origin of his being and was slowly sucking it out.

"We cannot win like this," Aramus said, breathing heavily beside Olórin.

With a fiery glance at Olórin, he purposefully stepped in front of the two dwarfs and their flashing weapons. He sheathed his sword as if he was about to surrender. Olórin's heart fell into his stomach.

"Aramus, what are you doing? Get back behind me," Olórin shouted, fighting to hold the shield in place.

Aramus ignored him and held his arms out wide, like he was trying to hold something very large indeed. Olórin was helpless. He couldn't let go of his staff to pull the young man back or the shield would fail and the queen's army would be on Aramus in an instant. The dwarfs were too busy slicing at the creatures that made their way through to notice what Aramus was doing.

Suddenly, Aramus thrust his hands forward and an inferno of fire burst from them. The superheated blaze tore through the nearest ogres and worgen in a wide arc. It was met by the howls of pain as the creatures fell to the uneven ground. Some of them were instantly incinerated while others ran away, screaming and searching for an escape through the flames that blinded them. Aramus turned to Olórin then with a devilish grin on his face, the fire of Dantet still burning behind his amber eyes. His powerful chest rose and fell with the effort of his actions.

"Did you see that?" he asked Olórin excitedly.

"I did," Olórin whispered, the cold sense of dread stirring wildly in his core.

*

"WHAT WAS THAT?" Aria demanded of Edwel.

Edwel gasped, even though he did not breathe, and muttered some gibberish about swap gasses and sparking metal. She watched in horror as half her army fell to the ground, their charred remains blackening the moss around them, while another few died moments later. This was no swamp gas. Had she been aware that Aramus possessed powers like this, then she would have made her move much sooner. As it was, she had enjoyed the carnage too much.

"You remember what we discussed, Edwel?" she asked, bracing her feet in the mud.

"I do, but I have to say that I'm not comfortable with it," Edwel replied with a sullen look.

"I didn't ask you to be comfortable," Aria snapped, raising the Etherium arrow in her right hand and taking aim at Olórin. "I only asked you to be quick."

Aria nodded at the stone golem and he took off running toward the silvery dome. Just before he reached it, she let fly the blue tinted rod, and it took off with a zing toward her target. As Mullrode said it would be, it was immune to the wizard's magic and sailed through the shield effortlessly. But before it could hit the old wizard's heart, the powerful dwarf Luscious had referred to as the king's right arm, leapt into the air between the arrow and Olórin.

The dwarf crumpled to the ground, clutching at his chest and writhing in pain as the arrow refused to be deterred from its path. Aria held her breath as Aramus ran toward the dwarf. Just as the arrow left the half-man's body with a zing, Aramus dove in the direction of the wizard and grabbed it, but he wasn't quick enough. It reached the old wizard and dug into his shoulder. The wizard fell to the ground with Aramus as the young man's momentum wrenched the arrow from his shoulder. He let out a cry of pain and collapsed, so too did his shield, and Aria could almost taste the victory.

Undeterred by what was happening around him, Edwel pushed passed the remaining ogres. He lifted Aramus from off the ground and pinned him to a nearby tree with the full might of his stone arm. The young man gasped and choked as Edwel crushed his neck under his weight. But despite the kicking and flailing wings of his prey, the stone golem would not kill him. Aria had been careful to make sure he understood that *she* would have that pleasure.

With a deep satisfied sigh, Aria gripped her necklace and called for her army to be still once more. Without the wizard, her enemies would easily fall, and she had no intention of allowing one of the stupid ogres to take what was rightfully hers.

*

"NOOOO!" Bernard roared amidst the chaos.

Olórin lay on the ground, clutching his shoulder. Pain shot down his arm and blood oozed between his fingers. But regardless of the agony he felt, he was instantly alarmed by the sound of anguish he heard in Bernard's voice. It was all the more alarming because the battle around them had become still and silent.

Bernard rushed to his brother's side and turned him over. Even from where Olórin lay, he could see where the queen's weapon had worked its way around Angus's Etherium chestplate, piercing through his chest like he had been nothing more than a detour instead of a man.

Bernard cradled his brother's head in his arms, and stroked his fiery red hair tenderly. The moss beneath the mighty dwarf turned red, and Olórin could only watch as he saw Angus fight for breath.

"No, no, no, no. Brother, stay wih' me," Bernard's words were drenched with sorrow. "Please, hold on. Please."

Angus clutched at his chest and gasped desperately as he coughed up blood.

"You must," Angus bubbled, "you must take… my place."

Bernard shook his head adamantly, and held his brother closer to his chest.

"No, I willnae." Bernard turned to Olórin and shouted. "Wizard, do something. Wave yer magic wand and make him better."

Olórin felt the coldness in his wound quickly seep into every corner of his body. He also felt the desperation of

Bernard's plea and tried to lift his staff. But his limbs refused to obey him as if they weren't his own. The same weakness that he had felt in the dwarven mines, now clutched and tore at his very being. It was all that he could do to just breathe.

From the corner of his eye, he saw the queen take purposeful strides down the hill toward the stricken dwarf, and her stoic army parted way for her without needing to be asked. Her intense blue eyes scanned the destruction she had caused. The golden sword in her right hand glinted in the hazy morning sunshine, a colour too bright for the occasion. She stopped beside the two dwarfs and looked down on them with a heartless smile.

"Olórin cannot help you," she said to the rotund dwarf. "The Etherium arrow has pierced his skin and syphoned his magic from him. The only thing that stops it from ploughing through his heart is the hand of that evil creature you protect."

Olórin heard Aramus struggling for breath from behind him. He turned and saw a stone golem, he knew only too well, pinning Aramus's neck against the tree. The young man gritted his teeth and pushed hard against the golem with every muscle straining, but to no avail. In his hand he held the Etherium arrow the queen had spoken of. It dripped with Angus's red blood, and strained against Aramus's grip, trying to free itself to finish its task. But Aramus refused to let it go. But it was powerful and Olórin could see it slip, bit by bit, from his slick grasp.

"Bernard." Angus's chest heaved to find air. "I name you… the king's right arm. Give me your word…" His voice was lost as he arched his back and pain etched across his face as it slowly turned blue.

"No, no, Angus…" Bernard couldn't stop the tears from rolling down his face.

"Promise me," Angus croaked out, "that you will complete… whot the king as asked of me."

"No, I willnae," Bernard replied angrily. "Thas is no time tae be thinking about yer duties, brother. The king can shove his task where the sun dinnae shine. Breathe, please just keep breathing."

“Promise me brother, or I willnae have… a restful slumber.”

“I… I… cannae. I won’t. If I do that then you’re free tae go tae the next world, and I dinnae want tae lose ya, brother.”

Bernard’s voice crackled with sorrow. He swotted away the tears that fell freely from his eyes. Angus smiled weakly and rested his hand gently on his brother’s face. Olórin knew the look of death as it hovered over a mortal soul, and his heart ached as he recognised it in Angus’s face.

“I am already lost,” Angus whispered. “Promise me.”

Bernard shuddered as he stifled a deep sob. It took him some time to regain his composure enough to answer his brother’s final request.

“I promise, brother,” he said. “I promise tae see thas through till the end. The wizard and the winged man will have my axe until my return tae Balbuldor, or until we meet again in the hereafter.”

Bernard’s voice trailed off into a whisper at the end.

Angus smiled and after one last painful breath, his hand gently fell from his brother’s face. His gurgling chest quietened, and the king’s right arm fell silent. Bernard lowered his head and wept into his brother’s chest. All around them, the moment seemed to resonate with comrade and enemy alike. The silence of the mire, and the stillness of both parties, was only interrupted by the sound of Bernard’s pitiful sobs.

*

Aria hadn’t meant to sever the dwarven king’s right arm, not that it matter much as she had intended to kill them all once Aramus’s head was cut from his body. Whatever ill-feelings the self-appointed king of the dwarfs might harbour against her for killing his champion, he was just another treasonous subject she would have to deal with at a later date. She was still his monarch, after all, and siding with the wizard was nothing short of a betrayal against the crown.

Despite the fact that these half-men were now her enemies, she still felt Bernard’s deep sorrow hang in the heavy mist around her as he sobbed quietly into his brother’s chest. From behind, she heard Luscious hiss at her to “get on with the job”, but she ignored the worgen. Reminded of her own bond with Pearan, a small side of her recognised Bernard's pain. She wasn't so heartless that she couldn't give this fiery haired dwarf a moment to grieve for his brother, before she killed him too.

As Bernard laid his brother's head gently on the soft moss, Aria didn't see him pick up his axe again. She didn't see his stout figure move quicker than a striking snake, and only barely noticed the sharp edge of his axe swing for her head. She leaned backward and the dwarf's blade scraped her chestplate, sending a shower of sparks into the air, and missing her neck by a hairs breath.

Bernard swung again, and again, and each time she blocked his attacks with her sword. His strikes were powerful and the fury in his wet, steel-blue eyes told her that as long as his heart still beat, he would not stop swinging. Flashing gritted teeth from beneath his red beard, Bernard showed no sign of tiredness, and dodging his swings was becoming increasingly difficult.

"You there, subdue this dwarf," she ordered the nearest ogre.

The ogre looked on stupidly and snarled a toothy sneer at her. The dwarf swung again and Aria had to take a step backward to avoid being sliced in half. As she stumbled a few paces away from the grief-stricken dwarf, one of the ogres pushed her roughly back into the fight. She reached for her necklace.

"Are you deaf? I said to…"

Aria felt the blood drain from her face as she searched her neck. The golden pendent she had used to control the Dark Ones was no longer there. Her heart took off in a gallop and her stomach formed a painful abyss that swallowed everything but her fear. It seemed that the dwarf's axe did *not* miss, and buried somewhere in the soggy ground around her was the only control she had over her army. The ogre's stupid minds caught up with the events and, one by one, they joined in the battle as bloodlust took hold.

A cleaver barely missed her ear as she spun around

searching for any glint of gold amongst the mud. The dwarf fended off two ogres before lunging at Aria again. His mighty axe ricocheted off her sword in a blurred frenzy of dwarven iron. All the while the worgen looked on with apathy. Aria's sword swung in wide arcs as she fended off the attacks.

"Luscious, what are you waiting for? Help me," she shouted.

Luscious sat on his hind-quarters and watched the scene unfold. He cocked his head to the side and curled his lip, revealing his missing canine. His red eyes followed her lazily. For a moment she thought that he was enjoying watching her stumble to the floor as another wave of ogres came after her.

"My Queen," she heard Edwel's voice call out.

"Stay where you are, Edwel," she commanded. "If I should fall and cannot take his head myself, then you must do it."

"But Aria…"

"You *will* obey me," she shouted whilst ducking another cleaver.

From the corner of her eye, Aria spotted the old wizard standing up again.

'Oh, no,' she thought. *'The Etherium must be wearing off.'*

"Luscious, we both want the same thing." Aria stumbled over a severed limb of an ogre and fell onto her back. She only just managed to get to her knees before the next wave of deadly blades came after her. "There is no time for this. The wizard is regaining his strength."

Luscious shot a look at the old man, who was now rummaging through his tattered hat, and howled. In a flurry of deadly claws and snapping teeth, the worgen began to fight their way through the ogres, ignoring the furious dwarf. But Luscious had waited too long and Aria knew it.

*

The weakness that had consumed Olórin to near the point of death had begun to fade. His chest, however, still ached from the effort of breathing, blood still oozed from his shoulder, and his limbs still begged to collapse. He was virtually powerless to do anything about the battle that raged in front of him, or of the stone golem that was slowly choking

Aramus to death.

It was in this desperate moment that a voice whispered in Olórin's mind. He recognised it at once as the voice of his beloved Goddess Edwina. "I have cried enough," she whispered. Just as suddenly as he had heard her, and was filled with her loving light, she left again and the reality of the cold, misty morning returned to him. The air, laced with the clashes of weapons and the cries of dying ogres, brought him back to his senses. He knew what he had to do.

Rummaging through his old tattered hat, Olórin found the phial containing waters of life, the tears that Edwina had cried. She had given him four tears, but the potion only required two. Whilst fumbling a gem from the glass bottle, Olórin couldn't help but marvel at the Goddess's foresight. *'She must have known that I would need this,'* he thought. If that was true, Olórin wondered what need he might have for the other one.

Finally gripping one of the shining stones between his muddling fingers, Olórin place the phial back into his hat. Just as he did, he saw the ferocious figure of a worgen come hurtling toward him. His claws dug into the mud, propelling him forward, and his teeth flashed viciously in the morning sun, all except one missing canine.

Olórin placed the tear snugly into the burl of his staff and held it up high.

"ILLUMINOUS," he bellowed.

Like a creature that had suddenly come to life, the tear shot out a blazing light. The worgen and ogres stumbled backward, whimpering like they had been burned, and abandoned their queen as they ran into the mire. Olórin knew that the light of Edwina most probably *had* burnt them, like it had done to Aramus in Darzithal. But he couldn't tell for sure because his eyes were transfixed on his staff.

Like molten gold, the tear dissolved and gushed over the wood, turning it from a brown colour to a dazzling white. It snaked under his hand, sending a wave of power and warmth through his body. The pain left his wounded shoulder and when he looked down, only a hole in his purple robes remained as evidence that it had ever occurred. Even as a young apprentice Olórin had never felt so strong or alive before, and it took his breath away. It was the sound of Aramus gasping, and a sword meeting an axe, that drew his attention back.

Apart from his iron armour, Bernard was a vision of red; his fiery hair matching his furious red face. Tears flowed freely over his cheeks and he bared his teeth as he swung again and again at the queen. Her long, curly hair flailed around as she met his attacks with a trained hand, but she could not best his vengeance despite her skill.

Olórin, satisfied that Bernard would keep the queen at bay, strode calmly toward the golem. Aramus's eyes were beginning to roll back in his head. Just then, his grip loosened on the Etherium arrow and it shot out of his hand. It rocketed toward Olórin's chest with a tinny hum. Olórin's staff glowed and, as though time itself had slowed down, he calmly reached out his hand and caught the arrow before it struck. The arrow, etched with dark runes that no good wizard should know, struggled to escape his grip. The markings glowed brightly, sending a burning ache all the way up his arm.

"Abomination," he whispered to the arrow. "Be gone."

Olórin touched the arrow to his staff and the markings melted away like they had never been there. The arrow lost all fight and all power to move, and he dropped it into the marshy ground before continued on his way toward Aramus.

*

"Edwel," shouted Aria, panting hard with the effort of containing the half-man's fury. "You must kill the winged man."

She had seen Olórin's advance and, in a last ditch effort to complete her task, relinquished her desire to kill Aramus herself. But the stone golem hesitated as Olórin touched his shoulder.

"Release him, golem," Aria heard Olórin say between parries.

"I cannot. My queen has ordered me to kill him," he replied flatly.

"But you do not want to kill him, do you?"

Edwel looked blankly between Olórin and Aria. His stone

mouth turned down. Aria tried to command Edwel to kill Aramus *now,* but exhaustion had long set in. Every time she took in a deep breath, the dwarf's axe would be on top of her again.

"I do not. But I have no choice," she heard him say.

"Then you understand what I must do?"

Aria's eyes widened. *'What, what must he do?'*

"I will be sad about it, but yes, I understand."

"You may rest peacefully knowing that you have been a faithful servant," Olórin said, touching his staff against the golems head. "Reliqua."

Without warning, Edwel fell apart. His head rolled backward, toppling to the ground. His arms and legs came away from his stone torso and they all followed his head. The two black stones, that were his eyes, rolled into the marshy bog, leaving only the turned down mouth-hole on his square head to show that it had ever been anything more than just a rock.

Aramus fell to the ground, clutching at his neck and gasping for air. His black wings fell limply by his sides. From where he knelt, Aramus stared at Aria and she could see that the fire in his eyes was now gone. She was alone, surrounded by her enemies, who would surely kill her now. But she wasn't going to give up without a fight.

"NOOO," she screamed.

Butting the dwarf in his bulbous nose with the hilt of her sword, she took off in Aramus's direction. The dwarf was unperturbed by her assault, despite the blood gushing from his nostrils, and swung the back of his axe at her legs. Aria stumbled and fell onto the marshy wetland under her feet. Her sword flew into the air and landed a few feet away from her. She spun on her back and came face to face with the half-man whose axe was raised above his head, ready to strike.

"Bernard, stay your weapon," Olórin shouted.

Bernard didn't listen, he strained hard to bring down his axe. His eyes burned brightly with the desire for death and his muscles quivered with the effort. But no matter how hard he tried to complete the movement, he could not. Aria glanced over at Olórin. His staff was pointed at Bernard, somehow holding the furious dwarf's axe in place.

"I willnae," the dwarf seethed, nearly foaming at the mouth with fury. "I will have her head. Do ya hear me, wizard?"

"The battle is over, Bernard," Olórin said kindly. "I cannot allow you to murder an unarmed soldier, no matter how much you might want to."

Olórin walked toward the two, keeping his staff pointed at the axe, and rested a hand on the dwarf's shoulder. As though the kind gesture opened a flood gate, Bernard suddenly dropped his axe by his side and sobbed deeply. Olórin too let his staff fall and Aria breathed a sigh of relief at being allowed to live.

"Fine," Bernard said, wiping his eyes tersely with his beard. "I won't kill her, but I can at least hurt her."

The last thing that Aria saw was the butt of Bernard's axe as it came down on the side of her head. Stars filled her vision until the blackness of oblivion came to take her.

Chapter 19

Aramus had insisted on digging Angus's grave so as to allow Bernard time to say goodbye. Olórin was surprised to see Aramus leave his thin satchel on the ground, next to his feet, just before he started digging. The old man took it as a sign that Aramus now trusted his travelling companions enough to lay down his only possessions. *'Strange how death can bring people closer.'*

Aramus used the dwarfs axe to lift large chunks of mud from the ground, but the soggy dirt would not let him dig deep. In the end, they were left with little choice but to lower Angus's body into the mire, along with his Etherium sword, and watch him sink to the bottom. It was no kind of burial for a brave dwarf, Olórin knew this. But with the queen's army still nearby, and with no dry wood for a pyre, they could ill-afford to carry his body back to Balbuldor from where the king had expelled them. Right arm or not, the king would not be pleased to see them, or their pursuing worgen.

While Bernard stood solemnly by the mound of dirt, that was once the king's right arm, Aramus spent some time searching through the bog for just the right pieces of wood to create a marker for Angus's grave, collecting his satchel along the way. Using rope Olórin had stored in his hat, Aramus tied two pieces of wood together in the shape of an X and placed it at the head of the grave. With the remaining rope the young man tied up the unconscious queen's hands. He slipped her golden sword from around her waist and strapped it safely to his side. Satisfied that she wouldn't budge, Aramus joined Bernard and Olórin.

As dusk encroached on their private moment, the three travellers stood next to the grave in a moment of silence. The sound of frogs croaking, counted the many seconds they stood.

In that time Olórin couldn't help but smile at the compassion Aramus had shown toward the grief stricken dwarf. *'The kindness of one's actions is often more powerful then condolences,'* he thought. Bernard too seemed to appreciate the young man's efforts, giving him a grateful nod.

Now adorned in the ill-fitting Etherium armour, and carrying the Valefire around his neck, Olórin couldn't help but wonder if Bernard's rise to the top of the king's army hadn't had something to do with the potion of fortune he had given him. Although the potion should have worn off by now, Olórin still felt a wave of guilt as he glanced at the half-man, his hands clasped firmly in front of him.

"I am no' one fer many words," Bernard began, sniffling loudly and wiping his nose with his beard. "Angus understood them better than me. He did a lot of things better than me, but he was never big-headed about it. He was a good man, a brave soldier, and a great brother. He took on the weight of the king's woes and carried them proudly. His sense of duty never left him, no' even when it meant his life, and I can only hope tae be half as brave as he."

Bernard's bottom lip quivered and he let out another loud sob before clearing his throat.

"I dinnae know whot life is wih'out me big brother. He has always been there from the beginning of my time. But I do know that the world will be colder now that he's no' in it. And whatever people have said about him, whatever thoughts have wandered through their bigoted minds, I *know* that Angus will be the first one that the Goddess chooses to stand by her side."

Bernard shifted the Etherium chestplate awkwardly, which only covered half his torso, and tried to speak again. But his words were lost to the sorrow that so evidently weighed on his chest. The sorrow was contagious and Olórin found himself wiping a tear from his own eyes too. He didn't have to guess what small-minded people had said about the king's right arm, he knew only too well. But it was those people who would lose out in the end. They would never truly know the hero that had laid his life down so they could live.

"In death," Olórin continued for Bernard, "we find our

place. We see all those who have been touched by our living in the tears that they shed, and the great deeds we have done in the stories they tell of us when we are gone. Our deeds do not need to be mighty to hold an enduring place in the hearts of the living, nor do they need to stretch to the corners of the worlds for them to be felt. All that keeps us alive in this mortal realm, is what we leave behind. And, as all hero stories should, I vow that Angus's story will become the thing of legend. While breath still escapes my lungs, I will endeavour to tell all who will listen about the dwarven king's selfless right arm."

"Aye, and may the cold winds of death ner fly up yer kilt, brother," Bernard added with a satisfied nod and a sniffle.

The three travellers stood for a moment longer, bowing their heads, until the sound of the queen groaning disturbed them. Bernard shot her an evil look and spat in her general direction, like the mere sight of her breathing was an insult to everything he held dear. Olórin suspected that it probably was, and wondered if the dwarf would truly be able to keep his word.

"What should we do with the queen?" Aramus whispered to Olórin.

"Well, ye know whot I'd like tae do wih' her," Bernard replied, gathering up his axe and securing it onto his back.

"We cannot kill her, Bernard," Olórin said examining the young girl in red armour. "But we cannot let her go either. She would only find another way to gather an army, and, thus far, she has proven herself too dangerous to be allowed to do that."

"So, whot then? We tie her tae a tree in the middle of nowhere never tae be found again? That'll work fer me too."

"We should bring her with us," Aramus said. "She can't gather an army as a prisoner."

"Ha! Ye want me tae travel wih' that foul flange? I'll no' walk the same road as my brother's murderer, ya hear me, wizard?"

"I'm afraid that Aramus is right," Olórin said, touching Bernard's shoulder gently. "She is too dangerous to be allowed to go free. You are now the king's right arm, and as much as it pains me to twist it, we need you come with us. It is your duty, after all, and the last thing you promised Angus."

Bernard's face went as red as a beetroot and he mumbled unrepeatable curses under his breath. He pushed Olórin to the side, and, as he passed Aramus, gave the young man a quick punch in the ribs.

"Thanks a lot, clever clogs," he spat.

Aramus bent over, winded from the blow, and Bernard stomped off ahead of them.

"He is angry," Olórin said, righting the young man. "He is in a lot of pain right now, and it will take some time before the anger leaves him."

"How much pain will my ribs have to endure until then?"

"I do not know, perhaps just a little more. But until then, my strong young fellow, I would ask that you carry the queen before Bernard gets too far ahead of us. I am too old for the job, and Bernard would be more likely to strangle her."

Aramus nodded and walked toward the young queen. He picked up the girl who had tried to kill him with more gentleness than Olórin would have expected. Despite everything that had been said about the son of Dantet, Olórin was more determined than ever that he would succeed in curing Aramus. Then, the world would see the kind, passionate man that lay within him. But something still troubled Olórin.

As Aramus shifted the queen's limp body in his arms, the fire that had been behind his eyes was now well and truly gone. The memory of Aramus's excited face as he had used his powers against the ogres, however, was still firmly etched into his brain.

"How are you feeling?" he asked as Aramus walked passed him.

"Fine, why do you keep asking me that?"

"Well, the last time you were on fire, you were in a considerable amount of pain. Given that you incinerated half the queen's army, I expected that you might have some discomfort," Olórin replied probingly.

"No, I'm fine," Aramus said, keeping his eyes fixed on the road ahead. "It didn't hurt this time. Actually, it kind of felt good. Is that bad?"

Olórin was quiet for a moment. He suspected that being forced to burst into flames was unnatural, even for the son of Dantet, and wondered if the Dark God had done it to both free his armies and kill his son at the same time. But the residual power that had lingered in Aramus appeared to be extinguished now, and Olórin thought it best not to worry the young man.

"No, not at all," he lied to him, probably for the first time ever.

Satisfied with the wizard's answer, Aramus smiled and followed Bernard along the uneven path. Olórin couldn't help but wonder if his experience with his father might accelerate the maturing process of Aramus's powers. But there was little he could do about it now. Olórin made to follow Aramus, before remembering something and quickly began scouring the marsh between the fallen ogres.

"What are you looking for?" Aramus called back, pausing to cast Olórin a curious look.

"The arrow and the pendent that fell. Both are powerful weapons and we shouldn't leave them lying around to be picked up," Olórin replied. "But I can't seem to find them anywhere."

"The pendent?"

"Yes, a powerful weapon used to control Dark Ones called the, Amulet of Tenebris," Olórin replied, kicking over a few loose body parts. "As soon as I saw her command the ogres I knew that she must have had it in her possession, and I fear there is a dark wizard aiding her."

"I have not seen it, old man. They've probably sunken into the mud," Aramus called as he continued to follow the angry dwarf. "Come on, or Bernard will be half way to Elwood before we know it."

Olórin had a sinking feeling at the thought of leaving such powerful talismans lying about the mire, but Aramus was right. Despite his short stature, and his wide frame, Bernard had taken off at a great pace, leaving them some distance behind. Olórin supposed that the place of his brother's death was not a somewhere Bernard wanted to loiter. Taking long strides after Aramus, Olórin followed his two companions, and their prisoner, toward the home of the Elves, and prayed they would not slay Aramus the moment they saw him.

Chapter 20

"Whot do ye mean we're no' stoppin' fer lunch?"

The gruff voice rang out in Aria's throbbing head.

"We must wait until the mire is behind us," said a second, wearier voice. "Even now, I fear the Dark Ones are hovering nearby. There are very few places to run in this terrain that would *not* see us swallowed up by a gawping muddy maw."

Aria tried to open her eyes to see who was talking, but the bright, sunbathed world she saw, spun mercilessly around her instead. It left the figures blurred and unrecognisable. With the sky underneath and a grassy bogland whirling above her head, Aria felt her stomach churn and her eyes roll back into her skull. The voices in the bright world became muffled as they argued about whether dwarfs *actually* needed more regular feeding then humans, the loudest of them adamant that it was true.

As their disagreement dissolved, she was submerged into the blissful darkness once again. Unlike before, where it was unaccompanied by her consciousness, this time Aria saw images emerge in the dimness. Two figures wearing golden crowns coalesced before her. A man with curly red hair and brown eyes, drifted closer as though he glided on the air itself. Holding the crook of his arm, like she couldn't bear to let go of him, was a beautiful woman with blonde hair, piercing blue eyes and full red lips.

Aria recognised them at once as her parents, the king and queen of Naretia. The sight of them filled her heart with a warmth that felt like a long-lost comfort. Dancing around their legs was a small boy, her seven-year old brother Pearan. His brown eyes twinkled with mischievousness, and his wild, red hair bounced like a deranged cloud as he ducked and weaved beneath the feet of their parents, laughing loudly.

They watched Pearan's antics with adoring smiles, gesturing for Aria to join them. Aria couldn't remember the last time she saw her parent's smile, and her heart did a flip at their invitation. She tried to reach out to them, but her hands refused to obey. Straining to touch her parents, a rope snaked around her wrists and tugged her away. *'Why are my hands tied?'* she thought, glancing with alarm toward her parents.

Her mother and father, and even her brother Pearan, seemed oblivious to her plight as they each waved at her to come closer. Aria tried to call out to them, but only heard herself moan.

"Dinnae go blaming me if the hunger overwhelms me," her mother said in a deep voice. "And fer the love of the wee man, dinnae let that dirty fud come too close tae me, or I'll skin her!"

'What? Surely my mother would never say such a thing to me?' In that moment, a name circled at the back of her tumultuous brain, one that she loathed to hear. 'The Blood Queen.' Although she knew that the sound of it raised bile in the back of her throat, Aria couldn't remember why she detested it so much, or what it meant. Her mother, the queen, had never been anything other than a loving and kind ruler, same as her father.

As a bright light invaded her dreams again and melted the vision of her parents, Aria realised that the owner of the loud voice came from the upside-down world. She felt herself being jostled, as if someone was carrying her and needed to redistribute her weight. Her head swayed from side to side as her carrier took long powerful strides. Her hard metal armour dug painfully into her back as he did. She reached out and grabbed onto something to hoist herself up, hampered by her bound hands. Leaning her head onto what she could only imagine was a shoulder, Aria opened her eyes for long enough to see that she had grabbed onto someone's brown tunic. Beneath that tunic was the powerful chest of a man.

"Easy," the man's deep, cool voice whispered in her ear.

Aria tried to look up and see who had spoken to her so softly, but she only caught a glimpse of a strong jaw and shoulder length black hair before the darkness captured her once again.

The gloom wasn't so welcoming this time. It was laced with an ominous mist that pressed down upon her, making it difficult to breathe. From some indiscernible place within the deep recesses of the shadows, Aria heard Pearan scream in terror, and a panic rose up in her chest. She tried to run to him, but her feet wouldn't move. She tried to call out to him, but her voice was mute. Aria spun toward her parents for help, but was stymied by what she saw.

Aria watched in horror as their throats slowly opened, cut by an invisible knife, and blood spilled down their green and gold gowns. Their eyes disappeared from their heads, leaving only hollowed sockets. Bloody tears ran down their cheeks as they reached out toward her in a desperate plea for help.

Aria screamed as their heads toppled away from their necks and hit the floor with a sickening thump. She clutched onto a nearby green and gold banner and hid behind it. She was her fifteen-year-old self again, hiding behind a tapestry as her parents were murdered in the throne room. These images were no longer conjured daydreams, they were real, or as real as memories could get.

'No, I will not hide, not again,' she thought.

Her heart racing, she forced herself to emerge from her hiding place and glance tentatively to where her parents had fallen. The fiery oil lanterns of this acropolis of kings, lit the horrific scene far too brightly for her liking. It was too late, her parents were already dead, their bodies draped over one another and blood now carpeted the green marble floors. Her heart sank and a coldness cascaded from her head to her toes. Her parents had been murdered, and once again she had done nothing to save them. *'Coward!'* a disgusted voice whispered in her head.

A sound in the hollow room, let her know that she was not alone. Slowly peeling back the heavy banner from her vision, Aria was confronted by the strong, foreboding figure of a teenage boy. He stood over her decapitated parents and in his right arm he held her father's golden sword, now dripping with their blood. Large black wings extended to full width on his back, and his strong jaw muscles clenched as he breathed through gritted teeth. Her parent's splattered blood dampened his black hair and flecked across his slightly hooked nose. In his amber eyes, a malevolent fire burned within, and it sent a wave of terror through Aria.

Without warning, he turned and looked in her direction. A wicked smile crossed his face, one that promised she would be next. Fear released her feet and she ran from the room, her heart pounding so hard against her chest that it hurt. She remembered the day her parents died, and the vow that she had made to avenge them by killing this winged monster. But seeing that dreadful moment unfold again in all its horror, froze her intensions cold with fear, and she ran.

Each step through the limestone corridors of the palace rang out against the walls, whispering at her, telling her she had not changed, that she will always be a coward. Aria pleaded with the King's Guard who came across her path, to help her. But the suits of armour rusted in their place, cobwebs coated their helmets, and dust replaced the men inside. The sound of sparring warriors coming from the fighting arena outside, died into a nothingness until the palace was still. Even the servants began to disappear, one by one. Her only companions now were the voices of the all-powerful wizards ringing out in the empty corridors, over and over again, commanding all who could hear to abandon her.

As the voices died into the dust laden cobwebs, Aria called out for help again, but only the lonely echoes of her own voice replied. She was alone. She stopped running, and from one of the narrow windows of the palace she saw the powerful form of the winged boy take off into the sky. The fire in her heart reignited in a furious blaze at the sight of him leaving.

She clenched her hands until she felt her nails digging into her palms. Bolstered by the refusal to accept her failures, yet again, Aria ran faster than she had ever run before. She made her way down to the fighting arena to find a sword, or any weapon that she could lob at the disappearing figure. Instead she found Edwel, and the sight of him made her come to a screeching halt. Something about seeing him, jolted her out of the nightmare she was living. The golem was gazing lazily at the sky where the winged boy had now vanished.

"Isn't it a lovely day?" he cooed.

He turned toward Aria with the same stupid grin on his face that he always held. His stone arms crossed in front of him, and his square head tilting to the side. His usual nauseatingly pleasant demeanour held fast as, one by one, his limbs fell away from his body, and his head came loose from his torso. The mighty golem's stone body gave way like a rockslide, and he crumpled to the floor.

"*Edwel*," Aria whispered in horror.

Edwel didn't respond, how could he now that he was a mere pile of rubble in the middle of the fighting arena? The cobbled stone beneath him grew a thick layer of moss and encroached over his remains like a wave. Edwel's heavy body parts quickly sank into the mire beneath the moss. Standing over the grave of her only friend was an old man with a pointed grey beard, purple robes, and a floppy wizard's hat that looked as though it had seen better days. The wizard held a knotted wooden staff which glowed with an intense white hue. His blue eyes twinkled consolingly in the day's harsh light, and this irked Aria.

She remembered this old man. *He* was the one responsible for hiding her parent's murderer for so long, *he* had been the one to order her guards to abandon her, and *he* had been the one to kill her protector, Edwel. Aria balled her fists and charged him. She didn't care that she had no sword to slay him. If she had to, she would pummel him to death with just her knuckles. But as she reached his thin, stooped frame, he disappeared.

Aria went careening into a heaped pile of dead ogres instead. Green limbs, some of which were covered with black metal armour, fell on top of her. Ghastly faces with black beady eyes and malformed teeth, stared blankly at her as she sunk ever-deeper into their midst. They had been her army, the only ones who helped her try to slay the winged man, and she had sacrificed them all as though they were nothing.

Falling through the bottom of the pile of ogre bodies, Aria found herself out of the palace and standing in a grouse moor, with two dwarfs by her feet. One of the dwarfs was dead, and the other, more rotund dwarf, was weeping over his brother's fallen body. *She* had done this, *she* had been the one to fire the Etherium arrow to win a battle against the wizard. The memories of the atrocities she had committed during her quest to kill the winged boy, came flooding back to her then; the death of the dwarven king's right arm, the example she had made of the two worgen, the Mountainmen she had slaughtered in the mountaintop village of Tasadia, and the blood she had shed across Naretia. All in the name of her gentle parents.

Aria recalled that the moniker of 'The Blood Queen' had been given to *her,* not her mother. It was a heavy badge to bear, but she had never felt its true weight until now. The regret and sickness in Aria's stomach only lasted a few moments as the vision of the winged boy reappeared behind the dwarfs. He was older now, closer to becoming a man, and his eyes burned with the same fire she had seen the day he killed her parents. Now, more than ever, she wanted an end to all of this. An end to all of the pain, hurt, and death that seemed to follow him.

"Your Majesty?" the gentle voice whispered in her ear again.

Aria opened her eyes and this time the bright world didn't spin so wildly. The bogland was beneath her, as it should be, and the sky was thankfully above her. As she groaned into the shoulder of her carrier, she noted that her hands were still bound together with rope. Her head throbbed and with each pounding came the memories of her last battle. Most prevalent was the memory of the fat dwarf charging her, wanting to kill her for slaying his brother. In a moment of panic, Aria gasped and opened her eyes wide, expecting to see the dwarf's axe coming down on top of her again. The dwarf, however, had his back to her, and was walking ahead of the old wizard.

"Good afternoon, Your Highness," the cool, deep voice said to her. "Glad to see you have overcome Bernard's wrath so soon."

Aria's heart sank. If the wizard and the dwarf were ahead of them, then there was only one other person who could be carrying her. The idea of him touching any part of her filled her chest with a potent mixture of rage and disgust. Slowly, she turned to look at the owner of the voice and was met by the unwelcomed sight of a pair of slated amber eyes.

Chapter 21

"Get off of me!" she roared.

Aria let go of Aramus's tunic with a repulsed huff and swung her bound hands at his head. She caught his jaw with the side of her gauntlet. With a grunt of pain he dropped her onto the uneven path below. Winded for only a second, she rolled off her back and onto her feet. The world spun again, but she refused to let it unsteady her as she tried to bolt from her captors. A sudden jerk from the binds around her hands yanked her back toward Aramus. The tail end of her restraints were tied to two black belts lashed around Aramus's waist, one of which she recognised as her father's scabbard holding his golden sword.

"Give that back," she demanded, outraged. "I will *not* allow you to hold it again."

Aria rushed forward to grab the sword from Aramus's side, determined that when she caught hold of it she would remove his head with one clean sweep. But the son of Dantet was ready for her, and with the full force of both hands, shoved her backward again, sending her tumbling to the ground. Aria felt her breath leave her chest and she struggled to fill it again. His amber eyes rested torpidly on her as she lay on the ground, before wiping away the trickle of black blood that oozed from a cut on his jaw. Aria couldn't help but sneer in unobjectified pleasure at her gauntlet's handiwork.

"Numpty!" came the loud voice she now recognised as the dwarf called Bernard. "Are you three tankard's short of a good time, or some'ing? Whot, in the name of all things hairy, dae ye think would make us gave ya that? Yer a monster, a cold-blooded killer, wih' no regard fer life. Because of *you* my brother is… " The dwarf's voice broke and the last word his mouth moved to say, refused to come out. But Aria knew he meant it to be "dead".

Without warning, Bernard reached behind him and detached the broad-axe that was strapped to his back. Flipping it over into the wide palm of his hand, he raised it above his head and pushed passed Olórin. With powerful strides, the half-man charged Aria, his teeth gritted through his fiery beard and a deranged look in his steel blue eyes. Still on the ground, Aria had no choice but to raise her arms over her as her only defence. She peered between a small gap between them as the very ground itself trembled under the dwarf's enraged footfalls.

"Bernard!" Olórin boomed, raising his staff and pointing it at the storming dwarf.

The old wizard's staff glowed with an intense whiteness, and Bernard's axe was frozen to the spot. Aria recalled then how her plan had fallen apart, how the wizard had pulled something from his hat and put it into his staff just before her army ran away, terrified. The staff before this point appeared to be just a simple wooden walking stick. But now it hummed as a powerful white magic flowed over its smooth surface, like a multitude of tiny shimmering rivers. Whatever Olórin had done to his staff, it seemed to have imbued him with a certain vigour too. His stoop was gone, and his thin frame was fortified with a visible strength that Aria could not explain.

Despite Bernard's best efforts to break his axe free from the grip Olórin's magic held over it, he could not.

"No," the dwarf spat, nearly hanging from the suspended weapon now. "I'm wearing the Etherium armour, it's immune tae yer trickery. How can ye still stop me?"

"My dear friend," Olórin spoke calmly. "You buried your brother's Etherium sword with him. Your axe, although it is quite impressive, is made from simple iron, and therefore subject to the effects of my magic."

Bernard let go of his axe and dropped the last few inches to the ground. He breathed heavily and shifted the ill-fitting armour over his chest until it lay somewhere in the middle. His neatly plaited beard had started to come undone with the effort of his actions, and his thick red hair kinked in places.

"And so it should be," he panted. "No warrior should go tae the afterlife wih'out his sword, and Angus was the mightiest warrior tae ever walk these lands. Ye may have a hold over me axe, wizard, but ye have no hold over me."

Quicker than Aria thought possible for the wide-gaited dwarf, he spun on his heels and charged toward her again, leaving the axe hanging in mid-air. Before he could reach her, Aramus's lean frame stepped between her and the angry half-man. His large black wings opened out to full width and startled Bernard just enough to stop him in his tracks.

"Bernard," he began with a sympathetic tone.

Bernard ignored Aramus and punched him firmly in his stomach. The winged man doubled over with a grunt and Bernard tried to push past Aramus. But Aramus was quicker. He held out his strong arm in time to grab the stampeding dwarf. Aramus pushed hard against Bernard, who in turn pushed back against Aramus. It was a battle of strength to see who would win, and the straining of muscles and sliding foothold of the winged man told Aria that she was about to die.

"BERNARD!" Olórin thundered.

Bringing his white staff down hard on a protruding boulder, the marshy ground beneath them shuddered with the threat of giving way. Aria, unable to steady herself with wrists bound, toppled sideways onto the path and watched as the feisty dwarf gave up his drive, turning on the enraged wizard instead.

"Do not toil with me," Olórin seethed, walking toward Bernard with the floating axe now circling around his head like an obedient bird. "I may not be able to stop you, but I can conjure all manner of illusions that would feed on your worst fears, and no Etherium can protect you from that. I can ask the ground to swallow you whole, or the rains to wash you away."

Olórin reached Bernard and bent down until their eyes came level. Even Aria had to admit that if she were the dwarf, she would not be standing so fiercely against such an ominous figure. The axe slowly descended before landing gently on the ground as Olórin took a deep breath and regained some composure.

"But in doing that I would take away your ability to fulfil the last promise you made to your beloved brother. That is not my wish. You have promised to help us on our quest, and I heard from your own brother's lips, that if you give your word you will be true to it until the end. I hope you will not make a liar out of him."

"That's no' fair," Bernard said, giving the old man a poisonous look. "Dinnae use me brother against me. And fer yer information, I only promised tae no' kill her. I never said anything about letting that *cow* live a pain free life, now did I?"

Aria slowly sat up but daren't say a word against the irate dwarf. It wouldn't do her any good anyhow, and becoming headless was a surefire way *not* to escape.

"Don't you see, Bernard," Olórin said, standing up again, "that if I allow you hurt her, your rage might kill her. Then I shall die too, and our quest will fail. But if, by some chance, you do not kill her, you will only slow our progress. Time is not our friend, and by delaying our quest you might be putting the lives of everyone in Naretia at risk. By the ill-thought-out actions of your anger, you will end what your brother has given his life to protect."

Bernard opened his mouth like he wanted to say something. He raised his finger as if some important point he was about to make would refute what the wizard had just said. He even took in a series of deep breaths, and they all waited. But nothing came out.

"Promise me," Olórin said. "Do not have your brother's final request marred with the stain of vengeance. Promise that you will not attack the queen anymore."

Bernard hesitated. He took angry glances between Aria and Aramus, who was still standing at the ready between them. Looking as though lightning could erupt from his eyes, Bernard let out a low growl before throwing his short arms in the air.

“Och, fine,” he spat. “I promise tae behave. But if she should happen tae fall down a hole, or drown in a river, I willnae be saving her either.”

Bernard gave Aramus one last punch in the stomach before picking up his axe and stomping down the uneven path through the mire. Aramus clutched his stomach and Aria saw him grimace.

“That’s the third time he’s punched me, old man,” Aramus said, standing up again and rubbing his midriff. “One of these days I might just punch him back.”

“No you won’t,” Olórin replied. “His anger will pass eventually, as will his taste for punching things. We must be patient until then.”

“You mean *I* must be patient. I don’t see him punching you.”

“Ah, that is because I am old, and with age comes certain benefits… like not being a worthy target for a dwarf’s anger. Come, the day is waning, and night will soon be on us. We must find someplace more solid for our camp.”

Aria watched Olórin leave and waited for Aramus to order her to get up, but he didn’t. Not for a long time. Instead he waited, and by the furrowing of his brow he was evidently considering some other options. She became aware that it was just her and Aramus left behind as the others were nearly out of earshot. If he waited long enough he could tell them that she put up a fight, that he had no choice but to kill her, and they would believe him.

Aramus cocked his head toward her, his wings now neatly folded behind his back. His amber eyes rested on her as she sat on the ground, and she felt her heart take off into a gallop as he stepped closer.

“Come on,” he said, holding out his hand. “I assume you’re able to walk.”

Aramus took hold of the crook of her arm and helped Aria to her feet. She was slightly taken aback at the fact that he wasn’t shoving her, nor was there a sword drawn to shepherd her toward the others, nothing that *she* would have done as a matter of course. Once she was righted and her feet steady, he let go of her arm and followed his two companions, who were both a good distance away by now. Aria's bound hands, still attached to Aramus's belt, jolted her forward and she reluctantly followed them. She was determined to escape her captors, but now was not the time – not when the only place to run was into the morass landscape.

Aramus's pace was fast, it had to be to catch up to the others, and Aria found it difficult to match it. Her head still pounded from the dwarf's assault, and her body was still weak from having chased her prey with little rest. On more than one occasion she stumbled over the uneven surface of the road, and Aramus caught her arm to stop her falling flat on her face. Each time she was irritated at her gratitude that he did.

It wasn't long before they caught up to Olórin and Bernard, and their pace slowed again, for which Aria's weary legs were thankful. Perhaps it was the constant squelching inside her boots, or the loud clanging of her armour, or just her mere presence, which seemed to irk Bernard so much that he spent most of his time throwing scathing looks in her direction instead of ignoring her. Whichever was the case, she was determined to not let it bother her. But it did, and she couldn't help but see the irony of it all.

Aramus had slain her parents, and her whole life since then had been spent hunting him down and wishing vile curses upon him. She, in turn, had killed Bernard's brother and expected that he felt the very same hatred toward her. In some small way, she understood the winged man better now. As they had fought on the mountain peak, he had told her of how he had been vilified and feared all of his life, simply because of his likeness to his father. If that was true, Bernard had given her only a taste of the many years of torment which he had suffered.

The memory of their mountaintop battle came back to her then. The memory of Aramus kneeling down before her with his arms open wide, waiting for her sword to pierce his chest. If only she hadn't hesitated, if only Luscious hadn't interfered, he would already be dead, and things would be a lot less complicated. But now that she had this small understanding of the vilification he had suffered, she was beginning to know why he had asked her to kill him, asked her to rid the world of him, and it saddened her.

'Stop it,' she seethed. *'He is a murderer plan and simple. He killed your parents and he doesn't deserve your pity. He must pay for his crimes.'* The long walk through the mire was giving her too much time to think, so instead Aria decided to spend it looking across the vista for any means of escape. Detachment was much easier when not so close to the subject, and getting away was her priority now.

As the sun dangled just above the flat horizon, its light turned the mire's watery puddles into liquid gold. Spikey reeds poked their heads up from within the tufts of grass and Aria could tell, from the scent of flowers in the air, that spring was on its way. The days weren't so cold now. But even with that, the nights still clung to its beloved frost, unwilling to part with it. Nights always preferred the cold.

The four walked in silence, everyone save for Bernard who was determined to continue throwing back vile curses toward Aria for as long as he remained conscious. Aria hoped that they would make camp soon so that the dwarf might sleep, and she might get some respite. As if Olórin heard her thoughts, he stopped and examined a particularly large boulder that gave the impression of a desert island in the midst of a vast ocean of mud. It was just big enough to fit all four without needing to be on top of one another, for which Aria was grateful.

"We stop here," he said. "The worgen are still trailing us, but with a few well-placed spells on the outskirts of our camp, I am positive they will not attack."

"How positive are you, exactly?" Aramus asked, looking around cautiously.

"I am as sure as I know the sun will rise tomorrow. But if you doubt me, feel free to stay up all night and keep watch."

Supper that evening consisted of raw eggs, which only Olórin and Bernard ate, stale bread, and whatever dried fruits Olórin salvaged from the bottom of his hat. Aria's attack on them had sent their supplies to the bottom of the mire. It would have been a small victory in her eyes, to weaken them in any way, except now her own rumbling belly was suffering along with theirs too. There was no dry wood to create a fire, and no desire to alert the wandering ogres to their whereabouts either.

Aria was too hungry, and tired, to turn her nose up at the meagre offerings. She nibbled at something that once resembled a plumb, now wrinkled and chewy, secretly hoping that Luscious would make his presence known during their meal and rescue her. She had seen no evidence that the worgen were nearby other than the prickling feeling at the back of her neck warning her that she was being watched. But the worgen seemed to have his own reasons for following them, and it became apparent that rescuing Aria was not one of them.

Olórin and Bernard settled easily into sleep. Bernard's loud snoring disturbed the mating call of the surrounding frogs to the point that Aria saw them hop in the opposite direction of their camp. As she lay down on the hard rock, she focused her attention on Aramus – to whom she was still attached. He was the only one still awake, sitting up and staring out over the chameleonesque marshlands that had now turned silver under the moonlight.

His wings wrapped tightly around him as the night's frosty fingers caressed them all. Aria shivered against its touch, her armour absorbing the cold as the frost drew delicate patterns over the red metal. Olórin had rummaged out a heavy brown cloak from his hat, and thrown it over himself to keep warm. Bernard on the other hand, looked as though he needed no comfort and had simply found a spot to plonk himself down on and snore. Aria was positive that a sudden downfall of snow, or a bomb, would not dislodge this dwarf from his slumber.

"You cold?" Aramus asked.

Aria blinked, wondering why Aramus was asking.

"I'm fine," she said, trying unsuccessfully to stop her jaw chattering as she spoke.

"Oh, okay then," Aramus replied, wrapping his wings around him more tightly. "Only, I was going to say that if you are, you could sit by me and my wings would keep us warm. But since you're not cold, I won't mention it again."

Aria's mouth dropped open. She was expecting a torrent of vile words to spew from it at the mere audacity of this creature presuming she could stand to be anywhere near him. But nothing came out. The truth was that she had been near him for the last few hours and had only tried to hurt him once. In any event, the only curses she could think of were the ones Bernard had said to her earlier, and she daren't repeat those.

"Thank you, but I'm fine," she said.

Aramus looked over his shoulder at her and gave a crooked smile.

"Well, if things should change the offer is there."

Aria returned his smile meekly, more out of not knowing how to take his gesture than anything else, before curling herself into a ball as much as possible. She forced herself to close her eyes and try to fall asleep, confident that the wizard's request to spare her, and his close proximity, would keep her safe for the night. But between Olórin's nose whistles, Bernard's snoring, and the cold, Aria couldn't sleep. Giving up on the idea, she sat up and followed Aramus's gaze over the mire. Apart from mist rising off the water as it cooled, there was nothing out there that she could see.

"Do you not trust Olórin's spells then?" she asked.

Aramus half turned toward her and rested his amber eyes on her face for a moment. The moonlight muted their colour and he almost appeared normal to her then.

"No, I trust him," Aramus replied, shuffling back toward her until he sat only a few inches away. "I just don't want to sleep, that's all."

"Why not?"

"If I told you that, you might want to kill me again," he said, resting his arms on his knees and clasping his hands together.

"I thought you wanted to die," Aria said, examining his furrowed brow with some curiosity. "That's what you told me on the mountaintop."

Aramus sighed deeply, his lips pursed together, and his head hung as though something very weighty had suddenly landed on his shoulders.

"I did, and in some small way I still do," he said, picking up a pebble and tossing it into a nearby puddle. "But I think even *that* option has been taken from me too."

"What do you mean?"

Aria's armour had begun to rattle with the shivers that were now involuntarily coursing through her body. With her hands still bound she couldn't even wrap them around herself to try and stave off the cold. Aramus noticed, and, without asking, his nearest wing opened out full and wrapped itself behind her. Aria flinched, wanting to pull away. But she so desperately needed the warmth emanating from him. It was so warm, in fact, that Aria was sure Olórin had given the winged man some magical artefact to heat him.

"I suppose you've heard of the prophecy?" he continued.

"A little."

"Turns out that if I die, my soul, or whatever it is I have, will find its way to my father and he will use my powers to break free from his world. Then you will all die. I guess I am to have no peace in life or in death."

"But I thought he needed you alive to carry out his plans, that's what Luscious told me, and that's why he, as a traitor, wanted you dead."

"I'm afraid I can't tell you the motives behind my father's minions."

'If Dantet truly wanted Aramus dead, then why did Luscious interrupt me as I was about to kill him?' Aria's head whirled with the connotations that swam in there. She wondered then if Luscious hadn't made her one of Dantet's pawns after all, if he hadn't some ulterior motive for his attack on Aramus. If he did, she couldn't fathom a reason why.

"Who is Luscious?"

"The worgen who left me to die," Aria said, unable to hide her tone of disgust.

"I see," said Aramus.

The two sat in quiet contemplation for a while until Aramus broke the silence.

"I hear him, you know, in my head," he said quietly. "My father. He tells me things, things that he wants me to do.

Sometimes his voice is so strong that I find myself doing those things without realising. It's always worse when I dream, and I'm worried he will make me do something terrible while I am not conscious. That's why I don't want to sleep anymore."

"Does Olórin know about this?" Aria asked more loudly than she had intended.

Aramus nodded sheepishly, the weight on his shoulders slumping them further forward.

"He saw it in the dwarf city. I think he wants to believe the best in me, but I'm not sure that I would."

"So, you can't stop it, you can't fight your father's will? Are you aware of what you've done afterwards?"

"Not really. It's like living in a dream," Aramus said, wrapping his other wing around Aria as she shivered against the cold again. "Do you know the way that you try to run in a nightmare, but you can't, like your limbs just won't listen to your head?" Aria nodded, remember her own concussion induced dream earlier. "It's a little like that. I see myself doing things and I try to stop it, but I can't. When it's all over I sometimes think that it was all just a dream and none of it actually happened. Other times I'm not quite so sure."

Aria remembered the fiery glow that had been in his eyes the day he killed her parents and an unsettling thought raised itself in her head. *'Had his attack on my parents been one of these dreams?'* If that was the case then it changed everything. While he had committed this one crime, potentially without knowing it, she had committed many more whilst in full control of her senses. That would make *her* the only monster here. *'No, he admitted to killing them, so he must have known what he was doing.'* Aria's head spun as it argued with itself, but one thing had become very clear. For the sake of her people, and to protect her brother's life, she couldn't kill Aramus until she found out more about this prophecy.

Chapter 22

Olórin stretched his arms over his head and found his hands entangled in a wiry beard. He was sure it wasn't his beard as it was far too coarse. But just to make sure he ran one of his hands along the length of it until he reached a large fleshy nubbin.

"Oie!" came a gruff voice. "Get yer fingers outta me nose."

Olórin immediately retracted his hands and sat bolt-upright. Looking where his fingers had been, he found the furious features of Bernard staring back at him. The disgruntled dwarf gave a loud huff and turned onto his side, away from his travelling companions.

Olórin wiped his fingers on his cloak with a shudder, before glancing at Aramus. He found him sitting up and propped against a large bolder. Like a black-feathered cloak, Aramus's wings were wrapped around both himself and the queen. Her head was resting on his shoulder and her eyes were firmly shut. Aramus, on the other hand, was wide awake, and the small shadows under his eyes hinted that he had not slept all night. But Olórin thought it must be just a trick of the light because the young man always slept well.

He didn't quite know what to make of the sight of the two enemies cozying up together in the harsh light of a frosty morning. It was a sight he thought he would never see; Aramus and *any* woman in close proximity, never mind his mortal enemy the queen. Aria groaned and her bound hands became visible once more as they poked up beyond her feathered cape when she rubbed her eyes.

"What the?" she said, lifting her head and staring wide-eyed at Aramus. "Get off."

Aria gave the young man a hard shove with her shoulders and immediately Aramus unfurled his wings from around her.

'Ah, that's more like it,' thought Olórin with a little disappointment.

"Och, can't a dwarf get a bit of sleep?" Bernard grumbled, only half-turning his head toward Aria. "Would ye stop yer yapping. The sun's no' up over the horizon yet, and all I can hear is *you.*"

Bernard huffed angrily and turned away again. Olórin suspected that his brusqueness had more to do with the fact that it was Aria who had spoken and less to do with him wanting sleep.

"Good morning, Aramus, Your Majesty," Olórin said, inclining his head toward the two before fishing some browned apples and old bread form his hat. "Breakfast is served."

Bernard righted himself with enthusiasm, but his interest was lost when he saw the meagre offerings.

"That's no' breakfast! Ye wouldnae feed a baby bird wih' that garbage," he said. "Give me two minutes and I'll find the three of us a nice bit of boar, or a chicken at the very least."

"I think you mean the *four* of us," Olórin said, knowing full well that he had left out Aria on purpose.

"I'll no' stop ya if ye want tae share *yer* portions, but I willnae be sustaining the likes of *her*," he seethed.

Olórin could see the queen open her mouth to say something back to the irate dwarf and raised his hand to stop her. Much to his surprise, she closed her mouth again and instead satisfied herself by returning Bernard's vicious looks.

"In any event, we cannot light a fire to cook the meat, Bernard," he said. "Not yet, not until we are out of the mire and have some concealment from within the trees of Elwood."

"How much farther?" Aria asked, much to Bernard's obvious annoyance.

"Perhaps a day, but I am surprised you asked," Olórin replied. "I wouldn't have thought you would be so eager to join us on our travels."

"I'm not eager to help you at all," she said. "But there are a few concerns which I am not sure you have thought of. For one, the elves sole purpose in life is to balance the world by removing all things which don't belong in it, or threaten it. I assume that Aramus here would be one of those threats, and they will not help you in your quest. Also, if you are trying to prevent his death, and the fulfilment of the prophecy, I'd wager the elves would thwart you in that regard too. Tell me, is it true his death might see the kingdom of Naretia fall? Because if it is, then I am surprised no one has told me of it."

Olórin studied the young queen for some time. Her sweet-heart shaped face was a picture of concern, but he knew it had very little to do with whether or not Aramus lived, and more to do with how his death would affect her kingdom. From the corner of his eye, Olórin watched Aramus's interest pique as he listened in on the conversation. In a failed attempt to be nonchalant, he busied himself with trying to eat the hardened bread, his amber eyes only occasionally resting on the speakers.

"It is unclear, Your Majesty, so we must err on the side of caution. Only a select few have been told of the prophecy, to protect Aramus, you understand? However, I am confident his human side will prevail and the potion Edwina has charged me to make will cure him of his father's curse, and his hold over him too."

"Are you?" Aria asked, narrowing her eyes. "Sure, that is. If it should fail, if you are left with no other choice, could you see him killed? Could you sacrifice the lives of the wizard caste for the sake of the rest of Naretia?"

Olórin was slightly taken aback by the question and he opened his mouth to reply, but nothing came out. Edwina's words made themselves known in his head. *"...while there is one decision I cannot condone, you may have to take it regardless. If you do, know that I am at peace with it."* An odd weight landed in the centre of Olórin's chest as he wondered if this was what she meant. Edwina, thus far, had seen the need for an extra tear of life and it stood to reason that if she could foresee that, then perhaps she was warning him of the very real possibility that he would have to kill Aramus. But he had come to love Aramus, like the son he had never had, and the thought of killing him went against every fibre of his being.

"May I ask you, Your Highness, why it is you would see Aramus killed so readily?"

"'Cos she's a clag-tail," Bernard interjected, crunching the dried bread with ease.

"Bernard, don't," Aramus said.

Bernard shot him a deadly glance, but Aramus's brow had already been furrowed. His eyes shifted between Aria and Olórin, and Olórin could have sworn that there was a look of nervousness about him.

"Because he killed my parents," Aria answered flatly, as though it was common knowledge.

Olórin took in a sharp breath and fixed his eyes on Aramus. The young man bowed his head and let out a long weighty sigh. He dropped the bread from his hand and, after a few moments, looked sheepishly at Olórin.

"Is this true, Aramus? Was it *you* who killed the king and queen?"

"It was," Aramus replied quietly. "Although, I'm not sure how much of it was me."

"What do you mean?"

Aramus stood up, untethered the queen's binds from his belt and tossed it toward Olórin.

"I mean that it was the first time I heard my father's voice in my head, the first time I dreamed, and the first time I had killed in cold blood. You found me when I was eleven, surrounded by fully grown men who would kill me. I only killed those few to survive, and would have died if you hadn't fended off the other seven. But that day, when the king and queen stood before me, I had no reason to kill them. I just did it, and I don't really remember why."

"It's true," Aria added. "He had a fire in his eyes the day it happened, the same fire I saw as he killed the ogres."

"But why didn't you tell me this, Aramus? If I had known, if only I had known…"

"What? What could you have done, old man?" Aramus said, his voice a mixture of anger and sadness. Balling his fists he turned away from Olórin, like he couldn't bear to meet his gaze. "I didn't want to tell you because then you would look at me like everyone else did, like I was a monster. You were the only one who treated me as though I was normal, as though you actually cared about me, and I had never experienced that in my life.

"At the time, I didn't know Dantet could control me, I thought it was something bad inside of me, and I didn't want to lose your respect. I didn't want you to look at me like *that* – like you are now."

Without another word, Aramus took off into the sky and left Olórin still open mouthed. His head swirled with what all of this meant, and not all of it was about Aramus.

"This is bad, this is very bad," he muttered. "The wizard caste kept this information from me. Why, why wouldn't they tell me?"

"Perhaps they are not as united as you might think," Aria answered. "It was Mullrode, a member of the Order of Everto, who gave me the amulet to control the Dark One's. He agreed Aramus should be brought to justice at the very least. Perhaps he had a hand in it?"

"Mullrode? That snivelling little pest? His boots have always been far too small for his own liking, and his impatience has been troubling, but I never thought, not for one instant… I have been away too long from the wizard tower. Six years. This Order of Everto is most troubling, most troubling indeed."

"Sounds like thas Mullrode fella needs a good walloping," Bernard said, crunching on another morsel of bread. "Whot say we pay him a visit and give it tae him?"

Olórin stood and paced the small rock whilst stroking his beard.

"No, no, we have no time for that. We must get the last ingredient before we return to Lothangard," he said with a weighty sigh. "Come, this is no time to rest."

Olórin picked up the tail end of Aria's binds and helped her to stand.

"Whot about Aramus?" Bernard asked.

"He will find us when he is ready."

“And about my question, will you be able to see him killed if it comes to it?” Aria asked, walking behind Olórin as they clambered off the rock.

Olórin’s heart ached, but certain things were becoming clearer to him now.

“If it comes to it, yes,” he replied in a whisper.

Chapter 23

The sun was high by the time the soil underfoot became less watery. The grounds were blanketed in tall grass and dotted with the first colours of spring flowers as they poked their heads up to meet the sun. In the distance, Aria saw the unmistakable horizon of tall trees. The untouched, ancient forest of Elwood stood like the daunting wall of a natural fortress, stretching its green fingers into the blue sky. Not many travellers had entered the sacred sanctum of the elves, not many were welcomed. Even her father had not tempted fate, holding all of his meetings with the elves in Lothangard. Although they had a certain leniency for the sins of those living in the rest of Naretia, the elves were entirely intolerant of it within their own boarders. In the past, they had eradicated anything within their homeland deemed foul, with deadly force.

Aria spotted a dark figure gliding in the sky. With long, graceful swoops, Aramus circled overhead before descending and landing about a foot away from them. The tall grass bent under his feet and the disturbed wind tussled her hair. Aramus's wings tucked neatly behind his back again as though he was wearing a black cape, so long it swept the ground behind him. Although his expression was stoic and his jaw muscles were firmly clenched, he nodded to Olórin with an awkward half-smile, and Olórin mirrored him. The winged man said nothing as he reached out and took hold of Aria's binds again.

Aria rolled her eyes. *'Men!'*

They followed the dwarf as he razed through the thickened sward ahead of them with broad sweeps of his axe. All the while, Aria could see the muscles in Aramus's arms tensing and his knuckles turn white, as he clenched the rope tighter and tighter with each step. His eyes stayed firmly fixed on the green wall looming closer to him. She felt a small amount of pity for him then, knowing he was most probably walking to his doom. If it had been her, Aria wasn't so sure she would have been so compliant.

It wasn't long before they reached the outskirts of the forest. The green, dappled sunlight showed them the way over mossy trees, some of which had lost their battle to remain upright, and through brooks that laughed quietly. Stoic forest soldiers pressed in around them and rustled misgivings, while their fowl messengers screeched an alarm to no one in particular – their echoes dying some many miles beyond Aria's hearing.

No roads scarred the forest floor in Elwood because the elves believed a road would "encroach on the moss's right to grow". Aria had heard father complain about it many times to his visiting elves, wondering why they didn't want a road to Lothangard, at the very least. They had answered him every time with a question, "Why Lothangard?" The elves had no appreciation for the way the rest of the world put themselves on pedestals, and sighted her father as a self-important man. Their righteous attitude had never likened them to her, and even now, as Aria entered their inner sanctum, she felt the judgmental stares of their ideals follow her.

Aria picked her way across the foot-grabbing tree roots, desperately trying to keep up with Bernard's relentless pace. For such a little person, he was a powerhouse of determination and speed. Her bound hands made it more difficult to climb over the trees that had fallen, and the further in she travelled, the higher the hurdles became.

The clean smell of mulch and pine, filled her senses as she followed her captors deeper into the timberland. The trees grew wider, more dappled with lichen, and the sunlight fought hard to break through the thickening canopy. It was the kind of woodland she was unfamiliar with, as all the forests in Naretia were cut down for wood long before they got the chance to age and decay.

"Here, let me help you," Aramus said, holding out his hand to her at one point.

"Thank you, I can manage," she snapped.

Aramus withdrew his hand and waited patiently for her as she scrambled over the top of another tree trunk. Finally reaching the other side, Aria looked ahead and saw Bernard cupping his hands around Olórin's foot so that he could boost the old man over a mammoth bole the size of a Mountainman's house. It seemed that the dwarf needed no such help. In a series of axe swings and vaults, onto impossibly high branches, the dwarf made it to the top of the trunk alongside the old wizard.

Aria's heart sank, there was no way she could climb that with her hands bound, and she didn't think Bernard would be charitable enough to allow her to use his axe. Following Aramus's lead, she reached the felled tree just as Bernard and Olórin disappeared over the other side. It stretched a good distance either side and to walk around it would leave her alone in Aramus's company for too long.

"Aria, please let me help you," Aramus said.

Aria studied his face for a moment. His amber eyes were soft, his dark eyebrows were furrowed, and his hand was outreached to her again. With more than a little trepidation, Aria nodded.

Aramus shifted the satchel on his back and took a few steps toward her until they were only an inch apart. His powerful arms wrapped around her waist and pulled her in closer to him. Even through her armour she could feel a heat radiate off his body. So close to him now, she could see the small flecks of gold in his amber eyes, glint in the dappled tree light. He hesitated for a moment, like he wanted to say something, but he didn't. Aria watched him swallow slowly as though his throat had gone dry.

Without warning, Aramus spread his wings and, with one robust flap, propelled them toward the canopy. Aria felt her stomach lurch and hooked her arms over Aramus's head for security, hugging him tightly. Aria didn't notice their heads pressing together so much as she noticed the moss covered ground disappear beneath them. She couldn't help but take a deep breath in as they soared over the top of the fallen tree and over the heads of Bernard and Olórin on the other side. Gripping onto the back of Aramus's collar, Aria felt her eyes tear up as they refused to blink against the passing wind. From the corner of her vision she saw Aramus grinning.

She had never flown before, not many people she knew had. The nervous thrill in her stomach, along with the exhilaration of flying dangerously close between the tall trees, put a broad smile on her face that matched Aramus's. Soon, the trees became too thick to fly through and Aramus gently glided to the forest floor, landing some distance away from his companions. Aria gasped for breath and unhooked her hands from Aramus to wipe her teary eyes with the back of her hands. Her cheeks burned with the warmth of a flush.

"That was, that was…" she panted, brushing aside the hair that had fallen in front of her eyes to look at Aramus.

Aria froze as though she had been told a beloved family member had just died. She had meant to say that it was the most exciting thing she had ever done, before she remembered who she was speaking to. Even though he was smiling handsomely, and appeared to revel in her joy, she couldn't remove his face from the terrible memories that never left the back of her mind. Her smile faded, and when it did, so too did Aramus's.

Hearing branches breaking from behind, Aria was almost relieved to see a bushel of red hair hop its way toward her. Following closely behind, Olórin seemed preoccupied with the shadows between the trees then on their awkward moment.

"Having fun, are ye?" Bernard said, pushing past Aria and bumping a shoulder into her. Aria stumbled backward a few steps and Aramus caught her by the elbow to steady her.

"Looks like Bernard's found a new target for his anger," Aramus said with a small smile. "I can't say that my stomach isn't grateful, but I'd keep my distance from him if I were you."

"You think?" she said, not unkindly.

“Come, we mustn’t lose each other,” Olórin said from behind them. “The forest is growing denser and the light is fading fast. Water is the life blood of the forest, and if we follow it to the source, we should surely find the heart of it, and the elves.”

Aramus waited for the wizard to pass before following him. And by virtue of her binds being secured to Aramus’s waist, so too did Aria.

The forest around them grew claustrophobic, and even though she knew it was still day, the shadows made it seem like night. The moss gave way to rock, and slowly the trail grew steeper as they climbed, what seemed like, a mountain inside the forest. A turbulent river ran below them in a deep gorge, the sound of the disturbed birds muted by the thunderous roar of the water. Thick vines ran across the canopy above their heads, and at one stage, Aria was sure she saw a flicker of silver hair disappear behind them.

The sight of it made her heart beat faster. She scanned the timberland teeth at the other side of the gorge’s maw for any sign of movement. Once or twice she thought she caught a glimpse of a glinting bow as it flashed in the fading light. Vines groaned overhead and Aria saw their shadows move on the rocky surface below her feet. But when she looked up, they didn’t so much as sway in the gentle breeze.

Despite the fact she was the queen, it had always been made clear that the lineage of monarchs held no sway in Elwood. Aria’s cruel leadership had been the subject of condemnation from many an elf. Now that she was in their realm, she was subject to their laws, whether she liked it or not. It had only occurred to Aria, as they trudged ever upwards, that the arbitrating elves might see fit to kill her alongside Aramus.

“Olórin,” Aria said quietly, “I think we have some onlookers.”

“Indeed,” he replied. “They have been following us for quite some time now. I am hopeful, since they haven’t attacked us yet, that they don’t intend to. But I could be wrong. They may just be examining our actions, trying to determine if we should be allowed to live or die."

"Whot are they waiting fer?" Bernard said so loudly that Olórin felt the need to shush him. "Dinnae hush me, wizard, I'll speak if I want."

A sudden crack of a tree branch made all eyes turn toward the forest. But the sound had echoed against the rocky walls of the gorge and there was no telling where it had come from. Being the closest to Aramus, Aria noticed that his eyes had begun to glow in the dim light again. His Adam's apple bobbed as though he were swallowing something too large for his throat, and his hold on her rope tightened.

"Let us move more quickly," Olórin said. "Least our standing on the moss too long angers them."

Slipping on a rocky ledge, Aria found it difficult to keep up and had to steady herself on the jagged wall to her right. More than once, her hand slipped over a serrated wall and pain shot up her arm as it slit her palm. Aramus seemed unaware of her difficulties. Instead, he kept his eyes fixed on the shadows between the trees.

They had only been climbing for less than an hour when, without warning, an arrow whizzed through the air from the other side of the gorge and struck Bernard's Etherium armour squarely in his chest. It bounced off with an impotent twang, but weapons were instantly drawn.

"Keep yer back tae the wall," Bernard ordered.

Another arrow flew from the line of thick trees. This time Olórin fired a bolt from his staff to meet it. The arrow shattered into pieces before it reached its intended target, Aramus. The next instant, a hail of at least ten arrows flew in their direction. Aramus dropped Aria's rope to wield the two swords, his own and her father's, and blocked as many of the incoming projectiles as he could. The forest swelled with the sounds of Olórin's bolts cracking, as though they were lightening, and Bernard's vile curses. But from the other side came only the sound of arrows as they were let fly by unseen ghosts.

Aria had no sword to protect herself. Exposed on the side of the gorge, she ducked behind a couple of small boulders. She raised her hands over her head and curled into a ball as Aramus took to the sky. Peeking from behind her insufficient shield, she watched as he glided, twisted, and turned away from the deluge of arrows following him. Gold and silver flashed as the two swords met the arrows from which he could not escape. But no matter how hard he tried to reach the other side, the elves volleys' were too much.

Aria soon realised that the arrows were no longer flying in her direction. Aramus was drawing their fire, and Olórin was too busy protecting him to notice that she was no longer secured. The dwarf, who was now standing the closest to her, was distracted too as he delighted in deflecting any stray arrows that came his way.

This was her chance to escape and she knew it. She could run and reform her army. But the ravenous desire that had once filled her heart to see Aramus dead, was a dim hunger now. Too many things were at play, too many stories were conflicting, and Aria wasn't sure anymore that Aramus was the monster she had made him out to be. No, she had to stay, it was her duty as the queen to ensure that this so-called prophecy did not come to pass, if even just to protect her brother, Pearan, from it.

Without warning, the boulder she was leaning against gave way and Aria tumbled backward. She screamed as she plummeted toward the raging river. A sudden jerk stopped her descent and when she looked up, she found the rope around her hands had caught on a jutted piece of rock.

The rock shifted under her weight, and Aria screamed again. With the weight of her armour, and her hands lashed together, she knew she would drown if she fell into the river. Terror electrified her from head to toe.

"Save her," she heard Olórin's voice boom from above.

It was Bernard's fiery beard that poked itself over the edge and looked down to where she dangled. His steely eyes were hard and he made no effort to help, just as he said he wouldn't. Aria scrambled to find a foothold under the watchful gaze of the dwarf, but the crumbling rocks beneath her gave way every time she tried. A rush of wind, and the powerful sound of wings flapping, alerted Aria to Aramus's presence. His arms wrapped around her waist and before she knew it, she was soaring through the air once again. Turning this way and that to avoid the arrows, Aria felt his chest heave against the effort of it all, and his taunt muscles strain.

Flying with him wasn't as exhilarating as it had been before, this time it was just plain terrifying. Facing the winged man, Aria could see the strain clearly on his face as he clenched his teeth tightly. The elves were a good aim and, despite his deft flying, Aria could see black blood oozing from a cut on his arm, his shoulder, and his cheek. They weren't very deep, but it didn't reassure her that they would live through the ambush.

Aramus suddenly cried out in pain and they were sent tumbling through the air. Branch after branch whipped at their legs and arms as they fell, before Aramus managed to right himself again. Looking over his shoulder, Aria saw the ornate silver head of an elven arrow, now coated in his dark blood, poking out from one of his wings. She could feel his hands shake with the pain as he wrapped them tighter around her waist.

Aria feared that he would not be able to reach the ledge that was so close to them now, and they would both drown. He held her closer to him as though he knew her trepidation. His heart beat fiercely against his chest, against Aria's chest, and she couldn't help but press her head against his.

"Just hold on." His voice barely a whisper as the pain took the wind from him.

With more dips and pitches than she would have liked, Aramus finally made it safely to the ledge and the pair landed in a heap. But something was wrong, something was terribly, terribly wrong, and Aria new it immediately.

Lying underneath Aramus, his body crushing hers as he panted to regain his breath, Aria could feel the heat in him build. She had felt it the night before as he wrapped his wings around her, but now it radiated off of him like the glowing embers on charred wood, and it threatened to burn her. She unhooked her arms from around his neck and he slowly lifted his chest off hers, his two powerful arms either side of her head. When their eyes met, Aria caught her breath and her blood ran cold.

Aramus's eyes were ablaze with the fire she had seen the day he killed her parents. A panic rose in her stomach as he hovered over her. A cold sense of dread froze her to the spot and she was powerless to do anything but stare. *'Move you idiot!'* The burning heat making its way through her armour wasn't enough to melt the ice around her lungs so that she could warn the others. *'He has bested you again and made you a coward,* 'she thought.

Aramus groaned, his teeth grinding together, and lifted himself off of Aria completely. She watched him stumble to his feet, blood dripping from his wing, and face the enemy on the other side. To her right, Olórin fired bolt, after silver bolt toward the trees, whilst Bernard twisted and turned, catching arrows with his broad axe and an avaricious smile. Aria tried to call out to warn them, but the words wouldn't come.

"Stay down," Aramus hissed at her over his shoulder. "If you get in my way I might… I… don't want to hurt you."

"What are you going to do?" she whispered.

"Kill them all!"

Aramus clenched his fists and fire erupted from them. His hands trembled as he unfurled his fingers to reveal balls of fire dancing in his palms. The heat of it tingled Aria's skin uncomfortably, and she waited for it to engulf him, but it didn't. Aramus rolled the balls of fire over his fingers for a moment, before thrusting his arms forward: The weakness from his wound made him stumbled a bit as he did. The tree line on the other side of the gorge erupted into flames.

"Aramus, stop!" Olórin shouted.

Olórin's voice snapped Aria out of her frozen cocoon and she scrambled on her back toward the wall behind her, trying to put as much space between her and Aramus.

"Why?" he replied, taking aim at the other side of the gorge again.

Olórin fired his own silvery bolt, but it was no longer aimed at the elf's arrows. A deep, vibrating boom echoed through the woods as his magic blasted Aramus's attacks, destroying his efforts to end the lives of the elves.

"This power is not meant for mortal soil, you must not use it," Olórin yelled.

The old wizard panted under the strain of keeping up with Aramus's volleys.

"They want to kill me," Aramus hissed under his breath, "just like everyone else. Why should I?"

The question wasn't meant for Olórin, or anyone in particular. Aria couldn't be sure, but there was a hint of defeatism in his tone, like he knew that this was all he could expect from life, and it made her heart ache. Aramus fired a deluge of fireballs at the treeline, the muscles in his arms straining with every shot. The fire was coming more easily now, and Olórin wasn't quick enough to catch them all. The ancient wooden soldiers burned and crackled under his attack.

"Wait! The elves have stopped firing," Bernard shouted over the din of explosions.

He was right. For some reason the elves seemed to have ceased their attack, but Aramus was unsatisfied. He continued to blast the treeline, and every time Olórin attempted to thwart his attack.

"Aramus, they have stopped. There is no need for this. Control yourself."

But it was no good. Aria could see that Aramus was losing his battle to the alluring power of the fire. He couldn't take his eyes off the flames as they danced in his hands, it was consuming him. Each time he used his ability he seemed to grow in aptitude too, and the panic in Aria's stomach threatened to make her vomit. Should Aramus continue to ignore Olórin, there was only one course of action he could take to save them all, he would have to kill the winged man where he stood. If that were to happen then all of Naretia, and her brother, would surely be doomed.

Aramus braced himself and held his two arms out wide. Above his head an enormous ball of fire churned and grew.

Bernard eyes widened and he held his axe at the ready as he faced Aramus. Olórin too aimed his staff at the winged man, though it was not as steady as the dwarf's axe.

"Aramus, please don't," Olórin pleaded, his voice uneven.

From all around them, Aria heard the vines begin to move in the trees. The willowy whispers of the elves voices travelled along them, urging the liana to head toward Aramus. It was now or never. Aria had to do something before all was lost. She was the closest to him, and every time Olórin took a step toward Aramus, he was blocked by an arrow bouncing off the rocky path in front of his foot.

Without knowing exactly what she was doing, Aria stepped between Aramus and their invisible rivals. She teetered on the very narrow ridge, her heels suspended over the gorge. The heat of the churning fireball above them, beat down on Aria making it nearly impossible to breathe. The forest became quiet, save for the thundering of the water below. Aramus hesitated, fixing his fiery eyes upon Aria. There was a flicker of recognition, a semblance of Aramus beneath Dantet's curse.

Reaching up, Aria put her bound hands gently on Aramus's powerful chest. She winced against the heat radiating from it, but she did not waiver.

"All is well, Aramus," she said, her voice clear and gentle. "You will not die here today. I won't permit it."

Aramus shot her a dubious look as he breathed tersely behind gritted teeth. His chest leaned into her hands as if to warn her to get out of the way. Aria did not move. She could feel his heart pounding, and saw his arms strain under Dantet's power.

"I believe Olórin is right," she continued. "I believe you can be saved, that you *should* be saved. Despite everything, I have seen a side to you that proves it, and I am sure these elves will too. If your enemy can see this within you, surly there is hope. Please," she said, now sliding her hands up until they cupped his face. Aramus flinched against her touch. "Please, let us help you. Release your anger and trust us, trust Olórin."

Aria's fingers burned from the heat, but she didn't let him go. She slowly stroked his taunt lips with her thumb, and

Aramus closed his eyes in response. He let out a weighted sigh and leaned his mouth gently against her hand.

"I'm so tired," he whispered. "I can't keep fighting against a world that hates me."

Despite the terrible crimes he had committed, Aria felt a kinship toward Aramus then. She knew the pain of hatred, and her heart crushed in her chest at the sound of his weary voice.

"So, let us do the fighting for you," she whispered to him. "You're not alone anymore."

Aramus slowly trailed his gaze over Aria's face, the distinct sheen of tears in his eyes. After a moment longer, he lowered his arms. The fireball above him faltered and spluttered, before extinguishing altogether. Aramus slumped to the ground, exhausted from his efforts, and Aria caught him before he fell and pushed them both off the edge of the ridge.

Olórin lowered his staff and breathed a sigh of relief. He rested his hands on his knees, as though he would collapse, and audibly thanked the Goddess for bringing the queen to them this day.

Chapter 24

"Olórin, look," Bernard said, jabbing him in the ribs with a thick finger.

Olórin lifted his head and felt his breath leave him. The forest had come alive as its vines slithered through the trees. Each one wrapped itself around the waist of an elf and gracefully carried them across the gorge. They stopped a few feet away and hung precariously over the violent waters. The vines danced over the gorge as though a breeze swayed them, but the air was quiet now.

Ten elves, each one with long flowing silver hair, azure lips, and silver eyes, raised their bows and took aim at Aramus. *'How much they look like the Goddess,'* Olórin thought. *'A truly handsome race.'* They were not adorned in armour, but rather in simple clothes. Foraging for ore from the ground was seen as nothing short of rape to the elves. The only metal they used was for their weapons, and that was said to have fallen from the sky as a gift from Edwina herself.

While the women bore the most striking resemblance to the Goddess Edwina, the men had an androgynous beauty about them and Olórin couldn't help but stare. Each elf was different, some pale as the moon, others as tanned as Aramus, but it was the ones whose dark skin contrasted against the brightness of their silver hair, which attracted Olórin the most. As if to announce the equality between the sexes, the slightly pointed ears of both the men and the women were adorned with delicately crafted cuffs of tiny woodland flowers that most in Lothangard would regard as a female accessory.

Olórin heard Aramus take in a sharp breath. Turning toward his young companion, Aramus's face was one of lure and interest as he gazed at the elves. Struggling to his feet, he leaned heavily against Aria. To his knowledge, it was the first time that Aramus had seen an elf. *'Of course, why wouldn't he be attracted to them?'* It seemed that his father's genetics predisposed him to admiring the likeness of Edwina. Olórin wasn't sure if Aria had noticed it too, but her brow furrowed at Aramus's ostensive adoration.

"Why do you come here?" one of the elves asked.

Her vine brought her closer to Olórin, but her eyes, and arrow, were fixed on Aramus.

"We come to speak to your Elders," Olórin replied. "We are not an army, and we mean you no harm."

"But you attack us," a male elf said, joining the first. "Your companion wields the power of Dantet. Were it not for your attempts to stop him from striking us, and the queen's also, our arrows would have been more accurate, and you would have been slain. You say you are not here to harm us, but yet harm has been done to the forest around us. Why should we trust you?"

"Eh, I think ye'll find that it was *you* lot who fired first," Bernard spat. "Whot, did ye expect that we wouldnae fire back? Just lie down and die fer ya, is it? Yev got another thing coming if ye think that's what's going tae happen."

"Do not speak to me of lying down and dying, dwarf," the female said with a deadly tone. The elf's sliver eyes, punctuated with dark pupils, flashed a warning, and Olórin placed a hand on the dwarf's shoulder to tell him to be quiet. "Your people have raped and pillaged this land with your mining. Every night I hear the creatures you enslave, and the lands, cry in pain. Just be grateful that we fired at your Etherium armour, knowing full well that you would not be hurt.

"It was a test, to see how far your aggression would take you. And *you,* dwarf, reacted with anger, foregoing any intelligent thoughts your head might contain. You didn't even try save the queen when we dislodged her boulder with our arrows. You would have seen her killed."

Olórin wondered how the elves knew about Etherium when it had only come to his attention upon his visit to Balbuldor.

He surmised it must be because the elves were widely versed in all things natural and unnatural.

"*You* did that?" Aria almost shrieked. "You would have killed your queen, and all for the sake of a test?"

"We are ruled by none," said the closest elf to the queen. "The water would have lifted you to safety if we had asked it to."

Aria shot the elf a deadly look but said nothing to his denouncement of her title, for which Olórin was grateful. Instead, she occupied herself with trying to shift Aramus's weight on her shoulders, a difficult task with bound hands.

"Aria has shown her bravery when she stood between the winged man and us. She has shown she is capable of caring for her enemy and is, therefore, allowed to proceed through the forest," said the female elf. "Olórin Talfan, you tried to stop this demon from attacking us, despite the fact we were the aggressor. You may also proceed through the forest."

The female elf's vine swung her closer to examine Aramus, and for a long time she just stared into his amber eyes. Pain was very clearly etched across his pale face as he struggled to stay upright.

"You saved the queen, your prisoner," she said, slowly lowering her bow and slinging it onto her shoulder. "Even though you did, I can still see a great darkness within you. You hide something in the deepest places that I cannot see. I am not sure if it is simply a hurt that was caused to you, or if it is something more sinister."

The elf girl paused, and then reached out and roughly pulled the arrow from Aramus's wing. He cried out in pain and collapsed onto the stoney path again. Olórin gasped and started toward Aramus, only to be held in place by the sharp point of an arrow aimed between his eyes.

"What's wrong with you?" Aria shouted at the elf, desperately trying to stem the bleeding with her bound hands. The elf ignored Aria and lifted Aramus's chin to examining his eyes. He stared back at her for as long as he could before his eyes rolled backward his head.

“There is no fire,” she said, satisfied. “His father’s powers are subdued for now. He may continue with Olórin and the queen. However,” she said turning toward the dwarf again. “I cannot allow you through. You show no care for others, nor do you show any redeeming characteristics that I have seen. *You*, dwarf, may not enter.”

“Whot! Yer kicking me outta here cos I didnae save the growler who murdered me brother?” Bernard raged. “Yer a bloody, head-banging, cuddie-loving, oaf-looking, back end of a scrote, if that’s what ye were expecting me tae do? *You* dinnae know me, ye dinnae know any of us. Whot makes *you* the judge, jury, and executioner?”

“Do you hear any arguments?” the elf girl said, gesturing to her silent companions.

“You will have to forgive my friend here,” Olórin interrupted Bernard before he could say the litany of curses that were visibly teetering on the edge of his tongue. “There has been no time at all since his brothers passing, and I fear his emotions have clouded any normal reaction he might have. However, he carries with him an important item, one that I am loath to be separated from. Could you not see it in your heart to be lenient toward his manner, knowing his pain?”

Olórin had hoped that a vote of confidence from another caste of Naretia would sway the elves opinion of Aramus. But it seemed that they had a long seated resentment toward the dwarfs that Olórin knew nothing about, and Bernard wasn’t helping matters with his temper. Today, as with every other day, it seemed their puritanistic views would remain unsullied by outsiders.

“We could not,” replied the male elf. “He will not be harmed, but he shall travel no further either.”

Without warning, Bernard was lifted off his feet by a thick vine and carried back in the direction they had come. The air turned blue with the vile curses coming from his mouth, and time after time, he sliced his way out of the liana with his axe, only to be caught again by another.

“Bernard, wait for us outside of Elwood,” Olórin shouted after him.

“Whot do ye think I am, some kinda lap dog? No, I willnae wait. I will return to Balbuldor and inform the king of Angus’s passing.”

“You will remember your promise?”

“Aye, I’ll remember it all right. I’ll be back here wih’ reinforcements in three days, and if I have tae level the forest tae find ye, I will. Ya hear me elf? I’ll flatten thas place. Stick that in yer pipe and smoke it. Ha!”

Bernard disappeared through the thick trees and Olórin was sure he would cut as many vines as he would curse. It worried him too that the Valefire was carried away with the wilful dwarf. He wondered if Bernard would, indeed, return for them in three days’ time. It worried him more that Bernard might anger the elves by desecrating their sanctum if they were not there to meet him. But fate had seen fit to take this part of his quest out of Olórin’s hands. So, he had no choice but to trust, and fear, that Bernard would be true to his word.

“Come, your friend needs to be healed,” said the girl elf. “We must continue on to the city of Rhidwynn.”

Olórin glanced at Aramus and was alarmed to see that his tanned face was now a deathly shade of grey. Elf arrows were imbued with Edwina’s magic, poison to the young man. Dark veins pulsated down Aramus’s right arm, and as much as Aria tried, she could not stem the flow of black blood. Olórin rushed to his side, but before he could reach him, a vine wrapped itself around his waist and lifted him high into the air.

“No, wait. I must help him,” Olórin said as he came level with the dark skinned elf girl.

No sooner had he said it then Aramus and Aria were separated, and lifted into the air beside him, Aramus dangling limply in his vine.

“My name is Sudia,” the girl said. “I am one of Rhidwynn’s most formidable healers. I have seen these kinds of wounds before in Dark Ones, and can tell you he yet has some time. But not much. We must travel to the city where I can syphon the magic from his wounds. Then, and only then, will he recover.”

“You are sure?” Aria questioned. “It is imperative he does not die.”

It seemed to Olórin that the queen understood the nature of their quest, or perhaps she was just saying all the right things until she could be freed to kill him herself. Either way, it was too early to tell her true intentions.

“I cannot be certain. But, if he only had dark blood inside of him, our arrows would have killed him outright,” she replied. “It is only by his human side that he still lives, and only by his human side that we will cure him. It was his final test.”

With more grace and less haste than Olórin would have cared for, the vines moved through the forest and followed the gorge until it came to a thunderous waterfall. Sudia raised her hand and, without a word, the torrent parted in the middle, like the side-ways mouth of some watery beast. From within the darkened tunnel, more vines reached out their woody tendrils and took hold of the party. Aramus’s body fell limply into the waiting liana before they were all swallowed by the watery maw.

Chapter 25

The sphere-like prisons constructed of interlocking vines didn't feel as though they appreciated being balled up as they writhed beneath Aria's feet. Like a drip of water off a dewy leaf, they dangled precariously in the highest of branches of ancient forest trees. Moving and swaying in the breeze, the disgruntled groans sounded out the tree's objections. The woody spines murmured their secrets to one another as they leaned and bowed to the others conversations under the weight of it all.

To her right, Olórin rested his back against the wall of his small cell. Still wide awake in the depths of the cool night, he watched the silver haired elves glide through the trees in the twilight. They milled in and out of hollows and larger balls of vines, which hugged the very tops of the ancient trees. Although the elves appeared to live in these nests, Aria could not see a single bridge or evidence of any construction whatsoever. Like Olórin's unwavering gaze, she too couldn't help but be mesmerised by their ghostly appearances, disappearing and reappearing through the thick fronds.

To her left, Aramus lay unconscious in his own cage, the vines trying to writhe away from touching him too. She couldn't see his chest move in the dim moonlight, but the sound of his breathing reassured her that he was still alive. Even while so vulnerable, his silhouette was powerful, strong, and, were it not for the circumstance of his heritage, would have made him a champion of the King's Guard. Aria raked her eyes over him, wondering if his life, and *her* life, might have been very different if he didn't resemble his father so much. *'Perhaps if he knew love, even a small amount of it, he might not have been driven to kill my parents? Perhaps there might not be any change at all.'*

Aria shook her head, it did no good to dwell on "what if's" and she knew it. But no matter how hard she tried to think of other things, her curiosity drew her eyes back to Aramus. According to the elf named Sudia, his wing, now heavily bandaged, was healing rapidly, which surprised her. It was strange too that after only a few hours, the small cuts on his face, arm, and shoulder had disappeared. But there were a great many things that had surprised her lately. The first being that she had been brave enough to stand in front of Aramus whilst he was possessed by Dantet's power, not really knowing if she could calm him. The second, and more shocking, was that he *had* actually listened to her. Perhaps it was the touch of another human being that had broken through his rage, or perhaps it was her kind words and belief that he could be saved. *'Maybe that is all he needs, someone to believe in him?'*

Her thoughts were interrupted by Aramus's groaning as he began to stir.

"Aramus, are you all right?" Olórin asked, pushing himself against his cage to get closer to the winged man.

Aramus rolled onto his back and gasped as his weight pressed down on his injured wing. Grasping onto the sides of his cage, Aramus sat up – his arms shaking with the effort and his teeth clenched with pain. He gingerly stretched out his wing a few times within the confines of his prison.

"Sore, but I'm okay," he replied, winching. "Where are we?"

"The elven city of Rhidwynn," Aria replied, twisting her wrists to get some relief from the binds, to no avail.

Aramus leaned forward and examined his surroundings.

"Doesn't look like a city to me."

"That is because they do not harm nature to construct houses or buildings of debate. They live within their environment, or rather their environment provides what they need for them," Olórin said. "It's quite admirable really, but not a way that I would choose to live. These twigs are far too pokey to be called a bed."

Aramus laughed and in that moment Aria thought, despite what he was, he was actually quite handsome. *'I suppose even evil doesn't always have to be ugly.'*

In the silence, they watched the twilight fade, none of them able to sleep as they waited for their fate to be revealed. The silvery light of the moon gave way to suffocating darkness, just before the sun burned a hole in its shroud. It wasn't until the morning haze had all but disappeared, that Sudia returned. In her hand she carried a small bundle of light-blue cloth which, to Aria, appeared to be a dress of some kind.

"The Elders have gathered," she said. "You will leave all weapons and metal constructions of man here if you wish to meet them. This would include your armour, Aria."

Sudia waved her hand in front of Aria's cage. It opened just enough for her to reach in and untie Aria's binds, before handing her the dress and a pair of soft white shoes. Aria let the dress unfurl in her hands. It was long, flowing, and the kind of attire a queen should be used to wearing. But Aria had lived in her armour since her parent's death, always battle ready, and was as unyielding in her preference for armour as the metal itself. Her mouth opened slightly as she looked between the dress, Sudia, and the two men either side of her.

"You expect me to change here, in front of them?" she protested.

"If you wish to remain in the pod, it is your choice. I will be back when you have finished," Sudia said, closing the vines again and gliding away on her woody tendril.

"Never fear, Your Majesty, we shall look away," Olórin said, shuffling around and turning his back to her.

Aria glanced at Aramus. With a grimace at having to move, he too turned his back on her. She hesitated. After having worn her heavy armour for so long, she had almost forgotten what it felt like to wear proper clothes. She thought wearing it now would make her appear less formidable to her enemies, to Aramus. More so, she had never changed in front of anyone before, and the thought sent a nervous flutter through her stomach. But she had no choice and she knew it. Allowing her captors to speak on her behalf to the Elders was out of the question.

"If either of you look, I will slice off that part of you which makes you a man, do you hear?"

"You have nothing to fear," Aramus replied with a small laugh.

Casting wary glances at the two men, Aria quickly removed her armour and slipped the dress on. The fabric fit her snugly and the hem reached just below her knees. The gentle breeze blowing around her bare legs made her self-conscious of the fact that she was now entirely unprotected from both her enemies and roving eyes; her bulky armour had always hidden the slightness of her frame before. After declaring that she was "decent" Olórin and Aramus turned around again.

"My, I must say, you look positively beautiful," Olórin said admiringly, resting his staff to the side. Aria shot him a dubious glance.

Aramus became strangely quiet. He looked Aria up and down without a word, and Aria felt a moisture build up on her palms. She gripped the edges of her skirt to dry them and knelt in her pod, making herself a small as possible, so as to disappear from his gaze.

"He's right, you are beautiful," Aramus said.

He gave her a crooked grin and unhitched the scabbards that hung low on his waist, leaving the swords by his side. Aria felt an unwelcomed heat rise up in her cheeks and was thankful for the sudden reappearance of Sudia. With an airy wave of her hand, all three cages opened and they were once again gliding through the thick forest on vines. They descended to the forest floor where the brush had grown thick. Transferred from one vine to another they glided, untouched by the briars, toward a hollowed out tree.

The outside of the tree was smothered with lichen. It looked like an old man whose beard had cracked down the middle and let a gathering of elves inside. His rooty fingers twisted and turned with age, and poked out above the dark soil.

Inside the gargantuan truck was a chamber twice the size of Aria's throne room. It was filled with a large audience of silver-haired elves, who eyed them suspiciously. Through holes in the ancient bark, five elves were illuminated by the sun's rays. They stood on a raised bit of broken trunk and watched as the three prisoners were brought before them. Three of the elves were old and their hair had turned as white as snow, while one was younger – no more than a year or two older than Aria. The last of them was a small child, about Pearan's age, and Aria was certain that she couldn't truly be an Elder.

"Equality and wisdom knows no age limit," Olórin whispered to her.

His blue eyes twinkled with the acknowledgment of her disbelief. It was only as she looked at him that she realised Olórin and Aramus had been set free from their vines. She, however, remained firmly wrapped in the tendril. Sudia too had been released and melted into the sea of elves surrounding them. Thinking that her vine must be somewhat dim-witted or broken, Aria struggled to free herself.

"Your Majesty," the eldest female elf said, her skin as pale as her snowy hair, but her lips still as blue as the youngest elf. "My name is Mirathall, and I bid you welcome. I am to speak for the Elders, and as such, I must inform you that you are not our prisoner. However, you were the prisoner of Olórin Talfan, a wizard we have come to know over the years. It is not our place to undo what he has seen fit to do until we know the situation better. A hasty hand that moves too quickly can often do more harm than good. I would, therefore, ask you to be patient while we unravel the tale before us."

"But I am your queen," Aria spat, feeling an anger boil inside of her.

"You are *a* queen, yes. But you are also human, and humans are capable of horrendous deeds no matter their station. You are also responsible for the deaths of many innocent lives, and should you have entered Elwood on your own, your fate might not have been so favourable," she replied.

Aria opened her mouth to defend herself, but she knew that, in their eyes, she was the epitome of everything they were born to prevent. The elves would not hear her reasons, so she remained silent.

"Tell me, why is this girl your prisoner?" Mirathall asked Olórin.

"In truth, it was to prevent her from killing Aramus," Olórin replied.

"But from what I've have been told, she saved him as you entered our realm. She calmed his raging heart with her words, and he in turn listened. These do not strike me as the actions of someone wishing to see her enemy dead," Mirathall said. "Do you still wish to kill this young man, Aria?"

Aria hesitated, and mulled over everything she had learned about Aramus.

"I do not know," she answered finally. "He murdered my parents, and I am not sure I can forget that. But as the sovereign ruler of Naretia it is my duty to protect my people. If I am to believe the prophecy, it means I *must* help him instead. These are the sacrifices leaders must make, are they not?"

From the corner of her eye, Aria saw Aramus bow his head slightly as though he was disappointed with her answer. But it was the truth, and the elves acknowledged it with a slight inclination of their heads.

"And you, Aramus, do you wish to harm the queen?"

"No, I do not," Aramus replied, and with a little hesitation added, "My only desire was to earn her forgiveness, but I do not expect it."

Aria studied Aramus's face while the Elders conferred amongst themselves. The alarming greyness of his skin had disappeared, but he was still somewhat paler than before. She was searching for any sign he was genuine in what he had said, that he truly did want forgiveness, but his stoic expression never changed once.

She heard Olórin take a small breath in, and followed the wizard's gaze. It rested upon the youngest of the Elders. The girl had raised her hand over her mouth to whisper into Mirathall's ear and her sleeve had fallen away from her wrist. There, imprinted on the dark skin of her forearm, was the combined symbol of Edwina and Dantet. The birthmark of the sun and the moon shone with the same brilliance as her silvery hair.

"I ask you not to speak of what you know, Olórin," Mirathall said quickly, seeing his shock. "The prophecy you have seen about Aramus was yours to tell, this one is not. But now you understand why Thalia is an Elder. She is the living embodiment of equality, even amongst the Gods."

Olórin opened his mouth as if he was about to say something, but then closed it again and scratched his beard before becoming resolutely silent on the matter. Aria was a bit lost in the conversation. *'What is so special about this little girl?'* Aramus too looked bewildered.

"Thalia has come up with a solution for our little predicament," Mirathall said, gently stroking the girl's hair. The young girl called Thalia smiled sweetly and returned to her original place. "She believes, and I am inclined to agree, that the conflict between you two could be resolved with the simple matter of understanding one another better." Mirathal reached behind her and producing two thick, gold chains from a battered looking chest. "These will allow you to feel the other's heartache, joy, sorrow, and anger. Through the binding of your feelings, a deeper understanding can be achieved, and perhaps, even forgiveness too."

Mirathall walked toward Aria and Aramus, carrying the heavy looking chains, one in each hand. Her silver eyes rested on Aria first.

"We do not wish to imprison you. Whilst you wear these, you will be free to roam and make your own decisions. If you should not wear them, then I'm afraid that we will be left with little choice but to keep you in your cage. What say you, Aria?"

Aria wasn't sure she wanted Aramus to know how she felt about anything, but the thought of knowing more about him was too tempting. She wondered if someone without a soul, or half a soul, could feel anything at all. If he could not, then she feared that Olórin's plan would not work, and it was imperative that she find out.

"Fine," she replied.

Mirathall gently placed the chain around Aria's neck, securing it at the back. It was cold and weighed more then it looked like it should. The Elder then turned to Aramus.

"And what say you?"

Aramus simply nodded, but Aria could see his jaw muscles tense and relax repeatedly, like he was already trying to suppress his feelings. No sooner had the clasp snapped shut on Aramus's chain, then Aria felt it tighten around her neck. The vines around her waist retreated into the forest outside, but she was too preoccupied by the choking feeling to notice.

"It's too tight," she said, grasping at the metal trying to loosen it.

Aramus mirrored her actions and tugged at his own chains.

"They will loosen when you come to understand one another more. Eventually they will become so loose that you will be able to remove them entirely. But truly knowing the one you are linked to, will render the magic moot and they will simply fall from your necks. Until then, your hatred, your animosity, will only make matters worse," Mirathall said, returning to the other Elders. "It is a physical representation of the pain you cause one another."

Aria felt like she had been deceived into wearing it. Had she known it might choke her to death she probably wouldn't have agreed so easily. Her anger boiled inside of her, but it was Aramus who erupted.

"How *dare* you," he raged. "You have no right to treat me like this."

Aria was slightly taken aback by his reaction, as was Olórin, who stared at him with an open mouth. Aramus looked just as horrified.

"Sorry, I don't know why I said that," he said, pulling at the gold metal.

"*You* did not," Mirathall said, nodding in Aria's direction.

Aria felt the unwelcomed heat in her cheeks return. It was only made worse by the sight of Aramus's cheeks flushing too. *'For the love of... get a grip of yourself, Aria.'*

"You're quite an angry lady, aren't you?" Aramus said with a handsome grin.

"Shut up," she replied.

Secretly she was glad he was teasing her about her anger and not her embarrassment. The chains loosened of their own accord, but only enough to allow them to breathe more easily. Aria knew it had more to do with Aramus's understanding of her anger rather than the other way around.

"And now we come to the important matter at hand, the reason you have entered our realm," Mirathall said, looking expectantly at Olórin.

The old wizard regaled the story of his prophecy to Mirathall and the Elders. He told them how Aramus came to be, and the vision of the fiery carnage he saw in Darzithal with the Goddess Edwina. The elves whispered amongst themselves in an ever increasing crescendo when they heard what the Goddess had said. Concern was clearly etched across their delicate faces, and their silver eyebrows collectively furrowed; Sudia's being the most creased of all.

"The Goddess has sent me to find the sacred objects she left across Naretia to protect her children," Olórin said, over the whispers. "With these I hope to create a powerful potion that will syphon the darkness from Aramus and break the hold his father has over him."

For a moment Aria felt a nervous flutter in her stomach, but it only lasted for a fraction of time. She wasn't sure if it came from her, or Aramus. But the young man's expression was stony when she glanced over. Mirathall raised her hands to quieten the alarmed undertones echoing in the hollowed tree.

"Although I can guess what you have come for, because the Goddess has only left the elves with only one treasure, I must still ask you to name what it is you seek from us," she said quietly.

"The Geminum," Olórin replied.

The whispering rose inside the hollowed tree again, like a wave threatening to crash on a rocky shoreline. Mirathall raised her hands to calm them once more.

"What is the Geminum?" Aria asked Aramus quietly, who shrugged his shoulders.

“The Geminum, Aria, is all that is left of Edwina’s two children,” Mirathall replied. “It is the corporeal remains of what once housed their beings. The twin stars. Like all things that are balanced by the Goddess, one was a child of light, like Edwina, while the other was a child of darkness, like Dantet. But both were innocent children.

“When he killed them, everything that had truly made them exist was removed, leaving only a hungry vacuum that we use to contain the threats to our world. What was once Amor, the child of light, seeks out essences like herself, while Vesta consumes only the darker ones. Together they have aided us in ridding the world of great evils which should never have come to be.

“I see the same struggle of light and dark within you, Aramus, as I see within the Geminum itself. But such struggles were never meant to happen in mortal bodies, and I share Olórin’s concerns. The Geminum is a hallowed artefact that has not left the hands of elves since the dawn of our time. However, if Edwina has truly commanded you to seek out these treasures, Olórin, then I cannot see how we can refuse her request.”

Mirathall turned to the congregation of elves around them.

“If you object, make yourselves known now,” she said to the gathering.

The silence was only interrupted by the echoes of bird songs in the hollow tree. That was, until Sudia stepped forward.

“Visions, as we all know, are not set in stone,” she said, addressing the Elders. “If they were, then to set out on this journey would be a futile attempt to change that which we cannot. But we also cannot know for sure the outcome of this quest. So, to entrust such a powerful talisman to non-elves, to creatures who care little for the rights and wrongs of this world, would be unwise. I suggest that a voice of reason and balance accompany them on their journey, ensuring that man’s greed, his selfishness, does not corrupt the intentions behind their endeavour.”

Aria again felt the nervous flutter in her stomach and when she looked over at Aramus, she knew that it was clearly coming from him. His eyes followed Sudia as she paced, like she held him in a magical trance. His gaze only wavered when the elf looked directly at him. *'Perhaps he is nervous because of her?'* Aria thought. *'But why would he be?'* It hit her then. Sudia was beautiful, strong, and carried herself with a dignified grace that even Aria thought was attractive. Aramus was clearly enamoured with her, and this realisation set a weighty stone in Aria's stomach. She didn't know why, but the thought of the two of them together wasn't an idea she liked.

As though he could read her thoughts, Aramus suddenly looked over at her, the beginnings of a smirk edging across his face. Fighting a flush that threatened to spread across her cheeks, Aria squashed any emotions she felt into a deep, dark place inside that even *she* thought would never be found again.

After conferring with the Elders in hushed whispers, Mirathall turned to Sudia.

"Agreed. You have always been steadfast in our views and are a welcomed voice of reason. As someone I have known since your first breath, I would ask that you to accompany them, Sudia," Mirathall said. Sudia agreed with a small incline of her head. "You must know such a precious gift is not kept in the open, Olórin. Tonight, we hold the Awakening Ceremony, where all the living creatures that have slept through the cold and the darkness, find their way into the light again. For this, we will need to uncover the Geminum, and then you will have your final ingredient."

Chapter 26

Olórin couldn't help but think about recent events as they sat in a small hollow mid-way up an ancient tree. It was Sudia's home, but for now, it was also theirs. He had never liked heights, but not wanting to appear to be an ungrateful guest, he said nothing. Instead, he kept his back firmly against the farthest wall away from the small opening which, if stepped through without a vine, would see him plummet to the forest floor and to his death.

The hollow was warm and dry. This made it easier for Olórin to forget how high up they were, unlike the cages they had first occupied. As much as he had tried to sleep on the first night, he couldn't, the moving of the vines and the swaying of the pod was all too much for his nerves. And so, he spent the long hours watching elves mill about, trying to imagine that they were on solid ground, to no avail.

After the decision of the Elders, all their weapons were moved into Sudia's home. Olórin had felt quite naked, and weaker, without the newly imbued staff. Being creatures of balance, Edwina's gift had drawn a few disapproving looks from the elves, and Olórin decided it was best to keep it within the safety of his hat, for now. Aramus, on the other hand, had strapped his silver sword around his waist again and returned the golden one to Aria. Olórin wasn't sure that it was such a good idea, but he kept his objections to himself.

Aramus had also removed the bandage from around his right wing, his wound now almost completely healed save for a few missing feathers. He sat on the floor with his back against the wall to Olórin's right, while Aria, forgoing her usual weighty armour in lieu of the blue dress, occupied a small bed to his left. It was a time of quiet contemplation in the treetop home, while they awaited for Sudia to return with some food.

"Olórin, what do you know of that young girl, Thalia?" Aria asked.

Olórin had been waiting for her to ask this question for some time. The truth was he knew very little about her, other than what he heard in the wizard's towers of Lothangard. But if anyone deserved to know that small nugget of information, it was Aria.

"Mirathall has asked me not to speak of it," he replied, twiddling a small bit of moss between his fingers.

"But she has something to do with the quest, doesn't she? I mean, how could she not? She bears the mark of Edwina *and* Dantet," Aria said.

"Although her mark may not be as obvious as Aramus's affliction, bearing such a symbol would leave Thalia open to the prejudices of others, as it did with Aramus," he said. "I am not sure that I would want her to suffer as he did, and by telling people of *her* prophecy, I cannot imagine it would do anything but."

Olórin saw Aramus furrow his brow as he spoke, and Aria instinctively looked toward him. Although the young man was hard to read, Aria's expression was clear as his sadness turned the corners of her mouth downward. Finally getting a glimpse into Aramus's soul, even if it was only through the queen, Olórin was despondent to know his miserable life truly *had* affected him.

"All I can tell you, is that it is a very good thing she is here," Olórin said. "Whether we succeed or fail, Thalia will be a catalyst that will see your brother on the throne."

"This prophecy is about Pearan?" Aria almost shouted, hopping off the small bed to take a step toward Olórin.

Aramus's interest seemed to have been piqued too.

"I didn't know you had a brother," he said.

"You *have* to tell me about this prophecy," Aria demanded, ignoring Aramus. "I have a right to know. Is Pearan in danger?"

"No, he is not," Olórin replied. "At least no more so than the rest of us. But you have to remember that I am not the only one who can have visions. The prophecy about Thalia was from one of the elves own seers. I cannot tell you what they saw, and I doubt that they will be persuaded to tell you either. All I know is her fate is intrinsically linked to Pearan's, and to Naretia's too. But that prophecy is more fluid, changing, than Aramus's. For now, the only danger I foresee for your brother, is if we should fail."

Olórin watched as Aria paced the small hollow, running one hand through her curly red hair and clenching the other so tightly that her knuckles turned white. Aramus seemed to pick up on her agitation and shifted uncomfortably where he sat.

"Why, why does fate have to bring my brother into this?" she fumed. "It can have me all it likes, but not my brother."

"We are *all* brought into this," Olórin replied. "Whether fate sees us live or die, the events that take place, which we help to take place, will affect us all. But prophecies are not set in stone. Should we succeed, then I hope Thalia and Pearan's path might be very different. In fact, I should think that they would never meet at all."

Aria plopped herself back down on the small bed with a long sigh.

"You truly love your brother, don't you?" Aramus asked her.

"I would die for him," she replied without hesitation.

Aramus smiled, and this seemed to irritate Aria.

"Why are you smiling?" she snapped.

The young man's smile faded and he fixed his eyes on his boots.

"It's nice to see, that's all," he replied.

Aria didn't look convinced. She studied Aramus, her eyebrows knitting together so fiercely Olórin thought she might stay that way forever, but she said nothing. She didn't say anything when Sudia returned on a vine and glided gracefully into the hollow, either. Her furrow only deepened when Aramus's eyes couldn't help but follow the elf around the small room.

"Some food," Sudia said, placing a small leaf of nuts and berries on each of their laps.

"Good thing Bernard isn't here," Olórin said, attempting to lighten the mood. "I've never known a dwarf to be content if there wasn't a copious amount of roasted meat and ale at a meal."

*

The Awakening Ceremony was more beautiful than Aria could have imagined. The hollowed, old-man tree had been decorated with flowers Aria had not seen for many months. Fireflies drawn to the elves, twinkled around their heads, like stars in the night. They wore circlets of reeds, ivy, and moss, and each elf was dressed in white robes to mark the purity of spring. It was a time when plants and creatures were too young to bear the weight of sin, and was the elves most cherished season. Only Olórin, in his purple robes, Aramus, in his brown leather, and Aria, in her blue dress, sullied the sea of white and silver.

The large pedestal where the Elders had once stood, was now covered with all the culinary delights that the forest could offer, save for anything that had once breathed. But Aria didn't feel much like partaking in the celebration, despite her marvellous surroundings. While haunting music played and elves danced in flowing movements, Aria's mind rehashed what she had learned about her brother.

Prophecies were dangerous things. They so often led to misinterpretation, or only served to paint a target on one's back, as they had done to Aramus. It was a cloud she did not want hanging over Pearan's head. Although Aria hoped to see her brother take the throne and succeed her one day, she couldn't help but worry about how this would come to be. Olórin's words discomforted her. *'Should we succeed then I hope that Thalia and Pearan's path might be very different,'* he had said. This told her two things. The first, that Aramus's prophecy was linked to Pearan's, and secondly, that if she should fail, Pearan will have to take the throne. Which means she would either be jailed for her crimes, or dead. *'He's too young,'* Aria thought, absentmindedly examining the hilt of her golden sword as she sat on a large log. *'If for no other reason than for his wellbeing, I have to make sure that this prophecy about Aramus is stopped.'*

Something else bothered her too. When Aramus had asked if she truly loved her brother, there was a hint of something that she couldn't quite put her finger on. There was a certain excited thrill in her stomach that she was sure did not come from her. But the more she thought on it, the less she could find a reason for the strange feeling. After all, what was so important about the fact that she loved her brother?

"I hope you intend to spend more time with your hosts than with your sword," Olórin said, sitting down beside her.

Olórin took off his hat and rummaged around inside for a while, before producing a tankard filled with ale. Keeping the drink hidden within his hat, and looking sheepishly around him, he took a long sip before offering some to Aria. She shook her head and continued to examine the hilt of the sword she knew only too well.

"Am I going to die?" she asked him quietly.

"We are all eventually going to die," Olórin replied, hiding the ale in his hat once again and plopping it back on his head. "I am two hundred and ninety-eight, but if you had asked me in my youth how long I thought I would live, I might have said sixty. There have been many prophecies told about the wizards, and about my death, that would curl the hairs on your chest. But yet here I am. And if I were to have spent my life worrying about what *might* be, well then, I wouldn't have lived at all. However much time we are given in this world, it is important to spend it wisely and not allow our fears, our hatred, or our prejudices, to stop us from enjoying what we have been given. *That* is the true measure of living."

Olórin placed a gentle hand on Aria's shoulder and she didn't shrug him off. He was right, and she knew it. Although Edwel had all but told her the very same thing, she had been too angry and impatient to hear it at the time. This thought only raised another question.

"Can I ask you something?" Aria said, looking Olórin in his eyes. "If wizards can't kill, how then did you kill Edwel?"

"Ah, I am not in league with Dantet, if that's what you mean to ask me," he replied. "In order to be killed you must first be truly alive. Edwel, although he had a longing to know what it was to live, was nothing more than a conjuring. He was a collection of stones brought together to carry out orders given to him thousands of years ago. He did not fear his own death as all living creatures should, how could he when he was never born? I merely disassembled him, undid the spell that created him in the first place, as I would undo a jinx or a curse."

"He was neither a jinx nor a curse," Aria snapped. "He was the only one to stand by me when no one else would."

"As he was created to do," Olórin said softly.

Aria felt a sudden nonsensical wave of happiness and she tugged at the chain around her neck, wanting Aramus to feel her irritation. Glancing over at him, she saw him dancing with Sudia. The two of them moved elegantly in the centre of the hollow as if they had danced together for a lifetime. His handsome smile mirrored her pretty one as they held hands, dipping and twirling in time with the other dancers. His strong arms guided the elf girl and held her closely. Even with his wings, Aria knew he was a handsome man. She furrowed her brow and wondered what made Sudia so special. *'She's just a girl, same as me. Looking like the Goddess Edwina is no excuse for him to be so doe-eyed.'*

At that moment Aramus seemed to sense her irritation, and their eyes met. Aria felt a heat rise up in her cheeks, but she couldn't look away – to do so would be to admit something she daren't. He smiled at her over Sudia's shoulder, and Aria felt a giggle want to break free from her mouth. *'What is the matter with you?'* She hardly knew, but the more she watched Aramus and Sudia dance, the more she couldn't look away from him.

"Can you believe that he only learned to dance recently, and was taught by a seventy-year-old dwarf too?" Olórin said. Aria didn't respond, her eyes followed Aramus as he glided around the elves. "Come, it is time for you and I to dance," Olórin said, taking her by the hand.

"No, I don't want to. Wizard, let me go."

The warning tone in her voice did nothing to deter the old wizard. Despite her objections, she found herself amidst the elegant dancers, attempting to salvage some dignity whilst Olórin wobbled and twirled with elbows and knees akimbo. They weren't a sophisticated pair, or at least Olórin wasn't, and her attempts to contain his flamboyant gambolling was met with a daft smile. It was as if he was trying to embarrass her on purpose, and Aria couldn't walk away no matter how hard she tried. Every time she did, he would frolic around the dancefloor and block her exit.

Without warning, a firm hand grasped Aria around her wrist and twirled her away from the eccentric old man. Aramus pulled her in close to his chest and wrapped his other arm around her waist. Aria, momentarily stymied, swayed gently with the winged man as the music slowed. She rested her free hand on his chest as if to push him away, but her hand refused to obey. So close to his face now, she had no option but to stare into his amber eyes.

"You looked like you needed rescuing," he said with a small smile.

"I…" Aria had lost her words and had no idea where they had gone.

Aramus eyes examined her face and she saw his smile fade. His head bow just a fraction, and he swallowed deeply.

"It's okay if you don't want to dance with me," he said. "I'll understand."

Aria felt a sudden tug at her insides as though a sadness was weighing her down. But *she* wasn't sad. In fact, she was more nervous than she thought she ought to be.

"No, I want to dance with you," she heard herself say.

A slow smile spread across Aramus's handsome face again and Aria's heart did a flip before coming to a screeching halt. *'Oh Goddess,'* she thought in disbelief. *'I have feelings for him. No this can't be right, can it?'* The chains around their necks loosened.

*

Olórin found the edge of the dancefloor and did one last twirl before stepping off. He watched Aramus and Aria dance together, and admired his handiwork with a large amount of pride swelling his chest. *'I knew there was a reason their paths had crossed.'* Taking another sly sip from the contraband in his hat, Olórin sighed with contentment. Aria had been the only girl who had not feared Aramus, the only one to have ever spoken to him in a kindly manner, or as kindly as she could have manage. Although he couldn't be certain, he was hopeful that she was also Aramus's chance for true love. His only wish for them now was that they would have enough time to realise this before it was too late. *'Love can be so stupid and slow sometimes.'*

Despite the young man's fixation with Sudia, Olórin knew his lust would only ever end in obsession, not love. Being the son of Dantet, the elf would never love him in return, nor would her puritan community have allowed it either. No, it was definitely best to steer Aramus in the right direction, toward the queen. Even if that meant making a fool of himself on the dancefloor so that Aramus would feel compelled to rescue her from his floundering.

For the rest of the evening Olórin watched as Aramus and Aria glided in each other's arms. She laughed as he dipped her unexpectedly, and Olórin had never seen the young man so happy in all of the time he knew him. Their eyes only left each other's when the solemn, warm tone of a hollowed horn brought everything to a halt. The music stopped, and everyone turned to face the matriarchal elf, Mirathall. Even the bats, that had been clicking high above their heads in the old wooden tree, became oddly silent.

"My family," she said, raising her hand. "It is time for the awakening."

Without needing another word, the elves cleared the dancefloor and formed a circle. Olórin was ushered forward by random hands that disappeared when he looked. He soon found himself at the edge of the circle beside Aria.

"Where's Aramus?" he asked her.

"Gone to get a drink," she replied with a flush in her cheeks and a coy smile.

Olórin looked over the sea of silvery hair and saw Aramus's black wings hovering next to the food. Sudia stood beside him, and Olórin couldn't help but feel slightly annoyed he was still staring at the elf despite his obvious connection to Aria. But he was grateful that the queen wasn't tall enough to see Aramus over the crowd.

"The time of dying is now over," Mirathall began, drawing Olórin's attention back as she paced around the inner circle. "Soon the abundance of life will break free from its icy grip, and once again the world will be filled with colour and the coming of new souls. So too will our time of rest come to an end, as we see that this new life is balanced."

Mirathall chose five elves, some of them young, some of them old, to stand in the centre of the circle. Each of the elves joined hands and began to chant a haunting lyric that reverberated within the old wood of the tree. Olórin felt strangely peaceful when they did, as though he was once again standing in Darzithal.

"It is our duty to see that the world Edwina created does not do itself harm," Mirathall continued. "With Vesta's endurance we syphon the darkness from those who would destroy the kingdom, and with Amor we draw off the light which would blind us. Buried for so long in a place that even we cannot find, we ask that the light and the darkness come forth from the soil, and grant us the ability to safeguard this world."

The chanting crescendoed as the entire elf community joined in the chorus. Beneath his feet, Olórin felt the ground rumble and move as the inner circle of five elves lowered their hands to the mossy surface. The soil in the centre of their circle began to bubble as though a moleman was making its way up. Without warning, the mound of dirt burst open and a crystalline object shot out of the ground. Two glassy spheres, each the size of an ogre's fist, joined together at the centre, sparkled in the night like a star. One side of the object was brilliant and white, like Olórin's staff, while the other was smoky and black. The Geminum hovered in the air for a moment, before gliding gently into Mirathall's outreached hands. The Elder elf gazed into the brilliance she held, as though it were a new born child.

"This season, however," Mirathall said, turning to Olórin, "the Goddess asks us to give our most sacred possession to a wizard who says he is to save the kingdom. We trust in our Goddess, that she knows more than our mortal minds could fathom. We are, therefore, compelled to obey."

Mirathall walked toward Olórin and presented him with the Geminum. Olórin could feel hundreds of silver eyes watching his every move. Fearing that the crystal would shatter the moment he touched it, Olórin took hold of it gingerly. It felt both cold and hot to the touch, but it didn't burn. Mesmerised by the swirling light and darkness within the crystal, which never crossed into the others sphere, Olórin wasn't quite sure how long he stood there holding what was left of his precious Goddess's children. There was a certain morbidity to the whole ordeal, and Olórin couldn't help but feel like he had perpetrated some kind of crime just by being there.

"Take with you one warning, old friend," Mirathall said. "If the Geminum should shatter, then the world would fall to chaos. If it should find its way into Dantet's hands, then he would surely snuff out all of the light, and we would be lost to the darkness. Protect it and return it quickly, because time is not a friend of the equipoise our world has obtained."

"I will guard it as though my life depended on it," Olórin replied, placing the crystal into his wizard hat where it disappeared from sight.

"Good, because your life, and the lives of everyone in the kingdom, may very well depend on it," Mirathall warned.

At that very instant, the hollowed tree was filled with a terrifying shriek which echoed and reverberated against the ancient wood. All eyes turned and faced the direction it came from, and Olórin's heart beat ferociously in his chest when he realised what he was seeing.

Sudia was grabbing her head between her hands as if it would explode. She doubled over in agony as her hair began to turn black and dark veins ran the length of her body, turning her skin a sickly grey colour. Large talons erupted from her fingernails, and her slightly pointed ears now protruded grotesquely from her head. Sudia screamed again and it filled Olórin with a primal terror. Her cries bore only a slight resemblance to her former voice, as the deep, foreboding sounds of a Dark One took over.

Chapter 27

Chaos erupted and within minutes, a legion of elves with drawn bows, surrounded Sudia. As the closest person to the turning elf, Aramus had drawn his weapon too and readied himself for an attack. With little warning she spread her claws wide and took a swipe at Aramus, catching him across his face as he ducked. Olórin saw black blood pour from the cut on his cheek as he backed away from the shifting, writhing form of Sudia. Whatever motivated her in the midst of the agonising, bloating of muscles and bones, it seemed to have focused all of her viciousness on Aramus as she swung at him time, and time again. The young man ducked and dived away from her attacks, only barely avoiding the talons that came for his neck. Forearm length claws ricocheted off his sword, but they did not break against the sharpened metal.

Panicked, Olórin rummaged through his hat and produced his staff, but there were too many elves in the way to take aim. He only occasionally caught glimpses of the battle between the silvery heads that stood in front of him.

"Out of my way," he heard Aria shout.

Beside him he watched the young queen, now armed with her golden sword, try to push past the elves. But they refused to move, and both he and Aria were kept out of reach at the point of many arrows.

"This is not your concern," one of them hissed at her. "She is an elf and will be dealt with by elves only."

"Well, what are you waiting for then? Kill her," Aria screamed, panic and concern clearly audible in her voice as it reached pitches Olórin had never heard before.

Not a single arrow was let fly as Sudia and Aramus fought. A wide swing of his sword clipped Sudia's right ear and Olórin was horrified to see part of it now missing. Grey blood ran down the side of her deforming face, bleeding into the white linen clothes that stretched across her bulging form. Through the row of newly protruded sharp teeth, she howled with pain and cupped her ear with her hand.

"Mirathall, please," Olórin said to the Elder, who was contently observing the fight beside him. "Whatever it is you need to do, please do it quickly before she hurts Aramus."

"We must see if she is capable of reasonable thought," Mirathall replied, keeping her eyes fixed on the battle. "If her mind is still intact, then there is a chance we can save her. But if she should turn and fight her own people, despite being out numbered, then she is without reason and is lost to us. At that time, and only then, she will be killed. As of yet she seems to be only attacking Aramus. Perhaps there is a reason behind her actions?"

Panic rose up in Olórin's chest as he watched Sudia's powerful arm strike Aramus across his head, sending him careening into the ancient tree. Aramus tried to stand up again, but his legs went from under him and he crumpled to the floor.

"The only *reason* she's attacking him is because she must be under the influence of Dantet," Olórin shouted at Mirathall. It was the first time in nearly two hundred years that he had raised his voice to the point where it hurt his throat, and Mirathall seemed taken aback by it. "His father wants him dead and she is merely following his orders. I will *not* allow you to risk his life for a hypothesis."

Olórin's voice must have been louder than he thought because the nearest elves all turned to face him, as did their arrows. The fear he felt for his young friend, and the anger at the elves moronic need to weigh everything until all that remained was a neat bundle of black and white, saw him raise his staff and forcibly part the sea of elves in front of him. The elves didn't like to be defied and arrows zipped through the air in his direction. Olórin misdirected them all with a wave of his staff. Silver-haired warriors came after him and Aria with swords drawn, but they too found themselves sailing through the air in the same direction as the arrows.

“Do not harm her,” Olórin called after Aria as she charged through the parted elves.

Sudia, by now, had Aramus’s neck in her broad hand, pinning him against the tree and was choking the life from him. With his weapon knocked from his hands, the young man grappled at her powerful grip to free himself, to no avail. Not even the vigorous flapping of his powerful wings could loosen her hold.

Olórin could see his face turning an alarming shade of purple, but was unable to help him as his concentration, and staff, held in place the elves who ventured forward to stop Aria from interrupting the battle. Aria raised the hilt of her sword and hit the back of Sudia’s leg. Sudia’s knee buckled and came crashing to the ground. With another severe blow from the butt of Aria’s sword across Sudia’s startled face, she cried out and released Aramus from her grip.

Aramus fell to the ground and arched his back as he gasped for air, holding his neck. Aria rushed to his side while keeping her sword trained on Sudia. The monster that had once been their escort, lunged at them: Her teeth were gritted and her talons poised to strike. But before she could reach them, Olórin pointed his staff at her and power surged through his body as the full force of the magic Edwina had bestowed upon it, met with the enraged orc. Sudia stopped, motionless, speechless, her neck only a few inches from the tip of Aria’s sword.

“You have no right to interfere with elf matters,” Mirathall hissed at Olórin as she joined him at the edge of the circle.

“And you have no right to be so flippant with another’s life,” Olórin replied, keeping Sudia firmly stuck in her place.

It was an age-old argument that had raged between the wizards and the elves, one that Olórin knew would not resolve itself today. The wizards despised the emotionless judgment of the elves that saw them take a life when it suited their reasoning. The elves, in turn, thought the wizards weak and lacking in true devotion for the Goddess by allowing an unbalance to thrive.

Mirathall’s silver eyes rested on Olórin and he could see the fury behind them. If it wasn’t for Thalia pulling gently at her white robes to whisper into her ear, Olórin was sure that her anger would have burnt a whole into his skull, if it could. He was thankful that the Goddess Edwina had seen fit to not given them that ability too.

With Aria's help, Aramus stood again, and Olórin breathed a sigh of relief. Dark bruises wrapped themselves around the young man's throat, but he was alive and recovering quickly enough to walk under his own steam after a few moments. Taking wary glances at the frozen orc who continued to stare at him with the promise of vengeance, Aramus made his way toward Olórin.

"Aramus," Mirathall said, as the little girl skipped away behind the taller elves again. "Tell me what has happened here?"

"I don't know," he replied, his voice strained and gruff as he rubbed his neck. "One minute I was handing her a drink, and the next… well, you saw."

"But I did not," she said, narrowing her silver eyes. "In fact, no one saw. When the Geminum came to us I'd wager that everyone's eyes were on it, and not on you. Therefore you are the only one who could know how this happened. But the timing of it all makes me wonder if it was coincidences, or convenience, which saw it happened when it did."

"I don't like what you are implying, Mirathall," Olórin said, struggling to keep the beast that was once Sudia in place as she tried to break free from his restraints and come at Aramus again.

"There is no implication here, merely questions that need answering. And, so far, I am not satisfied that I have heard the truth."

"I've told you already, I really don't know what happened," Aramus said, raising his hands defensively.

"Look!" one of the elves standing behind Olórin shouted, pointing at Aramus's hand.

There, on the tip of his first finger, was a cut that couldn't have been caused by his battle, or by Sudia's large claws. It was too small for that, and, although it was mostly healed, the dried black blood was still a visible incrimination.

"You have poisoned her on purpose. That is why she was attacking only you," Mirathall hissed, grabbing a bow from the nearest elf and aiming an arrow at Aramus's head.

"No, no, I didn't. I don't remember cutting myself. I swear. Perhaps some of my blood got into the drink when I handed it to her, but if it did, it was an accident."

Aramus backed away as the elven community took aim at him. Aria stepped between Mirathall and Aramus, her sword drawn and a determined look upon her face.

"I have more cause to mistrust Aramus than any of you. I should be the last person in Naretia to come to his defence, but I do believe him. I can feel his fear, and I believe that he is telling the truth," she said, lifting the chain around her neck. "As devastating as it might be for Sudia, he did not turn her on purpose."

Olórin knew only too well that fear was not an omission of guilt. The truth was that even *he* wasn't convinced of Aramus's innocence, and was not able to speak in his defence, unlike Aria. But the young queen's protection might have had more to do with her fears for her brother, or perhaps some underlining affections she may have for Aramus, rather than the truth. Either way, Mirathall was right about something. The coming of the Geminum was indeed a convenient time for underhanded deeds to take place.

Slowly Mirathall lowered her bow and the elves behind her followed suit.

"Though I do not entirely believe you, Aramus, Thalia has once again shown wisdom beyond her years. As she has said, there are too many powers at play to know the real truth of it all. Therefore, we must do what is least likely to bring about the prophecy and to cause harm to the people of Naretia," Mirathall said, gesturing for the elves behind her to take Sudia before turning to Olórin. "It would be a long and complicated matter for me to cure an elf who had accidentally consumed meat. But with the potency of Aramus's dark blood, this is no ordinary turning. I fear it is beyond my abilities, and I would ask that we put aside our differences for now, so that you might help me cleanse Sudia of this infection."

The elves secured Sudia with countless vines and Olórin released her from his spell. Once again the quietness of the forest was shattered with Sudia's monstrous screams as she writhed against her restraints.

"I will do everything within my power," Olórin replied.

Before following Mirathall out of the hollow, Olórin turned to Aramus and Aria. He grabbed the young man's hand roughly and pulled it closer to his face. The cut on his finger was almost healed, but even still, it looked like a clean cut as though it had been made with a sharp blade.

"You are sure you had nothing to do with this?" Olórin demanded of him in a low voice so that Mirathall wouldn't hear.

Aramus snatched back his hand and stared at Olórin for a long time. His lips pursed into a thin line and his eyebrows furrowed. The moonlight, which found its way into the elves meeting place, illuminated the look of betrayal in his amber eyes, so much so, that Olórin couldn't have missed it. Neither could he have missed the fact that his chest rose and fell tersely with the offence of his words.

"You don't believe me?" he said quietly. "I knew you would think me a monster when you heard of my crimes in Lothangard. Now you can see why I didn't want to tell you. I am guilty by the mere fact that I am me, aren't I?"

"That's not what I meant, Aramus."

"It is very clear what you meant," Aramus said, walking to the back of the now empty hollow and turning his back on Aria and Olórin. "Go, just go and leave me be, wizard."

"Aramus," Aria said, reaching a sympathetic hand out to him.

"No, just leave me here. The elves won't want me around Sudia in any event, not after this. Just go and help her. I'll be fine."

Aria ignored Aramus and placed a gentle hand on his shoulder.

"Please, Aria," he said, resting his hand upon hers for a moment. Aramus's tone softened a little when he said her name and he let out a long sigh. "They may yet turn on Olórin if he can't heal her. I can fly away at any time, but the old man might need your sword. Go with him."

After a slight hesitation, Aria nodded and reluctantly slid her hand away from Aramus's shoulder. Olórin felt the weight of guilt in his chest as he left the hollow with Aria. *'Am I wrong to suspect him? Would I have blindly believed him if I hadn't known about the murders he committed in Lothangard?'* There was no way to know for sure. But despite the disappointment or hurt Aramus felt toward him for his doubts, the young man had still cared enough to make sure that Aria was there to protect him.

The vines brought them to a large cave just outside the city of Rhidwynn. Within the cavern was all manner of herbs, potions, and healing tools, resting on makeshift shelves. Enormous barrels filled with well-cared-for poisonous snakes, leaches, and vernaks (a small creature whose bite contained a powerful tranquiliser), lined the walls. An acrid smell overwhelmed Olórin's nose as he entered, but his nose was soon distracted by what his eyes saw.

In the centre of the cave, illuminated by oil fires on six stone pedestals, four metal spikes protruded from the stone floor. Secured into the thick metal hoop on top was a chain and manacle. This was where Sudia was tied, and she didn't appear to be pleased about it; her screams echoed loudly in the small cave.

Olórin hung behind the elves as they began their healing rituals, content to only be an onlooker until he was called for. Five elves sat around the orc, including Mirathall, holding hands and singing a tune that raised the hairs on the back of Olórin's neck. The language they used was not elvish, nor was it any other language that the old wizard knew how to speak, but he recognised the tune instantly. It was Dantet's song. A melody that lured darkness toward the singer, and the sound of it turned Olórin's blood cold.

For hours they sang dark words. Sudia writhed as the lyrics hit her misshapen ears, and her powerful arms tugged against the chains that held her to the ground. Her black eyes scanned the room and found Olórin's shining staff. She hissed and spat at the staff, and when that didn't work, her long, black tongue shot out of her mouth trying to reach it.

Olórin was transfixed on the scene. He couldn't take his eyes off the darkness that was spreading into the whites of her eyes, the pulsating veins that traversed her face, or the pointed tongue that was trying to reach him.

"What are they doing?" Aria whispered beside him.

Olórin jumped at the sound of her voice. He had almost forgotten that she was there.

"The song is an ancient and dark siren's song, one from the harpies I would imagine," he replied. "That, along with various herbs and a leech or two, can halt the darkness's march inside an elf, and usually see them cured… in a few days."

"A few days? But we don't have that long," Aria said. "Bernard will be here tomorrow. If he's as good as his word, he'll flatten the forest and start an all-out war between the elves and the dwarfs. Besides, I don't think it's wise to keep Aramus here much longer."

Amidst the screams, Olórin turned to Aria and studied her features.

"Am I mistaken," Olórin said with an impish grin, "or is that a hint of concern for our winged friend I hear in your voice?"

"What? I think you must be going deaf in your old age. No, definitely not," Aria replied, but Olórin caught the faint hint of pink in her cheeks. "I only meant that if we don't want him killed by vengeful elves, and our quest failed, that we should get him out of here. That's all. Honestly."

'Our quest?'

"Indeed," Olórin said, smug in the knowledge that Aria, at the very least, didn't hate Aramus anymore.

"Olórin, we have tried everything within our power, but she is only getting worse," Mirathall interrupted.

Her long snowy hair, which until now was as neat and straight, was dishevelled as she approached Olórin. There was a sorrow in her silver eyes that couldn't have been missed, and the task of helping Sudia had lined her old face with more wrinkles than Olórin had remembered seeing before. He wondered if it was the close proximity to such dark energy which had changed the Elder so quickly. He remembered only too well how his energy was syphoned from him in the mines of Balbuldor.

"Please, will you try your wizard magic?" she asked wearily.

"Would you but fight so hard to save the lives of non-elves, then we, as comrades, would be better companions," he replied.

"Now is not the time, wizard," she snapped, her eyes glistening with the threat of tears. Olórin got the distinct impression that Sudia meant more to Mirathall than any of the other elves. But in the spirit of equality, she would never admit to it.

"It seems that it is not. I cannot guarantee I will succeed where your expertise has failed, but I will try."

Olórin walked closer to the creature that was once Sudia. Her mammoth grey form thrashed and twisted against the restraints. Black tendrils snaked their way toward the edges of her eyes that had turned almost completely black. It was then that Olórin noticed Sudia following the movements of his staff as if it would reach out and burn her. She hissed at it, whilst at the same time backed away as much as her restraints would allow.

"I wonder," Olórin said to no one in particular.

Olórin rested the tip of his lustrous staff against Sudia's shoulder. She arched her back and a screamed in a way that Olórin had never heard before. It echoed through the forest around them, terrifying the creatures within into silence. Slowly the black veins receded from around the area which his staff touched, and the skin underneath lost its grey hue. A hint of silver fought its way back into the nearest eye and Olórin could see terror within it.

"Please, stop, it hurts," she whimpered between gasps of pain.

Olórin removed his staff at once and the poison seeped its way back.

“Don’t stop,” Mirathall said urgently to him. “Whatever you were doing, it was working.”

“My staff is too slow and painful. She will die before it has worked,” he said, taking off his hat and rummaging through it. “She knew, she knew. I cannot fathom how she knew that I would need just one more, but she did.”

“What are you blathering on about?” Aria asked.

“I only needed two,” he said, producing a small phial containing three gleaming stones. “She gave me four. One for my staff when I would need it the most, and now one for Sudia.”

Olórin stepped closer to the orc, and placed his staff firmly in the centre of her forehead. Once again the darkness receded and Sudia’s terrible screams rang out through the forest. Olórin bent down to her, keeping his staff firmly in place.

“You must swallow this,” he said, showing her the tear of life. “It will cleanse your body of this poison and you will be born again.”

“I, can’t,” she choked.

“You must,” he replied, popping it into her mouth and holding her jaw firmly closed.

Sudia fought against the darkness that reviled the light of Edwina in its mouth, and swallowed the gem. Almost instantly she arched her back, screaming and flailing in her restraints as though her insides had been set alight. Her powerful arms strained against the chains and she managed to break one free.

“Hold her,” Olórin bellowed at the surrounding elves.

Just as three elves laid their full weight on her free arm, the ground under Olórin’s feet rumbled violently as though it were going to break in half. The elves became oddly silent, and their eyes grew wide as though this was not a normal occurrence during a healing session. In fact, only a few paid any attention to Sudia as she struggled against the dark poison inside of her. After a moment of hesitation, Mirathall made her way out of the cave and fell to her knees, plunging her hands into the dark soil outside. Silvery strands of magic ran from her finger tips, disappearing deep into the loam.

“No, it cannot be,” she whispered, disbelief clear in her voice.

Just then, the willowy figure of a small elf child descended through the trees, and came to hover three feet away from the crouched Elder. Despite his struggles to restrain Sudia, Olórin still managed to turn long enough and see that it was Thalia who had arrived.

“They are free,” she said in a quiet, whispery voice.

Suddenly, Thalia was dropped to the ground and the forest was plunged into darkness. If it wasn’t for the oil fires dotted throughout the city of Rhidwynn, and in the cave, Olórin would have been completely blind.

“Something is very wrong. Find Aramus,” he said urgently to Aria. “Find him and bring him here.”

Chapter 28

Aria ran faster than she had ever run before, only slowing enough so that the torch she carried wasn't extinguished by her speed. Save for the alarmed cries of the elves, the forest was unnervingly silent, and every snap of a broken twig under her feet, sounded out like a firecracker. Although she could not see them, she could feel the terrified stares of four legged creatures hiding in the thick brush, as they watched her run all the way back into Rhidwynn.

Reaching the hollowed tree again, Aria was relieved to find Aramus still there. He seemed unaware of the commotion that was happening outside as he adjusted the leather strap of his satchel in the brightly lit meeting place.

"Aria, what's the matter?" he asked, stepping toward her.

"Didn't you hear the ground tremble?" she said, trying to catch her breath again.

"I did. But why do you look so terrified? It's not as if the ground has never shook before," he said with a small smile.

"No, not like this. Something is wrong, something is very wrong. Come outside and see." Aria grabbed Aramus by his arm and dragged him out into the pitch-black woodland. "Look at the sky, the moon has gone, and I can't see the stars anymore. Even the vines have disappeared and the elves cannot call them back again. I had to run all the way here."

Aria breathed heavily as she searched the canopy where the night sky should have poked through, but her eyes failed to see anything other than the darkness. In all of her years alive, in all the stories she had heard about her kingdom, she had never encountered such a thing, and it terrified her. Her mind raced as she tried to make sense of their situation, but it ran too fast to give her a reasonable explanation.

Aramus turned toward her and his amber eyes rested on some indiscernible place on her face; her nose, her lips, she couldn't tell which. It was only then that she realised she was still clinging tightly to his arm.

"Don't be scared," he said. "Olórin will know what to do."

Aramus reached up and pushed some of the red curls away from her face. His hand followed the line of her jaw until it rested gently under her chin. Stepping closer to her, he raised her head until it was only a few inches away from his own. Aria felt a nervous thrill start in her belly and a deep flush ignite a heat in her cheeks. She was grateful for the darkness in that moment.

"I won't let anything happen to you," he said, with a handsome smile.

Aria couldn't help but smile in return. The chains around their necks loosened again and if she tried hard enough, Aria was sure she would be able to squeeze it over her head. But she didn't want to, not yet. She wanted to see if Aramus reflected any of the feelings that she seemed to have developed for him. Like a tidal wave that withdrew at the beginning, recoiled at the coast being so close to it, her feelings for Aramus had washed over her and destroyed the hate she had for him. But Aramus was always so irritatingly calm when they were in close proximity. The amber eyes she gazed into now, only served to remind her that he was still the son of Dantet, and her parent's murderer, no matter what she might feel for him.

"Olórin said I am to bring you to him," she said, quietly wishing that Aramus would refuse to go for just a few moments longer. Aria was disappointed when he withdrew his hand.

"Come on then, best not keep the wizard waiting. He might die of old age if we delay," Aramus said, taking hold of her around her waist and spreading his wings wide.

Within seconds they were soaring through the air at a speed which Aria was sure would see them crash into an unseen tree. She dropped her torch and wrapped her arms around Aramus's neck, her eyes wide with fright.

"Slow down, Aramus. It's too dark to see where you're going."

"My eyes see through the darkness," he said, pulling her closer to him.

Aria rested her head against his and closed her eyes tightly. It wasn't until she felt his powerful wings become still and they glided gently downwards, that she opened them again. She was relieved to see that they had arrived at the cave, safely. Olórin was waiting for them outside. He rushed toward them just as Aramus let her go.

"Aramus, thank the Goddess you're safe," he said, the obvious worry on his old face now replaced with relief. "Do you know what has happened here?"

"How could I know, old man?"

There was still some animosity in Aramus's voice as he spoke to the wizard. Aria expected that it would take some time for the feeling of betrayal to fade.

"What I meant was, can you see what has happened to the moon?" the old wizard asked wearily. "You have always had better eyesight than a worgen in the darkness."

The children of Dantet were named Dark One's not only because of their allegiance with the Dark God, but because they preferred to hunt at night – their eyes able to see as clear as if it was day. It appeared that Aramus was no different. He stepped away from the cave and stared long and hard into the nothing.

"All I see are vines," he replied. "Thousands and thousands of vines. They seem to be interlocked tightly with each other over the trees, as though they were some kind of shield. That's what is blocking the sky."

"He's right. I can see them too," a strange female voice said from behind Aria.

Followed by Mirathall, Thalia, and a few other elves who eyed her charily, was Sudia. Her long silver hair had turned a dirty grey colour. Only one eye was silver now, the other remained pitch-black. The veins that had pulsated across her body had all but disappeared, save for a few that still framed the edges of her face. Her once azure lips were a dusty grey, and her voice still hinted at the monster that once lay within her.

"I can see much better in the dark now, hear much better too," she said, twisting her head from side to side, listening to all that was around her.

"You could not cure her?" Aria asked Olórin quietly.

Olórin didn't have time to answer. Sudia moved more quickly than Aria could see, and in the next instant, Aria found herself three inches off the ground, her neck clasped in Sudia's strong hand.

"What did you say about me, whelp?" she hissed.

Aria grappled at Sudia's hand trying to free herself. The elf had an unnatural strength about her, and no matter how hard she beat Sudia's arms, she couldn't loosen her grip. Aria gasped for air and stars began to dance around her periphery. It wasn't until Aramus's fist met with the elf's jaw, that she breathed freely again.

"Keep your hands off of her," Aramus shouted, steadying Aria.

"Ha! I should have seen it earlier," Sudia said, picking herself up off the floor and rubbing her jaw. Her deranged eyes followed Aramus's hands which were gently holding Aria by her waist. "You have feelings for this girl, don't you?"

Aramus said nothing. He let Aria go and stood his ground, clenching his fists so hard that his knuckles turned white. Aria could only feel anger coming from the necklace.

"That is enough," Mirathall boomed.

The old elf glided between the two with the drifting grace of a ghost. Her despondent silver eyes reflected the light from the oil lamps being carried by the other elves, and her expression was grave.

"Sudia, there are terrible things afoot here today, some that we might never get answers for," Mirathall said, facing the elf. "But perhaps you might answer one of them. Can you tell me who did this to you?"

Sudia's mood switched dramatically as she went from enraged, to distressed in an instant, like there was still some part of her that was still struggling against a darker side.

“I… I don’t remember,” she said, holding her hand over her injured ear that was now missing its tip. “I remember the Geminum being handed to Olórin, but everything after that is a blur; snippets of memories that make no sense. But there was a voice, a dark voice that taunted me, told me to do things and… and I couldn’t stop.”

“I see,” Mirathall began, not looking directly at her. “Sudia, you have become like a daughter to me. Were it not for that fact, I do not believe your life would have been spared. This fact has made me guilty of favouritism. As it is, your purity is tainted by the dark blood of Dantet, but it seems that we cannot completely heal you of it. Your aggressive behaviour is not your own, and it does not belong within the elf community.”

“What are you trying to say?” Sudia asked, trying to catch the old woman’s gaze, to no avail. “Are you going to try and kill me now?”

“No,” Mirathall replied quietly. “If we have seen fit to allow the half-breed of the Dark God to live, then balance dictates that we must also allow you to live too. But it cannot be within Elwood. There is no place for a grey-elf here.”

“A grey-elf, is that what I am? Neither light nor dark, but with the capability to turn to either side? You, of all people, should know that I would never turn my back on the elves. This wasn’t my fault,” Sudia barked, turning her furious gaze on Olórin. “I did not break my vows. I did nothing wrong. So why am I being punished for it?”

“You are not being punished, Sudia, but we must protect our people. I am hopeful that Olórin’s cure will continue to work within you,” Mirathall said, drifting back toward Thalia. “But the wisest of us has decided that you should leave Rhidwynn, leave Elwood, and not return until then.”

Aria felt a sudden pang of pity for the elf, and she wasn’t sure if it came from her or Aramus. Seeing as how the elf had just tried to choke the life from her, Aria assumed it did not come from her.

“What am I to do? Where am I to go? If my own family won’t accept me, who will?” Sudia said, her eyes wide, searching the fellow elves around her for an answer. They gave her none, and her lips curled around her teeth viciously. "So, you're going to let a child decide my fate? An impudent, smug, little rat like *her*? No, I will not allow it."

Without warning, Sudia lunged for Thalia. The young girl ducked behind Mirathall's white robes and let out a squeak of fright. It was Olórin who stopped her, his long white staff pointing directly at the enraged elf, freezing her in place.

"You may come with us," he said, releasing Sudia once she had calmed down.

Aria's mouth dropped open.

"Are you sure that's a good idea?" Aria asked him. "The children of Dantet have only ever wanted Aramus dead. What makes you think that she won't try to kill him too?"

Sudia hissed at Aria, like a feral cat would hiss at its enemy. Her one silver eye and one dark eye burned into Aria as though she would love nothing better than to plunge a blade into her chest.

"I am *not* a child of Dantet," she spat.

"No, indeed you are not," Olórin replied. "If I have hope that Aramus can be cured, then it must stand to reason that you too can also be cured. This tragedy which has fallen on you, that occurred only because of our presences in your realm, is ours to resolve. If you swear your allegiance to our cause, your loyalty to me, then I promise to search for a way to cure you until my last breath leaves my body."

Aria thought that Olórin looked suddenly older, like the weight of another burden had aged him. She also suspected that Olórin felt guilty for what had happened to Sudia, like it was his duty to rectify every mistake which Aramus had made. She also began to wonder if that was the true reason he had also brought *her* along, instead of releasing her. After all, they had already dispensed with her army of ogres and worgen, how much more damage could she really have done?

"Fine," Sudia said. "I'll help you stop this prophecy if you promise to cure me afterward."

"Agreed."

*

The rest of the night was spent preparing for their departure from Elwood. Without the vines Olórin knew it would take them nearly an entire day to reach the eastern edge of the forest. He allowed the younger members of his party to gather the supplies needed as a weariness washed over him. He watched, with a certain amount of sadness, as the other elves gave Sudia a wide berth. They seemed afraid of her, and she didn't help matters by hissing at them whenever one came near.

Sooner than his old bones would have liked, they were prepared, and set off for the edge of the elven stronghold, accompanied by three armed elves: Mirathall had insisted on the extra protection. But Olórin suspected that her concern wasn't for them, so much as it was for whatever crossed Sudia's path.

Olórin wasn't sure if it was morning when they left, as the thick vines covering the forest let in no light. He only hoped that Bernard would be patient and wait for them on the other side, but he expected that patience wasn't one of his virtues.

As it happened, however, Olórin was glad to hear the dwarf's curses coming from the other side of a thick wall of vines. The slithering tendrils that trapped them inside, refused to open at their escorts command. If it wasn't for the large broadaxes on the other side, they may not have been able to leave at all; every time a liana was cut down, another grew in its place. And so, this gave the companions only a few seconds to leave the arboreal tomb.

"Wizard, where in the name of the wee man were you?" Bernard said.

Olórin's mouth dropped open when he saw the hirsute dwarf standing in front of him. His fiery beard had be neatly plaited again, and atop his head rested the spikey dwarven crown that king Thrais had once worn. Although his Etherium armour still did not fit his rotund figure, he was an impressive sight – made all the more impressive by the army of dwarfs standing to attention around him.

But as impressed as Olórin was, it was the colossal Beasties that hung in the background which took his breath away. They towered near to the top of where the tall trees of Elwood should have been, replaced instead with a wicker dome of vines. Unlike the female Beasties he had seen in the mines of Balbuldor, these creature's maws of undulating teeth could have swallowed a man riding a horse, whole. Their exoskeletons were grey, toughened, with spikes as long as he was tall. Riding atop of each of them was a single dwarf in iron armour. Once again, the behemoths were being controlled with heavy metal chains driven into the sides of their heads. The ground rumbled underfoot as the six legs of the Beasties shifted impatiently. One of them let out a primordial roar, and it made the hairs on the back of Olórin's neck stand on end.

"What has happened here?" Olórin asked, only barely able to close his mouth enough to form the words. "Why are you wearing Thrais's crown?"

"Dinnae get me started on that fool," Bernard answered as Aramus, Aria, and then Sudia made their way through the vines. "Seems that the king had many allegiances with the wrong people, and it came back tae bite him in the arse. He betrayed you, he betrayed his own people, and I suspect that he attempted tae betray the followers of Dantet. If ye promise yer word tae too many people, I suppose it would be impossible tae keep it. I dinnae know how it happened exactly, but we are in fer a world of hurt now, wizard." Bernard paused for a long time, a look of utter fear crossed his face. "The seal tae Dantet's world, has been broken."

Olórin felt a coldness wash over his insides as though Bernard's words had a powerful magic laced within them. He quickly realised that the rumbling sound which reverberated through Rhidwynn, and had alarmed the elves so badly, must have been the seal breaking. *'No, this cannot be. This was not meant to happen. Something has started events that were not in my vision.'*

"I came back tae Balbuldor too late," Bernard continued. "When I got there, I found that the king had been poisoned by a dark magic. He was jabbering on about some wizard making him break the seal, but I saw no wizard there. The only thing I saw was a legion of Dark One's as they emerged from the mines below; Dark One's the likes of which I have never seen before.

"In the end, Thrais died, and as his right arm and his only successor, it was my job tae see the dwarfs' tae safety. And that's whot I've done. I've sent them on tae Lothangard while I travelled here. It's the only place left that is strong enough tae withstand the monster's that are coming."

"Did he give you a name?" Olórin asked, stepping closer to the dwarf, his chest tight with panic. "Did Thrais name the wizard that had made him break the seal?"

"Aye, but I tell ye there was no wizard there. It was just the ramblings of a poisoned and dying mind," Bernard replied, only now noticing Sudia and throwing her a cautious look. "I thought elves were supposed tae be pretty."

"I thought dwarfs were supposed to be strong, not fat," Sudia snapped.

"Och, I ought tae knock the two queer eyes outta yer head fer that," he said, huffing and puffing under his beard.

"From what I heard there was only one queer thing you knew, your brother," she said with an ever widening grin.

Bernard lunged at Sudia, followed by ten equally enraged dwarfs who wanted her blood to spill. But they were all stopped with Olórin's magic as he raised his staff, all except Bernard in his Etherium armour. Olórin blocked his path to the grey-elf by stepping in the way.

"Outta my way," he snapped at Olórin. "Angus was a more formidable fighter, a more loyal subject, and a better person than she could ever hope tae be. She has no right tae sully his name like that. I willnae have it. I willnea let him be remembered for something like that. I'll cut out her tongue before she says these vile words tae another soul. Outta me way, wizard."

"Bernard," Olórin said, placing his hand upon the dwarf's shoulder, calming him with a silent spell. "Aramus and I know only too well the pain of discrimination and bigotry. Even Aria has felt the sting of a prejudice tongue. So, we understand your anger. Sudia, I fear, will also know your brother's suffering soon enough, and will come to regret her words. However, none of us shall live long enough to regret anything unless we work together to end the prophecy. With the seal broken, Dantet needs very little to rise up into our world. But I am sure that he is still lacking in something, otherwise he would already be here. And so, I ask you again, Mighty King of Balbuldor, what was the name of the wizard that enslaved Thrais?"

"Mullrode," Bernard answered.

Olórin heard Aria take a sharp breath in.

"That was the wizard who gave me the amulet, and the Etherium arrow," she said.

Olórin's heart sank so low into his chest, he was sure he might die then and there.

"Then it is true," he said, unable to hide the sorrow in his voice. "The wizard caste is no longer whole. Like a house built upon shifting sands, it has broken into two without me realising. Dantet's fingers have reached into the cracks to wrap around the greedy hearts of the ambitious wizards within. I am certain now, Aria, that your ill-thought-out actions have been as carefully orchestrated, and incited, by the same dark wizard that killed Thrais. Mullrode has worn many masks and you mustn't feel bad, or stupid either, for not having seeing through them. Even I did not see the dark eddies turning under my own feet. Perhaps I did not want to see them."

"So, what do we do now?" Aramus asked.

There was a quiet tremble in the young man's voice that Olórin had never heard before, and he knew it to be fear. It was reflected in the arch of his wings that just would not lie flat on his back anymore, and the clenching of his jaw muscles. *'He must know that his time is running out. How I wish he had longer to discover love.'* Had it not been for the betrayal of the wizards within the tower there might have been enough time. Olórin knew it did no good to dwell on what was no longer possible, so instead, he focused on the certainty of their situation.

"Now, we must make haste and return to Lothangard where I can brew the potion," he replied, releasing Bernard and his dwarfs. "I fear that all the Dark God needs is one last piece of the puzzle to fall into place so, that he can rise from his world. But I will not allow him to have that piece. I will not allow him to have *you,* Aramus."

Chapter 29

Aria was glad that the dwarf no longer directed all of his animosity toward her. Bernard, instead, was occupied with keeping a watchful eye on the grey-elf that rode the Beastie in front of him. The mammoth creatures moved with a belying speed, an advantage to having six legs. They groaned and vibrated with a deep, soulful sound that resembled the rapid beating of a drum inside their chests. Aria felt the vibrations travel up her legs and into her own chest as she sat astride the Beastie she shared with Olórin and another dwarf. But that was the only discomfort she felt as the animal's six legs ensured a smooth ride.

"Marvellous creatures, aren't they?" Olórin said from behind her.

"Kind of scary actually," she replied, holding on tightly to the sharp prongs either side of her, even though she had no fear of falling off.

"Despite their ferocious looks, Beasties are actually a very docile creature. It is only by the persuasions of the dwarfs, and their chains, that they become deadly," he said, glancing toward Aramus who had decided to fly instead. "They mate for life, these Beasties, and will defend their mate and young with their lives. An honourable trait for such a scary monster, yes?"

"I suppose so," she said, knowing full well that he wasn't just talking about the Beasties.

She followed the old wizard's line of sight and was surprised to find that he was no longer watching Aramus fly. Instead he was looking toward the northern horizon where a wall of ice could just be made out.

"The water in the Stonyfields is a little higher than normal for this time of year, don't you agree, Your Highness?"

"A little, what of it?"

Olórin didn't answer for a long time. Instead, he squinted against the bright light of the mid-day sun like he was trying to see something very, very, far away. The Stonyfields consisted of large canyons that scared the hoary stone, like old battle wounds on an ancient soldier. Even from so far away, Aria could hear the thunderous sounds of the water coming from the glacier, as it tried to deepen the scars. But in her seventeen years of life, little had ever changed in this place.

"As queen, I'm sure you are familiar with the landscape of the northern ice fields?"

"I am," Aria replied, turning her head around to look at him questioningly.

"Good. Aramus, come here," he said, ignoring her probing stare.

Aramus dutifully glided next to the Beastie.

"I am an old man who does not like to fly," Olórin said, gesturing for Aria to go with Aramus. "We are approaching the Giant's Chasm, but before we get there, I would like you to fly ahead with Aramus and check that the water level hasn't been made unnaturally high."

"*Unnaturally?*" Aria said, tentatively stepping on the back of the Beastie before wrapping her arm around Aramus's shoulder.

"I am hoping that I am wrong, but I believe that the dragons under the ice have been disturbed by Dantet's seal being broken, and their fires are melting the ice that surrounds them," he replied.

Aria was about to scoff at the old man when she felt Aramus wrap his arm around her waist and lift her off the Beastie's back. The sudden surge of air over her face as they took to the sky, and the loss of anything stable under her feet, made her take in a sharp breath instead. Together, they soared toward the icy plains of northern Naretia.

It took over an hour to reach the colossal glacier that stretched as far as the eye could see. Aria had always thought that the stark difference between the grey, stony landscape and the towering wall of ice, resembled a line drawn across two different realms. One was bountiful and rich with life, while the other was barren and unwelcoming. She had always felt an unease around the border to the north, like she wasn't supposed to cross it. But now, high above the ground and safe in Aramus's arms, Aria surveyed the endless expanse of white for the first time. A nervous thrill inside of her was half-hoping that Olórin was right, that there were dragons living below the glaciers.

Water flowed more quickly than Aria had ever seen before, but the crevasses and peaks of the frosty north refused to give up the secrets that lay beneath. After an unfruitful exploration, Aramus turned and headed back toward the Stonyfields.

"He doesn't really believe that there are dragons, does he?" Aria asked Aramus as she scanned the glacier behind them. "They're just fairy tales, myths from imaginative minds with nothing better to do."

"Olórin has a tendency to believe in the impossible," he replied, turning his gaze toward Aria. "After all, he believes that he can cure me."

"You don't believe that he can, you think it is impossible?" she probed. Aramus's gaze avoided Aria and, instead, followed the horizon as they soared back toward their companions.

"I don't know," Aramus replied eventually. "I used to believe that he could. Youthful innocence perhaps, but for a time he was the only hope I had of not being… well, *this*. Now, I'm not sure anymore. Too many things have changed, and even if he can cure me of the curse, I might always look…"

Aramus's voice trailed off and the sorrow that filled Aria, crushed her chest. The sting of tears burned at the edges of her eyes, even though Aramus's were dry, and she was sure her feelings came from the necklace.

"There's nothing wrong with, with *this*," she said, gesturing to Aramus.

"Really?" he said with a disbelieving smirk.

"Yes, really," she replied, letting go of him with one hand to brush away some of his black hair and look him squarely in his eyes.

Aria felt herself slip when she did, and Aramus grabbed her around the waist with two hands, pulling her in closer to him. Despite her fear of falling, Aria's hand never left the side of his face and her eyes never wavered. Instead of flying forward, Aramus pivoted upward until they hovered in place. His powerful wings disturbed the air around them and tussled her hair. He leaned in, his face so close to hers now that she could feel the heat of his breath on her lips. She watched, as a fire rose in her belly and her heart quicken. He opened his mouth slightly to say something, but nothing came out. His slatted, amber eyes searched hers intensely and, for a moment, everything around them seemed to slow down.

"Aria, I…" Aramus whispered, running his hand up her back until it rested gently between her shoulders.

Aria felt a jolt of electricity surge through her body as he pulled her in closer to him. His Adam's apple bobbed as he swallowed deeply, and she felt a small tremble in his fingers. Aria took a small breath in as she felt his lips brush against hers. After a moment of hesitation, he kissed her.

She closed her eyes and kissed him back, running her fingers through his hair. A heat built under his skin, not as hot as the day he attacked the elves, but still there nonetheless. Never in her wildest dreams, or nightmares, did she ever think that she would someday kiss the man who had murdered her parents.

That thought stayed with her as she felt him pull her in closer. The image of his fiery eyes stayed with her too as she desperately tried to ignore it. But she couldn't. Her heart felt the weight of her parent's dead eyes as they watched from her psyche, and it made Aria pull away.

"I, I can't," she said in a whisper, leaning her forehead against his.

Aria felt Aramus's body tense under her. His shoulders became rigid, and even the beating of his wings took on a more terse sound. But she felt nothing from the necklace; no disappointment, no sadness, no anger.

“Do you think you could ever love me?” he asked so quietly that Aria wasn’t sure she heard him. “Do you think that anyone could ever love a creature like me?”

Aria felt a small part of her heart break for him. Aramus hadn’t asked to be born like this, he didn’t volunteer to be controlled by the Dark God. All he had ever wanted was to be normal, of that much Aria was certain. But no matter how much she tried to move past the image of him standing over her parents decapitated bodies, his eyes ablaze with a terrible fire, she couldn’t.

“I think I have come to forgive you, Aramus,” she said, lifting his chin with a hooked finger until his eyes met hers. “I have even come to care about you too. And if you had told me some weeks ago that I would be saying these words to you, I would have cut off your head thinking you were mad. But that gets me wondering that, if in such a short time I could have come to care about you so deeply, maybe I might also come to love you too… in time.”

Aramus gave a half-grin but the sadness in his eyes was evident, even if she still could not feel it.

“But you could never forget? No matter what your feelings for me might be, you would never be able to forget the wrong that I have done to you, would you?”

“I’m not sure… I…” Aria grasped for an answer, but there was only one. “No, I don’t suppose that I could.”

The words were so final, like hearing the sickening thud of an axe through someone’s head and knowing that there was no hope of avoiding death. There was no way around it, and she didn’t want to lie to Aramus. The memory of her dead parents was too deeply ingrained in her mind to ever be forgotten, and along with it came that devilish image of Aramus.

“I understand,” he said, tearing his eyes away and looking behind her instead. “There are some things that cannot be overcome, and I am grateful for the chance to have at least tried to make up for my mistakes. I can’t say I’m not disappointed though. You are beautiful and strong. Out of all the girls I’ve met, you were the only one who I thought might… ”

"Aramus, I…"

Aria was cut off by Aramus shushing her, which shocked her somewhat. But the sight of his eyes locked on to a target somewhere below them made her realise he wasn't being rude because of her rejection.

She followed his gaze, and in the darkest shadows of the canyons Aria spotted a movement. She couldn't make out the form of the creature no matter how hard she squinted. Whatever it was, it was large, bubbling in the shadows, and was making its way toward the surface of the Stonyfields through the gawping gullies of the Giants Chasm. It took a determined pace toward the stone bridges which crossed the hungry canyons; the very same ones Olórin and the rest of their party were traversing in the distance.

"What is it?" Aria whispered.

"I don't know, I've never seen them before. But they don't look like the cute and cuddly kind."

"I can't see anything, bring me closer."

Aramus swooped toward the wide mouth of the canyon and glided at the precipice of the darkness below. The gloom seemed unnaturally dark for the high sun. Aria saw the shapes of monsters she had only ever heard of in fairy tales, claw their way up the side of the canyon walls, filling her with terror. It was the two white tusks glinting in the sunlight either side of their mouths, some broken or missing, that gave them away.

Wide hands with long hooked claws dug into the grey stone walls, dislodging chucks of shale. A set of equally ferocious clawed feet secured the creatures as they surged along the walls of the gully. Their grey skin almost blended them into their surroundings, like a chameleon. Their approach was quiet for such a large mob. The only noise she heard was the scuttling of their claws and the falling stones dislodged by their movements. The bubbling river of deadly creatures, moved like raging whitewater, and she knew it wouldn't be long until they reached Olórin.

"No, it cannot be," Aria whispered, fear taking most of her breath away.

"What?" Aramus asked. "What are they?"

As the first few emerged into the brighter light, Aria knew she was not mistaken. Green eyes searched the surface of the Stonyfields, elongated noses sniffed for the scent they had been given to find, and craniums, too small for their owners impressive size, obeyed the silent commands Aria knew they had gotten from Dantet. Hundreds, maybe even a thousand of these creatures scurried across the crumbling wall of the canyon, like spiders. The party of dwarfs and Beasties Aria could just make out in the distance, were unaware of their approach.

"Take us back to Olórin," she said, grabbing Aramus's tunic. "NOW!"

*

Olórin had never liked the Stonyfields. In his opinion there were far too many bridges to cross over the ravines that were far too high. Of course, he also knew that his distaste for the place might have more to do with the gulches and his fear of heights, than anything else. Riding on the back of a weighty beasty as they crossed the first few overpasses didn't help matters either, and Olórin couldn't help but remember the reason for his fear. Being repeatedly dangled by your ankles off the tall wizard tower in Lothangard for being "different", was bound to have a negative effect on a young apprentice. But that was many centuries ago, back when he was just a boy, and public perception of all things "different" was less tolerant than it appeared to be now. Still, he couldn't help but feel as though he had been cheated because of the era he was born into.

Olórin had never been a popular apprentice wizard, but a potion of anti-gravity, or a curse of month-long incurable hiccups, was nothing compared to what Angus must have endured. Dwarfs were not the gentle kind, and embraced change slowly. Olórin's unpopularity had changed when his visions came, and for a while he was grateful for the reverence it gave him. Now, however, he wasn't quite as grateful as the weight of it all rested on his old shoulders.

Olórin could feel that they were nearing a point, a point so small and indiscernible in the long linage of time, that it would have been insignificant if it weren't for the sharp turn it was about to take. And it *was* going to take a sharp turn. But which direction was becoming more unclear as the darkness waded in to influence the outcome.

"Whot in the name of all things hairy is that?" Bernard shouted.

Olórin followed the direction that the tufty dwarf's thick finger was pointing. From some way off he could make out the shapes of Aramus and Aria returning. But something wasn't quite right. Aramus's wings were flapping much faster than Olórin had ever seen them before. In the canyon beneath them, something black followed, bubbling like a potion in a cauldron. Olórin heard Aria scream the name of the creatures before he could see them, and it made his insides go cold.

"Trolls!" she bellowed time and time again.

Almost as stupid as ogres, but twice as deadly, trolls were the last thing that Olórin was expecting to see emerge from the dark canyon below. But emerge they did. Rows and rows of tusky, savage beasts spilled over both edges of the ravine and made their way toward Olórin; each one of them tall enough to reach the Beasties shoulders. There was thousands of them, all recent escapees from Balbuldor, no doubt.

"Move!" Sudia yelled, kicking the sides of her beasty urgently.

Without warning, Olórin felt the creature beneath him take off at a fierce pace, quicker than he would have given the mammoth beast credit for. His mind raced as the reality of what he had just seen finally hit him. *'Dantet's strength is growing. The long forgotten monsters of his world are returning, and my time is running out.'* Aramus caught up with the galloping Beasties and carefully lowered Aria onto its back again. For the first time in the young man's life, Olórin saw panic and fear in the glances he took behind him, and in the wideness of his amber eyes. It terrified Olórin to know that his friend, his son, knew the end was coming. And Olórin could do nothing about it.

"What do we do, Olórin?" Aramus shouted, struggling to keep up with the Beasties pace.

Olórin looked behind him to see a wave of grey creatures with green eyes, engulf one of the Beasties that was lagging behind in a wave of claws, riders and all. Although the open maw of the Beastie made easy work of a few trolls who were unfortunate enough to find themselves serrated by its teeth, there were just too many of them to fend off. Despite their fast pace, the rest of the trolls were still able to keep up with them, even managing to catch up to another Beastie, and dig sharpened talons into its hide to slow it down.

Sudia stood up on the back of her mount and faced the rear. She fired arrow, after arrow, over Olórin's head and into the pursuing monsters. Two of her projectiles found their way through green eyes, while one made its way down the gullet of a roaring troll. But there weren't enough arrows in Naretia to kill all the trolls, and Olórin couldn't think straight because of the fear he felt for Aramus.

"Olórin, what do we do?" Aramus shouted again.

"All is lost," Olórin whispered. "This was never supposed to happen."

"Speak up, old man, I can't hear you," Aramus said, drawing his sword from his belt and flying back momentarily to dislodge the nearest troll's head from its body.

"He said we should run, as fast as we can," Aria shouted over the chaos that was thundering up behind them.

Olórin glanced at the young queen. A determined look in her blue eyes told him this was not a time to wrestle with doubt. She was right, and Olórin knew it. Now was not the time to lose faith. The Goddess Edwina herself had come to him and told him he was on the correct path. Now more than ever, he needed to believe that and must not deviate from his quest. But with the trolls loose in this world, Olórin was expecting there were a great deal of dark things making their way into Naretia. Perhaps they were already there, hunting for them, waiting for them at Lothangard: Things he knew he could not defeat.

"We will need an army," Aria said. "Sudia, do you think you can get a message to the elves and ask them to come to Lothangard?"

"I can ask," she said, shooting another troll in the chest. "But they will not come. Elwood has closed itself off to the world, and the elves will respect the forest's decision. The balance has been tipped far beyond what they can repair. They will remain in the safety that it provides while the rest of Naretia burns, and wait for the day that the darkness weakens."

"I knew I dinnae like those pointy-eared bampots fer a reason," Bernard spat. Sudia shot him a pointed look. "Dinnae worry about having an army, Aria. The dwarfs will defend Lothangard."

"And the King's Guard too," Olórin said, finally able to speak again. "When we reach the ramparts of Lothangard I will send word that they are to, once again, obey your command, My Queen. Together, with the dwarven army you shall have a legion to defend your people."

Olórin saw a slight quiver in Aria's bottom lip as she acknowledged his words with a small incline of her head. *'How things have changed,'* he thought. *'Once this girl was our enemy, too impetuous to command her subjects. But now, as the wick burns close to the end of the candle, she has become wiser, more tempered than I. A true leader and queen.'* Olórin smiled as he looked over the young girl with curly red hair who, in the face of a battle that whispered promises of defeat, appeared fearless.

"So the plan fer now is whot, run?" Bernard said, taking a swipe at a troll that had come too close to his mount with his broadaxe. The troll lost an arm for its troubles.

"Yes," Aria replied, "run!"

Chapter 30

To Aria, Dwarf arrows had a distinctly different sound as they zip through the air; heavier, louder than ordinary arrows. She was relieved to hear them as they reached the bulwark of sandstone that protected the city of Lothangard. High above them, she could just make out the iron helmets of dwarfs poking between the parapets. Their silver bows gleamed a fiery red in the reflected light of the setting sun, letting loose thousands of arrows toward the mass of pursuing trolls.

The wall, which had stood for more than three thousand years, had gargantuan sculptures of past kings carved upon it. Behind it, Aria could see the tall, limestone palace hang over the city like a displeased shadow as they approached. Although her mother and father had been gentle rulers, there was a long line of ancestors before them that would have disowned her for not having avenged her parent's death, despite the cost; a trait of impulsiveness she had inherited from them, no doubt. But Aria didn't have time to dwell on the displeasures of ghostly rulers past. They were fast approaching the iron portcullis, and the dwarfs, who had taken it upon themselves to secure the city, had it firmly closed.

"Open the gates," she yelled once they were within earshot.

The sound of metal chains running rapidly through the gatehouses signified the dwarf's obedience to her command, but the heavy metal gate was slow to rise. Even though the Beasties were unfamiliar animals to her, she could see that they were exhausted. Their six legs had been running full pelt for hours, and each one of their crimson mouths took on a dark purple hue. But she dared not slow them down.

With her bow constantly in motion, Sudia continued to strike down whatever trolls Aramus could not reach with his sword, and Aria had never heard such vile words uttered as the ones that poured out of Bernard's mouth. But the strangest thing to Aria was the silence from the passenger behind her.

Olórin, armed with his iridescent white staff, did not utter a single word as they fled the monsters behind them. Nor did he attempt to fend off any of the toothy fiends nipping at his ankles. This was left to Aria and her sword. His long grey beard whipped about his head in a deranged manner through the fast moving air, but even this, it appeared, could not distract him from his thoughts. The only movement she witnessed from the old man was when he placed his hand upon his hat to prevent it from flying away. Aria wondered what had disturbed the wizard so much, but remained answerless as a set of razor sharp claws dug into her leg.

In the same moment she cried out, she also swung her sword and detached the monster's hand from his arm. The troll squealed with pain and, clasping his spurting stump in his remaining hand, ran in the opposite direction. Clenching her teeth, Aria removed the motionless limb from her leg and tossed it to the side, whereupon the trolls fought over who was going to get to eat it. This bought them a small amount of time, albeit enough to just catch their breaths. In that reprieve Aria glanced at Aramus. Like Olórin, he too paid no attention to the fact that her leg had just been skewered, and seemed preoccupied with some deep thought. *'My heroes,'* she thought sarcastically.

The small party reached the gates of Lothangard, and the mammoth Beasties only barely made it through the still-opening gate.

"Let the gate fall," Aria bellowed.

A deafening rattle of metal chains echoed through the narrow cobbled streets of Lothangard, followed by the thunderous boom of the metal portcullis as it met with the ground. A few trolls made their way inside, some were crushed by the falling gate, while others met their end at the point of the dwarf's arrows.

Olórin was first to dismount, sliding off the Beastie's back before it even had time to collapse onto its quivering six legs. Out of the corner of her eye, she saw him dart into a nearby house whereupon two strapping men exited and made their way toward more homes along the streets. Aria didn't have time to try and figure out the old man's peculiarities. Her city was under attack and she had to find a way to defend her people.

"Aria, Aria, Aria!"

Aria recognised the shrill voice instantly. From between the billowing cloaks of people desperately seeking shelter from the battle, she saw a shock of red curly hair bounce its way toward her. Following closely behind the small boy, was the overweight female figure of one of the palace aides, desperately trying to catch him. Aria slid off the back of the Beastie and winced with the pain from her leg. No sooner had her feet hit the ground than Pearan jumped into her arms.

"Pearan, are you alright? It's okay now, hush don't cry," she soothed, as the young boy sobbed into her shoulder.

"They say something really bad is coming," he sniffled. "They say it's going to kill us all. You were gone for so long, I thought you were dead, Aria. I thought you had gone to mommy and daddy without me, and left me here all alone."

Aria's breath caught in her chest and for a moment, she couldn't move it again. To hear his worst fears said aloud dulled any pain she felt from her leg and, instead, sent an ache through her heart.

A hot tear ran down her cheek. She looked into her brother's watery brown eyes as his head rested against her shoulder. She felt both Bernard and Aramus's stares on her back as she took a few breathes to steady her voice. The chain around her neck loosen once again; Aramus obviously had come to realise just how much she loved her brother. Aria wiped away his tears with her hand, and tried her best to smile.

"I would never leave you," she whispered, not confident enough that her full voice would remain steady. "Never. But I would never lie to you either, Pearan. Something bad *is* coming, and I need to be here to fight it. As much as I would like to, I cannot have you nearby because I would spend all of my time worrying about you instead of fighting the monsters. It is very important that you do as I say now, no matter how scared you might be. I need you to be brave and hide yourself in the palace."

"But Aria…" he said, his bottom lip quivering as he lifted his head and wiped away tears with the back of his small hand.

"No buts, do you hear? I need you to hide like you did in the throne room. Stay hidden, and don't come out until only *I* tell you to. Do you understand? Listen to no one but me."

"Is he one of the bad guys," Pearan said, pointing behind Aria.

He was trying to change the topic and delay the inevitable, but Aria hadn't the heart to be too stern with him. Not now as the things of nightmares were about to come crashing through the gate. She glanced to where Pearan was pointing, and found the foreboding figure of Aramus watching them carefully, with one eyebrow raised.

"No, he's not," she said with a small smile. "Now go. Get behind the walls of the palace and hide so that no one can find you, Pearan. Do as I say."

Aria gestured for the careworn palace aide to take her young brother, the returning pain in her leg and the loud shouting from the dwarfs seeing an end to the intimate moment. Pearan sounded out his objections in desperate wails, and the elderly lady had to be helped by a passer-by as he kicked and squirmed, trying to fight their grip. He screamed after Aria as they took him away, begging and pleading for her not to leave him. His hand, so small, reached out as far as it would go, his face, tear-stained and frantic.

"Hide, Pearan," she yelled back at him, her voice breaking as tears began to trickle down her face. "Please hide," she whispered.

Aria stared in the spot her brother had disappeared through, long after he had left. It wasn't until Aramus's warm hand rested on her shoulder that reality came crashing down around her. The cries and the screams of her people, as they scrambled for safety, made their way into her ears once again.

"You truly love him, don't you?" Aramus asked.

Aria wiped the tears away from her face and nodded. She took a deep breath and turned to the line of dwarf's who adorned the highest parts of the battlements like shiny baubles on a festive tree. They were still, and their bows lay limply by their sides as they jeered at whatever lay beyond the wall. This alarmed Aria, and she brushed Aramus's hand aside.

"Why have you stopped firing?" she roared.

"They've lost their taste fer blood," one of them shouted back.

"I think dwarf meat is too chewy fer their liking," said another.

The second dwarf's statement was followed by a riotous uproar from the wall.

"Be quiet you fool's," Aria shouted at them, but they could not hear her.

Only a moment ago, thousands of trolls had come within a few feet of the city. '*Why were they not attacking?*' Aria had to find out, and the many steps up to the parapet seemed too long a journey right now, especially as her leg was beginning to ache once more.

"Quick, get me up there," she said to Aramus.

"Aye, me too," Bernard added.

Aramus gave the oversized king a weary look before he took off with Aria toward the celebrating dwarfs. Aria ignored the congratulatory claps of broad hands on her back as she pushed her way passed them.

"Shut it," she heard Bernard's voice boom over all the others.

Blissful silence ensued and all that could be heard was Aramus panting as he lowered the heavy dwarf next to Aria.

Beyond the horizon, silhouetted against the fireball that was the rapidly setting sun, Aria could make out the hideous figures of the trolls. They paced over and back against the last of the light as though they were trying to stamp out its fire with their feet.

"They're not leaving," she said to Bernard. "Their waiting."

"Whot are they waiting fer?"

"Reinforcements, and the darkness," she replied, trying desperately to hide the panic in her voice. "Their eyes have the advantage in the night."

"My Queen," came a voice from the streets below the wall.

Aria turned to see a small battalion of King's Guard, dressed head to toe in gleaming gold armour and armed with swords and bows, staring up at her. On each of their chests they bore the symbol of her linage, the head of a dragon, and across their faces was the same look of determination she had seen when her father had been the one to rule them.

"The King's Guard are gathering as we speak and are awaiting your orders," he said.

Aria took quick glances at Bernard and Aramus, each of whom inclined their heads slightly toward her as if to acknowledge that *she* was now the one in charge.

"About bloody time," she roared back. "Gather as many able men as possible. Set the archers up high, and be prepared to light the oil fires. Get the defenceless into the Palace where they might have some protection, and then position and hitch the catapults, ready to let fly."

"Aye, Your Highness," they roared in unison.

"You there," Aria shouted at the nearest soldier, who stopped instantly and saluted her. "Seal all exits to the city and find me the wizard called Mullrode. I believe he might be a spy for Dantet. I give you permission to remove whatever limbs you must to keep him here, just as long as he remains alive so that I can question him after you're done."

"Yes, Your Majesty," the soldier replied.

"Aria!"

The sound of Olórin's voice was as weak as the dying light that tried to illuminate the streets of Lothangard. As the King's Guard disappeared through the city, Aria picked him out more easily. His eyes were despondent and his frame more stooped than she had remembered as he stood in the cobbled street below.

"Now comes the time that you must do what you were born to do, protect the people within these walls," he said. "Now is also the time where I must fulfil my part in this prophecy and make the potion. But to do that I will need Bernard and the Valefire."

"Och, sure ye can just have it. I have no need fer shiny things anymore, and Thrais willnae be wanting it back. If ye haven't noticed, I'm the ruddy king now," Bernard said as he started to remove the leather pouch from around his neck.

"I would not part with such a talisman so easily, if I were you," Olórin warned. "Even though it is small, it possesses a magic far greater than mine, and I would hate for it to fall into the wrong hands. It would be better if you kept it next to your untainted heart, and came with me instead."

"Don't worry, Bernard," Aria said, clasping the dwarf on his armoured shoulder. "I will command both armies fairly."

It was only then Aria realised this was as close as she had ever gotten to the dwarf without him trying to lop off her head. Her chest was filled with a sudden weighty feeling, and she knew that it did not come from Aramus.

"Bernard, I…" Aria fumbled for eloquent words that would in some small way describe what she truly felt. But there were none that would come near. "I'm sorry, about your brother. I was wrong, so very wrong. I know nothing I can say will ease the pain you feel, and nothing will ever undo the terrible things that I have done. But for what it's worth, I just wanted to say that I'm sorry."

Bernard's fiery beard billowed and fell as he huffed tersely beneath it. Aria wasn't sure if he was about to run his axe through her, or start crying. Eventually, the dwarf gave a sheepish nod of his head toward her, before turning and making the arduous journey down the many steps of the battlements with his short legs. Aria watched him disappear into the palace with Olórin, before turning her gaze back toward the dying sun. As she waited for the inevitable, she began to wonder if it would be the last sunset they would ever see.

The heat of the day receded into the dusk. Her body ached from the tension of waiting before she realised the night had crept up behind them. Large barrels of fire oil were positioned and held fast by the King's Guard, ready for use on top of the sandstone heads of the past kings. Their gaze was unwavering as they glared into the darkness, waiting to obey their queen and defend Lothangard until their last breath.

The mammoth catapults groaned in the bailey behind the wall, each one loaded with stingers; a weapon her father created. The stinger would be set alight just before being loosed and the flames would burn quickly through oil-soaked rags. Each stinger contained a bombardment of shrapnel and sharpened knives wrapped in their own oil rag. With the night as darks as it was, the stingers would be imperative in finding the enemy.

Aria listened to the archers flexing their bows, testing the strength and durability of their strings, and the clatter of freshly made arrows being landed at their feet. But aside from those small interruptions, the city of Lothangard was as quiet as Aria had ever heard. The ancient cobbled streets were empty, the rows of wooden buildings were darkened, and the street lamps had not been lit. Aria had never seen the city like this, and it whispered doubts of survival in her head.

The night waned on, and the cloud-covered sky refused to clear. In the darkness she couldn't help but look at Aramus. Despite having just kissed her, he was more distant toward her now than he had ever been. He wouldn't even look in her general direction, and Aria surmised that the sting of rejection was the reason.

"There," yelled Sudia unexpectedly. "I see movement."

Sudia had positioned herself on the highest spire of the turret to Aria's left. Wrapping her leg around the metal prong, and leaning dangerously over the rampart, Sudia pointed toward the darkness. It seemed that her new persona was one immune to the natural fear of falling that most would have.

Aria squinted, trying to make out the something she was pointing to, to no avail.

"Do you see anything?" she asked Aramus.

"No," he replied, squinting as much as Aria. "All I see is darkness."

"What are you waiting for? It's over there," she shouted again, pointing toward some indiscernible point.

"Your Majesty," one of the King's Guard beside her said. "We could send out some lighted arrows to help us see better?"

"And show your hand too early?" Aramus scoffed. "I tell you the grey-elf is mistaken. They are not here yet."

Aria furrowed her brow and pursed her lips tightly together. Should she fire arrows into the darkness, her enemies would have a clearer picture of their numbers. But by the very nature of Sudia's condition, she knew that she had the same ability as Aramus to see in the dark. Perhaps she had a better vantage point than Aramus. But her abilities were new and, as of yet, untested.

"Send a volley," she said to the line of dwarfs beside her.

"Aria..."

Aramus was cut off by the whooshing sound of a hundred lit arrows as they sailed through the air. For the longest time Aria watched them soar gracefully into the darkness, unhindered, and she breathed a sigh of relief as they descended. But her relief was short lived. Somewhere along their path a few of the arrows stuck into something, mid-air, whilst the rest fell to the ground. That something let out a shriek, and Aria heard the distinct sound of wings flapping as it tried to get away.

"Harpies!" yelled a dwarf.

"I thought you said..." Aria started, looking toward Aramus.

"I... I didn't see them. Aria, I swear I didn't see them," he replied, trying, without success, to convince her of his innocence. "I don't understand, he must have stopped me from seeing. He must know what is about to happen."

From where the arrows hit the harpies, Aramus should have been able to see them. Either something was blocking his dark abilities, or Aramus had wanted his father's army to gain ground for some reason. Whatever the case may be, Aria had no time to decide which.

"Archers, take aim," she roared, turning back toward the wall and raising her sword above her head. Now more than ever, she wished that she had kept her armour on, but there had been no time to change out of the dress the elves had given her.

There hadn't even been enough time to tend to her leg, but thankfully it had stopped bleeding on its own. "Fire!"

Hundreds of arrows flew past her head and into the darkness. Only a few of them met with the creatures in the sky.

"Pour the oil," Aria shouted at the King's Guard who waited by the large barrels of fire oil. The guards dutifully tipped the contents of the barrels into the hollows in the stone king's heads. "Archers, take aim, fire!"

Another volley of arrows sailed into the sky, and this time they hit something larger than a harpy. The burning arrows outlined a creature on the ground that rivalled the size of the dwarf's Beasties. Aria felt a large stone land in her stomach with the sight of what came next.

From within the darkness she saw red, slatted eyes, as large as horses, flare into life and stare back at her. A rumbling bellow reverberated through her bones as the creature opened its glowing, crimson mouth, and fire swelled inside its gullet. It shot out a ball of lava, and when it did, the creature was illuminated enough that Aria could make out its shape.

Large horns, the size of tree trunks, twisted and turned on top of the creatures black head. On all fours, its mammoth paws turned in on themselves and ended in talons that appeared to have been dipped in molten iron at some point. Its chest, only slightly larger than its head, and gargantuan in size next to its skinny waste, heaved as it prepared to fire again. It was a creature that Aria thought could only have ever been conjured from a nightmare. But yet here it was, living, breathing, and trying its best to kill them all.

A fireball hit the palace walls behind her and erupted, splattering the wooden houses beneath with great globules of sticky magma. Aria panicked as the walls of the palace were coated in multiple molten spittle's from at least ten horned beasts. She feared the limestone would crumble with the heat and everyone inside, including her brother, would perish. Thankfully the glowing gobs ran off and burned the empty houses around the palace instead.

"Light the oil," Aria shouted, turning her attention back to the battle at hand.

From the heads of the dead kings, the guards lowered torches and Aria watched the flame disappear through hidden channels. It lit up the kings' hollow eyes and flowed down their swords. It crisscrossed over shallow channels carved into the sandstone walls, and set the battlements alight. The fire burned and hissed as it made its way across the oil soaked ground in front of Lothangard, like a lake of flames, and illuminated the night as though it were day.

Horrific howls of pain rang out in the crisp air as ogres, horned beasts, and any other dark creatures that were too stupid to run away, burned in the oil fire. From the corner of her eye, Aria saw a large group of worgen narrowly miss the lapping tongues of the flames. Leading that group was a worgen she knew only too well, Luscious. In the brief moment that Luscious's red eyes met hers, she saw him snarl and flash the hole that had once held his canine tooth. It was clear then he was not on their side, if he ever was at all.

"Catapultiers, aim your weapon now that you can see," Aria commanded.

"Aria, the harpies!" Sudia shouted from the spire.

Aria looked to the sky. The flayed forms of what once appeared to be women, now adorned with fleshy wings, made their way toward the parapets. In each of their clawed hands was a sword, and from each of their mouths came a terrible cry. Aria flinched from the noise as it almost made her ears bleed.

"Archers, Archers, at the ready," Aria screamed, to no avail.

All the male King's Guard, and dwarfs alike, were staring open-mouthed and dreamy-eyed at the hideous beasts approaching; every man save Aramus. Only the female soldiers stood in their place and obeyed her commands, but there was only a handful of those.

"Allow me," Aramus hissed, spreading his wings and taking to the sky with his sword in hand.

"Aramus, no," Aria called after him.

If Aramus heard her he didn't respond. He shot into the sky with blistering speed and, in the glow of the emblazoned walls, all Aria could make out was the flash of his silver sword as it met with some of the harpies throats. Their song was quietened as they turned on Aramus, and the men on the ramparts suddenly snapped back into life, hitching their bows. The air was rent with the sound of the hag's cries as more fiery arrows found their targets.

Aria heard Luscious let out a brutish roar. Within a matter of seconds, the remaining ogres ignored the city of Lothangard, and hurtled their spears at Aramus instead. This was followed closely by lava balls from the remaining half-burnt, horned creatures. It seemed to Aria that Luscious appeared to be commanding the mammoth army, a General in-lieu of the Dark God, as it were. Luscious must be high in Dantet's ranks to have been afforded such a role, and Aria felt stupid for not seeing it sooner. It also seemed that when Aramus was in their sight, the assaults from city of Lothangard were nothing more than an annoyance in the periphery of the dark militia.

"Aramus, come back," Aria shouted at him. "It's *you* they want."

"The stupid fool can't hear you," Sudia roared back.

Without a word to Aria, Sudia jumped from the spires and landed squarely on the back of a harpy in mid-air. With her sword placed at the harpy's throat, she persuaded it, with a few well-placed kicks and pulling of hair, to fly closer to Aramus. With a single sweep of her sword, Sudia sliced its neck and jumped off its back. Aria held her breath as she watched the grey-elf fall through the grasping claws of Dantet's mistresses, and through the dwarven arrows that whizzed past her head. She plummeted fast until she landed on Aramus's back with a thump. Aria lost sight of them as they tumbled toward the ground, encircled by a mass of wings and terrible screeches.

"Aramus!" Aria screamed, her heart beating so fast it hurt. "Sudia!"

Just as Aria leaned over the battlements to scan for the pair, a sooty cleaver flashed across her face. If she had been slower at pulling back she might have lost her nose to it. Aria drew her sword straight up and, gripping onto the hilt with both hands, she drove it down over the wall where it met with something hard. Quickly glancing over the edge to see what she had hit, Aria was horrified by the sight that unfolded beneath her.

Propped against the blazing wall of the city, was the burning corpse of one of Dantet's massive horned beasts. More horrifying was the ogres clambering over it, setting themselves alight as they scurried up the ramparts, desperately trying to get inside the city. The dead ogre, whose head now housed Aria's sword, was half-burnt and still on fire. It's death mask, a picture of agony. The ladder of ogres it had climbed up to reach her didn't fare much better, and the smell of it all made Aria's stomach turn.

"Archers, defend the ramparts," she shouted, removing her sword from the ogres head.

The archer's focused their next flight of arrows toward the ogres that were climbing the walls like ants. Line after line of them fell back down into the lake of fire below, but it didn't deter their efforts to reach the top. Waves of green skinned monsters, too stupid to realise that they would die, vaulted over the burning carcass of the horned monster, and climbed the fleshy ladder of their comrades. It was a gruesome battle, the worst she had ever seen or heard tales of. The individual screams of agony from the ogres, rang in Aria's ears long after they had perished.

"Light the stingers," Aria roared toward the King's Guard.

She felt the heat of the giant balls of oil soaked rags as they were ignited behind her. She scanned the sky once more looking for any sign that Aramus and Sudia were alive. If she sent the stingers over the wall now, they would surely hit them as they emerged. But the encroaching army of Dark Ones closing in on the parapets, meant she couldn't wait much longer. In a matter of seconds, the thin lining of oil rags would be consumed and the deadly payload released. Aria couldn't wait any longer.

Aria breathed a sigh of relief when she saw Aramus break through the smoky entanglement of harpy wings and ogre cleavers. Dangling below him, and being carried by her ankles, was an infuriated Suida who sung her sword wildly at the pursuing harpies, spitting vile curses in their direction.

"Release the catapults," Aria said as soon as the pair reached the wall.

Aria paid little attention to the deadly balls that soared overhead as Aramus collapsed beside her. His face was scratched on one side by a harpy claw, and he breathed heavily as he tried to regain his composure. Other than that, he was unharmed.

Aria brushed back his dark hair and examined his face. But Aramus knocked off her hand muttering that he was "fine". He didn't meet her eyes, and Aria knew why. From what little she could see, Aramus's eyes were alight with the fire of Dantet once again. No doubt his proximity to the dark creatures, and the battle he had just fought, did nothing to suppress his darker side. It wasn't a good omen, and Aria knew that the last place he should be, right now, was fighting alongside her.

A thick dwraven arrow protruded from Sudia's shoulder, but it made little difference to her temperament as she struggled to her feet again.

"Give me my bow," she yelled, before clasping her shoulder and wincing as she collapsed back behind the wall again. "I will take off their heads one by one if I have to… dirty scum," she panted.

"You will not," Aria said.

"I beg your pardon? Who do you think you are that you can give *me* orders?"

"I am the sovereign leader of Naretia, and commander of this army," Aria replied, edging closer to Sudia and narrowing her eyes. "*You* are injured, and Aramus draws their attention too much. You are both a liability, and I order you to make your way to Olórin. Find him so that he can heal you, Sudia. You should wait with him so too, Aramus, so he can cure you. The sooner he can do that, the sooner this will all be over. Do I make myself clear?"

Sudia looked at her with an open mouth. She fully expected that one, or both of them, would argue with her. But to her surprise they didn't.

"Well, if you're going to be like that then I'm not sure I want to stay," Sudia mocked, stretching her good arm toward Aramus so that he could carry her. "Besides, I don't think you need me much here anyhow. You seem to have everything in order."

Aria couldn't help but smile a little.

Aramus glided off the edge of the battlements, Sudia scooped in his arms, without so much as a "be careful" toward Aria. She was slightly taken aback by his lack of concern as he left her to face an army of Dark One's. It seemed to Aria that he was almost relieved to get away.

"Your Highness!" a dwarf shouted urgently from behind her, interrupting her thoughts. "Ye need tae come and see thas."

Aria stood next to the dark-haired dwarf and followed his pointed finger.

"No!" she whispered, all blood draining from her face. "Surely now all is lost."

Chapter 31

Olórin rooted himself into the highest room of the wizard's tower. To be precise it was the north-west turret of the palace which had been home to the wizard caste since Olórin could remember. He had spent nearly his whole life milling in and out of the dusty, scroll-laden rooms and, before today, it had been mostly in the company of a warm, homely feeling. But it had been so long since his last visit, and so much had changed, that it had become unfamiliar to him now.

Getting in had proven difficult too. A great number of charms, incantations, and explosions were needed to bypass the magical booby-traps someone had left for him; someone, no doubt, who no longer favoured the rule of Edwina and had no qualms about killing intruders. Bernard nearly lost his head to a Pugione curse, which let loose twenty, or so, determined daggers that changed direction of their own accord to follow them. Olórin surmised that the daggers had been enchanted to follow any target that lacked a certain mark.

Etched on some of the limestone walls, as they had ascended the narrow spiral staircase, was the mark in question. He knew it only too well and the sight of the upside-down triangle with two lines curving out in the centre, like a pair of horns, was one he had wished never to see again. It was the mark of the dark wizards who followed the rule of Dantet. He had not laid eyes on it since the time of the ogre's uprising in the Saraethian mountain villages.

"My eyes have been diverted for too long," he muttered over the bubbling cauldron.

"Eh?" Bernard said, raising one bushy, red eyebrow.

"A Supreme Wizard's place is not gallivanting across the kingdom. It is here, watching over his caste and protecting the magic from those who would taint it, even if it is from one of their own."

"Whot could ye have done?" Bernard said, throwing cautious glances out the door, his axe gripped tightly in his hand as though he was expecting another booby-trap, or an invader. "Ye couldnae have refused a request from the Goddess herself."

"No, but I could have sent someone else to find him, or at the very least brought him back here when I did," Olórin replied, dropping two of the tears of life into the iridescent liquid that bubbled like tar. "Instead I kept him locked away in a small cabin with me for six years, when other wizarding minds might have been able to help. But this was *my* quest, wasn't it? It was my arrogance and self-importance which led me to think only *I* could be the one to carry out her orders. It was my selfish need to be accepted which led me to abandon my charges, and my duties, so I could be favoured in her eyes."

"Now, listen here," Bernard said, stepping closer to Olórin, wagging a thick finger. "We've all done things for glory and bumptiousness. I think ye might recall the bribe I took tae let ye in tae Balbuldor. If I had no' been so greedy, maybe none of thas would have happened… maybe me brother might no' be dead." Bernard voice trailed off into nothing before he cleared his throat and continued. "But ye cannae live in regrets because they will do nothing but drown you, and whot use will ye be tae yer charges and yer duties then? We've all made mistakes, and Goddess knows, I've made more than my share. That flaw is no' exclusive tae just you, old man. So get over it, and do whot ye must tae finish this. There'll be time for lamenting and regrets when this is all over."

Olórin couldn't help but regard Bernard in a different light then. His sometimes inappropriate candour, and wiliness to act upon impulse, were qualities that Olórin had come to admire recently. They were also the qualities that made dwarf's immune to the persuasions of the Dark God. Although, it seemed that his predecessor, Thrais, was not as immune to the rather mundane curse of greed, and the persuasions of a certain silver-tongued dark wizard.

"You will make a fine king, my friend," he said to the dwarf.

Bernard huffed and puffed beneath his immaculately styled beard. Olórin was sure that he saw his eyes glisten in the candle light, but he didn't have the opportunity to find out for sure, because in the next moment, Aramus burst into the room with Sudia in his arms. The grey-elf looked decidedly greyer than Olórin figured she ought to. And protruding from her shoulder, was the thick wooden shaft of a dwarf's arrow.

"What the hell was that?" Aramus asked, gesturing toward the staircase he had just come up. "You afraid that someone will sneak up behind you?"

"Ah, you mean the curses. No, they were left here by dark wizards trying to protect their secrets."

"A fine shot," Bernard said, gesturing to Sudia's shoulder with a wide grin.

"I have a finer shot. If you like, I can pull the arrow from my shoulder and show you," she seethed. "And I'll shoot it somewhere where the sun *dinnae* shine."

"Yer a vile creature," Bernard huffed, righting his Etherium armour. "And ye need tae work on yer accent before ye try tae take the piss out of a dwarf. Otherwise ye'll just end up looking like a twat. Oh wait, I guess it's too late fer that."

"Enough you two, we haven't got time for this," Aramus snapped. "Olórin, please heal her. I have to return to Aria, she needs my help at the wall."

"But she said…" Sudia began.

"She needs my help," Aramus said forcefully.

"Is it bad out there?" Bernard asked.

"As bad as you can imagine it," he replied.

"Olórin, hurry up would ye. Take the Valefire already and let me be off," Bernard said, snatching the pouch from around his neck and holding it out to Olórin. "I need tae be wih' me army. There's no way a young whipper-snapper like Aria can protect the city on her own."

"Oh, so now *you* are the one who is prejudiced. Is it just because she is young, or is it because she is a girl that you doubt her ability? Because from what I can see, she's doing a better job than most of the swaggering men that came before her," Sudia said.

"It's because she's only a wee one. She might have some experience wih' small battles, but defending a city is a different matter. The dwarfs have defended Balbuldor from enemies above and below. It's in our blood. Anyhow, whot do *you* care whot I think of her? I thought *you* were only here fer a cure."

"Believe it or not, the outcome of this war affects more than just your fat arse," she replied.

"Right, that's it. I'm outta here," Bernard said, throwing the small leather pouch on the table beside Olórin and making his way toward the door. "I've had enough of yer insults."

"You must stay, Bernard," Olórin boomed, using his staff to magically seal the door shut and prevent Bernard from leaving. "I will need the Valefire very soon, but until then you must be the one to guard it, not I."

The Valefire could be used to make any number of powerful and terrible weapons; ones that could flay the flesh from a man where he stood, or crush an army as it approached. Such was the might of a shield that could hold back a powerful God like Dantet.

The latter was the most tempting of all for Olórin, and that kind of temptation he could physically feel like someone tugging at his sleeve. But there was no time to create those weapons, and he knew it. The lure of the Valefire would divert him from the task at hand, and he wasn't even sure that he had enough time to create Edwina's potion as it was. Even if he crushed Dantet's army, Aramus would still turn and Naretia would still burn because of him. Olórin was also sure the Valefire was the prize Mullrode had sought from Thrais before he poisoned him; a prize Thrais could not give him because he had sent it away with his right arm. *'Perhaps there had been some loyalty in his heart after all.'*

"Don't go far," he said to Aramus before releasing the door again.

Aramus nodded, rummaged through some of the dusty cupboards nearby, and shoved a wad of bandages into Bernard's wide hand. "Make yourself useful while you're waiting, and fix Sudia up."

Before the dwarf had a chance to sound out the objections that were spluttering on the end of his tongue, Aramus had disappeared beyond the door again.

"Oh yes, please do," Sudia scoffed. "Fix me."

"No amount of anvils on the head could fix *you*," he muttered.

Olórin left them to their bickering and concentrated instead on the potion. He ignored the cries of pain as Bernard pulled the arrow from Sudia's shoulder. He ignored the foul curses that she swore at him, and the worse ones that he swore back. He was watching the potion bubble slowly, much too slowly for his liking. With every thunderous sound of something large hitting the palace walls, and there were many, he grew more impatient and wished he could bolster the small fire underneath. But he couldn't. He had to wait for the potion to display the right shade of pink before he could add more mundane ingredients like Farthal Fall – a rare fungus that would bind most potions together.

When he went to fetch the Farthal Fall, however, there was considerably less of it in the glass jar than he thought. He was sure that only a moment ago there had been enough for him to complete the potion. Dust had thickened over the multitude of jars lining the wall, so that their contents were obscured. Perhaps he had mistaken one jar for another? As it was, the Farthal Fall jar, which rested on a cupboard by the door, was all but empty, save for a few scraps left at the bottom.

Olórin scrambled through the cupboards beneath the grimy shelves, and breathed a sigh of relief as his hand rested upon another jar. Examining it closely he was even more relieved to see that it was filled to the wide triangle stopper with small, dimpled, green balls. Popping a few balls into the bubbling cauldron, the iridescent liquid turned muddy.

"Bernard, I will need you to hold the Valefire over the potion now."

From his left side Bernard's hand appeared and it was splattered with Sudia's grey blood. Between his thick fingers, Olórin saw the impossibly white stone gleam. It reminded him of the same dazzling haze that encased Darzithal, only this light was tangible. Almost as though he were in a trance, Olórin found himself reaching out to touch the stone, dreaming of the wonderful things he could do with its power. As his fingers came within inches of the talisman, he wondered if he could actually rule the kingdom of Naretia. He would certainly make a better ruler than those who had come before him. He would preach kindness, equality, and tolerance between the castes… and cut down those who would opposed him. Any ignorant fools standing in his way would feel the wrath of his righteousness, and justly so.

"Olórin?"

Bernard's voice shattered Olórin's dreamy utopia. He snatched back his hand and fixed his eyes resolutely on the dirty potion instead. Torn between the possibilities of an ideal world and the corruption the power of the Valefire had wrapped around his heart so quickly, Olórin was fearful of looking at it again. He closed his eyes for a moment to gather himself.

"Are you okay?" Bernard asked.

"Just rest the tip of the Valefire into the liquid," he replied, stealing a few more deep breathes.

Bernard did as he was told, and the viscous potion began to swirl slowly as Olórin recited the words he had heard whispered to him in dreams. It was a language that was unfamiliar to him, but the sounds rolled off his tongue as though he had spoken it since birth. He knew it to be as ancient as the foundations of Naretia itself, for it was the God's language. But no sooner had the last sound left his lips, the words left his memory as Edwina had told him they would be. Forgotten in an instant, and try as he might, he could not remember them. He knew it was probably for the best because the vernaculars of deities had a power unto themselves and were never meant for mortal lips. The potion continued to swirl, but now two distinct colours emerged. Like snakes coiling around one another, one side was dark while the other began to shine.

Olórin nodded to Bernard then and the dwarf removed the Valefire from the potion, quickly putting it back in its pouch with a cautious eye toward Olórin. Just as he did a ruckus erupted from the staircase beyond the door. Olórin heard the distinct sound of magical projectiles zipping through the air, followed by the numerous clangs of metal swords. The sounds of dark words activating darker spells found their way into Olórin's ears too, and he recognised the voice that had spoken them.

"Sudia, guard the potion and bring it to me when the darkest part is as black as night and the brightest shines like the moon, do you hear?" Olórin shouted. "It cannot be moved until then, not a bump or a tremor."

"Why me?" she asked glancing toward the door.

"Because I fear I may need Bernard's axe, and your shoulder has yet to heal. Do not argue with me, not now."

Sudia narrowed her deranged eyes, but did not argue.

It took Olórin only a moment to fly down the narrow, winding steps and find the source of the noise. Surrounded by the King's Guard was a junior wizard with shoulder-length black hair and a nose that stuck up into the air no matter which direction his head turned. The booby traps, which had nearly cut them down as they entered, lay dormant now that their creator was present. The soldiers fought bravely against Mullrode, but their swords were no match for his magic. One by one, they fell to their deaths.

"Congelo!" Olórin boomed, pointing his staff at Mullrode who had not seen him approach.

Mullrode's arms slowed to a halt. As his face turned toward Olórin, it froze, along with his body, in an expression of surprise and anger. The junior wizard, immobilised in mid-motion with one leg still in the air, he came crashing to the ground with a dull thud as though he was a statue tipped over. Bernard was on him in an instant, kicking away

Mullrode's staff and pressing the sharpened blade of his axe against the wizard's neck. Mullrode huffed and puffed behind his clenched teeth, but could not utter a word.

"Do not kill him," Olórin ordered.

"Couldn't ye let it go just thas once?" Bernard said, keeping his axe firmly in place. "I'm sure yer Goddess will understand if thas eejit loses his head."

"I do not spare his life for that reason," Olórin replied. "He must be questioned. There are many hands at play in this war and I believe he knows the truth of it all. Bernard, please go get Aria. She will be able to confirm or deny his truthfulness, and may be better at persuading him to tell it than I."

Bernard looked thoroughly put out at not being allowed to lop off the young wizard's head, but obeyed Olórin's wishes regardless.

*

"There's just too many," Aria whispered under her breath.

Despite the diligent efforts to push back the dark army, the labours of the dwarf's and the King's Guard had little effect. Now that the lit contents of the stingers had dotted the land around them, it was easier to see the numbers of dark creatures below. The ogres and the horned beasts were only the first wave. Beyond them was a sea of monsters that swayed from side to side with anticipation, like a hive of blackened bees. They huddled together, and their collective form took up nearly the entire horizon. Most alarming, however, was the creature that glided in the sky.

With a wingspan half the width of the entire dark army, and illuminated by the oil fires of the burning ramparts, was the mammoth form of a dragon. Its golden body gleamed against the darkness of the skies, and its red eyes burned as though they were coals. *'How are we to defeat this? All must surely be lost.'*

Aria found herself suddenly wishing that Edwel were still around to advise her on what to do. She had never faced such daunting numbers, or heard of a successful attack against a dragon (not even in fairy tales). Her fear had galvanised her ability to command.

“By the great, hairy plumb-sacks of the king, whot is that?”

Aria was never so relieved to hear Bernard’s voice as she was at that moment.

“A dragon, what are we to do?” she replied, hearing the uncertainty in her own voice.

Bernard’s steel-blue eyes searched hers for a moment, and the hardness she had always seen in them before, softened. He rested a reassuring hand on her shoulder and Aria felt the sting of tears of relief burn at the edges of her eyes. She was too young for a war of this magnitude, to inexperienced, and they both knew it. Gripping onto his axe again, he turned his eyes to the sky and watched the dragon for a long while before he answered her.

“Dinnae worry about the dragon, it’s no’ attacking us just yet,” he said. “I’m no’ convinced it’s on Dantet’s side either, look.”

Sure enough when Aria examined the scene again, with less panic in her heart, she saw that the dragon was encircling them all, as though it was trying to decipher the going’s on below. The harpies gave it a wide berth and even Luscious seemed to be eyeing it warily. It appeared that neither side of the warring parties had expected to see the dragon appear.

“Better tae just concentrate on whot’s in front of us and keep our heads.”

Aria nodded and took in a deep uneven breath, before ordering another volley of stingers to be let loose.

“Let me take over,” Bernard whispered to her. “I’ve been fighting me whole life, but if I start barking order’s while yer still here, y’ell lose the respect of yer army, and maybe even yer crown.”

“I, I can’t,” Aria replied, looking around to see if any of her army had heard him. “I’m the queen, their leader. How can I abandon them?”

Bernard raised a clenched fist to his mouth and cleared his throat.

“Yer Majesty,” he yelled as loudly as a dwarf could. “Olórin has captured the traitorous wizard named Mullrode in the wizard’s tower. He needs yer expertise in loosening tongues. He knows that ye might have better luck than he with finding out who within these walls have sided with Dantet, and brought thas war upon us. I will follow the orders ye have given me and command yer army while yer gone."

Aria's heart leapt into her chest. *'Mullrode has been found?'* There was a large amount of guilt and feelings of ineptitude at the idea of leaving her army in the middle of a battle, but she had a lot of questions for the wan wizard that needed answering. Those answers might just lift the murkiness of this war from around them all, and help them to see it clearly. They would know their true enemies and would strike them down within the shadows they hide.

"So be my orders," she shouted just as loudly. "Bernard, the mighty king of the dwarf's, shall be my voice, and you are all to obey his commands."

A deafening uproar sounded out from the two armies. Despite their loyalty, they looked relieved to have Bernard as their general. She smiled and nodded appreciatively at the feisty dwarf, before turning toward the stairs which lead down the wall.

"Aria," he called after her when she was half-way down. "Where's Aramus?"

"He went inside with Sudia," she replied. "Why?"

"He's no' there now. He said he was coming out here again tae help ya, but I dinnae see him anywhere. He should have been here by now."

Aria felt her stomach lurch. Aramus had definitely not returned from the palace. She knew because she had kept a watchful eye on it, to ensure that the walls did not crumble and her brother was safe. She had seen him enter, of that much she was certain, but he had definitely not returned. *'Oh Goddess no,'* she thought, feeling her insides go cold. *'Has he been captured by another dark wizard?'*

Aria ignored the pain in her leg and turned on her heels to run as fast as she could toward the wizard's tower, the last place she knew he had been.

Chapter 32

"You are going to lose so you might as well give up now. Dantet will be arriving soon, and when he does, you will all *burn.*"

Aria recognised the whiny voicc instantly, and the sound of it made her blood boil as she thought of how he might have hurt Aramus. She also recognised the triangular markings on the limestone walls of the staircase as the same one he bore upon his arm. The same mark that had driven an ogre mad enough to plough a cleaver through his own head. She felt the shame of her stupidity for believing that the mark was a protection spell against Dantet's army, knowing now that it was merely insurance for his followers so they wouldn't be caught up in the war that raged outside.

When she came upon the owner of the voice, she was met by a most welcomed scene. Mullrode was tied to an old, high-backed, wooden chair, looking as waxen and superior as ever. His binds, however, were invisible; no doubt created by Olórin's glimmering white staff, which he held pointed at the junior wizard. For all intents and purpose it appeared that the Mullrode's legs, arms and torso were glued to the seat. His sickly grey eyes met hers as she entered the room, and a wicked smile spread slowly across his face.

"Ah, if it isn't little Aria," he said. "Actually, I'm glad you're here."

Aria stopped dead, momentarily stunned by his condescending but pleasant tone.

"Many wouldn't be," she hissed at him. "Tell me, why are you glad?"

"Because I was always taught to have good manners and, to that end, I would like to thank you."

Aria found it difficult to believe that such a wretched man would have a mother, never mind one that would care enough to teach him good manners.

"Thank me?"

"Yes, you see, without you none of this would have been possible. Without your eagerness to see Aramus dead, and your youthful rashness, I would have never been able to carry out my plan. You were a very useful little puppet, thank you."

Aria lunged at the officious wizard with no warning at all. Balling up her fist, she ploughed it into his jaw with as much force as possible. As a seething rage filled every ounce of her being she hit him time and time again, feeling the back of his head hit the wooden chair. She didn't stop until Olórin pulled her off.

"While I appreciate your gusto, we must keep him conscious to answer our questions," Olórin said.

Aria gritted her teeth together tightly and tried to control her breathing, to no avail. She was at least satisfied to see that she had managed to split Mullrode's lip and a nasty purple bruise was beginning to form under his right eye. A faint throbbing in her knuckles was her medal, and she did nothing to ease the pain. But Olórin was right.

"Fine, where's Aramus? What have you done with him?" she demanded.

"Did he not return to the battle outside with you?" Olórin asked.

The old wizard's face was a picture of concern, and Aria was sure she saw a great wad of his grey beard turn suddenly white.

"He did not," Aria replied. "Who is working with you inside Lothangard, and where have they taken Aramus?"

Mullrode leered at Aria before spitting the blood from his mouth, missing her face by inches, and remaining resolutely silent.

"How *dare* you," Olórin roared at him. The old man's eyes gleamed with a viciousness that Aria had never seen before. "How dare you spit at your queen, you arrogant, officious, pompous, puffed-up little rat. You *will* answer the questions. What have you done with Aramus?"

Mullrode smiled maliciously and said nothing. Olórin slammed his white staff into the ground so hard that Aria was sure he was trying to waken the tower, as though it were a sleeping giant.

"Verax Coactus," he chanted over and over again.

The words bounced off the walls as though each limestone brick memorised what he had said and parroted it long after the old wizard had finished speaking. Mullrode's eyes grew wide as the whispering continued to sound out from mouthless shadows within the bricks and mortar of the wizard tower. Olórin waited until the many voices dulled to a gentle whisper. If Aria hadn't been there when it was created, she would have mistaken the sound as the rustling of trees from outside the palace walls.

"Now you will answer my questions, won't you?" Olórin asked.

The whispers grew in volume.

"Y…yes," Mullrode answered.

The voices died down once the answer had come. The junior wizard looked pained, as though a great many needles had suddenly been prodded into every inch of his skin as he tried to refuse to answer.

"The spell will compel anyone within these walls to answer questions truthfully, whether they like it or not. That means it will also affect you, Aria. It will not allow you to answer a question with a question either. Only the truth will stop the pain. So, do not give him the opportunity to ask you a question you do not wish to answer. Do you understand me?" Olórin said.

"Yes," someone with her voice replied.

Aria clasped her hand to her mouth. The whispering remained steady, and Aria suspected that it was because she had not resisted the question.

"You're a charlatan, aren't you Olórin?" Mullrode asked quickly. "You made up the story about the prophecy to gain favourable attention, didn't you? All because you were about to be found out and lose the respect of your peers. You made it all up so that they would think the Goddess Edwina favoured you, didn't you?"

"I am neither a charlatan nor am I a liar," Olórin replied firmly before quietly adding, "It is true that I sought the favour of Edwina, yes, but of no one else."

"What does he mean "about to be found out"?" Aria asked, before she remembered the spell that was cast around them.

Olórin shot her a pointed look and winced as the answer was slow to come out.

"I am eccentric in many ways, including in my choice of preferred companionship. My preference is also the reason why I never married, or had children of my own. A great many people are objectionable to that way of life, as Angus would have attested to if he were still alive."

Aria felt a searing heat rush up into her cheeks. She knew the wizard didn't appreciated her curiosity, especially not in front of a dark wizard when he had no choice but to answer truthfully. From the corner of her eye she could see Mullrode open his mouth again to ask another question, trying to prevent his own questioning, but she fired one at him before he had the chance.

"What have you done with Aramus?"

"Nothing," he replied easily.

"I don't believe you, are you lying to me?"

"I am not," he laughed. "If Aramus has disappeared, perhaps he has been shot and left to die in a corner somewhere out of sight… or perhaps he has *made* himself disappear."

"What do you mean by that? Why would he make himself disappear?"

Mullrode closed his mouth and Aria could see pain crawl across his face. The whispers of "Verax Coactus" grew louder and louder. His high-arched eyebrows furrowed together over squeezed eyelids, and his teeth clenched. Aria saw a bead or two of sweat on his brow as he gripped the weathered scrolls of his armrests with both hands.

"Why would he make himself disappear?" Olórin asked again.

Mullroded groaned and writhed on the chair as the pain now consumed him. The voices were no longer whispering, they were shouting at him. He breathed tersely through his clenched teeth but, as Aria suspected for such a cloistered wizard, he didn't last long against it all.

"Because he has been give his own mission from Dantet," Mullrode blurted out, taking deep breaths with the last of his words. "You don't really think that Aramus is on your side, do you? Do you honestly believe that he wants to be good, that the son of Dantet wants the mundane life of a mortal?"

"Yes," Aria replied.

"I don't know," Olórin said quietly.

Aria's mouth dropped open as she stared at the wizard in disbelief. She only barely remembered not to ask him any questions, but seriously considered asking him just one regardless. Why? It was Olórin, after all, whose blind belief in the Goddess Edwina's quest, had reassured her she was doing the right thing for the kingdom of Naretia, for Pearan. '*How could he, of all people, have doubts?*' Aria had seen him doubt Aramus in the city of Rhidwynn, but never once thought it was anything more than a need to reaffirm his belief in the winged man, and that his fears were only superficial.

Now, she wasn't quite as sure. This brought back her own misgivings that she had discarded for the sake of Naretia, for the sake of her feelings toward him, and, more importantly, for the sake of her brother who might have to face a terrible future should their mission fail. Aria knew it was a distinct possibility that she *chose* to believe the best in Aramus because she had to, just as she had once convinced herself that her cruel reign was necessary to bring a murderer to justice.

"What mission has he been set?" Olórin asked Mullrode.

"The same as you," Mullrode replied. "His father has commanded him to make a potion, a dark potion, one that will give his father's physical being enough power to walk upon this soil. Oh, don't look so surprised, Olórin. You and I both know that where there is light, there will always be shadow. One cannot exist without the other, for without the darkness, how can we know the light?

"Your elf friends can attest to this. They, with their physical resemblance to Edwina, and steadfast policing of the world, are the perfect example of the balance I speak of. They are the antithesis of the Dark Ones. Well, all except that grey-elf you travel with, but that abomination will feel the power of my God's hand soon enough, and her darker side will bend to his will. Despite his lack of power, Dantet still holds a knowledge of magic that would make me far stronger than you could ever be, and he has promised me that power when he rises."

Save for the gentle whispering of the voices from within the walls, and the occasional *boom* as a lava ball hit the palace, the air was so thick with silence that Aria found it difficult to breathe. Her mind raced with what Mullrode had told them and her heart refused to slow. *'No, this is all wrong, this can't be.'* Icy beads of sweat tickled her just under her hairline, and some niggling idea, that she couldn't visualise, kept prodding her racing mind. Something about Aramus's demeanour when they returned to Lothangard, now set off alarm bells. But no matter how she grasped for the origin of that thought, she could not get a hold of it.

"That's what this is about for you, isn't it?" Olórin seethed, pointing his staff at Mullrode. The staff hummed to life and a spark left its woody surface, hitting Mullrode's triangular mark on his forearm, making him wince. "You crave the power to reign over all the other wizards, to murder where you see fit. You were never content to follow the path set out by the Elder wizards. Your arrogance made you believe that you were better than it, and your impatience made a fool of you.

"Do you honestly believe that Dantet will let you live once your purpose has been served? You are *his* puppet, no more than Aria had been yours. And like all the toys that he has played with, and lost interest in, you will be discarded and left to burn with the rest of us. Dantet does not know loyalty, he does not know compassion, love, or mercy. Edwina has taken all these things from him. He knows only the emptiness that remains in his soul. And that emptiness will consume everything in its path."

"But you don't understand, Olórin. I *am* better than you. I am more powerful and more intelligent than any wizard that has come before me," Mullrode said. "I don't see why my progress was hindered by the traditions of longwinded fossils, like you. Maybe his other toys will be left by the wayside, but he and I have an arrangement. I'm more useful to him alive, because I am his right hand, and he owes me everything."

"He owes you *nothing*," Olórin shouted, placing the burl of his staff against Mullrode's chest. "Anyone capable of murdering his own children will not have the integrity to honour any debts, and you are a bigger fool than I thought if you think that he will."

"The only fool here is *you*, Olórin. Do you really think that your story, sorry, your prophecy, would have ever happened if it weren't for me? Dantet's world was sealed off by the Etherium and a dwarf wizard's magic. There was no way that anymore Dark One's could have passed in or out of his world. But yet, you pranced around, telling everyone who would listen, that it was going to happen. That someday Dantet's son would be born and we would all burn under his fire. That's what gave me the idea, you see? If it wasn't for you and your stupid prophecy, I wouldn't have thought of it. I realised that there was a quicker way to gain power, to be released from the mothering chokehold of Edwina."

Aria wondered if it were true, if the prophecy was, indeed, self-fulfilled, and that they all had been put in harm's way by the ramblings of a desperate old man. But Olórin's gaze never left the junior wizard, and the hand holding his glowing staff was steady. It was the staff that reminded her that Edwina truly *had* appeared to him, that she had given him the tears of life which created it; the same tears that saved Sudia's life. If he had made the prophecy up, then he would not have been granted these gifts.

"But don't you see? How my prophecy came into being was of little consequence. The fact remains that it did, which should tell you I was not lying," Olórin replied with a small laugh. "Were it not for you, some other fool would have set the prophecy in motion. You are no more an integral part of this tale than the proverbial shoe lace one might trip over to start a chain of events. And Dantet will not see you as anything other than that."

"No! You're wrong. *I* was the one who started all of this. I will be remembered for it, not you." Mullrode's eyes bulged and his clenched hands shook with the affront of Olórin's dismissal. "It was *me*. *I* made promises of uncountable riches to that greedy dwarf, Thrais. I was the one who convinced him to let me pass through his mines. *I* was the one who found Aramus's mother, eighteen years ago, and brought her to Dantet. *I* set in motion a great number of things that your prophecy did not foresee. And I was the one who gave Aramus the ingredients he needed to make his potion."

Mullrode's outrage seemed to be appeased with the appalled silence that followed.

"What ingredients might those be?" Aria asked eventually.

"Oh come now, I thought you of all people might have seen a hint of what was going on. You've always seemed more distrusting than the crumbling minds of the old men who surrounded me. Even I thought it terribly convenient that Luscious only bit Aramus on the shoulder and not on the neck. Thank you, by the way, for punching him in the muzzle and helping him to loosen his tooth. And, of course, I can't leave you out either, Olórin. You were the one, after all, who kept the tooth and handed it straight to Aramus. It's amazing the power contained in the poison of a worgen's tooth and how it can darken the very purest of souls."

If what Mullrode was saying was true then Aria's retaliation had been nothing but someone else's plot and she, their pawn. Everything she had done *had* been carefully orchestrated and manipulated by Mullrode. She felt suddenly sick and was determined that if she should throw up it would land in Mullrode's lap. But that niggling feeling in the back of her mind was not appeased with this revelation. This was not the thought she was trying to grasp.

Aria tentatively fingered the gold necklace that connected her to Aramus and wondered if she should take it off. It would be easy to slip it over her head now, and she had no desire to remain attached to him if he truly was working with Dantet. But Mullrode was not a reliable source, and although he answered the questions truthfully, it was *his* truth. She also wondered if this niggling feeling was coming from Aramus. If that was the case, she wanted to keep the necklace on.

"Of course, it was sheer good luck that your golem came and got me that day," Mullrode continued, his arrogance now freeing his tongue to gloat over his cleverness. "I wasn't quite sure how I would get the Etherium to him. Powerful stuff that, gives one incredible strength if used correctly. It would have looked suspicious if he had tried to take some from the mine, although I believed he did try. Pity that Dantet was impatient and bolstered his abilities before he was eighteen. I expect he couldn't control such raw power very well. But you made it very easy for me, my dear, and if you had killed Olórin in the process, all the better for me."

"You were the one who ensured Aramus would be alone with the king and queen too, weren't you?" Olórin hissed. "You made sure all of the guards had left the throne room. I remember hearing of it. Although I had not been around for many years, I still had, still have, some wizards loyal to me. They told me about a young, impertinent wizard giving orders that only the Supreme Wizard should give. It was you, wasn't it? You helped Aramus kill them."

"What!" Aria felt her heart jump into her mouth and her hand fly to the hilt of her sword. "Was it you? Did you betray my parents? Did Aramus take their eyes?"

Mullrode grinned malevolently and endured a moment or two of pain for no other reason, Aria suspected, than to make her wait for the answer. In that time the point of her sword found its way to the centre of his chest.

"Yes, to both," he chortled. "Can't have a dark potion without the all-seeing eyes of wise rulers, now can you? But that's not all. I was also the one who gave you the Amulet of Tenebris, if you remember. Olórin had interfered with my plan to have Aramus killed by taking your army away, so I gave you a new one. This," he said, gesturing with his eyes to the war outside, "was *all* because of me. Because I am more powerful than any wizard who came before, and I *will* rule you all."

A hot rage filled every ounce of Aria and tears stung at the edges of her eyes. Aramus *had* lied to her, to Olórin. She tried to plunge her blade into Mullrode's chest again and again, but no matter how much she pushed, it would stop an inch away from him every time. Aria spun around to face Olórin, tears beginning to trickle down her face. Olórin looked more haggard than normal and his eyes would not meet hers. Instead, they stayed fixed on Mullrode.

"Let me kill him!" she shouted, wiping away the tears. "He was the one responsible for all of this, he should die. Stop protecting him, old man."

"I cannot," Olórin said, his voice laced with despondency. "I cannot allow you to kill even him."

Aria flung her sword to the ground and it landed with a loud clatter. She screamed in outrage as her hands ran through her red hair and tugged at it, hoping to ease the anger and frustration as she paced the dusty room. Nothing helped and the sounds of the palace rumbling under the heavy fire of the horned beast's, only made matters worse. The urgency of that niggling thing inside of her made itself more pronounced too.

"You see the weakness of Edwina's rule," Mullrode laughed. "Now you see that if I was the Supreme Wizard, things would be very different for you, Aria. They still can be, if you help me."

"Help you?" Aria screamed. She rushed over to the contemptuous wizard and grabbed him by his robes, pressing her face close to his and gritting her teeth. "You were the one who let Aramus kill my parents, who bolstered my desire for revenge, and let me set these Dark One's on innocent people. What makes you think that I would ever help you?"

"Because if you don't, Aramus will not die, and Naretia will be in more peril than if I were to succeed."

"But your plan *is* succeeding, isn't it?" Aria hissed, tightening her fist around Mullrode's robes as if it were his neck she was throttling. "That's what you told Olórin, I heard you in the stairwell. "You will lose," you said. So if your plan is succeeding, why do you need my help, why do you want Aramus dead?"

Mullrode did not answer.

Under her hand, which was now pressed hard against his neck, she could feel him shake with the pain that was building through his body. Once more he clenched his teeth and refused to answer, the pain twisting his rodentine face. After a few more moments the whispering walls became just as stubborn and a monsoon of "Verax Coactus" filled the small room.

"Answer the question, Mullrode," Olórin boomed over the din. "Why is it important that he should die if he is, in fact, charged with making this vital potion for your God? Surely you would want him to finish it?"

Mullrode again refused to answer and this time he endured the pain with more conviction. Aria punched him in the jaw wanting to tip the balance of his threshold, to no avail. It wasn't until Olórin pointed his staff at him that Aria saw a twitch in his otherwise resolute demeanour.

"I see your pride is not allowing you to admit your failings," the old wizard said, taking a step closer to Mullrode. "Answer the question or I will use the Ultimum Maledictionem."

From what Aria knew of wizarding, and it was very little, the Ultimum Maledictionem was the spell wizard's used on the most hostile of enemies. It was as close to killing a person as the wizards could get. The spell cast delusions in the mind that would torment a person with their worst fears, whilst at the same time sear them with a pain more horrific than being burned alive. The victims were said to never be the same after it again, often left in a vegetative state, but never dead.

"You wouldn't," Mullrode hissed behind his gritted teeth. "Such a benevolent leader as yourself wouldn't have the stomach to use a curse like that."

As much as she hated to agree with a toad like Mullrode, she did. That particular curse hadn't been used in thousands of years and was severely frowned upon, for good reason. But to her surprise she saw Olórin step closer to Mullrode and hold his staff over his head, waving it in small, circular motions.

Aria let go of the wizard's robes and gladly gave way to Olórin's approach.

"Ultim…"

"Wait!" Mullrode interrupted. "Wait, just wait."

Mullrodes eyes were wide with panic and his breathing grew haggard as he fought through the pain of the whispering walls. As pale as he had been before, Aria had never seen a human go as white as he was then. Olórin's words drifted away, but he kept his staff over the young wizards head.

"Aramus and Dantet can hear each other's thoughts whether they choose to or not, such is the connection between father and son. Through his dark children I have been kept informed of Aramus's progress. For a time he refused to accept his father's will. Even after the death of the king and queen of Naretia when, with their blood still warm on his hands, Aramus grew to first know the lure of the darkness. He refused to succumb to it, no doubt as a result of some misguided loyalty to you, Olórin."

Still the whispering walls continued to murmur, waiting for the answer that Mullrode was trying to skirt around. The wizard's face contorted with the pain and Olórin kept his staff hovering steadily above his head. Aria felt the niggling at the back of her mind pushing its way forward, like it was trying to get a better view of the answer that would inevitably leave his mouth. Somehow she knew the two were connected.

"There *was* a flaw in my plan, one that I did not foresee," Mullrode said reluctantly. "I thought that the Amulet of Tenebris would be safe with the queen. I had not considered that she would lose it to a dwarf. Luscious was very foolish to leave it in the mire for Aramus to find, and he was punished severely for his mistake. The worgen has proven a very useful spy since then, tracking your every movement and reporting back to me. But Aramus now has a way of overriding his father's control over his children and building an army for himself. If that should happen, then no one will win this war and all will perish. *That* is the true prophecy that you witnessed, old man. Not the coming of Dantet, but the rise of his son."

"But he didn't find it," Olórin said. "It was lost in the bogland along with the Etherium arrow."

"Was it?" Mullrode asked rhetorically. "I think you will find Aramus used your blind trust in him to retrieve it whilst you buried that other dwarf. Just as he did to find the missing part of the grey-elf's ear whilst you tried to save her, another ingredient he required for the potion and the reason she was turned. The flesh of a turning elf, you see, is volatile and can be swung toward the darkness. It will alter the flesh of any that consume it too."

"No, he couldn't," Olórin whispered.

Aria felt sicker than she had ever felt before in her life. It was in Rhidwynn that she had come to trust Aramus, even liked him to a certain degree, and defended him against Olórin's doubts. She felt foolish when she thought back to how she had been jealous of his attention on Sudia, now knowing that it had been only for his dark potion. She also felt thoroughly disgusted at how her skin had tingled under his touch as they danced. *'Surely I could not have been so blind. Mullrode must be lying.'* The dying whispers of the wall told her that he was not lying, and the niggling notion in her head started a wave of panic in her stomach. He had been so calculating, so convincing, that Aria knew he must have come to Lothangard for a reason. But that reason was still far from her grasp.

"Whilst it would be better for Dantet to wait until he is eighteen, and at full power before he is killed, Aramus has forced his hand. For without Aramus's power, a copy of Dantet's own gifts before Edwina took them from him, the Dark God would be vulnerable and will not rise. It is true that up until your journey to Lothangard, Aramus could have been swayed either way, and this is why his father had held off his attacks. He only wanted it to appear that he desired Aramus death, so you might be more convinced and unwittingly aid him. I don't know what it was exactly that turned him against both your plan and his father's, but something did happen.

"Dantet has informed me that Aramus intends to make the potion for himself, so *he* will rule Naretia instead. But he is only half his father, and mortals were never meant to wield that kind of power. He is missing one last ingredient, and Dantet's army is here to make sure that Aramus does not complete it. So, now you see why it is in your best interests to help me, Aria."

"What is the last ingredient that he needs?" Aria asked quietly, almost afraid to hear the answer as the niggling grew more impatient in her head.

"Aramus needs a powerful substance to bind it all together," Mullrode answered.

"Farthal Fall," Olórin said, his eyes wide. "I knew there was more of it before he left me. He must have stolen it while I was distracted with Bernard, to complete the potion."

"No, no, Fathal Fall isn't strong enough," Mullrode scoffed as though Olórin were just a student in his eyes. "He might have tried to use that. If he did, it would be certain to fail. No, Aramus needs something far stronger, celestial, something that can unite souls – even after death. He needs to sacrifice true love, and obtain the blood that comes directly from the heart to be able to bind these ingredients. Unless one of you have fallen head-over-heels in love with him, there is no way he can complete it – at least not one that he has yet thought of."

"Aria, do you…" Olórin began, his eyes wide with concern.

"No," she replied, furrowing her brow. "He kissed me, but… but I couldn't forget what he did to my parents. Perhaps my rejection is what tipped him over the edge?"

Aria felt a wave of guilt wash over her for a moment before the niggling thing that was playing at the back of her mind began to jump around like an overzealous student with their hand raised. Mullrode's words set off a whirlpool of panic in her stomach. Something about love, about her love for him or lack thereof, had changed his demeanour toward her. That was until he had comforted her whilst she sent Pearan to hide in the palace.

"Oh, no," she said, her legs nearly faltering as she remembered how fascinated he had been in her brother whilst they were in Rhidwynn too. "Pearan. He was very interested in whether or not I *truly* loved my brother. But surely he cannot use Pearan? Surely he needs his victim to love *him*? Tell me, Mullrode, tell me that he cannot use Pearan."

The junior wizard's mouth dropped open for a moment and a look of intense concentration crossed his face before he spoke again.

"Love is love. I cannot see any reason that he couldn't."

Aria felt her gold chain unhitch itself, slide from her neck, and fall to the dusty floor with a hollow clinking sound. "To truly know the one you are linked to will render the magic moot," Mirathall had said. Aria knew Aramus now. She knew why he was here, and so too did Olórin by the look of the wide-eyed understanding in his wrinkled face.

"Aria, wait. This too might be a trap," Olórin said urgently.

Aria ignored him and spun on her heels, panic pumping the blood through her ears and making her mind dumb with fright as she bolted through the door.

"You must kill him, Aria, because Olórin will not. He will not sacrifice the lives of the other wizards for your brother, just as he would not sacrifice their lives to protect the Mountainmen of the east," Mullrode shouted after her.

That was the last thing that Aria heard as she made her way out of the wizard's tower. She feared she would already be too late to save her younger brother, the only living person in Naretia that she truly loved.

Chapter 33

Aria could hear the bloodcurdling screaming of both men and monsters from beyond the safety of the palace walls. The sound was so sharp in her ears that she knew the dark army must have breached the cities defences and made their way into the cobbled streets below the palace walls. Aria felt a wave of guilt for her absence wash over her, but the feeling was swallowed by the cold jaws of panic as she failed, room after room, to find her brother. Her heart beat at a rate that she knew could not possibly be sustained for long.

"Where are you?" she whispered to herself, afraid that talking too loudly would alert Aramus to her presence. "Why do you have to be so good at hiding?"

Aria's lungs ached, her legs burned, and her whole body shook, begging her to stop and rest for a moment. But she refused. Her mind raced with the images of Pearan's best hiding spots, the ones she knew of anyhow. Every time her eyes matched those images, her heart sank lower into her chest when she discovered that they were all empty.

Eventually she had no choice but to stop in the middle of a long corridor and breathe deeply before she passed out. Running her hands through her hair and crumpling to her knees with tears blurring her vision, Aria felt an overwhelming tied of nerves surge up from her stomach. *'Where, where could he be? I told him to hide, but he's so good at it I might never find him.'* The thought gave Aria a small amount of relief. *'If his own sister can't find him, perhaps Aramus can't either.'* Her relief was short lived as the bone chilling screams of a small child echoed through the empty stone corridors and reached her ears. Her heart stopped and everything around her became silent as she listened intently to the echoes that taunted her failing.

"Pearan!" she screeched, getting to her feet to follow the sound of the voice.

Aria reached for her sword, determined that this time Aramus *would* meet his end, but her hand met with empty space. It was then she remembered that, in her haste to find her brother, she had left it strewn on the floor next to Mullrode. She had nothing, no wizard to help her find her brother, no stone golem to protect her from the monster that had given her nightmares, no guards, or defence of any kind. But yet, as she made her way toward the palace throne room, a strange calmness came over her.

Rounding the corner and slipping into the dark marble hall through the large wooden doors, Aria took in a sharp breath and willed her heart to keep beating when her eyes met with the scene in front of her. Pearan had obviously taken her instructions literally and hidden behind the throne, as any seven year old would do. His eyes were wide with fright and Pearan's red hair disappeared as he dived around the golden chair, trying to avoid the tip of Aramus sword.

Aramus's eyes were ablaze with the terrible fire of Dantet and his wings were arched on his back, flames licking around the edges of them. More alarming was the murderous look that twisted his face until there was no part of him that Aria recognised as the man she had come to care about.

"Aria, help," Pearan shouted. "He wants to kill me."

Aria sprinted with every last ounce of her energy toward her younger brother. Aramus ignored Aria and caught hold of Pearan by his arm. He drew his sword into the air ready to strike the young boy just as she reached him. Aria heard herself scream. She felt the searing sting of sharp metal in her chest, and the trembling of a small child's body behind her. The hotness of Aramus, so close to her now, burned her as he leaned closer to Aria. Triumph was written all over his face, as she felt her lungs slowly begin to fill with something sticky and suffocating.

"You can go now boy, I have no further need for you," Aramus hissed, letting go of Pearan to grasp Aria more firmly, and stop her from collapsing. "Your sister has made the ultimate sacrifice for you, and inadvertently given me the final ingredient that I needed."

"Aria?" Pearan's sweet young voice was laced with a deep sorrow that she had not heard since her parent's deaths.

"Pearan, go, find the wizard Olórin," Aria gasped, keeping her eyes locked on Aramus's. She didn't want to show her brother the blood that was filling her mouth and drowning her. "Then hide."

"But Aria…"

Aria felt his small hand clasp hers and for a second she latched onto that feeling, knowing it would be the last time she ever felt it. Coldness and heaviness filled her body. She knew her time was running out as her chest rattled with the effort of breathing. She didn't want her brother's last memories of her to be the same awful ones she had of her parents. She didn't want him to be consumed by it, as she once had been.

"Pearan, go, be quick," Aria spluttered, feeling the muscles in her neck lose their strength and the need to breath burn at her chest. "Go, now."

Aria heard him sob deeply and felt his hand slip away from hers. The coldness that was left after his touch spread throughout her body, and when his footsteps finally disappeared down the corridors, Aria collapsed.

Aramus lowered her to the ground, his uncaring fiery eyes watching her as the world around her darkened. She didn't feel the crushing need to breathe anymore, or the pain as he pulled the sword from her chest. All she felt was the coldness, the empty coldness that pulled her away. The sounds around her were muffled as she watched Aramus untie the satchel from his back and retrieved a glass bottle, filled with a purple liquid. He uncorked it and held the tip of his sword over the opening, dripping her blood into it. The blackness around her encroached further until there was only a small pin point vision of Aramus smiling. The liquid in his phial turned so dark, that it might have been capable of extinguishing the sun itself.

He was consumed, and she was dying.

'So cold.'

*

Aria had only left the wizard's tower for a moment, but already Olórin had lost track of her. Leaving Mullrode tied up, Olórin ran through the long narrow corridors as fast as his wiry body would allow him. The palace was large, and he had no idea where to begin his search. His creaking bones protested at having to move at such an unnatural pace for a two hundred and ninety-eight year old man, but he kept running despite their complaints. He had no choice. It was, after all, his fault that the young prince was in danger. Had he just kept a better eye on Aramus while they travelled, or gone after him when he ran away at the age of fifteen, or left him to die the night he was attacked by those men, then perhaps none of this would have happened?

The guilt burdened his heart more than the exhaustion, and Olórin could feel his fingers and toes go cold. His head grew dizzy and his vision blurred until the world around him spun. The weight in his chest sank deeply into his stomach, and Olórin only just managed to stop running before he fell and heard the clatter of his staff hit the stone floor. *'Not now.'*

The silvery outline of the palace corridor dissolved into darkness and from within it, Olórin heard the voice of a young man fire out orders. The clashing swords sharpened his senses, and when the vision came into focus, he was confronted with the image of a burnt landscape. Again the cries of war came to his ears, but he could not find the owner of the commanding voice. Long silvery hair from hundreds of elves glided either side of him in a ghostly motion, their arrows zipping past his head. From high above him Olórin saw the silhouette of a golden dragon gleam against the night sky – the fires below bathing its shining body in a dangerous ochre hue.

Something huge rumbled the scorched ground underfoot. It was deeper and more numerous than the dwarf's Beasties or the horned monsters of Dantet. Beyond the peaks of a blackened mountain's to the east, Olórin spied the enormous heads of giants sway, unhurriedly, from side to side as they made their way toward him. From so far away it was impossible to tell if their swinging weapons were meeting with friend or foe.

Many things happened in his vision, and countless faces passed by Olórin, some of them recognisable, but all of them terrified. This was a vision unlike any other. Whereas before he only saw the outline of what was to come, an echo of things to happen, now it was as if he was there. He could smell the burning flesh of creatures, hear their shrieks of anguish, and taste the bitterness of fear in his mouth. His vision told him that a great war was coming, far beyond anything they had seen before, and from the looks of it, Dantet appeared to be winning.

It was then the colossal, winged frame of the dark God materialised through the smoke-ladened vista. His black, horned body loomed over the unseen warriors beneath the smog and towered over the distant giants. His fiery slatted eyes, as large as two moons, burned through ashen clouds and finally rested upon Olórin. Something pounded in Olórin's hand. When he looked down he saw a black, glassy stone pulsating as though it were a heart. His fingers and palm were blackened and fused to the bizarre gem. Dantet's roar shook the heavens themselves, and Olórin knew that this stone was what Dantet wanted.

Just as he felt the coldness of death's touch reach out to him, Dantet's face changed. Where his eyes were once fearsome and fiery, now they shone, pupil-less and silvery. His snarl turned into a smile framed by azure lips and was surrounded by a brilliantly white complexion. Silver hair tumbled from the gargantuan horns on his head, spreading out through the land until it enveloped both Dantet and the darkness.

Olórin gazed into the face of the Goddess Edwina and wondered if he was being shown the moment he was to join her in the hereafter. The Goddess shook her head as if to say "no" and furrowed her silver eyebrows. Olórin was suddenly filled with a sorrow so great he thought it might crush him. Edwina's eyes bore the anguish of a mother saying goodbye to her child for the last time. Her blue lips parted and Olórin waited expectantly for the voice that he had so longed to hear.

But the sound that came from her mouth was not that of a woman.

"Help me," it said. "Wake up."

The voice was that of a young child he didn't recognise. With some confusion Olórin found himself drawn to the desperation he heard in the child's loud sobs. He felt the dizziness return, the hardness of the stone floor beneath him, and the throbbing of his head, pull him reluctantly from the image of Edwina.

"Wake up," the child's voice pleaded.

Olórin opened his eyes and the world around him spun. Small hands grabbed at his robes and shook him urgently. When his eyes managed to focus again, and the clashing of swords was the only thing left ringing in his ears, he was met by the sight of a young boy with the same red hair as Aria. His brown eyes were bloodshot, and tears tumbled freely down his blotchy, terrified face as he shook Olórin again. The child in question looked so much like Aria that there could be no doubt that he was her brother.

"Wake up, wake up, wake up," he cried, grief and terror convulsing his lungs so he could only speak in hiccups.

"Pearan," Olórin said, sitting up and rubbing the back of his head. "What has happened?"

"Aria, Aria, please help her," he sobbed.

Olórin snapped back to reality, ignoring the pain in his head, and stared into the young boys terrified eyes.

"Where is she?"

"Th… throne room," he hiccupped before clasping his small face in his hands and sobbing so hard that Olórin knew he would not speak again.

"Pearan, listen to me. It is very important that you hear me," Olórin said grasping the young boy's hands away from his face. "I'm sure you know all of the secret passages in this palace, am I right?"

Pearan nodded, still gasping for air through his grief.

"You must get out of here, out of Lothangard, and hide. Do not tell anyone your name, never stay in one place too long, do you hear?" Again the young boy nodded. "I will come find you when it is safer. But if I should not come, if I should not survive, then you must keep yourself hidden from all and make a new life for yourself. Go now."

Pearan stood up and disappeared through the corridor, tripping over his own feet as he left. Olórin waited until he was out of sight before picking his staff up and, on unsteady legs, taking a short-cut through the central courtyard to get to the throne room. Once outside, the same burning smell he had had in his vision reached his nose, making it feel as though it had been instantly blackened with soot. He turned his eyes to the sky and his breath left his body in a moment of absolute terror.

Soaring above his head was the golden dragon he had seen in his vision, majestic, terrifying, and watching. Olórin quickened his pace, sure that at any moment he would see the figure of Dantet loom above the castle walls too. His legs wobbled and his chest ached from the effort. Thankfully no such figure appeared. But upon Olórin's arrival in the marble hall, he found an image more distressing than the face of Dantet could have ever been.

Aramus stood at the top of the hill of marble steps, his wings smouldering and his eyes ablaze. In his hand he swirled a small phial containing a dark liquid, which almost seemed to suck the light from every oil lamp in the room. Lying on the ground at his feet, a waterfall of red, curly hair cascaded down the marble steps, continued on by a river of bright red blood. Aria's face was a horrific shade of grey and the edges of her lips had turned blue. Any life or lustre that had once been in her eyes was lost now as they emptily stared at Olórin.

"Aria!" Olórin gasped, rushing to her side.

Her skin was cold to the touch and her distant eyes remained motionless. He was too late. His innards ran cold and the distant rumblings of war outside the palace became muted. As he knelt by her side, Olórin had to lean on his staff for support, for fear he would collapse.

He had failed.

"What have you done?"

"What needed to be done," Aramus replied.

His voice was indifferent, deeper, as he continued scrutinise and swirl the phial in his hands. Only taking a momentary glance toward Olórin and the dead body of the young queen, Aramus shrugged his shoulders as if all he had done was accidently trampled someone's prized flowerbed. Olórin felt an anger begin to surge in his stomach. He leaned over Aria's body and closed her eyes before standing to face Aramus.

"How, how could you kill her? She was on your side. She defended you when all others doubted," he roared.

"Why wouldn't I kill her?" he replied. "The blood from her heart was my final ingredient. It's not as if she actually cared for me, old man, she told me that herself. The only thing she wanted to do, was protect was her scrawny little brother."

"You… you…" Olórin was lost for words.

Olórin breathed deeply, trying without success to calm himself. He was at the point of no return and he knew it. Aramus stood, Dantet's potion in his hand, and the glint of the Amulet of Tenebris around his neck, beneath the gold chain of the elves. It seemed that Aramus had not understood Aria in the same way that she had understood him, and his chain had not broken.

"Why couldn't you have just waited until the potion was ready?" Olórin asked quietly, already knowing the answer.

"And what… become the pet of another God?" Aramus scoffed. "You have no idea what it's like, old man, to have one whispering in my ear, telling me I am nothing more than a vessel for his power, while the other despises me more than anyone who has ever clapped eyes on me. Is that to be my destiny then? Am I to die alone, or to live despised for an eternity, never fitting in, never having anyone truly love me? And because of what crime, because I was born?"

Amidst the anger that surged an energy through his old body, Olórin came to realise what was truly happening before him. They were puppets, all of them. Pawns that were being pushed around a board between the warring parents who presided over them: An eye for an eye. He remembered the vision granted to him before Pearan found him and knew that

Edwina *was* saying goodbye. She knew what was to happen and did nothing to stop it. Olórin felt a warm tear trickle down his face as he realised that Edwina had been just as guilty of manipulating him, as Dantet was of manipulating Aramus. He felt cheated, betrayed, and angry.

"I think that I will make my own destiny," Aramus continued. "With my father's potion I will be too powerful for anyone to ever oppose me. It is *my* turn to govern the condemnatory people of Naretia, and they *will* bow down to me, or burn for their defiance."

Olórin was almost inclined to agree with the young man then, save for the fact that many innocent lives would be lost if he did. His faith in his visions, in his Goddess, diminished within him. He vowed, then and there, that after this day he would no longer partake in the war between Dantet and Edwina. Should he survive, Olórin thought it better Pearan remained hidden and find a new life of his own, away from the self-fulfilling prophecies his head had been filled with. But Olórin would do this one last thing, not for Edwina, but for the people of Naretia.

"You stupid fool," Olórin said, raising his staff and pointing it at Aramus's chest. "Even if you succeed you will never know true happiness, not without the potion I have created. You will be forever lost in the *idea* of acceptance, the illusion of adoration. But the hole in your heart will never be filled, just as it will never be filled in your father." Olórin steadied himself and felt the power of his staff surge through his arm. "I ask you, please Aramus, do not drink that potion. Wait until Sudia comes. I do not wish to kill you."

Aramus turned to Olórin and glared at him. Without warning, his wings flared in a crimson blaze and that same powerful wickedness Olórin had witnessed in Darzithal, flashed across his face.

"You will not kill me, old man," Aramus seethed. "You cannot."

"We are all capable of murder," Olórin said, feeling an odd calmness wash over him. "My vows do not prevent me from killing you. While my brethren would suffer the ultimate sacrifice for my actions, it does not mean that I cannot. I am just as capable of becoming what the world regards as evil. It is only by my actions, my choices, that I stay on the path of light. But all that can change. So I say it to you again, Aramus. Please do not drink that potion because I do not want to kill you."

Aramus laughed loudly, his harsh voice echoing off the empty walls of the room. Outside Olórin heard the shouts of warring men in the corridors coming closer, and panic started to rise in his chest. Dantet's army had breached the palace walls and would be on top of them at any moment. But Aramus seemed unperturbed by the sound.

"I don't mean your vows," he guffawed. "I'm talking of your love for me. I am the only family that you have ever known, and your soft heart will not allow you to harm me."

A weight burdened Olórin's chest as he came to another realisation.

"As evident by the war between Dantet and Edwina, even the most loving parents must sometimes sacrifice their children for the greater good," Olórin replied, taking a step closer to Aramus.

It was then Olórin saw doubt in the young man's eyes, like he considered Olórin a viable threat for the first time ever. With a flick of his thumb, Aramus uncorked the phial and raised it to his mouth.

"Aramus, NO!"

As soon as the glass rim touched the young man's lips, Olórin released the energy from his staff. He watched, almost as if in slow motion, as the blindingly white electricity crackled at the burl and shot out, hitting Aramus in his chest. No sooner had the phial, and Aramus, been blown backward, then Olórin's staff shattered into a thousand pieces. It exploded with such force that he was blown half-way across the throne room too.

Olórin wasn't sure if it was the ringing in his ears muting all noise, but outside everything became strangely silent as he lay gasping on the cold floor. Weakness began to invade his old body, the likes of which he had never felt before. It sapped at the very essence of his being and he suspected that those who did not follow Dantet, were also feeling it. Death was peaceful, but it was slow.

Olórin lifted his head to see that the job he had been sent to do, was done. Aramus had fallen into the golden throne, his chest opened and black blood oozed down his trousers, pooling at his feet. His tanned face was as grey as the young queen's below him, and the fire of Dantet had left his eyes. He was still breathing, but only just.

"Olórin, Olórin, are you okay?"

Sudia's voice was a welcomed sound. It filled Olórin with comfort to know he would not die alone. But it didn't change the fact that he would die as soon as Aramus's heart beat for the last time.

"There were ogres and trolls in the palace, I couldn't get through any faster," she said, picking him up by his shoulders and helping him to sit. "It was the strangest thing, they just suddenly stopped fighting and stood in their place, like they had become statues. I chopped off a few heads along the way, but it wasn't as satisfying as I thought it would be. Here, the potion is ready."

Clutched in the hand held close to her injured shoulder, she held a phial which was now split into two distinct colours. While one side bore an unmistakable resemblance to Aramus's potion, the other shone more brightly than his staff ever could.

"It's too late," Olórin replied, turning away from her and pointing to Aramus. "I had no choice." Sudia let out a gasp when her eyes found where he was pointing.

"But that means you will die too," she said, turning to Olórin again, her one black eye and one silver eye both looking at him wildly. "No, I will not have it. You promised to find me a cure. Maybe if *you* drink the potion it will protect you, protect your soul and keep you alive?"

Olórin considered the notion and a sudden surge of hope swept over him. He took off his hat and rummaged through the contents, only barely able to keep himself upright as his energy continued to wane. From within its depths he retrieved the glistening Geminum. Turning the hourglass gem over in his hand he knew that it was possible to save himself by syphoning out the stain of darkness that the murder has left on his soul. But the idea of living on while the rest of his caste perished was too much to bear.

"Give it to me," he said, taking the phial from Sudia's hand. "Help me to him."

"To *him!*" Sudia gawped. "Have you lost your mind?"

"For the last time, my mind is perfectly sane. Now help me. If I can complete the task, then perhaps his soul might be spared after all. He will not suffer at his father's hands, and Dantet will be unable to rise."

With a few expletives muttered under her breath, she helped Olórin over to Aramus. The young man was still breathing in spits and spurts, and his terrified amber eyes focused on Olórin as he leaned against the throne next to him. The old wizard couldn't bear to look into them, so instead he uncorked the phial and focused on tipping its contents into the young man's mouth. He spluttered and choked, but he swallowed it.

Holding the Geminum over the gaping hole in his chest, Olórin began to chant. Slowly a dark mist rose out of Aramus and found its way into the darker side of the Gemium. When there was no more darkness to capture, Olórin felt his knees go weak and had to grip onto the throne to keep himself upright. He continued to chant despite the fact that he knew the spell was completed. All the while Aramus's ragged breathing became worse.

"Olórin?"

The voice was choked, soggy, pleading. Olórin went quiet and Aramus gripped onto his robes as he stared, wide-eyed, around the room as if he were seeing it for the first time. His gaze rested on Aria's dead body before finding Olórin's face again.

"What have I done?" he whispered weakly. "I'm sorry."

These were the last words that Aramus spoke before his eyes glazed over and his ragged breathing became still. Olórin felt the Geminum slip from his hand and heard it shatter on the marble steps. He ignored Sudia's cries of despair as it did. She abandoned him to gather the fragments of black and white glass at their feet. Olórin didn't care. He waited for his own death to come, for the time of the end to his soul and his being.

With his free hand he traced his fingers over the young man's amber eyes to close them. Then he lowered his head onto Aramus's shoulder and wept. That was the way things remained for a long time, the silence of the marble hall only broken by Olórin's mournful sobs and the tinkle of glass shards falling between Sudia's fingers. Olórin waited for the weakness to worsen, the pain of grief his chest to disappear, and the nothingness to envelope him. He waited, sobbing harder than he had ever sobbed before.

"Whot has happened?"

Bernard's voice rang too loudly in what had become a marble crypt.

"Why are you here, dwarf? Why are you not fighting outside?" Sudia snapped, her voice heavy with sorrow and despair.

"They've gone," he replied, the dwarf's voice quietening to a whisper. "The dark army has up and left, just gone, like a dog that has been recalled by its master. We won!"

Silence followed Bernard's statement. Olórin didn't care to ask the questions he might have before Aramus's death. It seemed too that Bernard needed no explanation for the horrific scene before him, and for that Olórin was grateful.

"Help me with him," Sudia said in an uncharacteristically soft voice.

Olórin heard Bernard's iron clad footfalls make their way to the throne. As though he his skin had turned to stone, he only barely felt the dwarf's rough hands hoist his old legs off the floor, while Sudia took him under his arms. Together they carried Olórin, weak with grief and magicless, toward the large wooden doors at the end of the palace. Olórin couldn't take his eyes off the scene they left behind and thought the image would stay with him for an eternity – the queen of Naretia slain at the foot of her throne, and her killer, the man he had come to think of as a son, dead in her golden chair by his hand. Both of them surrounded by the glittering fragments of the Geminum and his shattered staff.

"What happens now?" Bernard asked Sudia.

"Nothing," Olórin whispered. "I will not let fate, or the Gods, control me like this anymore. Pearan will find his own path, and Edwina and Dantet can fight their own war."

"But what will happen to Naretia?" Sudia asked.

"That is not my concern," Olórin wheezed, feeling his chest collapse. "But it seems that you are the only king left in Naretia, Bernard."

Bernard and Sudia glanced at each other, but remained silent as they carried Olórin out of the throne room. Although he saw the blood-stained corridors, the bodies strewn about the courtyard, and heard the cries of anguish from mutilated soldiers as they died, his mind was stuck on the last memories he had of his son.

He willed his heart to stop as he was carried up the spiral stairs to the wizard's tower, and past the empty chair that had once held Mullrode. But his heart refused to obey. It carried on beating while the rest of the wizard caste fell to their knees, while the magic of Naretia perished, and the kingdom came to know a new and frightening era.

A note from the author

Although it isn't customary, I wanted to take this opportunity to thank you, the reader, for deciding to pick up my book. I hope, in earnest, that you have enjoyed my novel and will look for the next instalment of the Naretia series. To keep abreast of the announcements, you can subscribe to my website or keep an eye on my social media sites listed below. I look forward to connecting with you all.

www.tpkeane.com

twitter @tpkeaneauthor

https://www.facebook.com/Anathemites/?ref=tn_tnmn

30052761R00220

Made in the USA
Middletown, DE
12 March 2016